REBIRTH

BOOK 1 IN
THE ROGUES SHIFTER SERIES

To Aarone,
Happy reading + thanks so
much for stopping by.

Best wishes,
Gayle Parness :0)

GAYLE PARNESS

Dedicated to my mom, my daughters, my brother and the friends who told me to hold true to my dreams. Because of you, I experienced my own rebirth as I wrote this book.

Thank you.

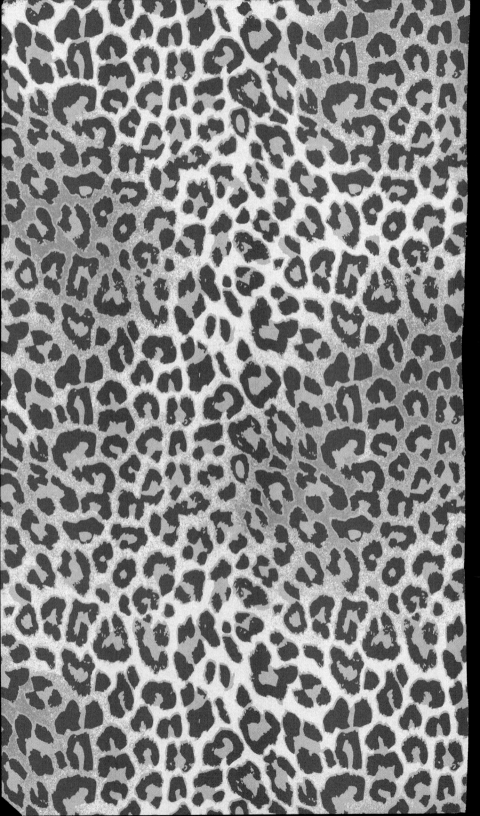

CHAPTER ONE

I LAY UNCONSCIOUS ON THE DAMP GROUND, my body still, my mind untroubled even by dreams. Awareness returned in tiny bits and pieces, each moment a battle to free myself from the mental fog. My heart pounded in my chest as I desperately gulped in small quantities of cold fresh air, burning my dry throat as it traveled to my lungs. Pine needles and rough stones dug uncomfortably into my arms and back. I shifted my body, trying to ease the ache.

Pungent scents assaulted my nose from every direction: the musky forest floor, wood smoke, the sea, a metallic odor: blood—my blood.

The shock jolted me to sit up and stare down at my body. My arms and hands were covered with splotches of dried blood. The knees of my black jeans were shredded and stained—my bare feet drenched in mud. I trailed a shaky hand over my chest and belly, finding no injuries except for the ripped state of my tee shirt. I gasped loudly then immediately slapped a hand over my mouth to stifle the sound. Someone had dumped me here, injured and unconscious. My attacker could still be nearby.

Wincing, I tried to smother my fear and concentrate on sorting out my frightening situation. Unfortunately, the sudden upright movement had my stomach competing for the gold medal on the uneven parallel bars. I lowered myself gently back to the ground and glared up at the stars, frustrated by my weakness. I swallowed hard to keep from losing my last meal—whenever and whatever that was—and shut my eyes to stop the trees from spinning.

If sitting up meant vomiting all over myself, I could hang out here on the ground for a little while longer, no problem. I took a breath and sifted through my hazy memories in the hopes of figuring out how I got here.

I remembered putting my bike in the shed after riding all day and seeing a man I hadn't recognized sitting on my neighbor's porch steps. It was strange, because the Reynolds had left for vacation the day before. He stood when I passed and smiled at me, so I'd smiled back automatically to be polite. He was tall, dressed in coveralls, with wavy dark hair that hung below his collar. I thought maybe he'd been hired by the Reynolds to do some yard work while they were gone. But how much yard or construction work is done in the evening?

The squeaky gate had sounded its usual protest as I passed through and walked up the gravel path to the side entrance of the house I lived in with Justin and Maggie, the couple who'd recently adopted me. As I was putting the key into the lock, the air behind me stirred, and a pungent wintergreen scent filled my nostrils. A muscular arm had wrapped around my waist and a calloused hand covered my mouth. I struggled briefly but couldn't call out other than to mumble a frightened grunt. Something sharp pricked my neck. Nothing else.

Still sprawled out flat on the forest floor, I shuddered. The man had drugged me and taken me—somewhere, but where? I listened intently but heard only a variety of squeaks and squawks, scratching and scurrying by the local smaller woodland inhabitants. Those creatures didn't bother me. It was the human variety that concerned me at the moment.

I was so angry with myself I could scream. A stranger on my neighbor's porch should have set off alarms in my head. I dug my nails into my palms, forcing my mind back online. *Think.*

Getting to the nearest road was my first idea, but I didn't know where I was or even if a road passed through this remote area. I listened as carefully as I could for the hum of passing cars, but heard nothing. Maybe I could follow the stream. It would most likely lead me to a campground or a town.

Of course, to accomplish any of that I had to stand up. I shivered again, remembering my recent attempt. Although the nausea had dissipated, I was desperately cold and thirsty. Whoever had attacked me must have left me for dead out here in the woods.

Think! No matter what the guy's motives, I was alive and I intended to stay that way. I bit my lip and forced away my fear, knowing better than most that panic was as much my enemy as the stranger was.

"Where are you running, sweetheart?" The man's breath smelled of cigarettes and beer. His hand stroked my hair.

"Stop it!" I whispered through gritted teeth. Reliving past horrors wouldn't help me. That attack was two years ago and those men couldn't hurt me ever again. Later, when I was safe, I could fall apart. Now, I needed to kick myself in the ass and get moving because lying here was dangerous. The smell of my blood could attract predators and I so didn't want a run-in with a bear. People sometimes died from exposure and shock, so I needed to find shelter. I took in another lungful and noticed once again the scent of woodsmoke. There must be a hunter or a camper in the area who could help me.

I tried to sit up but I was still too dizzy, so instead I called out, as loudly as I could, "Is anyone here? Please, I need help!" My throat sounded raspy and felt sore, probably from being so dry.

The forest quieted and the hairs on my arms rose. Something was moving toward me.

I forced my arms and legs to move into a hands-and-knees position and dredged up the energy to drag my exhausted body under some nearby brush and curl into a ball. I wished myself invisible, but understood how pitifully lame my effort was. Why hadn't I kept my big mouth shut? A frightened moan slipped through my lips, but I quickly covered them with my sticky hands and chanted mentally. *Don't panic. Don't panic.*

A pair of large hiking boots stopped inches from my feet, quickly followed by a masculine hand parting the bushes. A man crouched next to me, speaking in a soft voice, "You're safe. Are you injured?" I didn't speak. "Try to get up now. I won't hurt you."

Left without options, I forced myself to crawl out from under the bushes. After he helped me sit up, he draped an old wool blanket over my shoulders. I clutched it tightly to my body to try and stop the shaking. Maybe I was wrong and this wasn't my attacker, but instead some camper who happened to hear me call out. Why would my kidnapper care if I was cold?

"I'm too dizzy to stand up. I'll fall." I twisted around to look at his face and inhaled a too familiar whiff of wintergreen.

My breath caught in my chest as I stared at the man I'd seen earlier on the Reynolds' porch. He seemed taller, maybe 6'2", and was no longer dressed in coveralls. Instead he wore jeans and a brown long-sleeved tee, which fit tightly over his slim but well-muscled frame. His dark eyes took in my ragged condition and he shook his head, not smiling. Dried blood was evident on his hands and shirt and that worried me—a lot.

"If you try to run away, I'll restrain you. It's for your own safety."

Wow. Just what a freezing cold, thirsty girl who can barely sit up wants to hear, right? "I won't run." I didn't have a chance of outrunning him barefoot in my wobbly condition.

He held out his hand and after a moment, I reluctantly reached for it. It was large and warm and might have been comforting if the circumstances were different. Pulling me up without effort, he helped me wrap the blanket around my shoulders more securely, then brushed some leaves out of my hair. I didn't have the strength to pull away.

"I'm sorry this happened. How do you feel?"

I looked at him as if he were crazy. "How do you think? And what the hell do you care anyway?" My anger popped to the surface in a burst of venom. His mouth turned down, probably annoyed at my attitude. Well, tough. I'd rather he thought I was angry than... I looked down at my still shaking hands clutching the blanket. I was pretty much scared to death right about now, but he didn't need to know that. "Who are you?" I tried to look confident by taking a step on my own, but my traitorous knees buckled. He held my arm to steady me.

"Take it slow."

Did he just smile? Was he laughing at me? "You drugged me, right? Where am I?" Several tears ran down my cheeks.

Stop crying, you wimp. If I didn't keep my head, I may not survive the next few hours. I wiped my face roughly with a corner of the blanket.

His voice was soothing and deep, without even a hint of anger. "I'll answer your questions in a little while. We're heading to that cabin in the clearing. You can get cleaned up and have something to eat and drink." He held my arm so I couldn't pull away, placing his hand against my forehead. "You're dehydrated and your body temp's low. Just don't try to run and everything will be fine." I breathed in another mouthful of minty-flavored air and felt myself relax.

The cabin he'd mentioned was only twenty-five yards away, hidden behind some low hanging branches. He gestured in that direction and I found myself staring at it with longing. I was weak and thirsty. More than thirsty, my stomach was cramping up from hunger. I had no idea when I'd eaten last.

I stumbled forward with the stranger supporting my arm to help me keep my balance. As I walked up the wooden steps and across the narrow porch to enter the cabin, I shivered with fear and anticipation. One thing was clear. I had to keep my head and figure out a way to escape. He didn't know I was more than I seemed, not just a frightened teenaged girl. I was strong and fast and I was going to get out of this forest and back home, as soon as I figured out how to walk again.

CHAPTER TWO

W E ENTERED A COZY ROOM WITH multi-colored rugs and an old, comfy looking couch decorated with pillows and throws. A well-worn armchair sat near a lit fireplace, the moving flames decorating the walls with dancing shadows. The comforting smell of home-cooked meals lingered in combination with another musty odor, common to cabins occupied only on occasion.

He handed me a sports-sized water bottle and pointed toward a narrow hallway to the left. "Your room is the second door on the right. Do you think you can make it?"

"Yes," I snapped.

"There's a bag of clothes on the bed. The bathroom has clean towels on the shelf." I didn't move. "Go on, kid. No one will bother you. Just don't try to run away. There's really no-where to go and we need to talk."

I took a couple of swigs from the water bottle, but stayed where I was. He smiled and tried to sound reassuring. "I'm not going to hurt you. I'm going to make you something to eat and then explain everything. Go ahead." He gave my shoulder a squeeze and turned away, heading for the small kitchen to the right, opening the fridge and getting out a few bags.

Stumbling through the door he'd indicated, I locked it behind me and forced my shaky body to move into the small bathroom. After locking that door, I stripped and showered, my need to wash away the blood and warm up under the hot water taking precedence over my fear. It was important to see where I was injured and clean any wounds. The hot water felt like heaven, and I scrubbed my body hard, getting every bit of the blood and mud out of my hair and off my skin. The soap and shampoo worked their magic, and as I dried with a large towel I sighed with relief. I smelled human again.

Unwrapping the towel, I stood in front of the full-length mirror in the steamy bathroom and examined myself. Strangely, not one cut or scrape marred my skin, not even a bruise. Even more alarming, the scars that had marked my body after my attack two and a half years ago had disappeared as well.

Car doors slamming.
Two sets of feet rushing toward me.
"Where are you running, sweetheart?"
A rag shoved in my mouth.
A hand stroking my hair.
"So pretty."

My knees gave out and I sat down hard on the closed toilet seat. I covered my face with my hands and forced air into my lungs. When I finally stopped trembling, I visualized pushing the dark memory back into its box, the way I always coped with that particular horror. I rubbed my arms, tightening them around my body in a feeble attempt to banish the ghosts that still seemed to haunt me.

And there were plenty of them to banish. Raised within

the state foster care system, I was passed from family to family, never really fitting in anywhere. I'd heard the labels: Troublemaker, Disruptive, Self Destructive, the list went on. Sometimes I was all those things. Mostly I was lonely and angry.

At my various schools, I'd become pretty good at short-term friendships, but I moved around too often to hold onto even one. To survive, I threw my energy into schoolwork, getting good grades and even skipping ahead. But in most of my foster homes, I'd felt out of place and unwanted, unable to trust the adults who always sent me away without giving me the time I needed to adjust. I'd never lived in one place long enough to have a chance at a normal life.

The familiar feelings of hurt and rage began to build in my gut as tears ran down my cheeks. I jumped up and paced the room, scanning it for a way out, my spirit aching for a run. The window was large enough, but I wasn't an idiot. The kidnapper had left me alone and unguarded, so the cabin must be in a very remote area. If I ran, he'd follow me and bring me back. Maybe tie me up. And I still wasn't at my best. I needed food.

Grunting in frustration, I slapped my hand against the window frame hard, not minding the sting. I was never one to wallow in a pity party, but this day really sucked, even more than usual. No matter how crappy my life had been, I wasn't ready to die. I'd be seventeen in a few days, if I lived that long. I could still go to college. Maybe turn my life around.

The guy playing house in the other room said he wasn't going to hurt me, but could I believe him? I wiped away the last few tears and blew my nose with bath tissue.

Enough.

On the bed was a shopping bag containing clothes in all the right sizes. I was surprised to see that this was quality stuff, made of good fabrics, not discount store merchandise. Reluctantly, I dressed. My shirt and jeans were no longer usable and I wasn't about to stay wrapped up in a stupid towel. In a smaller bag were other items: toothpaste, a toothbrush, hairbrush, deodorant and more. Guess he figured I was sticking around for a while. I returned to the bathroom and brushed my hair and teeth, then scowled at the mirror.

I am such a jerk.

Grunting, I pulled my hair roughly back into its usual ponytail, finding some comfort in the familiar action. I peered closely at my puffy red eyes to see if my pupils were dilated from the drug he'd given me. They looked normal, and other than my raging hunger, I was feeling okay again.

I straightened my body to its full 5'9" and did a few stretches, just in case I caught a break. I ran often—it was how I dealt with the memories and the day to-day-pain, flushing away the rage and the loneliness with every stride. It was just me and the road, and I liked it that way. Sometimes a cruel comment or unfair situation had me lacing up my sneakers and racing out the door without telling anyone where I was going, escaping before my rage could reach the boiling point and turn dangerous. At least that was my fear. That a part of me could lose control and do serious damage.

But on the road, my body moved in a perfect rhythm, strong and powerful—and fast. Freakishly fast. So fast I had to hide the truth from everyone. I'd timed myself running on secluded roads where no one would see me.

I looked toward the door to the hallway, remembering the cold ground and the fear and the nausea. Maybe doing some damage wouldn't be so bad in this particular instance. Could this guy really catch me? He had long legs—that's for sure—and he looked fit. The thought of getting caught sent shivers through my bones. He was quick and quiet. And what if he had a gun?

I jumped at the two raps on the door. I hadn't heard him walking down the narrow hallway. My hearing was usually great. How did he do that?

"Kid, I made you something to eat. You need to get your strength back. It's been over a day since you've eaten." I listened for his retreating steps but heard nothing but the sound of the refrigerator door opening and closing in the kitchen.

Wait, did he say over a day? Was it Monday night? Maggie and Justin must be so worried. Knowing them, they probably already had the town turned upside down with search teams out in force and my face already on milk cartons. If only there was some way to let them know where I was and that I wasn't hurt.

The odor of food reminded me that I needed to eat to get my strength back. I stood, reached for the doorknob and froze. Decision time: run or stay. Something in my gut told me if the man had wanted to kill me he would have done it already.

I sniffed, my mouth beginning to water. It smelled like steak.

My empty stomach took over command, forcing my brain to send out orders to turn the knob. I peeked down the hallway toward the kitchen, brushing a few loose strands of hair out of my face and grimacing with resolve. Maybe I could somehow convince him to let me go. I'd talked myself out of tough situations before. I was actually pretty good at it. Tonight I'd need all my skills.

I smiled on the inside, my confidence building. I could always run away later, while he was asleep.

CHAPTER THREE

T HE DARK HAIRED STRANGER TURNED AS I walked into the small kitchen. "Sit here." He smiled and motioned to one of the three wooden chairs pulled up against a small round table. I sat down hesitantly and he handed me a steak knife, fork, and napkin. There was a pitcher of cold water on the table and he told me to help myself, so I drank down a glass, not minding the cold ache against my throat. He placed a large bowl of salad on the table followed by another with bread, then handed me a dinner plate laden with a steak and fries.

I watched him as he served up his own food, careful not to let him notice me doing it. His back was broad, but his waist was slim as were his long legs. He looked young when he smiled, probably around twenty-two or twenty-three. He'd managed to find the time to change his shirt and clean up while I was still in the bathroom. His movements were graceful like a martial artist's, but I sensed that underneath the smile and the elegance was a dangerous man.

He sat across from me. "Eat, Jackie, and I'll explain a few things."

He knew my name. Had he looked in my wallet? I glanced around the room hoping to find my backpack. My cell phone was in there, something else I hadn't thought about. Jeez, I'd definitely been drugged if I'd forgotten about my cell phone. Taking a big bite of the steak, I realized I was totally starving. I forgot about everything else, shoveling in mouthful after mouthful as fast as I could chew and swallow.

His voice was soft and soothing. "Slow down a little. There's plenty. My name's Rob. I'm not going to hurt you, but I'll have to lock you up if you try to run away."

"I heard you the first time." I glared at him over my water glass. Now that the drugs seemed to be mostly out of my system, my fear had turned to anger.

Still, he smiled at me, as if my attitude was no big deal. "Good. You understand. Makes things easier."

"Easier for you, or for me?" I continued to scowl between bites.

"Both of us, but mostly for you."

I was annoyed that he wasn't taking me seriously. I squirted out some ketchup and chewed on a fry, watching him as he took another bite of his salad. The food was making me feel a lot better, giving me the nerve to ask questions. "Why did you kidnap me?"

He just kept on chewing, watching me but not answering.

"They'll find me and you'll go to jail." I bluffed, not sure at all that someone would find me in this remote location. "Are we in the Sierras?"

He swallowed, hesitating for a moment as if wondering how to proceed. "What I'm going to tell you will be tough for you to hear."

"Spit it out." I kept shoving food in my mouth. I'd need this energy later when I made a break for it.

"No one will report you missing. Maggie and Justin told

your school that you were moving because Justin needed to start a new job in Colorado. They've already left town and a moving company is packing up your house. Your stuff is going into storage until you need it.

I stopped eating. "You're crazy if you think I'm falling for that bull."

"You'll be able to see them again in a couple of months." I didn't respond. "They wanted me to tell you they love you. They felt terrible about not being able to talk to you first. But we had no choice. Your situation was becoming dangerous."

"Dangerous?"

"I'll be calling them regularly to fill them in on your progress. They've actually helped us like this before, although you're the only child they've adopted. They think you're an amazing kid."

I'd been holding my breath, unable to believe what I was hearing. This can't be real. My family cared about me. They definitely wouldn't leave town without me. They wouldn't want me to get hurt or to be frightened or to be alone.

It was suddenly way too much to deal with. "You're full of shit," I yelled, standing and knocking the chair over. I started backing away, holding my steak knife in front of me and searching for a way to get around Rob and out of the cabin.

Rob moved so quickly I had no time to react. The knife clattered uselessly to the floor as he secured my wrists in a tight grip, his face only inches from mine. My nostrils filled once more with his cool wintergreen scent and I shuddered, my muscles relaxing against my will.

Intrigued by his strange ability, I looked up into his dark brown eyes. *Who is this guy? I panic, and he soothes me.* I was ready to explode ten seconds ago and now...

Oh no, I wasn't some weak little girl he could control with some spooky cologne. I gritted my teeth. "Let go of me,"

I demanded, trying to pull away without success. I hoped he didn't think I was really going to stab him with the knife. I've never been a violent person, but this experience was stressing out my sanity circuits.

He was having absolutely no trouble holding me in place. I tried a couple of moves I'd learned in self-defense class, but nope. No luck. And he was smiling at me. What a jerk. "I'll let go if you sit down and eat more of your meal."

"Fine." No use letting a perfectly good steak go to waste. I'd spent too many nights as a kid feeling hungry. "But I still don't believe anything you said."

He'd somehow righted my chair without me noticing. How was that possible? I sat, but didn't feel all that hungry anymore. I pushed the plate away.

"If you don't eat, it'll take longer to recover from the meds."

"What did you give me?" It had actually flashed in my head for a whole thirty seconds that Rob wasn't so bad, but then I remembered the dizziness, the nausea and the blood. I narrowed my eyes and fantasized about seeing him led away to jail.

He seemed to be amused by my anger, which annoyed me even more. "It's a new drug created for a specific purpose. You had your first dose a few hours ago and didn't exactly react the way the other trainees did. You ran off and I couldn't find you for an hour or so." He laughed at his own private joke. "You're pretty damn fast."

"You've done this to others?"

"Yes. There's a good reason, if you'll just listen."

No way was I listening to Mister Minty Fresh the serial kidnapper. "I should have kept running. You wouldn't have caught me." Slapping my hands down hard on the table, I glared directly at him, too angry to be afraid.

Rob leaned back in the chair looking kind of smug, but his voice was soothing. "You're wrong, Jackie, I would have found you." He pointed at my plate. "Keep eating." He frowned so I took another tiny bite. "I know this is very difficult, but the sooner you can recognize the truth of your situation, the easier it will be for you to adapt."

There was something compelling about him when he spoke in that calm clear way. I wanted to believe that he didn't want to harm me, but I was afraid to let down my guard.

My stomach growled again. I looked down at the delicious steak and decided to keep eating. I'd need my strength to escape, I reasoned, so if he wanted to talk while I ate, I guess I could pretend to listen. Later I'd run. Then he'd be eating my dust.

He handed me a clean knife and picked up the one I'd dropped, tossing it into the sink.

"I wasn't going to stab you. I was…what you said…hurt."

"Try to trust me, Jackie. I won't lie to you."

"Where are we?"

"We're on Isla Solitaria, which means lonely island in Spanish. We locals call it Solo Island. You're miles from mainland California—pretty much stuck here no matter how fast you think you are." He smiled at me and I crossed my arms. *Huh.* I knew exactly how fast I was and it would probably blow his mind. "You're here to be trained. When I'm satisfied you're ready to leave, you'll be able to live almost anywhere you'd like. I don't want you to think of yourself as a prisoner." He took another bite of his food and waited for my reaction.

I stopped eating as I tried to process what he'd said. He'd just told me that he was going to train me to do something and then let me go. Yeah, like that wasn't total BS. As I watched him eat, I tried to figure out what he *did* want. He hadn't tried to touch me, other than to keep me from running and to help me into the cabin, which was a good thing 'cause I didn't think I could fight him off for long if he wanted to rape me. I took another look at his biceps and broad muscular chest. Nope, my only chance was to run.

Rob glanced down at my plate then back at me, raising an eyebrow. I shoved a French fry in my mouth to placate him, then chewed and swallowed. "What do you want me to learn to do? And who the heck are you?"

"I'm getting to that. Think of me as a recruitment specialist. I work for a diverse group who share a similar interest. One person in particular has observed you on and off the last few years and is very interested in your potential. He called me in specifically to train you." He buttered a slice of bread as he spoke.

I snorted and almost choked on my next fry. "My potential? As what, a runner? That's about the only thing I do well."

"Running fast is one of your gifts."

Another non-answer. Must be one of his so-called *gifts*. "This friend of yours was watching me?" He nodded. I pushed away the stray pieces of salad and took a bite of the bread he'd handed me, shuddering as I remembered another day and other men who'd watched me.

"Have you ever heard the term shapeshifter?" He seemed to be scrutinizing my expression carefully.

"What, like werewolves?"

"No, not like wolves, although shifters do take the form of animals. Shapeshifters aren't ruled by the phases of the moon and are able to shift under almost any circumstances, as long as they've gained enough control and are physically strong. Also, shifters don't live under such a rigid societal structure as wolves, enjoying a lot more freedom within their communities. Werewolves are more powerful physically, at least when they're healthy, and are definitely more volatile. They make dangerous enemies but can also make loyal allies. It's important for a shifter to know which variety of wolf they're dealing with."

This must be some kind of weird joke. "You're talking like werewolves and shapeshifters are real creatures. Are you taking your own drugs?" *Why is he telling me this ridiculous crap?* I tried to figure out his motives as he sat and watched me. *Maybe he's just nuts.* That thought did nothing to relieve my anxiety.

"They are real. Vampires, witches, sorcerers, the fae and many other supernatural beings inhabit the world with humans. I know you don't believe me now, but in a few months it'll all seem pretty mundane."

I was not gonna be anywhere near this guy in a few months. "You said the fae? Like…fairies?" I almost laughed at him, but then thought better of it. He could be seriously crazy and laughing at him was probably not a good way to get him to let me go.

"They're more like Galadriel than Tinkerbelle. The ones I've met are extremely powerful. Many of them have lived for thousands of human years."

"Oh. That's interesting. Like Tolkien elves, huh?" Speaking softly, I asked, "But what's the training for?" Keeping him talking was probably the best strategy, at least until I could think of something else.

That eyebrow had arched up again, the corner of his mouth lifting slightly. "I see the wheels turning. I'm not crazy."

"Oh, yeah, I know."

"I'll be training you to shift, to feel comfortable in your new skin."

"New skin?" Whoa, that sounded really creepy.

"You're a shapeshifter. Usually shifters make their first change a couple of years after puberty, but some are late bloomers. You and I are here on the island to force your first change away from anyone who could get hurt. It'll happen eventually anyway. I'm just going to bring it on a little faster. That's what the drug is for. I'll get you through your first shift as safely as possible." He watched me carefully, waiting for me to bolt or cry or react in some way.

Wow. This guy should design role-playing games. I decided to pretend to play along with his strange little fantasy. "Why not just wait until I change naturally?" I pushed my fries back and forth, my appetite having suddenly disappeared. I glanced at the door and he laughed.

Rob continued, "Two reasons: If your first change occurred in school or your home, you'd have been terrified and could've hurt someone. Also, shifter populations are thinning out. We're always on the lookout for shifters, like you, who've slipped through our radar. We have dangerous enemies and most of us feel that bringing strong young recruits into the mix will only help strengthen the community."

Rob stood up and moved slightly away from the table. "I'm a shifter. A black leopard."

I felt a strange electric charge in the air, my body tingling pleasantly as energy filled the small room. I watched in complete astonishment as Rob's hands turned into enormous black paws with lethal looking claws. He flexed them slightly, retracting the claws when he noticed my wide-eyed expression. Just as quickly the paws transitioned back to his large human-looking hands. The change seemed effortless. He wasn't even breathing hard.

Stunned, the reality of the situation hit me like a two-by-four in the face. "But I don't want to change," I pleaded. "I'm human, not an animal. I won't let you drug me again. You can't force me to change!" I'd stood without thought, rage and fear smoldering in the bonfire of my jumbled emotions. There was no way I was going to let this pseudo-nice creep inject me with some weird drug to make me turn into a bird or a bear or whatever. Maybe this was some kind of governmental test site, although Rob didn't really look like a scientific geek. More like a Land's End model.

"Please sit down." His soothing voice and comforting wintergreen scent made most of my tension float away. Suddenly my knees were bending and I was sitting again.

He rubbed his hands, maybe massaging away the effects of the transition. "The drug I've given you doesn't turn you into a shifter. Shapeshifters are born, so you must have had at least one shifter parent. The drug simply encourages your body to do what it would probably do in a few days or weeks anyway. I just don't see the point in waiting around for it to happen. You shouldn't have to stay on the island any longer than necessary." He smiled kindly. "I know this is rough for you to take in."

I crossed my arms over my chest and looked down, trying to bury my fear where he couldn't see it. His hands had definitely changed to a leopard's paws. That wasn't some hallucination. I should have been screaming or crying, but instead I wanted some answers. I lifted my chin. "Where did all the blood come from? I don't have one cut. And why can't I remember anything?"

"Amnesia is a side effect of the tranquilizer I gave you outside your house. You probably won't ever remember your trip to the island. You struggled quite a bit after I administered your first dose of the experimental meds four hours ago. Your hands began to shift and you did some damage with your claws. Some of the blood was yours from self-inflicted injuries and some of it was mine as I tried to subdue you, but most of it belonged to my other guest in the back bedroom. Come, I'll introduce you."

As I followed him, my head was spinning with ideas. Someone else was here? Was there another prisoner like me? Maybe we could team up and get off this island. Of course I only had his word that we were even on an island. He might be lying. What did he say about my hands changing? I looked down at them and they looked perfectly normal to me, except for the missing scars.

We walked quickly to the back of the cabin, opening a door on the left. I couldn't believe what I saw.

Chapter Four

THE ROOM WAS SMALLER THAN MINE, STILL managing to fit a double bed and an old pine dresser. The walls were freshly painted a pale green and a multicolored rug covered a portion of the worn wooden floor. Two windows overlooked the woods behind the cabin, giving its occupant a slightly different view than mine.

The scent of eucalyptus was strongest near the bed so I turned in that direction. Suddenly I was face to face with a beautiful cougar lifting his head to return my startled gaze. His ears perked to attention as he stretched like a typical cat, then jumped down, opening his mouth in a yawn to give me a good view of his very sharp teeth. His furry coat was a lovely sienna brown across his back, turning a lighter shade as it traveled toward his stomach and down his legs.

One of his front legs was cuffed, attached to a thick chain leading to a metal plate bolted to the wall. Even though Rob was in front of me, I found myself inching backwards into the hallway, wondering if the restraint was in place because Rob thought he was dangerous.

Rob nudged me forward. "You're safe."

Uh, huh. This crazy shifter dude kept wild animals as pets. Very large wild animals.

The cougar's head tilted as his large golden brown eyes seemed to take me in with typical feline curiosity. He growled softly at Rob, perhaps in greeting, then blinked once and shifted his weight from giant paw to paw, flicking his thick tail and sniffing the air. I backed against the wall, worried that he could smell my fear or hear my much faster heartbeat.

Rob spoke. "Jackie, meet Ethan. Ethan, why don't you change back to human form so you can introduce yourself? You may want to turn your back for a minute, Jackie." Uncertain, but really curious, I turned to face the wall. A similar electric type charge made my body tingle in the same cool way that Rob's change had done earlier. I heard a few grunts and the sound of clothing being pulled on. "Okay, you can turn around now." Rob said.

When I turned back, I looked in surprise at the young man standing next to the bed. Slightly broader than Rob, he was about 5'10" with shining chocolate brown hair tossed around his head in messy waves. Because he was only wearing sweatpants, I noticed that Ethan's arms, chest, and stomach were sculpted with muscle. His eyes took on a mischievous glint when he saw me checking him out, and I could feel my face heat up in a blush. I was really relieved to see that the cuff around his cougar's leg had adjusted to fit his human wrist, although I couldn't figure how Rob had managed it. Ethan's left forearm was etched in ink, a cougar lounging on a tree branch.

"Ethan is chained because he didn't believe there'd be consequences for trying to take off before he finished his training," Rob explained. Ethan rolled his eyes, but didn't appear angry at all. "While he was running off, he ran into you. You made quite a mess of him, unintentionally, I'm sure. Served him right." Ethan's eyes were back on me, an amused smile making him look less predatory. Rob smiled as he continued. "I was able to get him back to his room easily after that. I suppose I have you to thank for his capture." He and Ethan both laughed.

I looked Ethan over, puzzled by his uninjured chest and arms. "I guess I should apologize, but I don't remember doing it and you don't seem too beat up."

Ethan took a step closer causing the chain to clunk loudly. "Shifting helps me heal faster. Jackie, huh? What kind of shifter are you?" He looked me up and down and smiled again. His voice was rich and easy on the ears, as the rest of him was easy on the eyes. He took in my scent as if he were still in animal form, and that's what brought me back to reality.

Checking out the hot guy had suddenly lost its appeal. I clenched my fists in annoyance and scowled. "I—I'm not a shifter. I'm not going to be changing into anything." I brushed my a few loose strands of hair off my face and frowned at him. He continued to smirk.

Just my luck, an arrogant asshole is the other prisoner. Well, he looks strong at least. Maybe he can be useful. Or maybe I should just leave him here chained up. He's probably more trouble than he's worth.

"Oh you're not a shifter, huh?" Ethan laughed softly. "A few hours ago those hands of yours were lethal weapons. You're some kind of big cat like Rob and me. Jaguar maybe?" He turned to Rob who shrugged, "Although your coloring may be too light." He looked me up and down as he smiled again. "Your body is typical female feline."

"Ethan, stop making her uncomfortable. I just might unlock the chain tomorrow morning if you can behave. Jackie, come with me. It's late and you need some sleep."

"G'night, Jackie. Grrr." I heard him laughing as Rob closed

the door.

What a jerk that guy is. A gorgeous jerk. I smiled to myself.

Lost in my thoughts I almost ran into Rob who was standing in the hallway holding a water bottle. "Take this; you'll probably be thirsty again later. I'm sleeping on the couch tonight. Get some rest, you'll be busy tomorrow."

"Aren't you worried that I'll run off?" I frowned, but still accepted the bottle.

"Nope. Shifters have excellent hearing." He pointed to one of his ear and smiled.

Lucky me. Two arrogant jerks in one house. "I still have a lot of questions." I yawned, turning away, embarrassed.

"We have plenty of time to answer them tomorrow. Try to get some rest." He smiled and walked toward the couch, his strong body moving silently down the hallway.

I flicked on the light, then closed and locked the door behind me. The room was small, but clean and smelled of fresh lavender, probably because there were a few sprigs in a vase on the dresser. The walls were cream colored, the curtains on the two small windows a pale blue cotton. There was a simple wooden dresser and a comfortable looking chair near the window. For maybe ten seconds I thought about running. I might be faster, but this guy was a freakin' black leopard, and if he caught me he might be hungry.

I took care of some personal stuff, and crawled under the covers, intending to spend time sorting through the mess of jumbled information dished out along with my steak.

Instead, I couldn't stop thinking about Justin and Maggie and everything I was being forced to leave behind. Much of it I'd be grateful to turn my back on, but Justin and Maggie had been real parents to me. I'd finally felt like I had a home and a family. And now everything had been wrenched away just when I was beginning to feel somewhat normal.

The real kicker was that the couple I'd thought loved me and wanted me in their lives, had handed me over to Rob and left town. Maybe they thought they were helping me, but they could have handled it a lot better. They could have sat me down and explained the situation rather than agreeing to have me kidnapped. Waking up on the ground, scared and miserable, sucked eggs.

I wasn't surprised when a tear wet my cheek, then another. Soon I was crying steadily, my head buried in the pillow in an effort not to wake anyone up. I curled up tightly on the bed and tried to squash the sadness and the anger by thinking about running through the woods, feeling the wind in my hair and the ground racing by under my feet.

I heard a soft knock on my door, and I knew it was Rob before he spoke. "Are you all right, Jackie? Can I get you anything?"

"Yeah, just … just get the hell away from me," I managed to gasp out between sobs. Rob had no other questions for me that night.

CHAPTER FIVE

I DREAMED.

It was the last few minutes of dusk and I was on a darkening forest trail running very fast. Giant tree branches loomed overhead casting sinister shadows across my path. I was barefoot, but the carpet of sorrel plants cushioned my feet as I sped along past fallen branches and fragrant shrubs. I saw movement up ahead so I ran toward it, curious, but also afraid. Three men were arguing about something. One of them had a gun. Suddenly I realized that I was no longer on the trail, but looking down on them from a great height, safe for the moment, yet still exposed if the man with the gun decided to take a shot at me. A beautiful male cougar lounged on a thick branch in the tree next to mine. He winked at me. When I looked down again, a large brown wolf stood on the path where the man with the gun had stood a moment before.

Suddenly I was awake. What kind of crazy dream was that? I shook my head to clear it, disturbed by the vision. Through the window I could see a trail winding off to the right, but I didn't have a clue where it led and I still felt weak from last night's adventures. The rumbling noises coming from my stomach reminded me that I hadn't eaten much yesterday, maybe only a third of the steak and a few fries. I stood and stretched, hoping there might be cereal or toast available in the kitchen.

I gasped to see my backpack on the small chair by the window. Apparently, locking the door didn't make any difference around here. Rummaging through the bag for my cell phone, I wasn't surprised to find it missing. At least my Mp3 player was still in its usual pocket. I made use of the bathroom and then unlocked the bedroom door and peeked out. Taking a deep breath to bolster my courage, I walked down the short hallway, rounding the corner to the kitchen.

As I entered the combination living room/kitchenette, Rob was typing on a laptop at the table and Ethan was stretched out on the couch with a book. Both of them looked up when I entered the room. Rob had a concerned expression but I stubbornly refused to meet his gaze.

Ethan closed his book and smiled charmingly. "So, Cinderella, what are you cooking us for breakfast?"

I sat at the table across from Rob and snapped back, "Didn't you get your cat food this morning, Garfield?"

"Garfield?" he scoffed. "I'm definitely more like the Cheshire Cat." To prove his point he grinned widely and then disappeared behind his book.

Rob smiled. "He's kidding. He ate six eggs, eight slices of bacon and four pieces of toast an hour ago. He definitely eats like Garfield."

Ethan groaned in protest, raising his hand and waving it around. "Growing cougar here."

"There are leftovers in the oven. Help yourself." Rob went back to working at his laptop.

I didn't want to cooperate with Rob, but the smell was making my mouth water. Hey, I could always eat first and then try to sneak away afterward. Deciding that this was an extremely intelligent plan, I opened the oven door and breathed in the heavenly smell. Eggs and bacon—yum. I scooped a mound onto a plate and sat down to eat.

Ethan closed his book, pulled a chair over to the table and sat beside me. He was wearing jeans and a navy blue sleeveless tee, his hair still a messy jumble and his golden-brown eyes shining with curiosity. I was still in the sweats I'd slept in, feeling kind of grungy, so I ignored him and kept on eating. Ethan reached out hesitantly to brush a strand of hair out of my face, watching me warily for any hint of a violent reaction. Feeling more confident, he started gently twisting the long lock in his fingers. When he leaned in to sniff it, I quickly pushed him away with a firm, "Down boy."

He sighed. "How old are you?"

"Seventeen on Wednesday." Not wanting him to catch me smiling, I stuffed a piece of bacon in my mouth. He was really kind of cute.

"Hmm. You seem older." He stood up and plopped himself back on the couch, humming the tune to, "A Very Merry Unbirthday."

Rob looked up from his laptop, smiling. "You can't take him too seriously. He's a young male shapeshifter and he just turned eighteen. They're always on the prowl. He's relatively harmless."

"I'll keep that in mind." I'd actually had plenty of experience discouraging healthy young human males. How different would a shifter be? I'd been the "New Girl" in three different high schools, always attracting the attention of the guys who were looking for something fast and easy. The key was to let them keep their pride intact while you backed away gracefully. Otherwise it could get ugly.

I looked at my hands as I scooped up another forkful of eggs. Had they really changed into paws? "How did I hurt you and Ethan the other night? If you're both shifters then I'm not stronger than you are. Was it the drug? Not that you didn't deserve to bleed a little." I glared at Rob, who answered.

"Yes, the first dose of the drug, which was only supposed to balance your body chemistry for the next dose, caused your hands to shift. You were upset and disoriented and flailed about in panic. I tried to calm you down so you wouldn't hurt yourself and finally managed to get you to fall asleep on the couch.

"But while I was with you, Ethan decided it was the perfect opportunity to make a run for it. I figured you were out for the night, so I ran off to look for Ethan. You woke up, ran into Ethan before I did and sliced him up a little. I discovered him passed out in the woods. Apparently he'd hit his head on a rock when he fell. He'd definitely had an unpleasant altercation with your long claws. Ethan, what happened exactly?"

"I'm too much of a gentleman to kiss and tell." Ethan beamed at me. His gorgeous eyes sparkled with humor, but I pretended not to notice, going back to concentrating on eating my breakfast.

Rob continued to tell his story, shaking his head at Ethan's joke. "When I went back for you, you were nowhere to be seen. I searched around and finally heard you call out for help."

I frowned at him, feeling tension growing inside me. "I saw the blood all over me and hoped that my attacker had left thinking I was dead and that some nice hiker or hunter might find me." Rob looked guilty. Good. "I know you think that I'm going to be a good little house pet and go along with all this shit, but that's not going to happen. You can chain me up and throw away the key. I'm not going to change into an animal for your messed up idea of entertainment."

No one spoke for a while. I chewed my food, Ethan turned the pages of his book and Rob tapped away on his laptop.

Ethan finally broke the silence. "Rob's a good guy. He's trying to help us out 'cause he had a bad experience when he first shifted."

I scowled and ignored Ethan's accolade. "Why couldn't you just come to Maggie and Justin's house and tell me all of this without drugging me? You say they knew what I was."

"Think about it. You probably wouldn't have believed me, and because of your history, we figured that your reaction would have been extreme. You do have a temper, running when you get upset. Being in the center of a human community is not a good place for a shapeshifter to flip out. If you'd told a human cop or neighbor, we'd have had a real problem on our hands. We would've been forced to go around scrubbing memories."

"You can do that?"

"Not me, but my associate can."

I saw Ethan scowl. "Garrett—he's a vampire."

"Are you saying that the one who watched me when I was younger was a vampire?" Rob nodded. *Okay, that is flat out creepy.* I stared at my hands, twisted together in my lap. "How is it that every scar I ever had has disappeared?"

"Shifters have an amazing ability to heal. I'm fairly sure your older scars went away because of the strength of this particular serum. I hope you weren't too attached to them." He tried to sound lighthearted, but I could tell by his expression that he was worried.

"No, Rob. I wasn't." My sharp tone jarred them into silence. I'd never willingly dredge up that experience again, having buried it in hell where it belonged. I walked to the window and looked out at the dreary day. This part of the country was prone to a lot of rain and fog, which matched my current mood just fine.

Rob spoke. "Look, I don't want you to go through what a lot of other rogue shifters have experienced. Ethan can tell you that shifting isn't so bad. In fact changing into your animal form can be liberating."

"What's a rogue shifter?"

"A rogue is a shifter who doesn't grow up with a family of shifters—one who doesn't expect the change and has no support system in place." I caught a quick wince, maybe from a remembered experience of his own, before he continued. "I'll be giving you another dose of the meds tomorrow. Today we need to do some preliminary blood tests and physical agility tests."

That was so not happening. "You can test my blood and my physical abilities, but you're not giving me another dose of that crap." I walked outside, fuming, giving in to the familiar tightness that usually had me running as fast as I could. *I'm getting out of here. I'll swim if I have to, or float on a tree branch until some boat comes along.*

I yanked on the bottom of my tee shirt and twisted it to tie it into a knot. I tried to roll up my sweatpants, preferring to run in shorts, but the legs kept falling down. In frustration, I took a pair of scissors down from the hook on the wall. I cut and ripped a jagged four inches off the bottoms. The morning was getting warmer and I could feel sweat start to bead at my hairline. I leaned down to tighten the laces on my sneakers, which had been cleaned and left outside my bedroom door.

Must've been the elves.

"There's nowhere to go." Ethan had followed me out and watched me adjust my clothes with an amused expression.

I stretched out my hamstrings, calves, and quads the way I always did before a run. "Says the guy who tried to escape the other night."

"You don't want to end up chained to a bed, believe me. It's really boring." He watched me stretch for a few moments longer. "On second thought I could come and visit you. I'm sure we could think of something fun to do." His impish smiled annoyed me enough to throw a small rock at him, which he dodged easily. Too bad his reflexes were so good.

"I'm going for a run, so tell the big bad leopard to chill. I'm not trying to get away; it's just what I do for tension, although if I really wanted to get off the island, I could." I narrowed my eyes in challenge, but Ethan wisely chose not to argue.

Rob yelled from inside the cabin. "You two will be back here in an hour. Stay on the trails." Not a question, just a statement.

"Whatever."

I took off at an even pace, moving along a forest trail with Ethan loping next to me.

"You're nuts if you think you can keep up," I taunted.

"You're crazy if you think I can't." He grinned and winked. I kicked into first gear and sprinted off. Ethan did his best for a while, but was tiring quickly. His muscular body was designed for strength, not speed, and although I'm sure that he ran for exercise, he was totally outclassed.

It had started to rain and the path was softening. Ethan disappeared for a minute or two, only to reappear in his cougar form. "Cheater," I yelled, smiling. He actually stuck his tongue out at me, or was he licking his nose?

His brown and tan body was a streamlined work of art. I admired the way his powerful muscles bunched and relaxed as he ran beside me, passing me gracefully. He seemed to be having a great old time making me stare at his tail, until I decided I was warmed up enough, kicked into super gear and left him behind me in the dust. He could watch my human tail for a while.

CHAPTER SIX

AN HOUR LATER, I APPEARED ON THE cabin porch, soaked from rain and sweat, yet much more relaxed. I'd come back because, well, I wasn't an idiot. I needed their help if this was really going to happen, and more and more I was starting to believe that it might. And if it was true that I wasn't human, then so many things I'd hated about myself, strange quirks that I'd always considered to be freakish, were all a natural part of who I really was. This was huge and scary as shit.

Ethan was sprawled out in cougar form growling at me softly. He rolled over onto his back practically demanding that I rub his belly. Nope, not happening. His bright eyes were pleading with me for attention, so instead, I scratched under his chin and behind his ears while he purred loudly. Just keeping that male pride intact. I smiled at him in superior female satisfaction.

Suddenly he leaped up, licking my face with his rough, gooey tongue. I raced into the cabin, laughing, heading for the shower to wash off the sweat and cougar saliva. *Bleah!*

Rob was waiting for me when I came out and suggested that I throw my dirty clothes in the washing machine by the back door. I was not excited to see he had the blood test kit set up at the table. Sighing, I sat, slumping in resignation. He relieved me of three vials of blood in a very professional manner, giving me a good whiff of his familiar wintergreen fragrance to relax me.

He smiled, his dark eyes glittering with humor. "It's a strange gift but it's come in handy many times," he joked. Sitting so close I was able to look at his face while he was busy taking my blood. A small dimple popped up on the left side of his mouth when he smiled, and his skin was smooth and perfect, not a wrinkle anywhere.

"Why do you call me kid? You're not much older than me." He didn't look a day over twenty-three.

"Sorry, I'll stick with Jackie from now on. But I'm older than you think." We both laughed as the sound of gentle snoring drifted in from the porch. Try to be patient with him. He's a good kid too."

"You'll be using that minty scent often with me. I get pissed off a lot."

His expression turned serious, giving him a slightly older appearance. "We didn't know you existed until around three years ago when Garrett discovered you running on a deserted road alone. We know you haven't had an easy life, and whether you believe me or not, we can all understand and relate to your anger. In fact, we're kind of counting on that controlled fury of yours to become useful."

I frowned at him. "Are you breeding an army?" I hated the idea of being secretly observed during the last few years. I spoke quietly, my voice tight with emotion. "Maybe you should've thought about showing up earlier and saving me from—some hard times." I stood and walked to the window, hoping he hadn't seen my eyes tear up. "I sure could have used a white knight."

His voice softly echoed his concern. "Our laws and our community dictate when we can step in. Garrett and I waited for specific physical markers that indicated your change was close, like those headaches you've been having and the change in your scent. You've only been experiencing headaches for the last three weeks. We couldn't make assumptions without that kind of strong evidence. It was still possible that you were human."

"I've never felt … normal."

He stood, giving my arm a squeeze. "You're smart and you're strong. You channel your anger and usually make it work for you in a positive way. We're going to help you through this."

I thought about what he'd said as I watched him label the vials and pack up his blood kit, bundling up the medical waste in a special container. "Do all the new shifters get this kind of treatment?"

"No. Most of them grow up in shifter communities and know what they are at a young age. A few slip through the cracks like you and me. Changing for the first time outside of a community of supes can be dangerous for the humans who witness the change and also the new shifter. Occasionally someone dies."

"Supes? Like in supernatural creatures? Jeez, this is so messed up." I groaned and leaned my back against the wall. "Vampires? Werewolves? Really? I feel like a character in a graphic novel. I don't want to run into any other *supes*, if it's all the same to you."

I stretched my arms over my head to relieve the stiffness in my shoulders just as Ethan walked through the door, having changed back into his human form, his sweatpants twisted and his longish hair a crazy mess.

He watched me stretch for a moment and sighed. "Time for a shower." This time I giggled when he passed me and winked.

CHAPTER SEVEN

ROB GAVE ME ORANGE JUICE AND TOLD ME to rest up. In an hour or so he was going to give me several physical agility and endurance tests. I lay down in Ethan's spot on the couch, and caught a whiff of eucalyptus, Ethan's signature scent—kind of an outdoorsy spicy odor. I picked up the book that he'd been reading and read the synopsis on the back cover. It was a mystery about a park ranger who works to solve a murder in one of the US national parks. Ethan was definitely a guy who liked his outdoor drama. I laughed to myself and started to read.

The next thing I knew, Ethan was sitting on the edge of the couch poking me gently in the stomach and saying, "Wake up, Speedy. You have to get tested." I yawned and started to stretch, thought better of it, and stood. He'd already run out the door to the front yard, so I followed him.

Rob put me through my paces all right. He timed me running, although I didn't run as fast as I could—no reason to give everything away—and measured the distance and height of my jumps. He had me doing sit-ups, pull-ups and running in place for what seemed like hours. Ethan lounged on the porch grinning and laughing. I wanted to drop kick the annoying asshole over the cabin roof.

Finally Rob pointed to the right indicating an enormous oak tree and told me to climb it. Now here's something I may not have mentioned. I really don't like heights. When I was around eight years old, one of the other foster kids pushed me off the top of a tall slide in the playground. I broke my wrist and never climbed up another slide. From that day, I've freaked when I was up high and too close to an edge.

"Uh, sorry, but heights aren't really my thing."

"You can do it; just push yourself past the fear." He looked at me confidently.

I shook my head. "I don't like heights ... ever. How about asking me to climb it when I'm a jaguar or whatever it is I'm going to be? Maybe it won't be frightening when I'm an animal." I shrugged and started to turn away.

"Your human fears will affect your abilities in animal form. You need to get over this one fast." His voice had taken on a sterner quality and I felt beads of sweat form along my hairline. Just thinking about climbing that tree was making my throat dry up.

"Oh, c'mon, Jackie," Ethan chimed in pushing me toward the tree, "This is easy!" He started climbing. He was like a freaking machine, pulling himself up smoothly branch-by-branch, until at last he sat smugly near the top, maybe 100 feet in the air, grinning down at me.

My eyes narrowed as I looked up at him. What an arrogant ass. He'd heard me say that I didn't like heights and he pulls this move in front of Rob? I looked up. He was actually waving at me.

"C'mon up." If anything was going to get me up that tree, it was Ethan sitting there taunting me with his no-fear-of-heights attitude. My fear drained away as anger spilled in to

take its place. I glowered and stretched my arms in evil anticipation of shoving him off of that top branch and hearing him
scream as he fell.

Up I went, all the time keeping my eyes on Ethan, never
looking down at the ground. Before I knew it, I was sitting on
the branch right next to him. But instead of making a snide
comment, he patted my shoulder, smiling and saying, "You
can really climb fast! That was cool."

That remark destroyed my murder-by-pushing plan as I
stared into his gleaming brown eyes in surprise, seeing only
genuine admiration in his gaze. Rob called out from below,
"Good work, both of you! Now you can come back to Earth."

Stupid me glanced down and the world instantly flipped
and spun in a nauseating tumble. I grabbed onto Ethan's shirt
for dear life and closed my eyes, shocked to hear myself whimpering a little. He put an arm around my shoulders to steady
me, his other hand on a branch above us.

My voice sounded squeaky but I was too scared to feel
embarrassed. "Ohgodohgod! I can't move. I'm gonna pass
out." I was shaking so hard I thought I'd break the branch in
half.

*Don't think about the branch breaking. The branch is stur-
dy. The branch will not break. We are sitting on the strongest
branch ever grown on a tree. This is the freakin' super branch of
all branches.*

My head was nestled so close against Ethan's shoulder I
could smell his uniquely spicy scent, and for some reason it
calmed me. He held me securely, murmuring words of encouragement into my hair. He seemed very calm, not fazed
at all by my fear, but I could've used a double dose of Rob's
wintergreen tranquilizer to stop the trembling.

Ethan continued to speak softly. "Relax. You're going to
get down one branch at a time exactly the same way you got

up here. And I'm going to help you." Placing a finger under my chin, he forced me to look at him. "You'll have to trust me." He spoke to me calmly but with authority, not like the goofy, flirting Ethan that I'd seen so far.

"I can't do this, I really can't." My eyes were glued shut as I dug my face back into his chest and desperately clutched at his shirt. I think I heard a seam rip, but I was way beyond caring.

"How do you expect to get down if you don't climb down?"

Sweat dampened my brow and palms. Trembling, I continued to cling to his shirt as I answered him, my voice sounding muffled against the material. "I don't freakin' know, Ethan. Maybe you can knock me out and carry me down unconscious? I definitely can't do this the normal way."

"Nah, you're too hard-headed." I knew he'd meant it as a joke, but I wasn't in the mood to laugh. He grunted, taking a firm hold of my chin, forcing me to look him in the eye. Our faces were only inches apart. "You will do this. You will climb down and I'll be behind you the whole time. I won't let you fall. I'll keep you safe." He let that sink in for a minute. "Tell me you trust me." I shook my head up and down quickly. I did trust him. He was channeling Rob or something, but I didn't care, as long as he could get me down again.

"Say it. Out loud."

"I trust you." The words came out a shaky whisper, but he seemed to hear them.

"Good. Face the trunk." I did what he said, although I was whimpering again. Put one hand next to mine and the other on that smaller branch. I'll be with you for every step. Don't look down at all."

His calm manner and reassuring voice gave me a touch of confidence, and after a very shaky start, I was able to follow his orders all the way to the ground with only a few tearful, frozen pauses along the way. When my feet touched the forest floor beneath the tree, I sat down hard, wrapped my arms around my knees and sobbed with relief and embarrassment.

I looked up to see Rob glance at me with concern then pat Ethan on the back and walk back to the cabin. Ethan sat down on the ground next to me and reached out to hold my hand in support. "You really did great. If it makes you feel any better, I can't swim. I start to panic in about three feet of water." He reached out to wipe the tears off my cheeks with his ripped shirt.

"I guess an island is a great place for you to be a prisoner," I sniffled.

He laughed. "Yep, without a boat I'm stuck here. But I don't really feel like a prisoner and neither should you. We're here to train and then we're free to leave." He brushed a stray leaf out of my hair and tried to do the same for his own.

I looked up at him and attempted a smile. "Thank you, Ethan. You—"

"Rob would have caught you, but you're welcome." He leaned over and kissed me gently on the forehead. Then he got up and walked in the direction Rob had gone, making sure that I could see how cute his butt looked as he walked away. Back to the old Ethan, I sighed and smiled.

A few minutes later I followed his spicy scented trail back to the cabin.

CHAPTER EIGHT

R OB WAS COOKING A BIG POT OF PASTA and Ethan was making a salad. To help out, I figured I'd get the washing machine going. I wandered around the various rooms picking up everyone's dirty clothes and towels, sorting and then starting a load of darks.

We ate dinner quietly, no one wanting to bring up what had happened unless I did. As I watched them eat, I realized that the dynamics in the room had changed. I wasn't angry with them anymore. I was sad about my parents, but I didn't feel the rage that had made me lash out at them. For some weird reason, Rob and Ethan seemed to care about me. And even stranger, I was starting to care about them, too.

"It was my anger that got me up that tree," I said to no one in particular. "I was mad at Ethan for acting so smug."

Ethan raised his eyebrows in pretended shock. "Smug? *Moi?*"

I ignored him and asked Rob, "Is that what you meant about using my anger for a purpose?"

"It's not just your anger. It's also your determination to succeed and your ability to focus on a task. You go after a goal without hesitation. Your strength at that moment, physically and mentally, is increased tenfold. Most shifters stay at an even balance, they're this strong or this fast all the time, but you have these incredible spurts of power. I wish you could have watched yourself climbing up that tree." Rob looked at me like a proud teacher. "There was nothing human about what you accomplished today."

"Yeah, she's definitely unbalanced." Ethan laughed. I threw a roll at him and he caught it without even looking, taking a slow bite to taunt me. "Yum. Thanks." He licked his lips.

"Does Ethan still get doses of the crazy serum? 'Cause he seems kind of unbalanced, too." *Bite me,* I mouthed in his direction.

"No, he's finished with that. Now he's here working on his control, which occasionally is sorely lacking." Rob sighed and shook his head good naturedly as Ethan chomped at the air in response to my taunt. "Speaking of the serum, you'll be getting another dose tomorrow morning so you need to get a good night's sleep. You'll be transitioning into your animal and that takes a lot of energy."

I slumped in my chair and thought about what tomorrow would bring. Certain animals were definitely more appealing than others. If I were a seagull I could fly off this island and go home. Sadness washed over me in a wave, my throat burning. No one waited for me. I had no home. I tamped down the tears and thought about what Ethan had said about me being some kind of large cat. That would be cool, I guess. I mean seagulls didn't have sharp claws and I'd already shifted my hands. I was kind of hoping there were no shapeshifter giant sloths.

I threw the load of dark laundry into the dryer and started a load of lights. "What day is it?" I asked Rob who was putting away the leftovers while Ethan did the dishes, all the while humming "Go the Distance."

"Today is Tuesday," Rob answered. Without comment, I grabbed a throw blanket, walked out the front door and sat on the wooden bench on the porch. It was chilly out, but I wanted to think. Tomorrow I'd turn seventeen. Two weeks ago when I thought about my birthday I'd imagined eating cake with Justin and Maggie and a few of my friends from school, then maybe going out to a movie together. What movie had I wanted to see? I couldn't remember.

I was supposed to be graduating in a couple of weeks, getting out early because of all the extra classes I'd taken, a lot of them college level. I'd be missing the ceremony and the typical parties afterward, most of which I wouldn't have been invited to anyway. Maggie and Jason would have looked at me with pride as I got my diploma.

I pulled my feet up onto the bench and hugged my knees, wiping away a few more tears as I quietly mourned the life I was leaving behind.

But as the sadness played out with each salty drop, there was a stew of new feelings emerging: excitement, anticipation, fear, of course, but also hope. Throughout my life I'd balanced on a wire, dangling between normal and different. If I could turn shifter and be accepted into a community of people just like me, maybe I could learn to like who I was.

And tomorrow I'd be turning into an animal.

Rob sat next to me on the bench. I hadn't heard him come through the door.

"Do you know who my birth parents were?" This is the question I'd wanted to ask all day, ever since he mentioned that there were shifter communities. Maybe my parents lived in one of them.

"After we see what you shift into tomorrow, I can put you in touch with someone who can help you search."

"Could they still be alive?"

He hesitated. "I'm sorry, Jackie, but I don't know."

"What happened to you when you first changed?"

His eyes lost their sparkle and his mouth thinned out as he remembered. "I was eighteen and living in a town in Southern Oregon with a family who had adopted me when I was an infant. I was pretty happy and looking forward to graduation and college. I had a younger sister who was also adopted as a baby. At the time she was fifteen and had gotten hooked up with a bad bunch of kids. She'd been missing for about 24 hours when I found her drunk in a rundown house. I grabbed her to take her home and this guy she was with punched me and started kicking me while I was down on the ground. His two friends joined in and I could hear my sister telling them to stop. One of them started punching and kicking her too. Suddenly my clothes were ripping and I was changing into a monster, or so I thought.

"I had no control over my leopard. I attacked them in front of my sister, then ran out the door leaving her collapsed and crying on the floor. There were woods nearby and I headed there. It was late and I thought no one had seen me. I ran all night until I passed out from exhaustion." Rob's face paled and his hands clenched in his lap, his knuckles turning white.

"In the morning I found myself back in human form chained up. I was now a captive of a man who ran a very different kind of program than I do. He explained what being a shifter was in only the briefest terms, then never explained anything again. He brought me food and water and left me in a boiling hot cell all day. He wouldn't tell me if my sister had survived and I couldn't remember how badly she'd been hurt. He beat me when I complained and continuously dared me to change again. When I finally did, he shot me with tranquilizer darts and beat me repeatedly. He didn't give a crap about training me; he was just into this whole power trip. At the full moon I found out he wasn't a shifter; he was a werewolf who enjoyed torturing shifters. I almost died that night. After three weeks, a group of shifters confronted him and convinced him by force to allow me to go with them. I found out later there were two other shapeshifters trapped in cages on the compound. They didn't survive the beatings."

I quickly wiped away a tear with my sleeve before he noticed. I couldn't imagine what he must have felt, cut off from his family, thinking of himself as a vicious monster. Rob had been kind to me, putting a lot of effort into easing my fears. I reached out to squeeze his arm and he patted my hand with one of his.

"I was wild at first. For everyone's safety, they kept me in a safe room. They taught me the basics of living as a shifter and how to cope with the anger. I learned to trust them and they helped me gain full control. I was free to leave, but I've stayed with them by choice. Maya, she's on the Shifter Council, noticed that I had this calming effect on others and recommended that I become a recruiter. At first I declined the offer, but," he hesitated, "for various reasons I ended up changing my mind.

"I eventually returned to my hometown to find out if my parents and sister were all right. They were fine, although they'd been told that I was dragged off and killed by the same *wild animal* that had almost killed the other men. None of them remembered anything from that night. Garrett scrubbed their memories once more and I never spoke to my family again."

We sat silently, both of us lost in our own memories of a life left behind. I finally crawled into bed around midnight, feeling sad, yet somehow hopeful.

CHAPTER NINE

THE NEXT MORNING I WOKE UP TO THE persistent hammering of a woodpecker outside my window. It was still early so I rolled over, covered my head with my pillow and tried to go back to sleep. Only seconds later, I heard a knock on my door. Annoyed, I got up to open it, running a hasty hand through my bed hair.

Ethan stood there holding a bag of clean laundry in one hand and what looked like a corn muffin stuck with a lighted wooden match in the other. He started singing "Happy Birthday" making me wince, not because he was off key, but because it was still very early. Putting my finger over his mouth, I leaned over and blew out the match. I felt bad when I saw his hurt expression, so I smiled and gave him a friendly hug.

"Thanks. I appreciate the thought, really. It's just kind of early and I'm not a morning person." I glanced at the tree outside my window. Maybe my animal, whatever it turns out to be, will like the taste of woodpecker.

"I didn't have the ingredients for a cake, sorry," Ethan said, handing me the muffin and throwing the laundry bag on my bed.

"This is perfect," I smiled, biting into the corn muffin. I hadn't realized how hungry I was. "You made this?"

"Yep, from scratch. I like to cook."

"Huh. So you're the Wolfgang Puck of the shifter rejects?"

He twisted up his mouth and shook his head. "We're not rejects yet. There's still a little hope."

I felt bad. "For you, maybe."

"Make a wish. Maybe a miracle will happen." Ethan grinned and turned away, twisting back halfway down the hall to say, "I am available this week to make your wishes come true." I almost threw the muffin at him, then realized my horrible error and grabbed my pillow and threw that instead. I took another bite as he caught it gracefully, and buried his nose in it, breathing deeply. "You know you're not getting this back." He sauntered off down the hallway toward the small living room. I sighed and took another bite of the muffin. *Well, you can't eat pillows.*

Giggling, I headed for the shower. When I finished my morning rituals, as basic as they were without any makeup or hair supplies, I followed Ethan's path down the hall and turned toward the kitchen, all the while nibbling on my birthday muffin. Rob and Ethan were seated at the table eating breakfast. I joined them while Rob poured me a glass of orange juice.

Rob smiled. "Happy birthday! Eat a light breakfast today. It works out better when you shift on a half empty stomach." I sagged, suddenly losing my appetite, putting the remains of my muffin down and sipping the juice.

Ethan smiled and pushed playfully on my shoulder. "So now you're legal."

"Legal?"

"Yeah, you can vote in community elections, own property, you can get married, too, although we call it mated. You're considered an adult at seventeen by all the supernaturals. It's 'cause most shifters transition for the first time between thirteen and fifteen and have to become responsible citizens, keeping their nature a secret from humans. If you mess up and hurt someone, you're tried as an adult. We mature a lot faster than humans."

"Oh yeah…you seem really mature." He pretended to glare at me, but then what he'd said hit me and I looked at him in shock. "How do you know all that? Weren't you raised by humans like I was? Didn't you just get here, too?"

"Nah, my parents are both cougars, still in Sacramento. I've been living with Rob for a few months in Crescent City." His expression had changed from happy to tense.

"But …." Ethan moved away from the table and looked out the window, crossing his arms over his chest in a protective gesture. It was obvious that he didn't want to talk about it. I let it go.

Rob cleared his throat. "There's something else I haven't mentioned about shifting that takes some getting used to for some people who've grown up outside the community. When you change form, your clothing rips to pieces and hangs on you in shreds, which makes it difficult to run, so we undress before we change. When we change back to our human form, we're still in the buff. Nudity is a natural part of the transitional process and it's nothing to feel uncomfortable about, although it can be awkward at first."

"Oh."

"I'll stay in human form when you shift in case anything goes wrong and you need help. Paws get in the way during a medical emergency. But Ethan's going to stay in cougar form and follow you if you run. New shifters like to test their limits. It's perfectly normal to take off, but please stay on the usual paths."

This newest information made me roll my eyes and twist my mouth up in irritation. I wasn't particularly self-conscious about my body, having been naked in many a women's locker room. Not being blessed with one of those curvy, womanly figures, my running kept me even leaner.

I raked my eyes across their faces. They looked really uncomfortable. If Ethan or Rob had been leering at me I might have felt differently, but for some reason I trusted them, even though I'd only known them a couple of days. After my initial shock and temper tantrums, Rob had been understanding and considerate and Ethan had practically saved my life getting me down that tree.

I looked from Ethan to Rob and sighed. "I think being naked in front of you two will be the least of my problems today. Let's get this over with." I walked back to my bedroom, stripped and threw on a robe. I pulled my hair back into a ponytail and walked to the front porch.

Rob grabbed his medical case and headed out after me. Ethan was already prowling around in cougar form. I sat on the porch step and Rob sat next to me giving me a reassuring smile. He pulled out a nasty looking syringe and I closed my eyes, trying to be brave. I hoped that it would all be over with quickly.

About ten seconds after the prick of the needle, I experienced a flash of nausea and then sharp shooting pains throughout my body. My robe felt heavy and uncomfortable, so I jumped up, letting it slide down my arms and pool at my feet. Every inch of my skin burned, even my earlobes and eyelids. Through eyes half closed I glanced at my hands, watching in horror and fascination as they began to change shape. Bones broke and rearranged themselves into a different scheme, making my skin heave with the motion. I cried out in pain and shock as tan paws speckled in black appeared where

I used to have hands and feet. I suddenly needed to crouch on the ground and flex my muscles, so I fell, hitting it hard with four feet instead of two. My jaw jutted forward as sharp teeth exploded from my gums, the long canines appearing last. Bones all over my body began to shift and fracture, elongate and bend, causing more excruciating pain. Fur erupted in waves of hot agony to cover my bare skin as a tail exploded out from my lower back. The transition took no more than a minute, but I felt like I'd been thrown into a giant mixer, ground up and spit out again. *Holy shit.*

As my body transformed, some senses became significantly more acute. I heard the bees in their hive forty yards behind the cabin and the beating heart of a small rabbit hiding under the porch. Salt air from the north shore of the island filled my nostrils, urging me to run toward the ocean.

Feeling sore from the violent transition, I stretched out my newly born shifter body and glanced at Rob, who was staring at me with a strangely astonished expression. I tried to laugh but only managed a strangled huff. Shocked by the odd sound, I trotted closer, interested to see what Rob thought of the new me. He crouched down and stretched out his hand. I rubbed my face against it and purred, allowing him to scratch me behind the ears, confirming the big cat theory.

He stopped scratching, laughing when I growled in irritation. "Garrett was right after all." When I tilted my head, he answered my unspoken question. "Your shift went well. You won't need the drug next time. Run with Ethan and stretch your legs. It's what you were born to do. Just try not to lose him. I'll shift and meet up with you."

Ethan, my much larger cougar companion, blinked, growled playfully, and took off running. *Huh, still cheating.* My nose picked up his spicy scent—so easy to track. I paced myself at first, growing accustomed to the movement of my feline form. I was sleek, with strong legs to carry me quickly over the ground and a long tail that acted as a rudder, helping me steer. I leapt over a fallen log and practically flew headlong into a tree, twisting easily at the last second to avoid the collision. I was flying through the air for yards and yards every time I leapt over anything.

What startled me the most was that I was still me—still Jackie—only in a very different form.

Ethan growled, probably telling me to hurry up, but instead, I churred with pleasure and relief, enjoying the primal noise that erupted from my throat, expressing my tremendous happiness.

Up ahead I caught a glimpse of cougar-Ethan's tail as he dove behind a cluster of large rocks, perhaps waiting to ambush me. Not wanting to end up on the bottom of a furry pile, I turned on the jets and flew past his hideout, leaving him too far behind to catch up. I skidded to a stop when I reached the shoreline of Solo Island and inhaled a deep lungful of the fresh sea air.

My senses were so sharp they overwhelmed me with the sounds and smells and even vibrations of the island: sea lions barking at each other on the far side, the sour smell of skunk cabbage from a swampy area to the west, the shuffling scrape of a crab making his way across the sand. I forced myself to sit on my furry butt and breathe in slowly, concentrating on finding a way to sift through the barrage of sensations and pull in my focus.

Ethan straggled onto the shore, cuffing me with his huge paw and plopping his furry body next to mine. He leaned his head on my back and growled, probably worried because I'd run off on my own and not stayed close to him. I flicked my tail in annoyance. He'd run off first! After a few minutes of resting comfortably together he got up, tossing his head to indicate that I should follow him. He led me to a still, clear pool of water and nudged me toward it. I drank my fill and when the water stopped rippling, wasn't at all surprised to see the reflection of an exotic cheetah staring back at me. My eyes were still emerald green, and the black tear stripes running down my face made them stand out beautifully. I admired my tan, sleek body spotted in black and my lovely tail covered in symmetrical black rings.

My long legs gave me all the advantages over the other big cats when it came to sprinting. I was the feline version of a thoroughbred and felt quite pleased with myself as I flicked my tail back and forth and twitched my ears. Ethan's reflection next to mine was destroyed the minute he stuck his enormous paw in the water and pulled it back to splash me on the snout. In retaliation I flicked my hip out to the side, knocking him off balance.

He was about to pounce on me when we both caught Rob's scent. Magnificent and terrifying, he strode toward us with stealth and grace, appearing out of the shadows as if he were a part of them. His muscles moved strongly beneath his velvety black fur and when he came to a halt, staring at us with his golden-flecked eyes, my cheetah shivered. He turned, growling softly, and we followed him back to the cabin, Ethan and I batting and nipping at each other like kittens.

The two larger cats disappeared when we got to the clearing in front of the cabin and I suddenly realized that I had no idea how to change back to my human form. The cabin door opened and Rob, clad in navy sweatpants and a gray tee shirt, walked over to me holding my robe. "I'll help you transition back. Relax and concentrate." He put his hand on my head and I felt instantly calmer. "Close your eyes and visualize yourself in human form again. Hear your human heart beating, breathe through human lungs …."

Rob's rich voice took my mind where it needed to go, because I began to feel that now familiar static attacking my body, then terrible pain as my bones shifted into a more familiar shape. My skin swallowed the fur, stretching and burning, the process taking less time in reverse. Just as I started to shiver, Rob draped my robe over my shoulders and helped me stand. I wrapped it snugly around myself, grateful when he offered me his arm to help me into the cabin.

Sore from my first shift, I dressed slowly in my bedroom then snagged a sandwich from a plate on the kitchen counter. Ethan was sprawled in his usual position on the old couch, my stolen pillow shoved behind his back. He grinned at me over the top of the book, patting the side of the couch still vacant. When I sat beside him he leaned down to grasp one of my bare feet, pulling it into his lap and massaging my sore muscles.

It was heaven.

"You'll be stiff and sore for a while, Speedy, especially your feet, legs, arms and hands. You were breaking the land speed record today," he chuckled loudly. "It was awesome."

Ethan worked the kinks out of my feet as I leaned back to speculate on what events might have taken this generous, funny young man from his home to Rob's boot camp. Was he still in touch with his parents, or was Rob his family now?

Rob sat in the armchair writing about the day's events on his laptop. "Tomorrow Ethan and I will show you how to hunt. You did very well today, Jackie. It's extraordinary for someone to adapt so quickly to her new form. Cheetah shifters are rare. I only know of two others."

I stared at him open-mouthed. "Did you say hunt? You mean like a real cheetah hunts, killing and then eating a RAW animal?"

I must have looked a little green, because Rob asked, "You

okay?"

"Uh, I guess so."

"Once you've hunted the first time you'll understand. It's not something you'd do daily, but the raw food eaten in animal form strengthens your body faster than our human meals do. You never know when you might need to regain your strength quickly when you're out on a job."

Ethan piped in, "It's really great. You hear their bones crunch in your jaws and the blood runs down your chin and their little hearts beat faster and faster until they stop forever."

I jerked my foot away and kicked him right in the stomach. "Ow." He pretended to groan. I knew I couldn't really hurt that rock hard body with a half-assed kick.

"You're a jerk!" He was just trying to get a rise out of me, but I was still feeling a little nauseated from his colorful description. I moved over to the table to sit in the chair next to Rob. "What kind of a job?"

"You may be perfect for a project I'm working on with Garrett. Cheetah shifters have other unique gifts, besides speed and tracking abilities. We'll talk about this more when you're finished with your training here on the island."

After resting for an hour, Rob took us back outside. We worked on the usual martial arts defensive moves, and learned multiple hand signals so we could communicate silently.

After dinner, Rob let me log onto his computer. I'd asked how it was that he got reception on the island and he mentioned that we had two serious tech geniuses on our team. He told me in no uncertain terms not to sign in to my email or social websites, but that I could listen to music or watch movies.

I behaved as ordered because …well…you just kinda did with Rob.

CHAPTER TEN

THAT NIGHT, I WOKE UP TO THE MURMUR of male voices coming from the direction of the front porch. I recognized Rob's right away, but the other was unfamiliar. It was late, after 2:00 a.m., and Ethan was softly snoring in the room across the hall. Curiosity got the better of my common sense, as I shook off the last vestiges of sleep and sat up.

I slid from under my sheets, threw a robe on over my sweats, opened my bedroom door, and crept as silently as I could manage down the dark hallway. The only light in the empty front room came from the glow of dying embers in the fireplace, causing ghostly shadows to move along the floor and the walls. I hesitated when I heard the conversation on the porch stop abruptly. Knowing I'd been discovered, I thought about turning around, but then a larger shade loomed in the open doorway. I took a quick step back in fright. The shadow moved with a graceful purpose, drawing slowly closer, and I was suddenly facing a man I didn't know.

My eyes had adjusted to the ambient light and I could see him more clearly now. He'd halted about six feet away, standing unnaturally still as if waiting for my reaction. I guess he didn't want to scare me. Too late.

His scent was different than any I'd encountered so far and I grew anxious, biting down on my lip so hard I could taste blood. His eyebrows arched as his full lips turned up with amusement, warming his expression. Thick auburn hair shone in the dying firelight, windblown from his meeting with Rob on the breezy porch, and although he'd dressed casually in a leather blazer, button-down shirt and jeans, he looked perfectly put together. He was a few inches taller than me, maybe 6', with lean muscles, long legs. and eyes so blue they stood out even in the dim light.

His chest rose and fell as he slowly took in my scent and I instinctively sucked in another deep breath of my own. His was strangely sweet and somehow familiar. This guy was Rob's vampire friend.

When he saw that I wasn't running out of the room screaming, he closed the distance between us. "Hello, Jackie. It's a pleasure to meet you officially." He didn't hold out his hand and I was glad, because I was afraid a vampire's skin might feel unpleasant.

"My name is Garrett." His voice resonated with a gentle persuasion as a tingle of energy urged me to look at him. I'd heard about vampires influencing others, at least in the books I'd read, forcing people to do things against their will. I looked down at my hands just in case any of that was true. I was so out of my element.

"Hi," I answered lamely, proud that my voice hadn't cracked even though my knees were shaking. I peeked up through my lashes to see him smiling at me again. Apparently he thought I was extremely entertaining. I realized with horror that I was in my robe with my hair sticking out in every direction while he looked the perfect runway model. *Just great.*

If first impressions meant anything in the shifter world, I'd be sent to an asylum rather than given a job.

I pulled the robe tighter around myself and ran a hand through my hair. "You've seen me before, haven't you?" I avoided his eyes, trying to look past his shoulder instead.

He laughed softly. "You can look at me. I won't glamour you." I didn't move. He took another step and lowered his voice. "Please, Jackie, I'm a friend of Rob's. You're safe with me." His voice was seductively rich and soothing, satin sheets against my skin. I shivered—and not from the cold.

Rob tried to put me at ease. "Garrett and I have worked together for years. I was just telling him about your progress. He'll be taking over your training when you get back to the mainland. Ethan's too."

Well, this was just stupid. I had to get over my fear, especially if he was going to be training me. I raised my chin and forced myself to look directly at his face. His eyes were shining with humor, not dead and lifeless as I'd imagined a vampire's eyes would be. His skin was pale, but not ashen, and his expression was warm, not threatening or frightening at all. He was, well, breathtaking was what came to mind. A dark angel, his power undeniable.

He spoke again as I watched in fascination. "To answer your question, three years ago I adopted you as a—well, not a project exactly—more of a willing responsibility. I've been looking forward to finally meeting you in person." His smile was brilliant and against my good sense, I found myself smiling shyly back, feeling slightly more comfortable. Even though, like Rob, he appeared to be only in his early twenties, Garrett spoke with a maturity that added years to my estimation of his age.

"Rob told me you shifted into a cheetah." I nodded and noticed a subtle change in the color of his eyes and the tilt of his head. He was excited by the news. "And he says you're adjusting quickly. It's something I'd noticed about you from the start, your amazing ability to adapt to new circumstances, even under extreme conditions."

He was suddenly standing only inches away, the closeness making me tremble. Because of his friendship with Rob, I trusted he wouldn't hurt me, so I didn't move away when he reached out to touch my cheek so gently with his fingertips. They were warm, not cold like I thought they'd be, and as they traveled down my face to hold my chin, my skin flushed with heat. I tried to look away, but his grip was firm and I was instantly drawn into the depths of his amazing sapphire eyes.

"I wish I could have stepped in sooner, but it was impossible." He released my chin and took my hands in his, inspecting them as if he expected to see my old scars. Was he apologizing? I must have looked confused because he gently dropped my hands and straightened up, smiling and appearing very young again.

"As much as I'd like to talk for longer, I have business to discuss with Rob. Therefore I must say goodnight. We'll be meeting again very soon." He nodded, turning and walking quickly out to the porch, leaving behind his sweet scent, still mysteriously familiar.

Rob said, "Please go back to bed. You'll need your strength tomorrow."

I walked back to my room, still feeling Garrett's feather-light touch on my cheek. I crawled under the covers and tried to sleep, but instead grew restless, attempting to sort through the fragmented memories of what had happened to me on that dark evening two years ago.

"Where are you running, sweetheart?"

I was two months shy of fifteen years old. I'd made plans to go to a movie with a really nice boy and a bunch of other new friends. I'd come home from studying at the library only to find my latest social worker in the living room telling me that once again, I'd be moving to a new town and a new family. I lost control and ran. Unfortunately, I didn't pay much attention to where I was going.

It was around 8:00 p.m. and I was on an unfamiliar road. Two men outside a house called to me as I ran by. I ignored them, so they cursed at me and I stupidly flipped them off. I was angry and careless but I was sure I could outrun them without a problem. They jumped into their car but I turned into a park and headed down a pedestrian walkway, knowing they couldn't follow me where there was no road. Unfortunately, they were very familiar with this particular park and were able to cut me off where the road intersected the path farther along. From that point I remembered only snatches.

Car doors slamming and the sound of feet rushing toward me

"Where are you running, sweetheart?"

My arms held behind me so tightly they hurt.

My head yanked back by my ponytail and a knife held against my throat

The scent of whiskey, beer and cigarettes.

A rag pushed roughly in my mouth.

My heels dragging along the hard ground as we moved farther from the path.

"So pretty."

I remembered kicking cigarette breath in the groin and him cursing at me. His larger friend released me, then stabbed me in the side when I tried to get away. God, the pain …. I stumbled back, managing to hold up my hands as I tried to block the rest of his attack. He sliced at my hands and my arms and I fell on the frozen ground. Cigarette breath kicked me in the ribs and I heard something break. Pain was all I knew and my blood was everywhere.

"You're dying tonight bitch."
As I was passing out, I heard him scream.

Later that night, I woke up in the hospital. The police asked me what happened to the men who'd attacked me, but I'd been unconscious and didn't know anything. Three weeks later, body parts washed up on the beach twenty miles north of my town. They were identified as belonging to both of my assailants.

CHAPTER ELEVEN

I DRESSED QUICKLY THE NEXT MORNING, intending to grab a cup of coffee and then a shower. Outside my room I practically collided with Ethan who held my shoulders so I couldn't pass him. After a few seconds he let go and backed up.

"I see you've met Garrett." Ethan scowled. "You reek of vampire."

I sniffed my hands. I liked the scent. "Not a fan?" I teased.

"He's okay at times, but I hate the stench. Most blood-suckers are trouble." Ethan grabbed both of my hands, sniffed them again and before I could pull away, licked each one, grinning hugely. He called out as he walked past, "Now you smell healthy, like a shifter." I laughed as I turned back to the bathroom to wash my hands, ridding myself of vampire and cougar.

After breakfast Rob took us out to the yard and had me place my hand on Ethan's shoulder as he crouched and shift-ed into his cougar and back again twice. Having a handsome naked guy under my hand one minute and a large furry beast under my hand the next was sometimes disturbing, sometimes cool and sometimes blush producing, but the two guys treated it like it was no biggie, so I tried to also.

Rob had Ethan explain what went through his mind as he shifted. "I see myself in cougar form, feeling each specific physical difference in my head before it happens. As soon as I sense the power surge, I force myself to breathe deeply and focus on my hands and feet changing form. They always transition first. There's pain but then the change itself flows naturally after that. It's gotten pretty quick with practice."

I tried to do the same, struggling at first. Rob and Ethan continued to encourage me. After several frustrating tries, I felt an overwhelming urge to allow the shift free rein. I was able to shift more quickly and less painfully if I relaxed into the pain, instead of fighting against it.

My larger feline companions led me into the woods to hunt for the first time. Opening my senses to the forest around me, I heard the heartbeats of several warm-blooded creatures in the area. I narrowed down my focus to one unlucky hare and set about the task of stalking it until I saw it up ahead nibbling on a loganberry bush. Lying in wait for the perfect moment to attack was difficult for me as I've never been patient when a goal was in reach. Rob had to practically sit on my tail to make me wait for the right moment to rush from the cover of the blackberry bushes. Happily, my instincts kicked in at the perfect time and I pounced on the surprised brown hare, biting into his neck to make a clean kill.

My human side might have cringed to see the cheetah kill and eat the terrified animal, but my appetite was satisfied in a way I would never experience as a human. The chase had given me an adrenaline rush unlike any other, and my physical strength seemed to increase with each bite as I shivered in ecstasy, licking the bones of the unlucky hare. When I'd finished and was grooming myself in the usual feline way,

Rob's leopard cuffed my head playfully with his giant paw and Ethan's cougar licked my face. Somehow, I didn't mind at all.

That afternoon, Ethan taught me to play backgammon while Rob emailed a few people and made some phone calls. Ethan turned out to be a good teacher, but after a couple of hours I was ready to stretch my legs and take a human run. Ethan said he'd tag along, so I slowed down my pace and we made it to the ocean together. We sat on an outcropping of rock and stared at the sea, both of us lost in our own thoughts for several minutes.

I glanced at Ethan's unusually serious expression and decided to break the ice. "Solo Island, huh? I guess I understand the name. It is kinda lonely out here."

"It's peaceful."

"It is, but why are you here? I mean if you're okay with shifting into your cougar then…?"

He shook his head and looked away. "Not now, okay? I'll tell you one day."

"Sure." I touched his arm hoping to offer some comfort. I'd never push him to talk about something painful when he wasn't ready. I had plenty of garbage in my past I wouldn't be sharing anytime soon. I changed the subject. "What do you know about Garrett?" Now there was a subject I could get my teeth into. Ha.

Ethan's mouth turned down. "He's dangerous. There's nothing else you need to know. Just stay away from him."

I frowned at his snippy retort. The memory of Garrett's concerned eyes along with the gentle touch of his hands on mine, still made me smile. "There's something familiar about him. I think we can trust him."

Ethan sighed in exasperation. "Even though he's Rob's friend, he has a bad rep, so it's probably better if we have as little to do with him as possible."

"We'll be training with him soon."

"Yeah, I know." Ethan didn't sound too enthusiastic; not surprising considering how he felt about vampires in general and Garrett in particular.

I decided to file away Ethan's words of caution, knowing that he meant well. But as I nestled under the covers later that night, I wondered when I would see Garrett again. I didn't realize it would be quite so soon.

CHAPTER TWELVE

I DREAMED.

It was evening and I was walking alone in a lovely garden surrounding a spectacular villa nestled into the cliffs above the Pacific. Waves crashed against a rocky shore, gulls screeched in their search for the last juicy meal of the day, and crickets warned off trespassers. As the garden darkened, my skin buzzed with electricity, and I caught a familiar scent.

Garrett walked toward me, all grace and style and looking like every girl's fantasy. Despite his beauty, warnings were flashing in my head, but I was already lost, my gaze locked on his, my heart keeping pace with each of his long-legged strides.

Was this his home? How did I get here?

His closeness made me nervous, his sweet scent strong, so I bit my lip as I had when I'd first met him. This time a single drop of blood escaped from the corner of my mouth and dripped slowly down to my trembling chin. He reached out and captured the red droplet with a finger, lifting it slowly to his mouth, sucking gently as I watched, enthralled. A slight shudder rippled over his body when he swallowed, a warm smile spreading across his *face, immediately putting me at ease. Silver flecks had appeared in his startling eyes the moment he'd swallowed, adding fuel to my sense of wonder.*

How could a man's smile make me feel so at peace? How could a man's eyes become eyes I needed to gaze into for eternity?

I knew I was dreaming, but at the same time I wanted the dream to never end.

With great care he grasped one of my hands and pulled me beside him, lowering us onto a bench overlooking the angry sea. He rested his hand on my shoulder and leaned closer. "Jacqueline," he whispered against my hair, "I was so afraid for you. Now you're safe with us."

No one had ever called me Jacqueline, I'd never liked the name, but spoken with Garrett's rich tone it was perfect. My heart beat very fast. "I don't understand," I whispered against his shoulder.

"You should know the truth. May I show you something? It's only a memory and cannot hurt you."

"Yes"

His eyes drew me in as the scene changed quickly. I appeared in the park of my nightmares, an invisible bystander watching a younger me being beaten and stabbed by my long-ago attackers. Only this time Garrett arrived like a hungry demon, ripping into them with sharp fangs and supernatural strength. The men screamed and died.

As horrible as it was, I couldn't look away because I was glad they were dead.

The dark angel crouched beside me, holding my horribly injured body with great gentleness. He bit into his wrist, encouraging me to drink his blood. I was pale, barely breathing, probably close to death. As I drank, the bleeding slowed and stopped, my color improving. I heard an ambulance in the distance as Garrett lowered me gently to the ground and disappeared into the trees in a blur of motion. He'd carried away the bodies of my attackers as if they were made of feathers and not flesh and bone.

The vision faded and I was once more leaning against him outside the villa, feeling both grateful and terrified at the same time. "I was almost too late. Je suis désolé. I'm so sorry." His eyes gleamed with anger and frustration and such sadness. I wanted to tell him that I was fine. That he'd arrived in time.

"Garrett—"

He brushed my hair away from my face, smiling his sad smile. "Sleep now, Jacqueline." And the velvet night swallowed me.

I woke up soaked in sweat and trembling violently. Reliving the attack had shattered me. I stumbled to the bathroom and splashed cold water on my face, sinking down to the tile floor and wrapping my arms around my bent knees.

I'm losing it. Did Garrett come to me in a dream and show me how he saved my life two years ago? "Ridiculous." I'd spoken out loud in the hopes of convincing myself. Dreams could not be real. That drug must still be affecting my mind. And the whole me-drinking–his-blood thing was just too weird.

But why did he seem so familiar? Could he have come to me that night? I opened the bathroom window and took in a few deep breaths of fresh air. This was just nuts.

When I stumbled back toward the bed, I looked at the small clock on the dresser. 5:00 a.m. What am I going to do now that I'm wide awake at 5:00 a.m.? I decided to get dressed and take a walk to straighten out my head. A narrow path snaked through the woods, leading south. Rob had said to avoid it, but since my night vision was excellent, and I wasn't usually big on following rules that made no sense, I chose to check it out.

Moving as quietly as possible down the forbidden path, I soon forgot the dream and became much more interested in my surroundings. Sheltered under oak and fir trees, the azalea and huckleberry shrubs colored the dark trail with blooms that would brighten beautifully in the early light of dawn. The first chirping and warbling of birds in the high branches caused me to glance up.

The moon was in its waxing phase. Before long it would be full, lighting up the woods with a silvery glow. *Good thing I'm not a werewolf*, I thought smugly. They'd probably be pretty jumpy right now, waiting for their forced change. Or maybe they liked the hunt as much as shifters did. I stifled a laugh with my hand when I realized how, in just a few days, I'd come to accept this crazy supernatural world.

Kinda hard not to when your own body made it impossible to ever think of yourself as human again.

I arrived at the beach and turned right, continuing to walk along a well-trodden path that followed the shoreline. The sky was growing lighter, yet some objects were still unclear, even to my more sensitive eyes. I saw a dark shape in the water, and crouched down, not sure what I was looking at. After another moment I stood, my mouth hanging open in shock.

A gentle breeze carried the scent of eucalyptus. I was startled, turning to see if it was some other cougar. Ethan had been snoring away when I'd left the cabin. "It's me," Ethan whispered, moving beside me. "I heard you leave. Are you okay?"

"I'm not sure."

"What's up?" asked Ethan.

"Well…look!"

Ethan glanced in the direction I pointed and then back at me. "What?"

"There's a boat. We could leave."

He laughed and sat down on a large rock along the path. "There are only a few problems with that idea. First of all, it won't start without the key and Rob has it. It's his boat. That's how we got here in the first place."

"Oh." I sank down beside him. "I hadn't thought about that."

"Second, if we left, he'd come after us."

I rolled my eyes. "How could he do that without his boat?"

"He'd call Garrett or one of his other friends to intercept us and bring us back here."

"Oh. Yeah. I guess he would." I pouted.

"Third, where would we go?"

"I don't … maybe … I guess nowhere." Ethan's words had reminded me that I didn't have a home to go back to. I could try to find Maggie and Justin in their new town in Colorado, but would they want me back? My body slumped against Ethan's.

"Do you still want to leave?" he asked, sounding kind of sad.

I watched the boat bobbing in the water. It looked like a nice one, practical like Rob, with a good sized deck and an inside cabin. It was definitely some kind of motorboat, since it had no mast or sails. Behind it, the sun was peeking out, the sky streaked with bands of orange and lemon and berry. That's when my stomach growled.

Ethan laughed, standing and stretching out his hand to help me up. "C'mon, I'll make you pancakes."

Rob was sitting on the porch when we got back. Ethan greeted him and headed to the kitchen, hopefully to get started on the pancakes. I sat on the bench next to Rob, still mulling over Ethan's question. *Did I still want to leave?*

"Early stroll?" Rob asked.

"I found your boat."

"Ah. Cheetahs are good trackers."

"It was an accident. I wasn't looking for it."

"They're also lucky," he laughed. "You decided to forego the attempted prison break?"

"Ethan's making pancakes."

"It's good you have your priorities straight." He managed to keep a straight face, but his dark eyes were glittering with humor.

Later, during breakfast, I announced, "I don't." They looked at me curiously. "I don't want to run anymore." They smiled and kept eating, feeling no comment was necessary.

We trained for three more days. On the fourth morning after the discovery of the boat, Rob sat us down at the table.

"I think I've done all I can with you here on the island. I'm sending you to Crescent City." He handed Ethan a key. "Take the boat. There are maps in the cabin under the logbook along with two cell phones. My number and Garrett's are programmed in. There are extra clothes in the bin over the bed and there's some cash there as well."

"Ethan, dock it in our usual slip at Sea Bright Docks. Tell Harry that I'll contact him in a few days. Directions to a house owned by my friend Carly O'Neal are in a manila envelope. She'll put you up while you're being trained. Call Garrett at three in the afternoon and he'll take over from that point. You'll be meeting a couple of other rogue shifters that I trained here on the island. I think you'll work well together."

I ignored everything Rob had just said, asking Ethan, "You can drive a boat?" I must have looked shocked, because they both laughed at me.

"Pilot, yeah. Rob taught me," Ethan answered like it was no big deal.

Rob continued, his expression turning serious. "Follow only Garrett's or Carly's instructions. There are some shifters in the community who don't believe kids like you are salvageable. They think you're dangerous and that you should be locked up, or worse. After you get to the house, stay out of sight as much as possible."

"Dangerous?" I couldn't believe anyone would think that I was a risk to their precious community.

"Garrett and Carly will explain. Just don't go wandering off."

"You're not coming?"

"I'm going out of town for several days." He shifted his gaze to Ethan. "Garrett's the best trainer you'll ever work with, so don't give him a hard time." His dark gaze returned to me. "Call him today at three. Don't forget."

We gathered up a few things, heading down the same path I'd discovered three mornings ago. Finally, I was going back to civilization. There would be TV and movies and unlimited internet. I bounced up and down with excitement as I walked along the narrow trail toward my newest adventure.

CHAPTER THIRTEEN

ROB HAD TAUGHT ETHAN WELL, SO THE boat trip passed without incident. He insisted that we wear life vests and I didn't argue, because I knew how unsure Ethan was around the water. It was pretty brave of him to take the boat out at all and I told him so. He laughed, saying that as long as he stayed out of the ocean, he was good.

Docking at Sea Bright, we stuffed supplies and clothes into two backpacks that we found onboard, left the boat with Harry, a short grizzled man, and took off hiking northeast through the town of Crescent City, California. We wore hats and shades, trying to remain incognito, but in Ethan's case it didn't seem to matter.

As we walked past quaint shops and official buildings, many of the people passing us on the street smiled and nodded their heads at Ethan in a familiar way, some of them using his name and saying hello. Most of them were female, no surprise there. I gave him a sly grin and he shrugged, saying, "I've met a few people since I've been staying with Rob, but mostly I've just crashed at his house."

I was dying to ask him more about why he was with Rob,

but he didn't elaborate any further, so I shut my mouth. He'd tell me when he was ready, although waiting wasn't my best thing. We stopped to eat a couple of burgers at the local coffee shop and after tipping the waitress and paying the bill, continued on to a small house nestled next to a grove of maple trees.

We knocked, and a pleasant-looking woman in her mid-twenties appeared at the door, a huge black and tan Rottweiler mix at her side. She was petite, maybe 5'1", with shiny short brown hair and pretty hazel eyes. The dog sniffed us suspiciously as she ushered us quickly into her living room. Dismissing Ethan with a snort, the big dog nuzzled my hand looking for some attention. I scratched him behind the ears. His stubby tail wiggled along with his entire rear end.

"Rob called a couple of hours ago. I'm Carly and that's Samson. I have a place for you to stay for a week or so until other arrangements are made. I'll drive you over there in a few minutes. Sit down in the kitchen while I get some supplies together. Help yourself to soda or anything else you can find. There's ham and cheese in the fridge and bread on the counter. Make some sandwiches for later if you don't want them now."

Ethan and I grabbed a couple of sodas, slapped together two sandwiches which we packed away for later, and sat at the table, too tired to talk. Our training had been rough the last couple of days and I was looking forward to taking a nap when we finally got where we were going. Samson sat next to me on the floor and I scratched his head distractedly, looking out the window at the view of the town below.

It was picturesque with a crescent-shaped beach and an island lighthouse. Spring flowers were blooming, but Ethan had told me on the boat thick fog was common at this time of the year. Shifters and wolves liked dense forests and when the fog rolled in, hunting became a lot more interesting. Ethan crossed his arms, stretched out his powerful legs, and dozed.

As tired as I was, I knew I'd never be able to fall asleep in that position, so I jealously stared at his sleeping form and continued to pet Samson, grateful that we'd be getting a ride to our final destination and I could pass out there. I'd been up since five in the morning.

Carly returned after about fifteen minutes rolling a wheeled duffle bag. "I've packed sheets, towels and extra clothes and supplies for you. My car is around the back." Ethan popped up, refreshed from his power nap, and we exited through the back door, Samson included. Ethan threw the duffle in the trunk and we headed off.

"I keep two safe houses for shifters who need help. The general population rarely tolerates rogues unless the council has cleared them. But many of us feel that shifters are shifters and should never be viewed as lost causes. I changed late myself and could have been in the same boat as you two if it wasn't for my supportive family. Communities are getting weaker because they're not letting in any new blood. You two are perfect examples. From what Rob says, you're really exceptional and our town could use your special talents, whether they know it yet or not."

"Thank you very much for your help, Carly." My remark brought a smile to her mostly serious expression.

"I'm sorry I can't have you stay in my house, but Garrett is a competent trainer and can certainly protect you better than I can. Just keep your eyes open around him, he's a vampire first, and always has a hidden agenda. You can trust him to protect you because he's invested in this project of his and Rob's, but no farther. I can't tolerate being around him for more than a few minutes." Ethan gave me a told-you-so kind of look, but I turned away feeling certain that they were wrong about Garrett.

We pulled up to a small house off the road, hidden by

four or five large black oak trees with low-hanging branches. Carly handed us the key, apologizing that the place was probably a little dusty. She also reminded us to set the alarm on one of our cell phones to wake us at three to call Garrett. She backed her car down the gravel driveway and took off in the direction of her home, Samson's head hanging out the passenger window, his ears flying out behind him.

When Carly left, we both breathed out a sigh of relief, glad that we'd finally be able to rest and shower. Ethan grabbed the bag and both backpacks while I unlocked the front door. We were pleased to see the small combination kitchen/living room was well stocked with the usual basic items, and since Carly had said she'd be bringing us a large meal every day, we wouldn't need to find our way to a market. A square table with four chairs was positioned near the door, and two arm chairs sat by a window and a bookcase. Down the short hallway was a tiny bathroom with a shower and through another door a small bedroom with one queen-sized bed, which both of us stared at longingly.

Ethan turned to me, a teasing smile twisting up the corners of his mouth. "I'll put the sheets on the bed and the towels away while you take care of the food and the rest." The cottage was warm, so he pulled off his tee shirt and started opening windows. I did what he asked, putting food in the cupboards and fridge, all the while becoming more and more aware of a painful vibration in my stomach and chest.

When I walked back into the bedroom, Ethan was spread out on one side, wearing only sweatpants, grinning and patting the space next to him. His hair was still damp from a quick shower, the scent of eucalyptus filled the room.

"Gee, Jackie, guess we have to share the bed. Did you know shifters usually cuddle together like a bunch of puppies or kittens? It makes us feel safe. It's nothing personal." His grin was infectious since I knew he was just trying to get a rise out of me. As much as Ethan liked to flirt, our relationship was basically a friendly one. I wasn't attracted to him in a romantic way and I was pretty sure he felt the same way.

"I'm not in the mood to cuddle, but its fine to share the bed as long as you stay on your side of it." I drew an imaginary line down the middle, making him sigh and lie back dramatically. When I threatened to use a sharpie marker to make the line more obvious, he grinned.

"Roommates it is."

Taking a quick look at my ragged reflection in the mirror, I decided a shower seemed like a good idea, especially since I'd be seeing Garrett later. When I came back out, dressed in clean clothes and feeling refreshed, Ethan was already snoring softly, his body stretched across the entire bed.

"Ethan, move. Maybe I should tie you to the bedpost on your side." I grumbled and pressed against his shoulder, nudging him over in a not so gentle way. He grunted and turned on his side facing away from me, still managing to stay asleep. I tried to get comfortable, but my head was still hurting from the strange pulsating energy that seemed to be seeping into my pores. After tossing and turning for another twenty minutes, I finally succumbed to sleep.

When I woke up, it was dusk. Ethan was quiet beside me, his arm stretched over my stomach, his breathing soft and steady against my ear. Annoyed that he'd moved to my side and that we'd forgotten to set the alarm to call Garrett, I moved Ethan's arm and sat up. A window was open, so the room was cool. A breeze blew the curtains around, bringing with it the sweet scent of vampire. *Oh, shit.*

Garrett stood by the bed glaring at Ethan. Dressed in black slacks, a black silk shirt and black leather jacket, he looked every bit the modern Hollywood vampire, but the look on his face held real malice. I was suddenly alarmed.

I tried to speak calmly as my heart hopped about madly in my chest. "Hi Garrett. We fell asleep and I forgot to set the alarm to call you. I'm really sorry. Rob said you'd be coming here to help us." My voice trembled slightly, but I hoped he'd think that it was because of the cold wind coming through the open window and not because I was afraid.

"Jackie." He smiled as I shivered. "A cougar," he glanced down at Ethan, "is not a fitting mate for a shifter with your abilities."

I stared at him in shock. His fangs were slightly extended and his brilliant eyes were sparkling with silver.

"Um, we didn't … we didn't do anything but sleep, Garrett." I steadied my voice, annoyed that I had to defend myself to this guy at all. "Look, we've been up since 5:00 a.m., walking miles and stressed out by the sudden move. We were exhausted. There's only the one bed and no couch." I swung my legs to the side and sat there rubbing my temples. My headache had returned with a vengeance. Where did Carly keep the aspirin?

He walked to my side, extending his hand to help me stand. The moment his hand clasped mine, the pain was gone. But he didn't know I had a headache. It must have been a co-incidence.

He led me to the small table where the delicious odor of Chinese food had combined with his own sweet scent, both of them making my mouth water.

"I brought you some take-out."

I sat down slowly, watching him warily for any hostile move toward Ethan in the bedroom. Instead, Garrett handed me a bottle of iced tea, chopsticks, and two Chinese food containers. He sat in the opposite chair. "I hope you like beef with broccoli and fried rice."

"This is great, thanks." I dug in, not realizing how famished I was. He sat across from me. "Did you eat?" I asked hesitantly between bites, immediately wishing I hadn't. I really didn't want to think about what or maybe who Garrett ate.

I watched him watching me, all the time aware of his quiet magnetism, which seemed even stronger under the lights in this small kitchen than it had in the cabin's darkened room. His amazing eyes invited me to take a plunge in their cool aquamarine depths, but he was a predator and I needed to keep my head on straight around him. I sighed between bites. It would be so easy to jump in headfirst.

Thankfully, he didn't seem aware of my reaction. "I fed a short while ago." He smiled, glancing in the direction of the bedroom. When he turned back to me, his expression was more serious. "One of you should have called me at three as instructed. I was concerned and on the verge of calling Carly."

"Do you know if Carly has aspirin?" I was rubbing my temples again, the pain in my head and stomach making it impossible to think straight, let alone eat. Garrett immediately took my hand in his and instantly the painful heat cooled and my headache disappeared. I glanced at our hands, then at Garrett, who was looking as excited as a kid with a new toy at Christmas.

"I knew it." His bright eyes glittered eagerly. "You are extraordinary."

"Why, because I have a headache—had a headache? Why did the pain and the buzzing stop when you touched me?" I heard Ethan snoring. "And why isn't Ethan awake? Is he all right?"

Garrett's expression remained neutral. "I wanted to speak to you alone first. He'll wake up soon enough."

I frowned. "What was up with you saying he's not good enough for me?"

He continued to hold my hand and I made no move to

pull away. "Normally shifters mate with their own kind, leopards with leopards, lions with lions, although there are always exceptions. Ethan will find a lovely female cougar to mate and raise cubs with."

"He's eighteen."

"It's a natural instinct, like with any animal. Cheetahs are rare and often develop unexpected talents. There's an energy that runs strong through this area and you're feeling its full heat because you don't know how to shield yourself yet. Most shifters feel it during their change but never have a permanent connection to the ley lines. This house happens to be positioned where two strong channels cross."

He removed his hand and the prickling static was back. "I use the lines often. I can help you if you'd like." His hand closed over mine once more, fingers twining, quieting the buzzing. "Right now I'm sharing my shield, but I'll teach you how to do this for yourself so you won't need me around."

"I like having you around." The words kind of popped out unexpectedly, making my face grow hot. I looked down at our hands twined together, resting comfortably on the table. They looked so natural.

He sighed, a lonely sound. "Other than Rob, I'm not well-liked by most shifters. But if you'll agree, I'd like to train you to protect yourself from the effects of the magic. I know it's painful for you right now and I'm afraid aspirin won't help." His fingertips were moving gently over my hand, my body responding with warm tingles.

Suddenly realizing the effect he was having on me, Garret stood, saying, "I'm going out to have a look around to make sure no one has followed you." He pulled an amulet attached to a chain from his pocket and handed it to me. "Wear this for now and the pain will lessen. I'll be back soon." He was gone before I had a chance to ask him about the necklace.

I heard Ethan groan, so I went back to the bedroom, happy to find that he was sitting up. "I must have been more tired than I thought," he yawned.

I shoved the necklace in my pocket. "Hey sleepyhead, I was worried about you. Garrett was here and you didn't even wake up."

"Yeah I can smell him." He made a face. "You set your alarm? I didn't hear it go off."

"I forgot about it too. Garrett said he wanted to speak to me alone so he didn't wake you. But I think he might have done something to make you sleep longer. Sometimes he's a little scary."

But also really hot.

Whoa. I needed to snap out of this fast. If cougar shifters weren't supposed to hook up with cheetah shifters, then vampires must really be off the menu. Not that he'd want a messed up kid like me. I glanced out the window, visualizing him standing on the roof, his jacket whipping around in the breeze, guarding us like some classy warrior.

"What do I smell?"

"Garrett brought Chinese food." I pointed toward the kitchen where another two containers sat on the counter.

"I'm telling you. He's dangerous." Ethan stood, wobbling, and headed to the bathroom. "I'll be back."

I walked to the bookcase in the small living room and read through the titles. A copy of Jane Austen's "Emma," well read and dog-eared, was all the motivation I needed to plop into a chair and settle down to read. She was my favorite matchmaker and I enjoyed her various misadventures.

Ethan returned, looking more than annoyed. "I think Garrett fed off of me. I feel shaky, I look pale and there's no way I wouldn't have gotten up when you did. My hearing is as sharp as yours and his stink alone has been known to wake me. I slept for three hours and still feel tired."

"If he drank your blood, wouldn't there be fang marks on your body?"

"I don't need to bite a shifter to feed from one," a rich voice replied. I jumped in shock as Garrett appeared in a chair at the table leaning back and looking almost smug. "To feed from a human, something I never do, by the way, I'd have to bite them, but to feed from a shifter I can gain nourishment by simply touching them. Because I'm fairly old, I need only take a tiny amount. Feeding from a shifter allows me to tolerate the sunlight for longer periods: a win-win situation for a vampire."

"You bastard...." Ethan moved threateningly toward Garrett, his jaw clenching and his hands in fists.

Garrett moved so swiftly, I almost didn't see the motion at all. He stood nose to nose with Ethan, his intense whisper sending prickling energy through my body, causing the hairs on my arms to rise. "You and Jackie are now members of my team and you failed your first test. You did not follow Rob's or Carly's instructions to call me. As you're the older and more experienced shifter, I hold you responsible. When you're careless in the field, people die."

Ethan straightened his body, meeting Garrett's gaze. "My mess-up did not give you the right to touch me, to feed off me."

"I could have killed you both." He scanned our faces, frowning. "This house is spelled to keep enemies out, but you left the door unlocked and the window open. Spells can be dispelled. If I'd been your enemy, I would have had an easy time of it."

"But ... we didn't know. We thought we were just hiding." I offered up.

"Your training with me began the moment you climbed

onto Rob's boat." He returned his gaze to Ethan. "For your own safety, it would be best if you showed Jacqueline the deference she deserves. Throw a blanket on the floor if you have to sleep in the same room."

The silver specs sparkling in Garrett's eyes were probably not a good sign.

Ethan responded with a matching intensity, not backing down, even though Garrett could probably break his neck in a heartbeat. "You're our trainer and I'll respect you in that capacity. But what goes on in this cabin is not your business. I'd never get out of line with her and I'm pissed off that you think I might. She's my partner and I won't treat her differently than any other female I'd train with. It's up to her, not you, whether or not I sleep on the floor."

"I'm fine with sharing the bed, Ethan." I frowned at Garrett who continued to glower at Ethan, his eyes still sparkling. Frustrated, I walked between them and put both my hands on Garrett's chest, giving him a nudge toward the door. "Can we please talk outside?"

The heated vibrations still making my nerves twitch calmed the moment I touched him. When the tension in my shoulders relaxed, he looked down to where my hands rested on his chest and I was happy to see the corners of his mouth curve up. No blood would be spilled tonight. But why did women always have to become referees? "Now, please, Garrett?" sweetly. He nodded politely and followed me out the door. I wasn't planning on staying sweet for long. I sat on a small chair in the yard and he stood a few feet away, leaning against a low brick wall, his expression curious. The buzzing heat was slightly less persistent outside the house so I took a deep breath for courage and began.

"You have no business telling Ethan and me how to behave when we're not working with you. I want to trust you, because Rob does, but feeding off shifters with your magic or whatever it is, gives me the creeps. I don't want you feeding off either of us. Especially since it makes us weak and we happen to be hiding from the council right now. I won't be able to work with you if you do it again." I crossed my arms to emphasize my words, lifting my chin to indicate I meant business.

Moving closer with a graceful stride, he sat on the bench across from mine. "May I explain myself?" I nodded. "I have a small group of volunteer donors who help me out. In return, I provide them with a service." I didn't want to ask what that might be. "I don't force anyone.

"Tonight, I arrived at your cottage before I had a chance to feed. I was worried when you didn't call me. When I saw Ethan's arm draped over you, I admit, I overreacted." He ran his hand through his hair and sighed.

"Try to understand—I feel very protective toward you, partly because of what happened two years ago. Now that you're both under my care, you needn't be concerned for your safety, although it's very important for you to learn how to protect yourself. I'll be keeping a close watch and sending others when I'm not able to be here myself. As predators go, I'm at the top of the food chain." To prove his point his eyes turned silver blue, his fangs extended and the huskiness in his voice sent icy shivers racing down my spine.

Memories of screaming men and washed up body parts flashed in my head. I didn't want this vampire as an enemy, but I wouldn't let him bully me either.

"Ethan didn't do anything wrong." I gave him my best stubborn look—and I was a black belt in that department.

I'd amused him again. Guess that was better than making him angry. "I'll strike a bargain with you. I will never feed from Ethan or you, unless you offer me your energy willingly.

In return, you'll work with me privately until you're strong enough to block the magic properly. When you've learned that skill, I'll teach you how to tap in and use its power."

"What is it exactly?"

"The ley lines are like rivers of magical power that flow all over the world, crossing each other in uneven grids. We supes tend to settle near the highest concentrations."

I felt nervous, afraid to look him in the eye, but I had to know. "Did you …? Did you really give me your blood when I was attacked by those two men?" He nodded. "Thank you. You saved my life."

He smiled: his gorgeous eyes crinkling up at the corners with real warmth. "You'll never come to harm again."

Standing, he reached down and pulled the necklace out of my side pocket, brushing my hip with his hand. He placed it over my head and fastened it. "I apologize for the scene I caused." His warm breath stroked my neck, my traitorous body responding with a shiver. "I'm here to help in your training, only I'm afraid I've started things off on the wrong foot. I'm usually an expert at controlling my emotions."

He walked back to the bench and looked me over with an amused expression. "Both of you put aside your fear and stood up to me."

"That makes you happy?"

"Actually, yes. It means we'll be able to work together. Rest up. In two hours, I'll be back to take you into the woods for your first training session with the other two shifters. For now, I'll be out here keeping an eye on things." When I stood, he leaned toward me. "But Jacqueline," he whispered, "if Ethan ever does anything to hurt you, I'll destroy him." He was gone before I could turn around.

Ethan leaned against the doorframe eating his Chinese food from the carton. He snorted, muttering, "Same here, vamp," turning and walking back into the house. I stared up at the moon and groaned. I needed this drama like a hole in the head!

Sitting again with a sigh I tried to puzzle out a solution to this ridiculous situation. Garrett was treating me like I belonged to him because he'd saved me, and Ethan was acting all macho around him.

Tonight I'd have a serious talk with these two. If I didn't straighten this mess out, our training sessions were really going to suck. I stood up and stretched my neck and shoulders, fingering the strange amulet that smelled deliciously of vampire.

CHAPTER FOURTEEN

TWO HOURS LATER, GARRETT PULLED UP IN a black Saab Turbo, the engine purring like a satisfied feline shifter. Ethan opted for the back, which put me in the front next to Garrett. That suited me just fine. We drove along a narrow twisting road into the mountains, none of us speaking. Garrett put on some music and started humming along with a few of the songs, so I stayed quiet, enjoying this peaceful time.

I tried to keep my eyes on the road ahead, but I'd occasionally sneak a glance at his strong hands on the wheel or his riveting eyes focused on the twisting road. I was hoping we wouldn't be seeing any of those silver dots tonight. Garrett chuckled when we heard Ethan snoring from the back seat and I was kind of surprised by the genuine warmth in his expression. Tonight, Garrett seemed to be just a young man enjoying a drive with a couple of friends.

Forty-five minutes later, we stopped at what appeared to be a summer camp closed for the winter, the buildings looking in need of paint and general repair. A red SUV was parked ten yards away and the two young shifters got out when we did, a guy and a girl.

The girl walked up to Garrett and kissed his cheek in greeting; the young man shook his hand. Garrett turned to us and introduced them. "Jackie, Ethan, I'd like you to meet Sinc Blakefield and Kyle Daro. They'll be training with you tonight." We looked each other over as people meeting for the first time do, and I recalled what Rob had said about these two being rogues like Ethan and me.

Kyle was slim and around my height, with beautiful dark almond-shaped eyes under a shock of bleached platinum blonde hair. He smiled brilliantly and extended his hand. "Hey Jackie, Ethan. Great to finally meet you guys." Tattoos covered his forearms and his eyebrow was pierced with a steel stud, yet he looked as put together as any corporate CEO in his black jeans and graphic tee. I liked him instantly and shook his hand, as did Ethan.

Sinc also stuck out her hand but said nothing in greeting. She seemed more the *I'll let you know later what I think of you* type. She was around 5'6", curvy in ways I wasn't, with gorgeous blue eyes and thick dark hair pulled back in a ponytail. She wore nice sweatpants, a tight-fitting purple V-neck tee and a rich-kid attitude that I'd seen many times before. They both looked to be around eighteen or nineteen.

"Let's go inside and I'll explain tonight's plan." Garrett led us to the locked six-foot-high chain-link gate and proceeded to climb over it with grace and strength. In seconds he was walking away on the other side. Ethan and Kyle started up together both making it over easily, although not quite as gracefully or as quickly. Sinc and I followed next and I managed to rip my sweatpants at the knee as I swung over the top. Ethan grinned and Sinc and Kyle tried not to notice. I just sighed, thinking, *I was gonna be some talented shifter, all right.*

We followed Garrett into a large well-lit wooden build-

ing, probably the recreation or dining hall, and sat at a long
table near the entrance. Ethan and I took chairs across from
Kyle and Sinc, none of us looking very confident about what
was coming next. Garrett stood at the head of the table looking us over thoughtfully, maybe cataloging our abilities in his
mind before we even began.

"Welcome. Our training sessions will be designed to find
your strengths and weaknesses but also to encourage you to
learn to work together and trust each other. Tonight, you'll
form two teams. The first will be given secret instructions to
follow to accomplish a specific task, the second will stalk them
in whatever form they wish, trying to gain as much information as possible without being caught by the first team. You
will do what you can to prevent them from succeeding. You
may defend yourself physically to stop the other team from
accomplishing their goal. However, no serious injuries will be
tolerated." Garrett looked at each of us in turn, his mouth set
in a flat line. "We'll be switching teams three times so you'll all
get a chance to work together. Each mission should take about
forty minutes. I'll be observing off and on. You won't see me,
or smell me," he glanced at Ethan, "but I'll be around."

Garrett paired me with Ethan and took us aside. "What
happened back at the safe house can't affect the way you approach this training exercise. I was wrong to do it and I apologize. It won't happen again. However that does not excuse the
rest. Are we okay?"

"Yes, Garrett, I'm letting it go." Ethan looked defiantly
into Garrett's eyes, but no real heat stirred between them. In
fact, I caught the corner of Garrett's mouth twitching as he
forced away a smile.

I was trembling from nerves and excitement. This was so
much more than I'd imagined—the real deal. I'd had to leave
the necklace in the car because I'd be shifting, but even the hot

buzz of the ley line energy couldn't dampen my focus. Garrett took my hand to quiet the sensation. "It won't affect you as strongly in cheetah form." He turned back to Ethan. "Trust your instincts. You're both strong and capable. In this round, you're the stalkers."

He walked away to talk to the other team, giving Ethan and me a chance to discuss our strategy. "Okay, let's play to our strengths," began Ethan. "Strategy, muscle and climbing are my department." He winked. "Speed, tracking and … swimming are yours." I laughed softly. We went over our hand signals and the group of signals we'd worked out for when we were in animal form. Stealth would be all-important.

Garrett spoke up again. "Stay on the campground property. You'll meet back here when you finish or I tell you to return. Kyle and Sinc, you have one minute's head start." They shifted into their animals rapidly: Kyle a gorgeous spotted leopard and Sinc a lovely snow leopard with those same striking blue eyes. They left through the doorway, seeming to head north. Ethan and I changed into cougar and cheetah a minute later. I breathed in deeply to catch their scents, taking off with Ethan close behind. Kyle's scent was a sharp lemony fragrance, much easier to pick up than Sinc's more subtle lavender. I tracked them heading west, using my human intelligence and acute cheetah senses in combination.

After playing cat and mouse for about thirty minutes, we were finally close enough to see and hear Kyle up ahead with a canvas bag nearby on the ground. Ethan gestured with a nod and a twitch of his ears for me to stay put and look out for Sinc while he snuck closer to Kyle, who was still in leopard form. Ethan padded away quietly, his tan coat blending perfectly with the dry brush.

I sat, senses alert, and waited. After a few minutes, my thoughts began to wander. I mused over how Sinc had greeted

Garrett and if that meant anything about their relationship. Maybe he was more than just her instructor? The thought made me cringe. I might actually be a tiny bit jealous. *Ridiculous.* A guy like that would never look at me twice.

I was distracted again by the quick heartbeat and snuffling noises of a nearby raccoon. I imagined what the plump little guy might taste like, remembering that I hadn't eaten anything since the Chinese food.

Suddenly, movement rustled the leaves in the tree above me. Before I could move, Sinc's snow leopard struck, smashing me to the ground and biting me deeply in my rear haunch, cutting easily through muscle with her razor sharp teeth. I snarled in pain and rage, my wound already bleeding steadily. Sinc's blue eyes shone a defiant challenge into mine before she growled and ran off. In one short bite she'd incapacitated me, preventing me from catching her, all because I hadn't been paying attention. Kyle had hidden the canvas bag before Ethan had chased him off, so I watched unhappily as Sinc snatched it up with her mouth and ran back toward the campground where Garrett would be waiting, ready to praise her for winning this round. *Crap.*

Should I stay here and wait for help? *Screw that.* I took off limping, pushing myself forward even though the bite was bleeding and the pain was intense. Feeling the sharp pulse of the ley lines beneath me, I concentrated on the power throbbing in my chest. My rage increased when I saw her up ahead, fueling my will to catch her. I was surprised to find that I could run more steadily now, the pain dismissed to the back of my brain and my focus on the view of her tail getting closer as I ran. Pushing myself harder, I visualized smashing her smug face into the dirt, snatching the bag roughly from her bloody mouth and finally Garrett's smile when I dropped the canvas bag at his feet.

Before I knew it, I was leaping onto her back and we were rolling in the dirt, stopping our momentum in a tumble of dried leaves and pine needles. Furious, Sinc twisted to bite me again, but couldn't without letting go of the bag. With a swipe of my paw, I slammed her head down hard in the dirt and grabbed it out of her now open mouth, racing as quickly as I could into the large cabin where Garrett waited.

I skidded to a halt, my claws scratching the wooden floor, panting from pain and the enormous adrenalin rush. Kyle and Ethan were already waiting for us. I dropped the bag at Garrett's feet and sat licking the wound on my leg. Ethan loped over in human form holding a medical kit. He crouched beside me and began cleaning my wound, telling me to stay in cheetah form until he finished. I hissed when he poured on the antiseptic, growling when he apologized. My wound was still bleeding slightly when Sinc strode in, shaking dirt from her face and snarling at me. I growled back, showing some teeth. Unfortunately, Garrett did not look happy.

Shit.

He crouched to take a look at my leg, telling Ethan he'd done a good job and he could bandage it up. When Ethan finished, Garrett said, his voice and expression hard to read, "Kyle, you and Ethan go out to hunt. I need to have a private talk with the girls." The guys looked at each other and left, stripping and shifting quickly to animal form. He pointed to a table. "Please transition and sit over there." He walked outside to give us some privacy so we shifted and dressed quickly. I was happy to see that I'd mostly healed, a small red welt the only evidence of the bite. We sat obediently at the table, not speaking and refusing to look at each other until Garrett returned and sat next to me.

"Sinc, Kyle told me the plan was to jump Jackie and stun her, not bite her, especially so deeply that she could have been in real trouble." My nervous stomach unclenched slightly, relieved that his icy blue stare wasn't directed at me. Sinc was trembling, and that worried me too. Garrett wasn't going to go all vamp on her was he? The bite had healed.

I put my hand on his to get his attention away from her. "She was trying to win the game. I'm fine now."

He turned his stern expression toward me. "It's not a game. There are killers out there—creatures you'll have to face together as a team." He turned back to Sinc and glared. "You disobeyed my direct order. Why?"

Sinc lifted her chin defiantly, "She's much faster and I had to keep her from chasing me. I didn't mean to bite her so deeply." She turned to me. "I'm sorry I hurt you. I never thought you might be in any real danger. I should have stayed with you to make sure." She turned back to Garrett, still nervous. "Accomplishing the mission takes precedence, doesn't it?"

Although my leg was still throbbing angrily, I was glad to see the scrape on her face wasn't serious. I'd dropped my anger as soon as I'd made her eat a little dirt. No reason to hold a grudge. Plus, I'd been the one to drop the bag at Garrett's feet.

Garrett arched an eyebrow, still looking at Sinc. "What else made you bite her so deeply?"

She sighed and twisted her mouth into a frown. "All anyone has been talking about is the new cheetah and how she's going to come in and magically save us all." She lowered her head, looking ashamed.

I laughed out loud. "Save you? I lost my focus when I should have been paying attention. I messed up." I smiled at her, knowing that making an enemy of this woman would not make my life any easier. And I definitely didn't want to be responsible for Garrett punishing her for disobeying him.

"How do you feel, Jackie?" he asked, real concern in his tone.

"It hardly hurts …." His expression told me he didn't believe a word of it. "Well, it still aches." An understatement.

"You're not off the hook either." He frowned. "In a situation like this where you know that backup is nearby, you should stay hidden, put pressure on the wound if you can and wait for assistance. Run only if your life or the life of a teammate is in danger. Shifter or not, you can still bleed out."

He reached across and pushed a strand of hair away from my eyes, tucking it behind my ear. I watched his perfect lips turn up into a gentle smile as I took in a deep breath to fill my nose with his scent. Realizing he might have noticed, I looked down, embarrassed, "Well, you know—the mission and all that. What she said."

Garrett grinned. "A little payback too, I think." He glanced at Sinc's scratched face.

I tried not to smile. "Yeah, I guess."

"You were incredibly fast, even injured. I couldn't believe you caught me." Sinc's tone held a grain of respect.

"We'll end this for now." Garrett looked again at Sinc. "The plans for the rest of the night have changed." His eyes met mine, still full of concern. "You'll need a good night's rest before you can continue to train in the field." His lips thinned. "But for now, go out and hunt together. Find something small and easy to catch. I expect you to work out your differences tonight, because I'm using the four of you to form a team. Your survival will depend on how well you work together."

Sinc looked me over. "We can handle it."

I watched him rise and walk to the door: a terrifying, seductive dichotomy. "I'll meet you back here in an hour." He was gone in a flash, leaving only a sweet breeze to mark his passing.

Sinc grunted. "He's probably hunting, too. I hope there aren't any humans around. He was really ticked off. Did you see his eyes?" Surprisingly chatty, Sinc looked at me with interest.

I nodded. "Yeah those silver streaks give me the chills. But he never takes human blood."

"Well, that's what he says, anyway. He's acting kind of protective toward you. It's weird." Her eyes narrowed. "Why'd you stick up for me? I wouldn't have done the same for you." She crossed her legs and waited to hear how I'd answer.

She was expecting me to get angry, but I wasn't rising to the bait that easily. I decided to be honest. "Because if Garrett lays into you for hurting me, you'll blame me and then working together will suck."

I saw the corners of her mouth twitch then quickly return to a neutral expression. "It might suck anyway." She shrugged, fiddling with the hem of her shirt, not meeting my gaze.

"Yeah, well, I'm starving and we only have an hour. Let's go hunt." We grinned and jumped up, tossing our clothes about haphazardly as we ran.

CHAPTER FIFTEEN

ARRETT, ETHAN, AND I PULLED UP TO Carly's little house and got out of the car, relieved to have gotten through the first session without any major disasters. Mumbling a goodnight to Garrett, Ethan stumbled through the door. He'd be snoring sometime in the next few minutes.

As the sky began to lighten, Garrett leaned against his car looking like a model from a print ad for sports cars. His pale skin took on a pinkish glow in the early dawn light. "The four of you did well tonight, once we got past Sinc's demonstration of what not to do during a training exercise."

We'd spent another two hours working out how best to utilize our different talents. Kyle was an amazing fighter and weapons expert: Sinc's talents lay in her stealth as a hunter and her brilliant technical and scientific skills. As Garrett presented us with different possible scenarios, we all agreed that Ethan's strength lay in working out successful strategies and communicating clearly how to approach each problem. Goofy Ethan was our natural team leader. Go figure. Plus, he was as strong as a grizzly. My extra-acute senses were the best for tracking and my speed was perfect for running down a fleeing enemy or delivering a vital message if tech wasn't available. Garrett didn't mention my connection to the magic, so I decided to keep my mouth zipped on that subject as well.

Kyle had also taken an hour to talk to us about some of his and Sinc's latest projects—all weapon related. This was high tech stuff the government might want to get their hands on, except Kyle and Sinc designed for the shifter community alone. The government would never hear about these weapons.

I took a step closer to Garrett and asked, "Will you give Sinc a pass on biting me? She made a mistake. She apologized. It's over."

He frowned and shook his head. "She disobeyed my order. Two inches deeper and you'd be in the hospital right now." Muscles moved under his shirt as he folded his arms across his chest. "In the field it may be Ethan giving the orders. If she doesn't obey me, why would she listen to Ethan?"

"If you hurt her, she'll follow your orders out of fear. If you let it go, she'll be loyal to you and free to give 100% to the team."

My insight disarmed him. "Sinc battles with her own personal stew of emotions. It's taken us some time to get her to trust or interact with others at all. Putting her on the team will help. But if I let her behavior go without consequences, she won't learn anything." He looked at me with curiosity. "How did you learn that particular lesson?" He pushed away from the car.

I dug my nails into my palms and looked toward the woods. Garrett probably already had access to my records. "I've lived with six different foster families. Most were fine, just average people. One foster father hit me when I didn't fall in line. His son was ... was worse. I swallowed and shuddered.

"I know what fear does to a person."

"Tell me their names." Garrett's voice had dropped an octave, his eyes swirling with silver.

"Why do they … do they do that? You're eyes …."

"Right now, because I'm angry with the males who hurt you so badly. Please tell me." I felt a tiny push encouraging me to answer.

I frowned, stepping back and shaking off his mental touch. "No. I've let it go. They can't hurt me anymore. I don't give them that power any longer."

Surprise flashed in his eyes. "I can find out."

"They're in jail." I turned away from him, my gut twisting into a knot. "I'd like you to stay out of my mind. I know you're trying to keep me safe, but I don't like it."

I listened to him breathe. He was so close. "I apologize."

"And will you lay off Sinc?"

"What do you think I'll do? Beat her? Bite her?"

"I don't know." I stared down at the ground. "Your anger scares the crap out of me. All that streaky silver eye stuff is terrifying."

I felt his breath on my neck without ever hearing him move. His hand touched my shoulder and I looked up. His eyes were filled with sadness. "Am I that frightening? Do you think me a monster like the men in your past? I would never hurt any of you. You're my students, not my enemies."

When he felt me relax, he continued, "Sinc pissed me off royally and I'm going to give her extra training assignments, but no blood will be spilled, I swear." He laughed suddenly and I was startled again by how young he looked when he smiled. "I can't control the silver in my eyes. It happens when I feel anger. It's an automatic response to freak out my enemies."

"It works. But why were your eyes silver in my dream?"

"It also happens when I'm feeling … amorous." My startled expression made him laugh again. "It was a dream. Get some sleep. I'll be back for our lesson tomorrow evening at eight."

He gave my shoulder a squeeze and opened his car door. I looked up at the sky. "Aren't you worried about the dawn coming?"

"No, I fed well tonight." Beaming like an angel, he slid into his car and drove away. I rubbed the shoulder he'd touched. It still felt warm.

Dragging myself inside, I forced myself into the shower and collapsed on the bed, happy to see that Ethan was on his side and not mine.

Around noon the next day, Carly and Samson arrived bearing groceries, extra towels and sheets, a few board games, a portable DVD player, and a few DVDs. She'd made us roast beef sandwiches and homemade salads, which we gobbled down immediately. After chatting for a few minutes, she gathered up the dirty laundry and left. Wow, I could get used to this.

Ethan announced that we should have a backgammon tournament, the loser relegated to washing all the dishes for the next three days.

We settled in to play, sipping sodas and munching on popcorn. Ethan, the master strategist, had me chasing him most of the time, managing to overcome my last ditch risky moves and win the tournament seven games to five. I washed the dishes while he gloated, which was only fair. When he wasn't looking I threw the wet sponge at him. That was followed by a knock-down-drag-out pillow fight, ending with us in a heap on the floor laughing and clutching at our sides.

Sinc and Kyle arrived later with Italian food in hand, and we enthusiastically dug into delicious meatball hero sandwiches and an enormous antipasto salad, talking amicably.

Apparently, shifters had fast metabolisms and needed to eat more often than humans. At least that's what we told each other as we gobbled down another big meal.

Sinc was decked out in her usual "designer casual," her dark hair pulled off her face and her blue eyes glaring at Kyle after some sarcastic remark he'd made. Kyle was sporting his black jeans, graphic tee, spiky hair, and huge grin. Because I was curious about them, I asked how they'd come to be a part of our strange quartet.

Kyle spoke first; obviously feeling relaxed when it came to talking about himself. "I was adopted from Cambodia by an awesome human couple. I'm a crazy mixture of French, Cambodian and Irish, no joke. My adopted dad taught martial arts, which was cool 'cause I rocked at it. His brother was an ex-marine who loved to hunt. I learned a lot about weapons from him.

"When I was around fifteen, I had these jittery episodes where my temper would flare up, and I'd feel like I had to punch something. I'd meditate or exercise, all my usual ways to relieve tension. Nothing worked. The worst was when I started getting horrible headaches. I ended up in the hospital having all kinds of tests. It sucked big time. The doctors, all human of course, were even talking about exploratory surgery.

"Rob and Garrett appeared in my room one night while I was sleeping. They talked to my parents and told them they were from a *special hospital* and that they'd like to take over my case. Garrett did his spooky mind control thing on them and me and before I knew it, I was in the cabin on the island and Rob was telling me that physically I was fine, but I wasn't really human. I didn't take it well at first. I loved my family and my life just the way it was. My parents think I've recovered, but that I'm working overseas. I call them every week and stop by every couple of months or so and stay a few days. They don't know I'm a shifter."

His expression turned angry. "I still have trouble working with Garrett. I hate that he went into my head like that. His power totally freaks me out, especially when he goes into vamp mode with his fangs out and his eyes all silver. I can't imagine how many people he's killed."

"I saw him rip two men to pieces." I quietly told them about my attack and how Garrett showed me what had actually happened. "I was bleeding all over from stab wounds and he had me drink blood from his wrist to help me heal."

The room was suddenly as quiet as a morgue. Kyle spoke up. "Honey, you are so screwed. He's gonna own you."

"Shut up, Kyle!" Sinc jumped up, fuming. "She was dying and he gave her his blood to save her life. You'd better hope that he'd do the same for you if you're ever in bad shape."

"Sure Sinclair, whatever you say. You've never been mind-controlled by him. Count yourself lucky."

Ethan and I looked at her curiously. "Yeah, I know. It's a stupid name, that's why I go by Sinc. A family of werewolves adopted me."

"Werewolves?" I was shocked.

"They were good to me at first. They thought I was a human kid and were going to make me a wolf if I decided that was what I wanted. You know the whole biting thing. Weres can't have kids. They can't carry a child because they have to change every month. Shifters can go the whole nine months without changing." I hadn't known anything about werewolves so this was all pretty fascinating.

Sinc continued. "Anyway, I started getting those same symptoms like Kyle described when I was fifteen. It was awful. Then one night I shifted right in the living room. It freaked everyone out. They locked me up and called Rob. He's one of the only shifters my pack trusts. I think it's that minty thing he does. Anyway, he came and picked me up and I haven't seen them since. They bought me a house and a car and they send me money every month, but it was like I was excommunicated or something."

"You call them?"

"They don't answer my calls. The alpha wolf won't allow it."

Even though she'd turned away to look out the window, we'd all seen the pain in her eyes. "I guess I was lucky that I didn't change during the full moon, because I'd have been dinner." She sat quietly, lost in her thoughts. None of us spoke for a few moments.

Kyle broke the silence. "Sinc and I trained on the island together with Rob like you and Ethan did. You two seem to get along pretty well. We fought all the time. Thank god we heal fast, otherwise I'd be covered in snow leopard scars."

"You got in a few good ones yourself," Sinc replied, throwing a pillow. They laughed together, sharing a private joke.

Ethan, Kyle, and Sinc left the cottage at seven thirty and headed to Carly's house. Meanwhile, I had a private appointment with a very hot, scary vampire.

CHAPTER SIXTEEN

AFTER CLEANING UP THE REMAINS OF OUR dinner, I walked into the back yard, nervous with anticipation. I had the necklace in my pocket instead of around my neck, trying to get used to feeling the magic, kind of toughening myself up. The night was cool so I pulled up the hood of my sweatshirt and waited, taking a few minutes to stare up at the stars surrounding the hazy half moon.

A large raven sat on the edge of the low brick wall that bordered the yard, watching me, ruffling its feathers, and cawing once. Blue eyes stared from its pointed black face, causing me to gasp and take a startled step backward. Magical energy suddenly crackled around me, biting into my chest and making me shut my eyes in pain. When I smelled a familiar scent, I opened them again.

Garrett sat where the raven once had, his thick hair mussed, with several strands hanging over his eyes, still managing to look amazing. Noticing my stunned expression, his lips parted in a smile. "Before I was made vampire I was a shifter and could use the ley lines as you will soon. In this present state I've lost my ability to transition into my original form, but on occasion I can pull a different change. Did you like it?" His expression was boyish with excitement, a kid showing off for his friend.

Sensing my mouth was still hanging open, I shut it with an audible snap. I guess that explains why he wants to help shifters. "Umm … that was cool, Garrett. Why a raven?"

"A raven is the easiest form for me to take as a vampire. It's a harbinger of death," he joked, using a spooky voice. When I didn't respond, he shrugged. "It's a good form for a fast escape and it's come in handy more than once."

"Can all shifters switch animals?"

"No. We usually just have the one form. I'm hoping soon I'll be able to transition to my original animal again."

I narrowed my eyes in irritation. "How is it that you're dressed after you change back?" This was a trick I wanted to learn, although I wouldn't have minded at all if he'd ended up naked the way the rest of us did. I tried to keep my lips from curling up as I felt my face grow hot.

"It's not magic. I can just put on my clothes faster than you can see me do it." He stood and walked in my direction, running his fingers through his messy hair. He was dressed in jeans and an unbuttoned black silk shirt showing off his perfect skin and hard abs. I closed my mouth and swallowed hard. This guy pushed every one of my buttons without even trying.

As he buttoned his shirt, I noticed that he wasn't breathing. "You don't have to breathe?"

"No, I do it to pick up scents. Also, humans tend to notice if you never take a breath, so I breathe when I'm around them." He came to a halt a few feet in front of me. Garrett made a point of breathing in deeply. "Your scent is unique. Lovely."

I couldn't resist taking in a quiet breath of my own. He'd

moved to the chair to retrieve the jacket he'd left draped over the back, and bent to pick up his shoes. My heart was beating faster, my eyes taking in his every motion.

Why was I drawn to this guy in such an intense way? Yeah, he was incredibly hot, but I'd always been able to keep my head around men. I had no illusions when it came to happily-ever-after and all that crap. Most men saw something they wanted and went after it. When they'd gotten their fill they moved on. I knew that love was out there, having seen it with Justin and Maggie and a couple of other foster families, just not for someone like me.

Was Garrett using his glamour on me? Vamps had the ability to make you want them physically, making it easier for them to convince you to give them blood. I didn't feel power coming off him, but then I wasn't really experienced with how the magic worked. But he hadn't tried to touch me except when the energy made my head hurt.

When I dreamed of him, he opened his arms and welcomed me inside. But a male like Garrett must have dozens of girlfriends, maybe even a wife, or a mate. I was only his student, not even his friend.

He spoke again, breaking through my jumbled thoughts. "What I've shown you tonight is between the two of us. Only a few shifters know that I can change form, and I'd prefer it to remain that way. Your magical abilities should be kept secret, too. When you're skilled enough to defend yourself, we can let your closest circle know. Until then, it would be dangerous for you to tell anyone. Certain powerful supernaturals would seek you out if they knew the truth."

Pain from the lines attacked me in waves. I rubbed at my temples, frowning.

Garrett asked, "Why aren't you wearing the amulet?"

"I'm trying to get used to the feeling."

"That's foolish. It will only get worse and then you won't be able to focus. You don't have months or even weeks to learn the skills I'll be teaching. You'll think I'm being cruel, because there will be pain, but manipulating the lines is dangerous and I take my responsibility as your trainer seriously. I will keep you safe." He lifted my chin. "Will you give me your full attention and follow my instructions?" I nodded, grateful that he'd decided to take the time to help me.

"Do you trust me? I'm asking because when I train you, you'll need to open your mind to me. Tell me now if you have any doubts."

He smiled to reassure me and I couldn't stop myself from smiling back, especially when I noticed the sweet way his skin crinkled up around his eyes. "I do trust you." The surprised tone of my voice made him laugh. I looked away. "Trusting someone …. It's hard for me."

"I won't betray your faith in me. You have the talent to become a great manipulator of the lines, a magical warrior, a lifeline for whatever cause you decide to champion."

His accolade was lost to me as a wave of hot static hit me in the belly. He reached out with his hand and I grabbed at it desperately, squeezing hard. The pain fled as quickly as it had appeared, and I found that I could breathe normally again. My gaze lifted up to meet his, my mind trying to communicate what my voice was too afraid to say.

Please don't let go.

I knew he hadn't heard my mental plea, but he kept contact with me anyway, as he led me into the house, his long fingers still twined around mine. I hoped with all my heart I wouldn't disappoint him, or myself tonight.

CHAPTER SEVENTEEN

G ARRETT PUT HIS SHOES BY THE DOOR, grabbed a water bottle from the fridge and guided me back to the circular burgundy rug under the window. We sat, legs crossed and facing each other. "It's important to remain hydrated." He handed me the bottle.

"Do you see yourself as a warrior?" I snuck a glance at his strong hands. Did he fight with a weapon, or was a vampire all about the fangs?

"Perhaps a warrior, but I'm no one's champion. I try to help out where I can, that's all." I wondered if he counted me as one of his causes. I managed to give him a shy smile, despite my jittery nerves.

I started to ask something else, but he interrupted. "Let's begin. I want you to breathe in and out in a steady rhythm. Find a song that speaks to you and hear it in your head. A child's nursery rhyme works too. Then breathe to that beat, four beats in, four beats out. Once you've found the right song, it will become your mantra for stilling your mind and your body and readying yourself to access the energy.

After running through various playlists in my head, I remembered someone singing a song to me long ago. I was very small and her voice had been lovely and comforting. I didn't know if it had been my birth mother, but I'd always imagined that it was. I chose that song and started to breathe in and out to the cadence of the tune.

Garrett released my hand and I instantly bent forward from pain as another hot jolt punched me in the stomach. "Why is it so much worse now?" I groaned. I reached out, but he snatched his hands away.

"Breathe, Jackie. Holding your breath will make it worse. The energy in the ley lines moves in currents producing waves of power, always getting stronger as the full moon approaches. This particular crossroads produces more than most others across the country. That's why the town was built here."

"Great." I grimaced, trying to breathe steadily. "Why didn't I have this problem before I transitioned? Or when I was on the island?"

"Your first shift brought on these abilities. The island is relatively far from a line. A powerful user could still access magic without a problem, but not a newborn shifter." He twisted his mouth looking slightly annoyed with me. "Please stop asking questions and breathe."

I shut up and concentrated, finally succeeding in gasping in rhythm. Four beats in and four beats out. Four breaths in and four breaths out.

"No, not short breaths, smooth. Try in through your nose and out through your mouth." He demonstrated.

I smoothed out my breathing and felt a slight lessening of the pain, although not enough to stop the single tear from running down my face. Why couldn't he teach me all of this while he was touching me? This sucked.

"Better, Jackie, but don't stop. Now I want you to close your eyes and visualize yourself standing somewhere out in the open. On a field or a beach is fine. Then imagine a strong solid wall, a shield of some kind. Whatever comes to you first will work best. There can't be any cracks or openings. I want you to visualize it brick by brick or stone by stone being built up around your body. Outside energy can't penetrate it no matter how strong the power. You control the magic to build your wall. It doesn't control you."

I lost count for a moment, wincing from the pain. "You must truly trust in your strength for the shield to work. It can be made of any material you choose as long as you believe it's impenetrable. And whatever you do, keep breathing in the same rhythm."

I hesitated, my muscles tensing up. Did I mention that I'd always been a tiny bit claustrophobic; enough to keep me out of small simulator rides or very crowded elevators? Building a wall around myself, even in my mind, was causing sweat to break out on my forehead. Another wave of pain hit me and I quickly went back to concentrating on my breathing.

"Don't wait. Do it now." His voice was urgent, even frustrated, irritating me. Jeez, *he* wasn't the one in pain.

Two more tears joined the other one. Maybe if I could see through the wall I wouldn't panic. What was see-thru and strong? I chose my material and started to build, pulling energy from the vibrations around me. Gemstone by gemstone, I created a wall made of smooth, clear diamond. It was beautiful as it rose up in front of me, glittering in the moonlight, and I was quite pleased with my choice.

As I was building, I was also visualizing myself very far away from Garrett. I placed myself on a grassy coastal cliff overlooking an ocean of rippling magic where anything was possible. Starbursts of colors glimmered on the swelling surface beckoning me to climb down and take a dip. I resisted the urge and quickly completed my wall, drawing a satisfied sigh from my trainer.

I was amazed that it was the strength of my mind that held the wall in place. I'd been able to use magic as a tool to shield myself, bending the power to my will. I grinned because the pain was gone and I wasn't afraid of it anymore.

"Perfect. Now open your eyes, only don't let go of your wall." His voice was as soft as velvet, caressing my fragile ego and giving me confidence. The vibrations and heat from the lines had stopped affecting me, and I was surprised when I looked down at my hands to see that Garrett still wasn't touching me. Inside of my mind I stood proudly on the cliff, looking out at the magical ocean of ley line power.

"Please look at me." His sapphire eyes were gleaming with pride. "Why the cliff?" he asked, smiling warmly.

"I like the ocean." He waited. "And I was angry and wanted to get away from you," I whispered, embarrassed that he might think I wasn't grateful for his help.

"Why create an ocean of ley line energy?" He seemed amused by my choices.

"I want to see what I'll be working with." I shrugged. "How can you see what's in my mind?"

"I tapped the lines and followed you mentally, until you finished your wall, then I was locked out."

"Any vampire can see inside my head?" I blinked several times, my eyesight blurring. My eyes widened. Garrett was starting to glow, looking even more like an angel. And boy, did he smell great. I took a really deep breath, sucking in his now familiar and very yummy scent.

"Only the older vampires can read thoughts. I think our blood bond makes it easier for me. But not when you have your mental shield up, like you do now. Clever of you to create a wall of diamond." He ran his hand distractedly through his auburn hair and I wondered dreamily what it would feel like to touch it. I was surprised to see that my hand had moved up toward his head, even though I couldn't remember moving it.

He grabbed it, laughing. "Okay, Jackie. I think you've had enough for one night." His voice was like a splash of warm soapy water, making my body tingle all over. "You're a little power drunk. Although you may not realize it, you used a lot of the line's energy to build your shield. It always affects cheetahs like this the first time. We'll be able to work for longer tomorrow. C'mon, I'm putting you to bed."

"You are?" I grinned stupidly.

"To sleep, Jackie." He handed me the bottle of water and I drank half of it down gratefully, not realizing how thirsty I'd become. I stood and swayed so he picked me up and carried me into the bedroom, lowering me down on the bed without effort. His grin was brilliant.

"Kyle told me that I was screwed and that you're gonna own me 'cause I drank your blood." I giggled, thinking that my words sounded a little slurry. I held out my hands and waved them around dramatically. "Master—I'm your slave."

He chuckled as he removed my shoes and tucked me under the covers. "I gave you my blood to heal you. It formed an unexpected bond between us. Now I can sense if you're nearby, or if you're hurt. We might be able to communicate mind-to-mind one day. But I don't own you, Jackie, and I won't feed from you. By using your wall you can block me from your mind anytime you want."

"You can feed from me. Go ahead." I giggled again only half joking. I was picturing his lips on my neck and it was making me feel warm all over, in a really good way.

He leaned slowly down until he was six inches from my foolish grinning face, my head resting on the pillow, his hands on either side. He smiled deliciously, silver sparkling in his vibrant blue eyes, his fangs just peeking out. His breath on my face was sweet and warm as he spoke. "Don't ever say that to a vampire, unless you know you won't regret it the next day. " He was gone before I could respond.

I sighed, a tiny bit disappointed, then rolled on my side and slept.

A pattern developed over the next two weeks. Ethan and I would get up between noon and one after a long night of training with Garrett, Sinc, and Kyle up at the campsite. We'd eat some of Carly's delicious leftovers and go for a run, or spar, or decide to take it easy because we were really sore from last night's training. On those days we'd watch a movie or indulge in another backgammon tournament.

Carly's arrival at four with more wonderful food was one of the high points of the day. She'd stay for an hour, always bringing Samson who seemed to crave my attention. Carly would leave and then Garrett would arrive around six. He'd work with me for a while out in the woods away from Ethan and then he'd take us up to the campsite for another training session with Sinc and Kyle.

Several things were becoming more and more apparent as the days passed. Sinc, Kyle, Ethan, and I were beginning to act and think like a team. We were also starting to bond, becoming more relaxed in each other's company. I was getting better and better at building my defensive mental wall so I was much more comfortable around the buzz of the lines. I didn't need to wear the necklace at all anymore. It now hung from the mirror over the dresser, reminding me of the vampire who'd given it to me.

Shifting to cheetah and back felt as natural as breathing, and some of my favorite times were when the four of us hunted together in our animal forms. If a hiker had happened upon us, he probably would have shaken his head in disbelief and then run like a bitch.

What I tried to ignore but couldn't, was how I felt toward Garrett, and it wasn't because of anything he'd done. His behavior was always professional and, while I was focused on the training sessions, mine was too. But then he would laugh and touch my shoulder and I'd have to bite my lip to keep from touching him back. He would smile at me because he was proud of what I'd accomplished, and I'd find myself staring at his lips and wondering if they'd be soft to kiss. He was doing nothing to encourage me, yet I was drawn to him totally, reading in his azure eyes what I wanted to find there.

And yeah, you could say this was a physical reaction to his spectacular looks, but you'd be only half right. He spoke to me with kindness and intelligence. He laughed at my jokes and teased me right back. He helped me see myself as a powerful, useful member of a community that needed my skills. I started to like and respect myself. I began to feel whole.

Once in a while I'd imagine that he was looking at me with longing, but then it would be gone and he'd be his usual steady self. I'd had a couple of schoolgirl crushes in my life, usually ending with my getting hurt, but this was so much more. The logical part of my brain told me that he would never feel the same way about me. Still, I was grateful for every moment we spent together, and when I crawled into bed at dawn, it was easy to close my eyes and dream about him.

CHAPTER EIGHTEEN

O N A QUIET MORNING, ABOUT A WEEK after I'd first learned to build my diamond wall, I dreamed again.

A huge wolf was stalking me. My leg bled from a wound on my calf, the scent bringing him closer and closer. I was running as fast as I could, trying to shift into my cheetah form, but unable to make the change. Now limping, I stumbled through a bed of sword ferns, sensing him almost upon me. I fell to the ground in a small clearing, shifting my body to face my enemy.

But Kyle, in leopard form, was suddenly growling beside me, protecting me. The large wolf who'd pursued me howled and other howls rang out in answer. Sinc's graceful snow leopard leapt down from the tree branch above me and Ethan's cougar barreled in through the brush, all three of them circling, facing the wolf pack that surrounded us.

I was injured too badly to change. We were outnumbered and I was useless. Frustration welled up in me. I picked up a large rock and threw it at one of the wolves, then another.

I woke up to Ethan shaking me. "Jackie, you're having a really bad dream and something crazy is going on here!"

I opened my eyes, grateful to see Ethan's concerned face, and not the snout of one of those wolves in my dream. Still feeling dizzy, I sat up slowly and looked around. My gaze wandered to the window where a cold breeze blew the curtains in toward the bed. I was startled to see that the window was smashed, glass scattered all over the bedroom floor.

"What happened?" I clenched the covers.

"I woke up when I heard you moan and then mumble. I think it was *run away*—something like that. The alarm clock went flying through that window and one of my boots smashed through this one. Is there a poltergeist in the house Carly didn't tell us about or is this about you?"

He was freaked out, but I didn't know what to tell him. Garrett had said not to talk about what my mind could do.

I could tell by the light that it was still pretty early, probably around six or seven. We'd only slept for a few hours.

I avoided his question. "I'll clean up the mess."

After locating the vacuum, Ethan helped me pick up the larger pieces of glass and vacuum up the rest. He was watching me suspiciously the whole time and I couldn't blame him, but what could I say? I wouldn't lie, not to Ethan.

When we finished, I made coffee and we sat across from each other at the small table. I looked at his worried face and reached across to hold his hand. He was startled and started to pull away but I held on tightly. Trusting my instincts, I made the decision to be completely honest with him.

"I have to tell you something."

"Does this have anything to do with your private lessons?" he asked softly.

"I think it might." I scanned his familiar face once more, but I already knew what I'd find. "I'm going to trust you with a secret."

"You know you can."

I released his hand and talked about the currents of ley line power flowing beneath us, something he knew about but had no experience with. I described the extra connection I had to this magic and what Garrett had taught me about focusing myself and building my diamond wall. Describing the dream, I explained that the broken windows were probably the result of me using the lines to protect myself.

I didn't mention any of Garrett's secrets.

"Will you swear not to speak about this to Kyle or Sinc or Rob or anyone else? I need to learn to protect and defend myself—how to use this ability to help people and not smash windows." We smiled at each other. "I'd also appreciate it if you wouldn't tell Garrett that I told you any of this. I'd rather tell him myself. Hopefully, I won't be doing any extra assignments for disobeying an order." I laughed halfheartedly.

"I won't say anything. You know you can trust me." He leaned over and gave me a hug, then picked up his cell phone lying on the kitchen counter. "We have to tell Carly about the windows. She'll have to send someone over to fix it. I'll just say we were throwing a ball around and the throws went a little wide." Within an hour, a repair team was there and the window was soon as good as new.

When they left, Ethan and I talked again about my "episode." "If I understand what you've said, you tapped into the power while you were dreaming. How are we going to keep this from happening again? I'd rather not wake up flying through the air and smashing into the window."

"I'll have to ask Garrett when I see him alone." I sighed, nervous about what he might say.

Carly and Samson arrived around three with their usual array of supplies. She cooked us a wonderful steak supper and joined us this time. I made sure to feed Samson a few bites and to scratch him behind the ears. He wagged his stubby tail and curled up on the floor next to my feet.

Carly looked curious. "Samson doesn't tolerate many people, but he's very attached and protective toward you." I scratched his head and rubbed his belly, pleased when he grunted in doggy satisfaction.

Twenty minutes later he was up, growling and barking at the door. At Ethan's signals, Carly grabbed Samson's leash and moved out of the way. Ethan went to the left of the door, prepared to defend us and I walked to the right, a frying pan raised and ready to swing.

"I don't think the frying pan will make a dent in Robert's hard head." Garrett laughed from behind Carly. She jumped and immediately moved to the window, dragging Samson with her.

After the initial shock, Ethan and I cracked up and opened the door for Rob. I gave him a huge hug, which surprised him, and motioned him toward the table. "How are you? Are you hungry? There's more steak." I deposited the pan back on the stove.

Rob dumped my old backpack on the floor near the couch. He'd brought the last of my stuff from the cabin. "Sure, Jackie, thanks." He gave Carly a hug then moved to the table to sit. I dished him up some steak and potatoes and Ethan sat across from him jabbering away and catching up on all the news.

I glanced over at Carly who stared straight down at Samson, avoiding Garrett's eyes. Garrett was sauntering toward her, an amused expression on his face.

"Hello, Carly," he greeted her. "How have you been?"

"Garrett." She was curt, obviously uncomfortable. She looked up, her anger giving her courage. "Judging from the hour, I'd guess you've been feeding from shifters again." She frowned and squatted beside Samson, petting him nervously and not looking at Garrett.

"Only the ones who ask me to. I'm quite popular, really. Don't worry. I'm not hungry at the moment." He smiled wickedly and squatted down beside her. Samson stopped growling and started wagging his tail the minute Garrett began scratching him behind the ears.

"Good boy, Samson." Garrett grinned at Carly, arching an eyebrow in a well-look-at-this kind of expression.

Furious, Carly yanked on Samson's collar, pulling him away from Garrett, grabbing her coat and mumbling as she headed out the door, "I'll see you tomorrow around noon." The door shut firmly behind her.

Garrett leaned elegantly against the large double window-sill, staring after her with a sad expression. I hesitated, afraid to intrude on his private moment, then gave in and walked over to ask quietly. "What's up with you and Carly?"

"We grew up together in Canada. Our parents were close friends, and she was like a sister to Marie and me. Both our families moved to Lafayette, Louisiana when the British kicked the French out of Canada. When I was made vampire and discovered that I could feed from shifters without taking blood, I did, indiscriminately. I never hurt anyone, but it was wrong and I made some enemies. Carly's never trusted me since. I like to tease her, but I wish we could get past it."

"How old are you?"

"I'm a child of the revolution," he chuckled.

"Umm, which revolution?"

"You know, General George Washington, John Adams. That revolution. My dad fought on the side of the Americans." His expression had grown serious again when he'd mentioned his dad.

I frowned. Those numbers didn't work. "How is that possible? Carly grew up with you? But she's not a vampire and she looks so young. That can't be right."

"Carly's a shifter, a leopard." When I didn't react, he stared at me strangely, turning to Rob. "I believe Rob has left out a vital piece of information regarding life as a shapeshifter."

"I can't do everything. You could have told her."

"Told me what?" I looked from Rob back to Garrett.

Garrett continued. "Shifters age normally into young adulthood after their first transition, but then they stop. As long as a shifter continues to shift a few times a year, they don't age. I know several shifters who are around four hundred years old, but look about twenty. And there are two-thousand-year-old shifters in Europe."

Feeling shaky, I sat down next to him on the wide windowsill, trying to wrap my mind around this newest bit of information. Seeing my reaction, he put his arm around my shoulders in support and I leaned into him, not even thinking about what I was doing. I couldn't seem to process what he'd just said. It was surreal, but then everything from the past couple of weeks had been out of some weird fantasy novel.

"Werewolves also stop aging as long as they continue to transition every month, which is not even a choice for them, unless they're ill. My cousin Aaron's a pack leader and he's two years older than me. We grew up together."

"He wasn't a shifter?"

"No. His mother was a shifter but his father was human. It can go either way. He chose to be bitten when he was around twenty-five. I think his latent shifter genes made him stronger and helped him gain the alpha position."

"But there are older people living in the town. I saw them."

"Some shifters decide to stop transitioning when their mates die, but our community is comprised of many human friends or mates of the shifters who live here in Crescent City. They all know about us and are sworn to secrecy. If it was all shifters, practically everyone would look college aged."

I laughed, imagining a town populated only by eighteen- to twenty-two-year-olds. "What about all the tourists or truck drivers, you know, the people passing through?"

"Would a human who ran into Rob on the street think he was anything other than human? The shifters here are good at hiding what they are. All supes are, and humans don't usually sense the difference. We gently discourage non-supernaturals from settling here if they aren't part of the community."

"Gently discourage, huh? Using magic?"

He only grinned in response. "How's your wall holding up?" He'd whispered so only I could hear, tightening his grip on my shoulder. Having his arm pressed against my back brought his face closer than ever, speeding up my heart. His breath smelled sweet and clean and his mouth, oh god. It was inches away. What would he taste like?

I whispered back, staring down at my lap. "I haven't had any pain the whole day. I sense the current, but it doesn't make me uncomfortable." His hand moved up and down my bare arm sending warm tingles over my skin. I wondered if he even realized he was doing it. I relaxed just a tiny bit more against him, hyper-aware of every place our bodies touched as we sat together on the windowsill. Rob glanced at us curiously, so I pulled myself away and moved toward Ethan, who was still chatting about our training sessions with Sinc and Kyle.

Garrett interpreted my standing up as a sign of impatience. "We should go, we have lots to do tonight. Rob will be working with the other three." He stood, offering me his hand. It was obvious he had no clue how his touch affected me, because if he did, he might never touch me again. He'd made it clear he wanted only a student/instructor relationship.

I smiled shyly and gave him mine, determined to enjoy it while I could. He smiled back, his beauty and his warmth breaking down the moment to its simple essence. A guy and a girl holding hands—nothing more. Was there any hope at all? I owed it to myself to find out.

CHAPTER NINETEEN

A S GARRETT DROVE, I PEEKED AT HIM nervously. My feelings toward him had changed so dramatically in such a short time. They'd gone from awe to respect to friendship to what? Desire? Or was I in love? I'd never been in love before. Can you fall in love in only a couple of weeks? He'd been my secret guardian for a few years but I hadn't known he existed until recently, at least not that I'd remembered.

For the hundredth time, I wondered if this was simply a physical attraction. I took another sneaky glance at his strong, lean build and his brilliant eyes that seemed to pull me directly into his heart. His mouth was turned up at the corners, those lips a siren's song to mine. Any normal girl would want a guy like Garrett.

But I was also drawn to what I sensed inside of him: his honesty and compassion. These seemed strange qualities in a vampire—not that I knew much about the undead—but perhaps not so strange in a shapeshifter. When he was changed, he must have retained much of his shifter self. Why had he decided to change at all?

But I was attracted to him on another level as well, so I tried to puzzle it out as he drove. He *got* me. We were connected on some deeper layer, maybe because he'd saved my life and given me blood, or because we could both connect to the magic of the ley lines. Or was it something else? Or all of those things?

I *got* him too. Hidden behind the professional calm and the occasional arrogant act, there was pain and self-doubt. Something inside him was broken. He was a rogue as much as any of us. I suddenly felt an overwhelming desire to touch him, to mend him. Instead, I clasped my hands tightly together in my lap and looked at the passing scenery.

"What are you thinking about? You seem a million miles away." His smile was warm, his eyes crinkling up at the corners in my favorite way.

I took a deep breath and began, not wanting to put it off any longer. "Something happened this morning that freaked me and Ethan out. I had a crazy dream and we woke up to things flying around the room. I decided that I didn't have any choice but to tell Ethan about my abilities. I didn't mention anything private about you," I added quickly.

Garrett pulled the car to the side of the road and turned it off. He faced me, giving me his full attention, saying quietly, "Tell me what happened."

I told him first about my dream and then about the smashed windows. I ended with everything I'd told Ethan and his promise not to tell anyone. As I spoke, I did my best to stay calm, but the thunder in my chest was probably waking the occupants of the nearby cemetery.

As if reading my mind, he said, "Your heart is racing. Are you still afraid of me?" His expression was sad, as it often was these days.

I thought for a moment about how to answer him. "I've

never been afraid that you'd hurt me, only that I'll disappoint you and you won't keep training me. I need your help. I'd be lost if you walked away now."

He huffed out a breath. "I'm not going to stop training you. I want you to be able to protect yourself and the team." His gaze burned into me. "You're blushing, Jackie. Are you troubled by something I've done? You can tell me anything."

Taking in a slow breath, I decided to go for it. "When I'm with you I feel—I feel kind of amazing." Okay, that was lame, but since his expression hadn't changed, I went on anyway. "I know you're not glamouring me, because I feel the same way about you even when my wall is up." I gave him a shy smile, hoping he'd respond in some way.

Still no reaction. I sighed and plunged ahead, figuring that I couldn't be any more embarrassed than I was already. "I know that this is one-sided and that you're not attracted to me." I lifted my chin, trying to drum up some more courage. "I won't let my feelings for you get in the way of working with the team." Jeez, could I sound any more pathetic?

He finally spoke, his voice a sad whisper. "As Sinc said, the mission comes first." I nodded, trying to figure out what he meant by that. Sitting so close to him was not helping me relax. I tried to open my window, but realized they were electric and the car was turned off. Breathing in his scent was making me hot and not just because of the car's temperature. I sat trembling in the seat, looking down at my hands, wishing I'd kept my mouth shut about how I felt.

"Jackie, please look at me." I bit my lip and twisted. His beautiful face was mere inches away, his intelligent eyes sucking me in like a whirlpool. "You did the right thing telling Ethan. I'll talk to him about it. Tonight we'll work on ways you can block the line energy when you sleep and dream. It shouldn't happen again."

He sighed, turning away, a deep crease forming between his eyes. "As for the other, you're wrong when you say I don't feel the same way. I'm incredibly drawn to you. Since I met you in the cabin on the island, I've thought of little else. Perhaps it's the blood or the magical connection between us, I'm not sure. You're a courageous and compassionate person. In the coming months, you'll meet other shifter males. I'm sure one of them ...."

"Garrett ...."

"It doesn't matter how we feel, because I'm not right for you. My lifestyle is dangerous and I have enemies. I feed on shifters. I kill when I have to. You've seen firsthand what I'm capable of doing in a fit of rage. You're young. You'll find another shifter who won't put your life in danger. I won't put you at risk."

After I'd heard the words, "incredibly drawn to you," I'd blocked out the rest and started inching closer to him, staring at those perfect lips, loving the way they moved when he spoke, wondering for the hundredth time how they'd taste when I finally pressed mine against them. I placed my hand on his arm, felt the firm muscles beneath his shirt and started tugging him closer. I mean, here was my chance and I wasn't going to spend the rest of my life regretting that I'd never had the guts to go for it.

He just kept talking and talking about how bad he was for me and how I should stay away from him when we weren't training—blah, blah, blah. I kept inching closer and tugging him toward me until I was only about ten inches away. That's when I struck, throwing my arms around his neck and kissing him for all I was worth. He was startled and pushed me away roughly. I slid across the seat, hitting the back of my head against the window.

"Ow," I rubbed the spot where a bump was sure to form.

Suddenly he was there rubbing it for me, looking a little angry and a lot scared.

"What - are - you - thinking?" His voice almost cracked. "Did you hear one word of what I was saying? I hurt you just now." Despite the pain, his concern made me smile.

He cares about me. My thumping heart was doing a happy dance.

"I heard you say you were drawn to me too. Anyway, it was my own fault; I kind of snuck up on you." Because he was so close, right where I wanted him, I reached up and touched a thick strand of his hair. It was soft silk, shining in the moonlight coming through the sunroof, smelling sweet and delicious. He grabbed my hand, maybe meaning to push it away, but instead he held it trapped in his as we stared at each other. His fingers twined themselves around mine as his gaze traveled slowly from my eyes to my lips to my neck. His chest rose and fell as he breathed in my scent, and I wondered for the first time what I smelled like to him.

Dots of silver popped in his lovely blue eyes, a sign that he wanted to kiss me, too. He leaned closer and whispered. "You have no idea what you do to me." His voice was a sexy vibration, his breath on my throat sending tiny shivers down my body. It certainly wasn't fear that made my heart jump around.

"Vampires, werewolves, shifters: we're all territorial. Once we lay claim to something, or *someone*, we'll kill to keep it. We don't share."

My dormant cheetah reared its head. *Mine.*

He touched my hair, hesitant, moving a stray lock behind my ear. "Any relationship between us would have to be exclusive. Is Ethan more than a friend or a team member to you? You seem very close."

I took a few moments and thought about Ethan. Did he have strong feelings for me? I loved him like a brother or a best friend, but never more than that. Garrett stayed frozen in place waiting for my answer, his face strung tight with tension.

"I don't know for sure how Ethan feels about me. I care about him, but I'm not attracted to him—the way I am to you. He's never tried to kiss me or anything." My face heated again and I looked down. "I can still work with Ethan and the team; it won't be a problem for me." I swallowed hard for courage and tentatively touched Garrett's silent chest while my heart continued its frantic drumming. His hand holding mine felt cool tonight and instinctively, I knew he hadn't fed before he came to the cottage earlier.

I looked into his eyes and found the courage to be honest. "I want to be with you." I was shocked by the intensity of my feelings, amazed by my brazenness. I wasn't acting like the old unsure Jackie, yet I'd never felt more like myself.

"You're seventeen and have no experience living in our supernatural world." He shook his head and moved away, staring out the windshield. "You don't know what you want or whom you want to be with."

That pissed me off, so I pushed on his shoulder and he turned his head to look at me again, eyebrows arched. "Don't patronize me. You think I don't know what I want? Then you don't know me at all. I've been through a lot more than most women my age or older. Anyway, back in your day, women were married off at 14." I scowled.

"Ah, yes, the good old days when we could sell our wives for a few cows or beat them daily if it pleased us." He smiled teasingly, indicating his hair, clothes, and his car. "In case you haven't noticed, I'm up to date with the customs of modern civilization."

I smiled and let go of my anger, reaching out to stroke his hand gently with my fingers. "You wouldn't be getting some gentle lamb, either. I don't give up when I set my sights on something." I rested my hand on top of his and felt him slowly wrap his fingers around mine, all the time staring at me, trying to gage the truth of my words. His expression was mixed: desire in his eyes but his mouth turned down with worry.

Feeling brave, I asked a question I wasn't sure I wanted the answer to. "What about you? Are you free? You said you had people that you fed from. Are they your...your lovers?" I looked away, expecting to hear the worst.

"Vampires feed to survive, but feeding isn't erotic unless both partners want it to be. I haven't had a serious relationship with a woman for a long time. I'm considered a freak; a shifter turned vampire. Not a particularly desirable long-term mate. Casual short-term relationships don't usually interest me."

He turned my face toward his with a gentle touch. Specks of silver glistened in his eyes. "This won't be like human dating. If we do this, I'm claiming you as mine. It doesn't have to be for always. You'll probably find that dealing with the reality of what I am is too difficult. This *claiming* is just a way of committing to remain exclusive while we're together. We can't be together any other way."

I nodded and smiled shyly at him, then almost laughed. I mean was he kidding? Who'd want to trade in a fancy sports car for a mini van? There'd never be anyone else, at least not for me.

"Will you still be able to work with me as your trainer?" He was stalling, trying to convince me that I shouldn't choose him, yet I knew he wanted me. My inner cheetah purred.

"Yes." I smiled and grabbed his shirt, tugging on it to try to bring him closer. This time he came willingly. "So in order for us to kiss each other, you have to claim me?" I smiled widely, amazed that this beautiful, elegant man cared for me and even more amazed that I felt comfortable enough around him to be honest about how I felt. I was slightly afraid that if

I looked in a mirror, I'd see someone else staring back at me. It was liberating.

"That's the deal."

"And then I can only kiss you and you can only kiss me, right?"

"Yes." He laughed.

"Then claim away."

A gorgeous grin spread slowly across his face, making him lose the serious, mature expression he usually wore and look like the young male he would always be. He took a moment to play with a thick strand of my blonde hair. "Would you like to guess what my animal was when I first changed?"

I knew as soon as he asked. "A cheetah."

And there it was, the other reason I'd spiraled toward him from the moment I'd met him on the island. He'd even said it himself when he was talking about Ethan finding a nice cougar to settle down with. We're attracted to our own and he was one of mine.

He pulled me even closer, his delicious scent filling the small space. One hand came to rest gently on my hip, the other traveled to behind my head, long fingers weaving through my hair. "Are you sure?" I nodded, never taking my eyes from his so he would know it was the truth.

Garrett whispered against my ear, "Jacqueline Crawford, I claim you as my mate." He pulled my mouth to his and kissed me very gently, almost unsure, his vulnerability making my heart ache and my body catch on fire. Pulling away from me again, he checked my expression one last time for any doubts I might have, but all he saw was me, smiling with unrestrained joy.

"And I claim you, Garrett Cuvier," I whispered. It was good to clear that up right from the start. He was mine as much as I was his.

He laughed softly, caressing my face with a gentle hand, his eyes sparkling with tiny silver gems, his nose taking in my scent as if it was his first meal in centuries. When he kissed me again, there was nothing tentative about it at all.

CHAPTER TWENTY

SEVERAL KISSES LATER, WHEN I TRIED TO unbutton his shirt, Garrett stopped me, grabbing my hand. "We have work to do tonight so you don't smash any more windows, although I may not complain too harshly if you hit Ethan on the head with a lamp." His hair was a little mussed where I'd dug my fingers into it, and his eyes were now streaked with silver; a sign of him feeling "amorous" as he'd explained before. I was flushed and tingling all over and really didn't want to stop, so against orders I stretched over to kiss him again.

However, Garrett had other ideas. He pushed me gently back in the seat and locked my seatbelt in place. "We'll be taking our relationship slowly." When he saw my pouting mouth he laughed and pulled the car away from the shoulder of the road.

"Garrett, you claimed me as your mate. Doesn't that imply we're actually...umm...doing more than just kissing?"

"We have time. For supernaturals, a mate is a true partner, not only a lover. Claiming you as mine for as long as we're together will protect you from other, less honorable creatures.

Today is a first step toward whatever is to come next between us. There's no reason to rush. Some supernaturals have a three-part ritual for creating a permanent bond with their chosen mate."

I sighed, knowing I wouldn't be changing his mind tonight. I could still taste him in my mouth, and I knew if I pulled out a mirror my smile would be on the smug side. He'd claimed me and I'd claimed him. Would I ever get tired of hearing that? I snuck another glance at his lips. Okay, I could wait, although it was never my best thing.

While he drove, I asked more questions. "Do you have a family?"

"The shifter family I was born to has been dead for over a hundred years. I'm close to my cousin Aaron, the werewolf I spoke about earlier. As a vampire, it's different. I'm bonded to my maker." His expression turned sour.

"What does it mean to be bonded to your maker? What's he like?"

He frowned. "Her name's Eleanor Howard. She's beautiful, clever in certain ways, and very powerful because of her age, which is over four hundred. She's also a brutal bitch. She uses her beauty as a weapon. She repulses me. Most of her creatures obey her without question—the others suffer constantly. I've watched her murder hundreds of innocents over the years just for amusement's sake.

"She kidnapped my father, mother, sister, and me because we were cheetah shifters and she wanted to know if we would survive the change. I did, barely. The rest of my family died. It was never my choice to become a vampire." His voice had lowered in volume and pitch, but its intensity indicated a rage that burned so deeply I felt frightened for him.

He pulled onto a dirt road that led farther into the woods and parked. "Eleanor spends most of her time at her villa in

Carmel. If she calls to me mind to mind, I'm supposed to show up, although these days, I'm usually able to block her out. It infuriates her." He managed a half smile. "She's also unaware that I can feed from a shifter without taking blood, which has come in handy the few times she's locked me in a cell to starve me into submission. She uses shifters as servants, so they're always around the villa. I'm kind to them and they don't mind helping me out.

"She doesn't know how strong I've become using the ley lines or that I can still change form. Apparently her little experiment has backfired on her. I've always been a pain in her ass." He tried to smile again but his eyes had clouded over as he opened his door and stood.

I went to him, putting my arms around his waist and nestling against his shoulder. My body conformed so perfectly to his, designed to fit like puzzle pieces. "I'm sorry you lost your family. Thank you for telling me." He was wrenched away from a happy life as a shifter and forced into becoming the kind of creature who'd killed his family. He was totally alone, surrounded by his enemies. I shuddered, imagining the horrors he must have endured.

He seemed surprised that I was supportive and not repelled by his past. Leaning down, he kissed me gently. "Very few people know what I've just told you and I need to keep it that way."

"You can always trust me."

"Yes, I know." He tucked a stray hair behind my ear and smiled. "Come, we have work to do." He kissed my forehead, taking my hand and leading me to a fallen log which we straddled facing each other.

We worked for an hour at strengthening my mental shield, visualizing it standing strong in the daylight and the moonlight. Garrett found he was able to pull extra line energy through me to enter that small part of my mind that was resistant to the block and help me fill in any chinks that might allow leaks.

Finally we were finished to his satisfaction. We walked back to the car where he took off his jacket and started to unbutton his shirt. His eyes gleamed with excitement. "Change to your cheetah because we're going hunting." When I didn't move, he grinned and said. "I'll turn around until you shift. I'm shifting too.

"Into your raven?"

"At first, but I thought that with your help I might try my cheetah again. It's been such a long time since I was myself. When I shift to animal form I can actually hunt and eat. It's incredible to enjoy food again."

He folded his shirt in half and placed it carefully on the back seat. My gaze skimmed over his broad back. "How can I help you?" He turned and I drank in the sight of his beautiful chest and abs, my gaze grazing over every plane and dip. I tried hard to swallow, but my mouth was a desert.

"I can add some of your line energy to mine, boosting the shift. It shouldn't affect you." He bent over and the boots came off. I enjoyed that angle too.

Who was this shameless female gawking at her guy's butt? Oh yeah, that would be me. I smiled, glad I was standing where he couldn't see me

Garrett continued, "We'll meet up at the clearing about a mile north of here. See if you can track a bird, little cheetah."

When he started to unfasten his pants, I walked quickly to the other side of the car, stripping and transitioning in record time. My cheetah stretched luxuriously at first, but my ears shot up the moment I heard flapping wings above me. He'd headed north. I ran after him, scenting Garrett and raven both.

He made it to the clearing before me, but not by much. Hunger gnawed at my stomach. My cheetah self was getting annoyed by the unreasonable delay. The scent of a plump raccoon was making me restless as I paced beneath the oak tree, growling softly and digging in the dirt. His raven had landed on a thick branch ten feet above, fanning his wings and ruffling his black feathers. I tapped into the lines in an effort to hurry things along, causing a familiar warm static to buzz through my chest. My stomach lurched violently as I felt energy being pulled through me and sent up to him, so I snarled and growled another warning.

I wondered idly how raven would taste.

Deciding I'd had enough, I called up my diamond wall and put myself behind it, only to realize that by doing so, I might have denied him the chance to change.

When I heard the growl, I looked up. Strikingly beautiful, a large male cheetah snarled playfully from the branch above. He jumped gracefully from the limb and landed next to me without a sound, his tail flicking with excitement. His large wet tongue licked my face, causing me to purr and rub against him. A strange sort of chirping sound popped out of my throat and he chirped back, butting his head into mine and cuffing my face with his huge paw. I bit him gently on the ruff and he took off toward the unlucky raccoon.

We hunted that night together under the gleam of the full moon, chasing each other, hiding then pouncing, sharing our kills. Several unlucky, but very tasty creatures filled our bellies while others were run down for fun and allowed to go on their way. I'd shifted and hunted a dozen times, first on the island and then while training with the team, but this night the experience was something more. Hunting with Garrett as cheetahs, sharing our unique magical gift, bonded us in a bone-deep, visceral way.

We sat in a clearing by a narrow stream, splashing each other and batting at fish as they swam by. He tugged at my wall, so I opened a small hole and let him into my mind. I felt magic flow between us in a loop, making my heart race and ache with a sweet longing. Our cheetah minds were only able to send short phrases or pictures to each other, but it was the most intimate experience of my life.

"Hurt you to speak?" he asked.

"No, nice."

He teased me by biting my ear, sending me happy memories of his childhood with his cheetah mother, father, and sister. He playfully bumped his head against my shoulder, making my cheetah attempt another smile.

I was so happy. Gone was the worried young man with the troubled past and the difficult self-appointed job of training a bunch of young rogue shapeshifters. Here, in the forest with me, he was free to be playful and carefree.

"Mine," he sent and my cheetah purred, content in a way I'd never believed was possible.

Garrett sat up suddenly, all senses on alert. We both sniffed the air and twisted our ears toward the faint sound of howling in the distance. He motioned for us to run back toward the car, so we raced over the terrain, only to realize that there were several wolves and that they'd surrounded us, closing their circle. He bumped me toward the nearest tree and indicated that I should climb. When I didn't, he bit me firmly on the leg, reminding me of who gave the orders and who should be following them. *"Climb now!"* he sent. I started clambering up, not too happy about it even in cheetah form. He followed and we hid, still as death, under the hanging branches of the black oak.

I smelled them long before they reached us. The smell was woodsy, but also rotten like carrion left in the sun. There were three wolves, huge and filthy, undernourished and ill-treated. One carried a pack in his mouth. Two of them were cut up and bloody, but all three were sniffing around the bottom of the tree, hunting us. They suddenly stared up and howled in triumph. They tried to climb, but wolf bodies aren't made for climbing trees. They soon decided on another tactic as one of them changed back to human, a relatively quick but very painful shift, judging from the man's loud moans. The others growled and snarled, circling the tree.

We were in trouble. I tried to indicate to Garrett that he should shift back to bird form and get away, but instead he rubbed his head against mine, looking me directly in the eye. "*Underfed and weak. Stay here.*" I was shocked into silence when he smoothly jumped down to face them. I sent out a warning chirp, but I'd forgotten, during our moonlit romp, what Garrett was.

I could feel him pull in the magic, buzzing through my body in huge waves even though it wasn't directed toward me. His shift was almost instantaneous, as if a magician's veil had been pulled away, revealing the surprise beneath. It seemed to cost him nothing in energy, unlike the werewolf who still panted from the pain of his transition.

Garrett stood silently behind the exhausted man, his eyes a swirling silver blue. Wicked fangs extended from his gums, curling his lip into a noiseless snarl. His fingers became claws as his muscles tensed to attack.

The man had pulled a gun from his pack and was moving to point it at me.

"Why don't you come down so we can play?" He squinted and looked in the higher branches. "Where's your friend?"

The next instant he was flying through the air, screaming, his gun on the ground and his broken arms flapping uselessly against his body. Garrett turned to the next were, the largest in wolf form, and in a blur which I could barely track, twisted his lupine neck, breaking it with a crack that made me cringe. Then the dead wolf was thrown across the clearing to land on top of his wounded comrade. The last wolf had jumped on Garrett and bitten the back of his neck, trying to slip around to the front and rip out his throat, but Garrett twisted easily and used his fist to crush the werewolf's skull. He dumped the body on the other two and crushed the skull of the man still screaming at the bottom of the pile.

When it was over, he crouched on the ground, resting. He was bleeding steadily from his neck wound so I jumped off the branch and ran to him, worried. He stood slowly and turned to me, his eyes still solid silver, his fangs fully extended, his hands clenched into bloody fists. A killing rage contorted his features, chilling my heart. I backed up slowly until the tree trunk stopped my progress and remained in cheetah form, waiting to see what he would do.

He took two steps in my direction, suddenly swaying and stumbling. Dismissing my anxiety, I ran to him so he could lean on my back to steady his legs. He must have used an extraordinary amount of energy tonight changing from vampire to bird to cheetah to vampire again and then fighting the three wolves. Plus his skin had felt cool earlier, so I knew he hadn't fed before he'd brought me to the woods tonight.

I nuzzled him gently toward the tree and was happy to see him sit, leaning his back against it and closing his eyes. I ran to the pack that the first wolf had carried and brought it to Garrett, hoping that it contained something that could help him. There was a water bottle, which he used to wash off his hands and face, and an extra pair of sweatpants. I was grateful to see that he no longer looked so fierce and I rubbed up against him to let him know that I was worried about him.

He stood slowly and said, "We'll have to walk back. I can

pull in some power from the lines but I need to feed. Hunting in shifter form is great for my cheetah but when I transition back, my vampire is still hungry." I chirred at him with concern. "I'll be fine; I just need to get home so I can call one of my donors." His wound had stopped bleeding but he'd lost quite a lot of blood, weakening him. "You'll be safer if you stay in cheetah form until we get out of the woods. There could be more weres roaming around since tonight's the full moon. You'll be able to outrun them."

I jumped on him and pushed him to the ground, which only worked because I'd startled him. I lay across his legs and bared my neck, trying to make it obvious that I wanted him to feed from me. I was feeling strong and healthy, but I couldn't protect us from weres. If he fed from me and I became weak, he could carry me to the car using his incredible vamp speed. If we did run into any other weres he could take care of them. It all made perfect sense to me.

"Jackie, I won't feed from you, I promised." I hissed at him and bit his hand just enough to hurt.

My green gaze pleaded with his. "*Feed now.*"

He sighed and nodded, "It makes sense. You're right. I can protect us." I licked his face. "I won't hurt you. I'm not taking blood. You'll just fall asleep. I'll keep you safe, I promise. Thank you, lovely cheetah." He buried his face in my back and hugged me, then sat up and rested both of his hands on my neck. My body vibrated with the first stirrings of ley line magic.

The sensation of energy being sucked out of me by Garrett was not unpleasant. I floated as my diamond walls crumbled and washed away in the magical sea. Then came an uncomfortable feeling as my skin stretched and bones twisted, shifting back to human form. I was too tired and feeling too euphoric to care. As I was drifting away into sleep, I thought

I heard him chuckle. My mind had opened to him fully, all barriers dissolved.

CHAPTER TWENTY-ONE

W HEN I WOKE UP, GARRETT WAS driving back down the road we'd originally traveled. I was feeling kind of fuzzy and tired but not too weak, dressed in his button-down shirt and seat-belted securely in place. The shirt had been fastened crookedly and fit me like a short dress—covering all the necessary bits. Also it smelled strongly of Garrett, a wonderful treat that made me smile. He was dressed only in his jeans, so I enjoyed the view for a few minutes until he noticed I was awake.

"I'm sorry about the shirt, but it was the fastest option." He was grinning impishly and it finally occurred to me that he'd carried me back to the car completely naked.

I covered my face and groaned, probably turning four shades of pink.

"Thank you for what you did. It was a smart strategic move and might have saved us if we'd run into any more wolves."

I didn't look up.

"Try not to feel embarrassed. You're lovely in both forms and it was my profound pleasure." He sounded so gentlemanly, which made it even harder to look at him.

A tear trailed down my cheek as we pulled into the driveway of the tiny house, and I wasn't sure if it was from embarrassment or shock. The wolves' deaths had been gruesome, but they'd been ready to kill us. Garrett had saved my life, putting himself at risk. The least I could do was thank him.

Garrett parked and was instantly on my side of the car opening my door. He noticed the tear, which had made it down to my chin. He pulled me up and kissed it away.

"You're the most beautiful naked woman I've ever carried in my two hundred and thirty-four years," he teased. "*Trés belle.*" He kissed me on my right cheek. "You were very brave when the wolves came." He kissed me on my left cheek. "And hunting with you was brilliant, little cheetah." He kissed my lips and I melted against him, my embarrassment completely forgotten.

The door of the cabin opened and Ethan stood there with Rob behind him. I pushed away from Garrett and smiled at them, but their surprised expressions caused me to quickly glance down at my scantily clad body. I felt my face grow hot once more as I grabbed my clothes from the car's back seat and moved toward the cottage, avoiding their eyes.

Not embarrassed in the least, Garrett had no problem switching into business mode. "I'd appreciate it if one of you could come with me. We have to dispose of a few dead wolves who were stupid enough to attack us. One of you should stay with Jackie. She's had a rough night."

Rob looked at Ethan's tightly wound expression and said, "I'll come with you. Ethan, make sure Jackie's all right and then get some sleep." Rob chuckled all the way to the car. "Can't wait to hear this story!" They climbed into the Saab and drove off down the gravel driveway, Rob laughing even more loudly as they drove away.

When I got out of the shower I dressed in pajamas and

walked into the bedroom to face Ethan. He was sitting up on his side of the bed, wearing PJ bottoms and a tee shirt, trying to look nonchalant. He pretended to be reading another mystery, but his jaw was clenched and there was a deep crease between his eyes. I sat on the bed next to him. "Okay, let's get this over with." I was tense myself, not knowing what to expect.

He lowered the book and asked in a soft voice. "Did he hurt you? Did he force you to do something you didn't want to do? I'll kill him if he did, vampire or no vampire." His woodsy scent was strong and reassuring. There was anger and concern, but no jealousy in his words or body language.

"Garrett and I were hunting together in the woods when we met three werewolves who attacked us. He killed them, but he was bleeding badly from a neck wound, so I let him feed off of me so we could make it back to the car and get home again. He took energy, not blood. I fell asleep and transitioned back to human and he dressed me in his shirt while I was sleeping. That's all."

He shook his head. "I saw you kissing him. There's definitely more."

I looked down at my hands. "Well, on the drive to the forest, I told him about my dream and that I'd told you about my extra ability. Then we talked about how we—how we felt about each other. He claimed me as his mate so we could be together. He doesn't think he's good for me but…."

I looked back up, but Ethan's incredulous expression stopped my explanation in its tracks. "He-is-a-vampire! What don't you understand about that? He's *not* good for you. He's dangerous and violent. He has some ruthless enemies who might use you to get to him. Claiming you puts your life in danger."

"I get the feeling he's not a typical vampire. He doesn't kill when he feeds. He cares a lot about our team and our safety. Anyway, I'm pretty sure I love him, so you're too late with the advice." I smiled at him sheepishly. "I appreciate it, though."

"How does he feel about you?"

I giggled. "He said he's drawn to me." I tried to make it sound dramatic, but Ethan wasn't smiling. "He doesn't go in for casual relationships. Claiming me is a big deal for him. Me too." I couldn't stop grinning.

Ethan narrowed his eyes in thought. "I meant what I said about him hurting you."

"He saved my life." If I were a firefly, I'd have been glowing.

Ethan shrugged, grumbling, "Look. If he's good to you and you love him, then I'm happy for you, Speedy."

I hit him with my pillow and we laughed together. It felt great. "Thanks, for being such a good friend." I turned off the light and closed my eyes; the two of us drifting off to sleep like a couple of oversized kittens.

CHAPTER TWENTY-TWO

AROUND NOON, CARLY ARRIVED WITH homemade fried chicken, mashed potatoes, string beans, corn, and biscuits. We were in culinary heaven. This time she didn't stay more than thirty minutes and she didn't bring Samson.

Ethan and I ate lightly, planning to work out. We sparred for an hour and Ethan took it easy on me. After that we went for a run and I set a pace he could match without too much trouble. After showering, we watched the old horror movie, "The Wolf Man" and laughed our asses off. We attacked Carly's chicken one more time, managing to devour every delicious scrap. By the time Sinc arrived with Kyle, we were ready for whatever Rob or Garrett threw at us.

Rob walked in around six, his face sober. "Garrett is meeting with some of his werewolf allies. The Western Pack Council reported some flak about what happened last night. He'll try to join us as soon as he can."

"His cousin Aaron?" Rob nodded. "Is his pack like the werewolves we met last night?" I cringed to think all wolf packs were as violent as that one.

"Werewolves are as different as any group. Those three you met were from the Pine Ridge Pack. That pack and the Brownlow Pack are causing all kinds of problems for shifters in our area. Both pack lands are located near Gasquet, a town not far from here. There's always tension between the races, but these particular packs are out for shifter blood. They feel we don't show them the proper respect. In other words, we don't pay them off or send them our young women or treat them like they're the lords of the manor.

"Garrett's cousin Aaron is the pack leader of the Greenway Pack from southern Oregon. Garrett also has close ties to Tony, the pack leader of the Danielson Pack from the Sacramento area. Those two alphas help us out when we need them. We've reciprocated a few times, too. Most shifters may not be as strong, but rogue wolves tend to rely only on their strength to win a fight. They don't use their most important weapon like we've been trained to do." He tapped his forehead. "We can outsmart most of them before a fight even starts."

Rob's cell phone rang, so he excused himself and walked outside to take the call privately. We could still hear Rob's side of the conversation. Perfect privacy was pretty much non-existent for a group of supernaturals, unless you put some real distance between you.

"Hey Aaron, what's up? He should have been there an hour ago … no I watched him get in the car and drive off … I really have no idea … I think we have to … Okay, we'll work on that from this end. Call you in thirty." He shut down his phone and turned to us, frowning. "Garrett never made it to the meeting. We're tracking him from his start-off point, so get your stuff together. We're leaving in five."

I ran into the bedroom and threw on loose sweats, thinking Rob might want me to shift to track Garrett. The shirt Garrett had dressed me in was in my top drawer, so I pulled it out and buried my nose in it, stuffing it in my backpack along with two water bottles. Ethan knocked and opened the door.

He must have seen the fear painted into my expression. "We'll find him. He's a big bad vampire. He'll be fine. Top of the food chain, remember?" I nodded and managed a grateful half-smile.

Ethan and I piled into Rob's SUV while Kyle and Sinc followed in Sinc's convertible. We drove to a lovely home set back from the road, nestled among maple trees and wildflower gardens. This was Garrett's house. This was where he spent his days, resting, and his nights when he wasn't with us. As we headed off from there, Rob told me the property had been owned by Garrett's shifter family and that he'd had this house built on it over one hundred years ago.

We drove the road he would have taken to Aaron's meeting. While Rob and Ethan kept their gazes focused on the sides of the road, looking for clues, I reached down and tapped into the lines, stretching my mental fingers in an attempt to touch his mind, unique and now intimately familiar. As we passed a narrow turnoff, I felt a distant twitch, so I directed Rob to follow that road, telling him to please trust my instincts. He didn't hesitate. We found the Saab on a narrow side road almost hidden from the secondary road by thick brush.

I jumped out of Rob's SUV while it was coming to a stop and ran to the car while the team went into action. Rob immediately got on the phone to alert Aaron that we'd found Garrett's car. Sinc searched her phone's database for nearby security cameras that may have caught something on video. Ethan was working with Kyle, pulling weapons out of two duffel bags that had been thrown into the trunk.

I opened the driver's side door and saw blood on the seat and the steering wheel, not a lot, but enough to scare the crap out of me. I stumbled to the other side of the car and got into the passenger's seat, sucking in a few short breaths. The tang of Garrett's blood was sharp, but other scents were mixed with his, disturbing scents—wolves and maybe something else. Yes, definitely something else.

A warmth from using the ley lines was evident, and the smell of magic was strong, although it had a sour, spoiled scent. Most disturbing was the scent of burned flesh. Bile rose in my throat and I jumped out of the car in a hurry.

Rob poked his head in the window to look around then turned to me with a questioning glance as I leaned back against the hood. "I smelled wolf, burned skin, Garrett's blood, and ley line magic. Also something else I couldn't identify." Shuddering, I turned to Rob. "If they wanted to kill him, how would they do it?" In my heart I felt that if he were truly dead, I would somehow know it.

Rob walked around the car to stand next to me. "Beheading is the surest way. The sun would take a couple of hours to kill him because he's over 200 years old. Fire is a sure but horrible death.

"I smell some kind of metal."

"Silver is used to restrain vampires, weres and shifters. It burns our skin and can poison our blood, but even a silver bullet to the brain wouldn't kill him, unless he was in a horribly weakened state. A wooden stake through the heart is a Hollywood myth. Their hearts no longer beat and the wood has no effect. Neither does holy water. Vampires have souls just like the rest of us. Tell me what else you smell."

"The werewolves were like the ones who attacked us before. They smelled like they never washed, and that other scent reminded me of the ley lines, only not really. Their magic smelled rotten."

"A black witch or a sorcerer, probably using blood magic." His shoulders slumped as he sighed.

I reached out and touched his hand, whispering, "I know he's still alive, I can tell." He looked up quickly and after a few seconds, nodded.

"Are you connected to each other?" Rob sounded hopeful.

"Sometimes we are. I'm learning to use the lines. I'm going to find him." I walked away and mumbled, more to myself than Rob. "Those shits are all going to pay."

I heard a car drive up and turned to see three people get out. The driver, Aaron, looked a lot like his cousin with the same lovely eyes and warm smile. His body was stockier and more muscular and he was probably an inch or two taller, putting him closer to Rob's height. He was dressed casually in jeans, sneakers, and a tee shirt. Sandy blond hair poked out of his baseball cap with a stray lock blowing over his forehead in the steady breeze. Rob only introduced him to Ethan and me, since Kyle and Sinc had worked with him in the past. He held out his hand and said, "We'll find him. I'm always bailing Garrett out of crazy messes." He chuckled and I managed to smile, appreciating his attempt to cheer us up.

To his right stood a taller, dark-skinned man, his muscles bulging unnaturally—maybe the result of lifting heavy weights for many years. His dark eyes glared at us, his mouth turned down in a frown. Aaron introduced him as Franklin, his beta or second in the pack, and explained that Garrett had saved Franklin's life and the lives of his entire family long ago. Franklin was extremely protective of "young Garrett" and had insisted on coming along.

The last wolf was a petite woman, slim yet curvy, with thick dark red hair falling past her shoulders. Her green eyes, lighter than mine, looked me over as she strolled past us to put a possessive arm around Aaron's waist. He introduced her as his mate, Catherine. She smiled and nodded like a queen greeting her subjects.

I told them what I'd come up with, omitting my ability to pull up magic. Sinc opened her laptop, showing us a video from a gas station security camera of a green van following closely behind Garrett's car, and also some data tracking Garrett's cell phone signal north of us. Ethan and Rob had already discussed my changing to cheetah to track more efficiently, so I transitioned and headed off ahead of everyone. They'd wanted to send Ethan or Kyle with me but I'd convinced them that they would just slow me down. I'd mark the trail with scratches so they could follow as quickly as possible.

My keen eyesight allowed me to make out the tire tracks way ahead of my position, so I was able to race down the path ahead of the breeze. I kept to the side road for about two miles until I came to a small clearing. The van was parked here, leafy tree branches piled on top of it in a hasty attempt at camouflage. The smell of unwashed werewolf was overpowering, but I could also smell Garrett and the other magic user. I crept forward hesitantly. The van was empty and more of Garrett's blood was pooled in the back where the seats had been removed. The odor of burned flesh was prevalent and I remembered what Rob had said about the effects of being restrained with silver.

I paced and tried to decide what to do. I could wait for the others, who were still a distance away, or head off on my own. I sensed that I was near him and didn't know how weak he was or if he could feel my presence at all. My wall was up for protection, but I could still feel the energy of the lines buzzing through my body. I toyed with the idea of reaching out to him mentally.

I was terribly afraid. Afraid of being overpowered by the lines if I tried to use them untrained. Afraid of what the violent weres who'd kidnapped Garrett had done to him or may do to me if they caught me. Mostly I was afraid that I might fail him when he needed me. I decided I wouldn't wait.

I sat on the ground and forced myself to recall my song, beginning to breathe in and out the way Garrett had taught me. I thinned out my mental wall rather than tearing it down, allowing only the smallest chink to appear near my heart. With a surge of will, I opened myself to more of the magic than I ever had before, having reasoned it out that larger amounts of power would be necessary. It cut into me sharply at first, like several small daggers, causing me to hiss in pain, but as I slowly regained my balance, the pain eased up. My senses extended out like a web, tendrils spreading, searching for Garrett's unique mind.

Suddenly he was there, connected to me so strongly I could feel his intense agony. I worried that it would be impossible for me to communicate with him since I was in cheetah form and he wasn't, but I tried anyway, sending him a picture of the team and our wolf allies coming to get him. *"Where?"* When I felt his answer I was overwhelmed with relief.

The message *"Old park lodge basement,"* was accompanied by a picture of a beat-up sign welcoming visitors to Redwood State Park. *"Blood magic. Dark witch. Can't use lines."* He was cut off abruptly and I couldn't get through to him again.

Blood magic. A dark witch. He needed me now. I scratched a mark on a tree, crouched down and followed the tracks left by his captors.

CHAPTER TWENTY-THREE

TWENTY MINUTES LATER I PEEKED AROUND a salmonberry thicket to survey the lodge below. Although I heard nothing, three cars were parked in the lot and lights were on in the building. I was downwind but still afraid one of the werewolves might be able to scent me, so I stayed low, regulated my breathing, and watched silently.

A woman, petite with light brown wavy hair and a man, stocky and tall with light shaggy hair came out the front door to stand under the porch light and talk. I caught a few angry phrases as their volume increased.

"This was agreed upon beforehand. The spell must be invoked now. We had a contract." The woman's voice was becoming strident.

"If you kill him now then we miss all the fun when the sun comes up. My pack will be very disappointed. They might even take it out on you, Miranda. Go ahead and torture him all you want, but you can't kill him until he's smoldering and almost dead from the sun, and that's final. There must be a few organs you can remove without killing him." He laughed, lowering his tone to speak. "He's going to pay for those three deaths last night. Then we'll go after his friends."

"I shouldn't have agreed to help you, John," she hissed and turned, storming to a black sedan in an angry huff. "Since I can't perform the ritual I'd planned, I'll be back at 4:30. I have another spell in mind and need a few more supplies." She drove off, her tires kicking up dirt as she left the parking lot.

The Pine Ridge pack leader glanced at the tree line. I flattened myself, afraid he might see or smell me. He sniffed the air and scowled. I hoped a wolf's sense of smell wasn't better than a cheetah's, because I could smell him on the breeze. He paused, looking straight at the brush where I was hidden, then moved on to scan the entire perimeter. He opened the main door of the lodge and called out, "Hank, up here, now!"

Hank, a very tall man with broad shoulders and muscular arms and legs, appeared at the door. "Take a look around. I thought I heard something. Can't have any of his shifter friends showing up, though I'd like to get my hands on a few of their women." He leered at Hank who grinned back.

"Sure John." He ran up into the trees to the right of where I hid.

John strode back inside the building, closing the door behind him. My ears perked up as I heard Hank heading away from me. Knowing I had less time than ever, I tried again to reach out to Garrett. I found him, weak and in pain, but awake again. "*Careful love*," he sent to me.

"*How many?*" I visualized him being captured.

"*Four plus a witch. Silver poison and a spell.*"

"*Feed from me?*" I pictured him taking energy from me as he had when he was a raven trying to change to cheetah form.

"*How close are you?*' He seemed so weak; it made my heart ache with worry.

"*50 yards. Try now.*" I dropped my shields and opened completely to the raw power of the lines, willing him to take whatever he could at this distance to stay alive. The magic burned through my chest and my stomach, directed through my mind to link with his.

I clawed at the ground and closed my eyes against the horrible pain—holding on for as long as I could before I felt myself on the edge of blacking out. Finally I was forced to pull down my shields and close myself off to the line energy.

Hank must have heard me whimper, because a few seconds later he was standing over me grinning. With the energy drain I had changed back to human form, and was lying naked on the ground at his feet, completely vulnerable. When he reached for me I made a feeble attempt at kicking him in the knee.

He laughed loudly and grabbed my leg before it made contact, twisting it roughly at the ankle. I heard a bone snap and screamed. The pain was excruciating and I sobbed in agony. He laughed and twisted my injured ankle once more, just so he could hear me scream again. I didn't disappoint him.

"You're a pretty one. When John's through with you I'll get a turn." He was still smiling when I heard a thud and looked up. Hank wasn't grinning any longer. He had a shocked expression on his face, probably because a long silver shaft was sticking out of his chest where his heart should be. He started to topple over on top of me as blood spewed out through the wound so I dragged myself away as quickly as I could, gritting my teeth against the pain. With a loud thump he fell across the bush I'd hidden behind, obviously dead, his eyes dull and his mouth still open in surprise.

Ethan, Rob and Sinc appeared a moment later, still human, followed by Kyle holding what looked suspiciously like a crossbow. Sinc threw a jacket over me and Ethan propped me up against him and held me so I wasn't lying on the cold ground. I sobbed and moaned as quietly as I could manage, trying not to give our location away to the other wolves inside the cabin. For some reason, they hadn't appeared when I'd screamed.

Bone protruded through the skin near my ankle and I was bleeding heavily. Rob took a look and said he needed to splint my leg before my natural healing ability kicked in and the bones healed unevenly. He gave me a thick stick, told me to bite down on it and to stay as quiet as I could for Garrett's safety. Ethan wrapped his arms around me to hold me still and I stifled the scream against Ethan's arm when Rob pulled on my foot to realign the bones. He attached my leg to the splint and immobilized my ankle using strips from his ripped shirt. Ethan whispered encouraging words into my ear and Sinc wiped away some of my tears with her shirt sleeve. I desperately wanted to close my eyes and drift off into unconsciousness, but I had to tell them about Garrett and all that I'd learned.

When I'd managed to stop sobbing and could speak again, I told them about the conversation between the pack leader and the witch but then hesitated to say more. Should I tell them how I communicated with Garrett and fed him through the lines?

I turned to Ethan. "I need to tell them about—you know. Is there an oath or a promise or something?"

He looked around at the others and smiled. "It's all about the honor of the team, Jackie. Kind of an 'unto death' situation." His eyes were deadly serious as he looked from Sinc to Kyle and back to me. Our lives depended on our integrity. In this world of incredible magic and corrupt power users, promises broken could end in death.

Sinc decided for me. "You're a cheetah. We know you have powers we can't begin to imagine. We'll keep your secrets." Kyle nodded in agreement. I told them everything about what

I'd learned to do.

Kyle's face lit up as he whispered, "Our team is freakin' unstoppable now." Sinc squeezed my hand and Ethan hugged me a little tighter. Despite the pain, I smiled.

Rob spoke. "Aaron and the others are circling to the north end of the building and will wait there for my signal. Can you contact Garrett to see if you helped him?" I nodded and sent out my mental fingers. Instantly he responded, his energy feeling much stronger than before.

"Are you all right? I heard you scream." His panic twisted my stomach into a knot.

I could talk to him more easily now that I was back in human form. *"I'm weak, but okay. Rob and the team and Aaron are here. The witch will be back in thirty minutes. Hank is dead, thanks to Kyle and his crossbow."* I smiled at Kyle and sent Garrett a picture of Hank draped over the bush. *"Are you all right?"*

"Much stronger, but I'm still bound with silver and the witch's block is in place. I'm in the basement near the stairs. There should only be three wolves now. Tell Rob to save me the witch."

I turned to Rob, "He says he's better and to save him the witch. He's still tied up with silver in a room near the basement stairs. There should be only three weres inside."

Rob pulled out his cell phone and sent Aaron a text. They agreed to move in on the lodge in one minute.

My leg felt better, but when I made a move to get up, Ethan yanked me back down, saying, "You're staying here with Sinc. Garrett's going to be furious if anything else happens to you." He walked over to speak to Kyle and Rob, assuming I would do what he told me to do. *Huh.*

Sinc plopped down next to me and handed me my clothes, which she'd brought along in her backpack. I took them back gratefully and she helped me put them on. It sucked to be sitting naked on a bunch of pine needles. We had to cut the leg of my sweats with Sinc's Swiss army knife in order to get the splint through the hole. She made me keep her jacket since I was still shivering even after getting dressed.

I glanced at her, puzzled. "Don't you want to fight with the guys?"

"I've kicked some werewolf butt in my time, but I'm fine with hanging here with you. They're all testosterone ridden right now anyway, and that makes them grouchy. I helped with the tech and the tracking so I've done my part."

She gazed at me appraisingly. "Are you and Ethan together?"

"No. We're friends. He treats me like I'm his little sister. I'm seeing Garrett."

I think her mouth dropped three inches before she snapped it back into place. "I don't want to crush your fantasy but Garrett doesn't really date. Many female shifters have tried to catch his eye, including me." She must have seen the shock on my face, so she shrugged, saying. "He's uber hot. A girl would have to be dead not to try. But lately he's all business. I can't remember the last time I heard him laugh."

"Well, he's dating now." Our night hunting together and sharing energy might not have been traditional dating activities I admit, but it was still amazing. And I'd seen him smile and heard him laugh plenty of times, mostly when we were alone.

We crouched in our hiding spot and watched tensely as our team and our allies crept down the hillside and entered the building. No one was standing guard on the first floor. Apparently these wolves were egotistical enough to think they could fight off whoever showed up, no problem. A few seconds passed before Sinc and I heard shouts and loud crashing noises, a couple of screams and a gun firing repeatedly. At this point I was ready to knock Sinc out and limp down the hill by myself to see if Garrett was okay.

I caught a sweet breeze half a second before I was lifted into Garrett's arms and kissed repeatedly all over my face and my neck and my hair and…well you get the picture. Finally his lips gently brushed over mine.

I pushed away to look him over. He looked shaken, battered, bloody and vulnerable, but he was alive. Not wanting to waste another second, I threw my arms around his neck and pressed my lips hard against his. He responded willingly and eagerly, helping me quickly forget all about my painful ankle.

I heard Kyle. "Jeez. Get a room."

We pulled apart, laughing, our foreheads pressed together. I'd almost forgotten anyone else was there. He sat down gracefully with me still in his arms and held me close. That's when my control crumbled and I started to cry. Sinc handed me some tissues as I sobbed from the release of hours of pent up tension. Garrett stroked my hair and whispered comforting words, some of them in French. I caught Sinc smiling and giving me a wink, then sauntering away like the cat she was to talk to Ethan, hugging him, playfully mussing his hair and kissing him on the cheek. He didn't stand a chance.

Aaron, Catherine and Franklin hiked back up the hill, splattered with blood but bearing no sign of injury. Garrett stood, leaving me leaning against the tree, and thanked them each personally.

"Man, that's three you owe us," said Aaron chuckling and throwing his arm around Garrett's shoulder.

"I think you're forgetting about the two sorcerers who had you by the short hairs last fall. They trump the three scraggly weres by a mile." Garrett pushed his cousin hard against the nearest pine, needles falling like rain and landing in Aaron's hair. He shook his head and grinned back, both of them laughing loudly.

Suddenly Rob quieted us all as the witch drove up in her car. Garrett disappeared in a blur before I could ask him to stay with me. Rob grabbed my hand to keep me still and tried to turn me away so I wouldn't see what was coming, but I had to look.

She stepped out of her car totally unaware of the danger appearing like a ghost behind her. Garrett stood as still as stone, a cold *otherness* turning him alien, fangs extended and mouth curled up in a silent snarl. She stiffened as she sensed him and turned, tracing a shape in the air and mumbling a spell, but it was too late. Garrett grabbed her chin, breaking her jaw so she couldn't speak the spell, reaching out to crush the hand tracing the symbols. She screamed in agony. He held her tightly and whispered something in her ear, then savagely tore into her neck, drinking her blood until she hung limp and dead in his arms. He threw her down on the blood-splattered dirt, spat on her body and disappeared into the lodge. All of this had taken about thirty seconds.

No one said a word, but they all turned to look at me. I felt the blood drain from my face as I managed to support my shaking knees by leaning against Rob. I was terrified I was going to barf right there in front of everyone. Instead, I forced myself to stand up and start limping back toward where we'd parked our cars, miles away from where we were. Rob caught up to me and lifted me as if I weighed ten pounds. Kyle, Ethan, and Sinc gathered up their things and passed us to take the lead, staying at least 20 yards ahead. Aaron, Catherine, and Franklin had agreed to stay to clean up the site and dispose of the bodies. Aaron was on the Western Pack Council and would be reporting both incidents to the rest of the council. In both cases where wolves were killed, we'd been attacked and would not be held responsible for the deaths according to their laws. Rob had explained each species lived by different laws, making dealing with supernaturals more challenging than I'd imagined.

After a few minutes, Garrett joined Rob and me. He'd washed the blood off his face and hands but seemed hesitant to touch me, as if he still felt dirty. We walked in silence for a few minutes, lost in our own thoughts.

His fingers combed through his hair, an anxious gesture. *"I'm sorry you saw me kill her. The blood of a black witch is powerful and I couldn't waste it. More wolves could have shown up and attacked us."* He watched me closely. *"I did warn you."*

When I didn't respond he spoke out loud so Rob could also hear. "Miranda knew you were a cheetah. She would have tortured and killed you when she was through with me. She's killed many humans and shifters over the years in order to work her blood spells." He waited for a response, but I couldn't bring myself to speak of personal things with Rob carrying me.

Garrett sighed sadly. "I'm a vampire. If you can't accept my darker nature, it's better you realize it now rather than later. I understand. I'll release you from my claim."

Garrett's expression was strained, his hands clenching and unclenching. Even after ingesting the black witch's blood he might still be feeling the effects of the silver poisoning. The ugly black burns from the silver restraints were healing, but it was a slower process than what I'd witnessed before. He reached out and touched my hand. "You shouldn't have come. It's my fault you got hurt."

"Are you able to hold me?" Surprised, he nodded. Rob carefully passed me over to Garrett's arms, joining the rest of the team and giving us some much-needed privacy.

Holding me against his chest, Garrett's expression grew

calmer, although he wouldn't look at my face. He just kept walking steadily along the path I'd taken to find him; the path I'd marked with scratches leading everyone to the lodge to rescue him. He could have rushed up ahead of the others with his vamp speed, but he probably thought I'd feel more secure with my team within reach. I breathed in his sweet fragrance to give myself a jolt of courage.

I stretched my senses to connect to his mind. *"I was so scared for you, even though I was positive you were alive. You knew I'd come, didn't you?"* I rubbed his shoulder, hoping it would offer him some comfort.

"I was hoping Rob had left you behind to keep you safe. But yes, I knew. Your injury...." He shivered with emotion.

He was drowning in guilt and wasn't hearing me. *"Garrett, listen to me. My ankle hurts, but it's nothing. It'll heal. Because of you and your training, I'll be able to help people, maybe even save lives. For the first time, I feel like I belong somewhere. You're alive, that's all that matters to me."*

He tried to smile, but worry still drew creases in his forehead. *"You were amazing, little cheetah. You'll do great things with your powers."* He hesitated before kissing the top of my head. It felt too much like a kiss goodbye.

"Will you talk to me?" I touched his face and he glanced down in surprise as I sent him a wash of my energy. *"You're hurting. I feel it. You can trust me."*

We walked for a few moments in silence. Finally he spoke, opening his heart to me in a way he probably never had, his voice in my head colored with sadness. *"I hate what I've become since I was changed. Ripping into Miranda was all about revenge and bloodlust and it went against everything I used to stand for as a shifter. I'm not against using torture to save innocent lives but that wasn't the case today. I could have taken some blood and turned her over to the council. The vampire in me enjoys the violence of the kill as much as the meal. It nourishes my darker self."*

"You were making sure we were safe." I argued. "She would have gone on killing people. The execution was legal, according to Rob, and if you can use her blood to help other people, it makes sense."

He shrugged. *"It's true I've accomplished some things as an undead that I couldn't have managed as a shifter, but I've never been able to accept what I am. I hide that fact from the world fairly well. Most people think I'm an arrogant asshole and I admit I've done things to earn that reputation."*

He looked into my eyes, his emotions raw. *"You seem to see through my feeble attempts to hide the truth. Until recently, I would have said that the day before my abduction by Eleanor was the last happy day of my very long life. Lately I feel there's some hope for me...."*

I recognized the yearning in his gaze, a longing from years of feeling like a freak. Yeah, he was powerful and drop-dead gorgeous, but he was mostly alone. He had friends, but he needed more. I could be what he needed.

I smiled and stroked his smooth cheek. *"I almost hurled when I saw what you did to the witch. Remember, I'm new to all this supernatural craziness. But what you did doesn't change how I feel about you. A vampire isn't all that you are. Your spirit is still cheetah, like mine."*

A shy smile cracked through his previously grim expression. Encouraged, I continued, *"I love all the different pieces put together."* I leaned up and kissed his chin, the closest part of his face. *"You should just resign yourself to the fact I'm not going anywhere, whether you drink from black witches or green aliens."*

He stopped in the path, his body shuddering as the terrible tension he'd been holding inside was released back into the universe. Before I'd taken another breath I found myself pressed against a tree trunk, his body pinning me there and his lips on mine. I opened my mouth and our kiss deepened deliciously. Feeling playful, I pulled in line energy and pushed it into him. He actually gasped, grinning as he pushed it back at me. I tingled everywhere as magical heat poured through my body and looped back to him again.

He pulled away, laughing. "Your cat is lively tonight. Maybe a little too lively for a man who wants to take this relationship slowly."

"You're the one who pushed me up against the tree and kissed me until my toes curled." I pretended to pout, but ended up laughing too. "Not that I'm complaining."

"I intend to make your toes curl on a regular basis." He picked me up again and started walking more quickly. "Ethan is probably leading a rescue party back this way."

I snorted, then covered my nose and giggled properly. "Ethan is going to have his hands full with Sinc, I think."

An evil grin spread across Garrett's handsome face. "Excellent," he smirked.

CHAPTER TWENTY-FOUR

A S WE DROVE BACK IN HIS HASTILY cleaned car, I leaned against the leather seat and watched him. His eyes were concentrating on the road, but his mouth was turned up at the corners, his long fingers drumming a lively rhythm on the steering wheel. He'd changed into clothes he'd had stashed in the trunk, so I didn't smell the witch's blood so strongly anymore, thank goodness.

"Are you driving me back to the house I'm sharing with Ethan?"

"Of course, where else?"

"We could go to your house. It looked really nice."

"It'll be dawn soon and I don't know exactly when I'll pass out and wake up again now that I've ingested Miranda's blood."

"I can just hang out there until you wake up." I slid my hand over to rest on the seat next to his leg, barely brushing up against his thigh.

"We've talked about this, *kitten*," he smiled at his joke. "You're seventeen."

"I'm an adult in the supernatural world, as you well know,

and you're only nineteen or twenty."

"Plus two hundred and fifteen." Huh, figured he'd be good at math.

I thought about what I could say to convince him, deciding to be honest. "I'm not a virgin, if that's what you're worried about." I looked down at my lap and waited for the inevitable words of disapproval. "It's no big deal," I whispered. I didn't sound very convincing, even to myself.

He glanced at me curiously, no hint of judgment in his gaze. "A boyfriend?" I shook my head and frowned. His expression changed as he realized what I was saying. "Was it your last foster brother, the one you spoke of? The family before the Crawford's?"

"If you tell anyone I'll kill you." The boy's hand was on my throat. "I'm gonna make you cry. No one will ever want you."

I nodded, trembling from the memory. When I saw Garrett's dark expression, rage beginning to burn in his eyes, I quickly blurted out, "I told you, he's in jail. He pleaded guilty. It's over and he's not hurting anyone else."

Although Garrett's eyes sparkled, a sure sign of his anger, his voice was laced with concern. He reached for my hand, squeezing it. "He's still hurting you, I see it. I'm so sorry. The state system took away your childhood, forcing you to constantly adjust to living with strangers." He raised my hand and kissed the palm, releasing it when a sharp curve in the road came into view. "You've coped with it courageously."

My voice lowered in volume, I turned away, not wanting to see his expression when I spoke about it. He was right. It still affected me, shamed me, even though I knew I hadn't done anything to encourage the rape. "I spoke to a shrink, and that helped me. I went to live with the Crawfords next and they were wonderful and supportive. I ran more often which helped me burn off my spurts of anger, just like always. Guess running is my own brand of therapy." I peeked at him through my lashes, anxious about how he'd react.

A deeper anger smoldered in his eyes. "Let me take care of him." I thought of the witch and the weres and the other men who'd attacked me.

"No. Please let it go. I used to have nightmares about him, but now I dream about you." He pulled me closer, draping his arm around me as he drove.

After parking in front of the cottage, he kissed the top of my head. "Rape is a very big deal." He kissed my mouth, this time too briefly. "But sex is remarkable when you're with the person you love."

"I'm not afraid. We should be together now. You claimed me."

"It was done partly to ensure no one else can lay claim to you. Even an older, more powerful vampire can't break the ancient laws." He lifted my chin with a long finger, forcing me to look at him. "I'm terribly possessive where you're concerned. Word has gone out you're now under my protection. A gifted cheetah could be a target for many others seeking a powerful mate."

"I'm under you now?" I teased, grinning at the vision.

He chuckled, twisting his mouth into a crooked smile. "Figuratively."

"So what's the rest of the vampire mating ritual and when can we do it?"

"Always in a hurry."

"I'm a cheetah." I shrugged.

"True enough. There are ritual words said while we share blood and connect mind to mind."

"Will it make me a vampire?"

"No. I'm the only shapeshifter I know of who survived the change. Enough talk. You need to sleep. We can talk about this another time."

Garrett walked to my side of the car, lifting me as if I were weightless. He carried me into the cottage and gently placed me on the bed. He took off my shoes and asked, "Would you like me to remove the splint? Your leg has probably healed well enough."

"Yes, thank you." I'd say anything to get him to stick around. Thank goodness Ethan wasn't back yet.

He sat on the edge of the bed and gently unrolled the bandages holding the splint in place. My ankle had started to heal, although I could still see the angry red welt where my bone had broken through the skin.

He touched it with his fingertips, looking thoughtful. "If I lick the wound, you won't have a scar." He glanced at me with his bedroom eyes, and speechless, I nodded, my eyes widening as I watched his every move. I wondered if I might turn into a puddle on the bed the moment his tongue touched my skin.

Garrett leaned over me, one hand holding my foot and the other resting on my knee. He licked my ankle, twice.

Oh my god. I didn't melt, but it was close.

When he sat up again his eyes were dancing with tiny stars and I was breathing heavily. "Good night, my lovely cheetah. Thank you for rescuing me," he teased, smiling with a certain degree of smugness as he kissed me on the forehead and left.

I was dreaming about him before his car made it to the main road.

CHAPTER TWENTY-FIVE

THAN AND I WOKE UP AROUND NOON AND
decided to head to the beach. The day was unusually
warm and it seemed like the perfect way to spend a day
off. My ankle was fully healed, due to Rob's quick work, my
own healing abilities, and some particularly potent vampire
saliva. Plus, I was in a terrific mood, probably because of the
attentions of the aforementioned vampire. Ethan asked Sinc
and Kyle to join us and I turned away with a little smirk. Was
Ethan attracted to Sinc? I hoped so. I wondered if Kyle had a
girlfriend.

I made sandwiches and gathered other snacks and drinks
while Ethan straightened up around the cottage. Kyle and Sinc
lived in town, so they'd know of a beach that met our main cri-
teria: deserted. We figured we'd be safest in an out-of-the-way
spot. Sinc and Kyle said they'd stop by the local store and get
us a couple of bathing suits and beach towels. I also put in an
order for sunscreen. My fair skin burned easily.

They picked us up right on time in Sinc's sports car, but
I was shocked to see Kyle was driving. I wasn't surprised to
find out they'd been bickering about it. Kyle didn't like the way

Sinc drove, but Sinc didn't like riding in his SUV, so it became a regular argument every time they went anywhere together. Turns out, she'd usually give in and let him drive her car, because she wasn't comfortable driving with him snarking at her all the time. They were more like siblings than teammates.

The beach Kyle chose was rocky with a small patch of sand where we could stretch out next to each other. The tide was out and Sinc remarked with a smile that the surf was fairly gentle, although the four-foot waves looked like they could knock you around if you weren't careful.

Kyle pulled out a Frisbee and we spent some time tossing it around, getting soaked in the freezing water and laughing crazily. Because the sea was so cold, Kyle, Sinc, and I shifted to our cats and swam for a while, encouraging Ethan into the water, where his cougar did very well paddling next to us. I'd happily discovered feline shifters didn't have the same aversion to water many other felines had.

When we'd had enough, we shifted back to our regular forms, dressing and eating everything Ethan and I'd brought in our bags, plus all the food Kyle and Sinc had carried in. Then we settled down like kittens on our towels and chatted.

Kyle started in with, "So, did everyone see my amazing shot with that crossbow? I think we can all agree your ass was up for grabs with smelly old Hank standing over you. Good thing I have such great aim. I was running at the time." He grinned proudly. "Of course that's nothing compared to what you'll be able to do with ley line energy once you're trained."

"She's already pretty amazing." Ethan smiled at me as Sinc's eyes narrowed just a little.

"Hey, now that you've dumped Garrett, maybe you and Ethan can hook up." Kyle looked like he'd just had the best idea of the day.

Sinc's expression turned icy, Ethan looked embarrassed,

and I sat up frowning, feeling more than a little peeved. "What makes you think I dumped him?"

"Uh—seriously? Because you saw what he did to the witch. And because you're not some dumbass vamp groupie getting off on blood loss and one-night stands—banging some vamp in the back room of a bar. Vamps are bad news."

Sinc opened her mouth to yell at him, but I lifted my hand to quiet her. "Kyle, I appreciate that you saved my ass, but I didn't dump Garrett. We're more together than ever. He doesn't hang out in bars banging vamp groupies. He spends his nights training us, including you, Kyle."

He ignored my anger and shrugged. "Sure, he's a great trainer. But he's gotta feed every day. Where do you think he goes?"

"He has donors, and he doesn't take blood from them."

"Hmm." Kyle shook his head. "You believe what you want. I still think you and Ethan should hook up."

"Ethan's my best friend." Ethan and I grinned at each other, both of us acknowledging the truth of our already close relationship. I turned the tables on Kyle. "So what's your girlfriend like?"

Sinc snorted, bending over with the giggles. I gave her a puzzled look and she blurted out, "His girlfriend's name is Peter." Kyle, Ethan, and I joined in the laughter.

"Yeah, he's cool. He's another leopard. We did the bonding ritual four years ago." Kyle looked so happy I couldn't be annoyed with him anymore.

"Peter is the stable, responsible one in the relationship," Sinc added. "He's a lawyer and he's almost as old as Garrett. I think they settled in the same town in Louisiana back in the 1800s. They're good friends."

"How old are you two?" I indicated Sinc and Kyle.

"In real years, Sinc's twenty-four and I'm twenty-five, but

we haven't really aged from when we turned eighteen."

"You haven't aged mentally since you turned twelve." Sinc gave Kyle the usual smirk and he responded with a playful snarl.

"How do you know when you stop aging?"

Kyle spoke up before Sinc had a chance. "It's weird, but you just do. You start looking the same in the mirror every morning, day after day. Plus, you heal faster. The main difference is you feel kind of settled, not antsy anymore."

Sinc made a derogatory noise. "You're still pretty antsy."

"Nobody asked you, Sinclair."

"Poor Kyle, since you stopped aging, you'll never be able to get plastic surgery to fix your face."

"Good thing you already had yours done before you stopped aging. Not that it took."

"Asshole." She was smiling.

"Bitch." He smiled back.

Ethan laughed. "You guys are like evil siblings." The two snarly shifters looked horrified at the thought of being related, which cracked Ethan and me up even more.

When we settled down again, Kyle looked at me seriously. "I know Garrett's smart and he's certainly hot, I can appreciate that, but he's freakin' dangerous. He was brutal with the witch, like they all are: vampires and wolves." Kyle lay down on his towel and closed his eyes. I wondered what had happened to cause him to hate vampires so much.

"You know, Kyle," Sinc said, sounding aggravated, "I think you should stay out of other people's personal business. You always manage to stick your foot in your mouth."

"Yeah, you're probably right. Sorry, Jackie. If I didn't care I wouldn't say anything."

"That's okay. And thanks again for the super shot with the crossbow. Maybe you could show me how it works?"

"Sure, that would be cool. Once you can use the lines, like Maya, you won't need a crossbow to defend yourself."

"Who's Maya?"

"She's kind of a shaman for our shifter community. She protects Crescent City from outsiders with this cool magical shield she has up all the time. Of course, what you can do with the ley lines might be totally different. You should think about studying with her."

"She's a cheetah, too," Sinc added.

"Garrett is working with me right now. Maybe one day I'll have a chance to meet Maya."

"Garrett is working *on* you. Before long he'll be feeding from you on a regular basis. You should see those vamp groupies. They're like drug addicts. They forget to eat because all they can think about is serving their vamp masters. Garrett will have you twisted around his fangs real soon, if you're not careful." Kyle turned over onto his stomach and closed his eyes.

"Just shut up," Sinc shouted. "Don't listen to him. Garrett is totally awesome." To Ethan she said, her voice dropping in pitch, "Do you want to take a walk along the beach?" She grabbed two beach towels and winked at me.

"Sure. You want to come, too, Jackie?" Ethan probably figured I wouldn't want to hang out with Kyle.

"No, thanks." I waved, winking at Sinc. "You guys have fun!"

"Kyle, keep your eyes open," yelled Ethan as he ran after Sinc, her hips swaying as she walked away. I watched them stroll down the beach chatting and teasing each other. Sinc laughed and reached up to mess with Ethan's hair, but he grabbed her hand and wouldn't let go, so they continued on hand in hand. Energy buzzed because of their attraction and felt so happy for them.

I lay on my stomach and pulled out the paperback novel I'd borrowed from Carly's cabin, chuckling as I heard Kyle's soft snoring. The author drew me quickly into the plot and before I knew it, an hour had passed. The sun was moving closer to the horizon and a beautiful pink glow was reflected across the sand. Kyle got up to take a swim, leaving me alone on the beach, but the story was so engrossing, I didn't mind.

Twenty minutes later, fog had started to move in, darkening the late afternoon sky and cooling the air temperature dramatically. A long shadow fell across my book and suddenly Garrett was sitting on the sand next to me, lifting my salty, sandy hand to his mouth and kissing it gently. I put the book away and stood up, stretching to relieve the stiffness in my back and neck. I saw him watching me stretch in my bikini, all the time smiling while little silver flecks whirled around in his eyes.

His rich voice brushed across my body. "You are exquisite, little cheetah." Unfolding himself gracefully from the sand, he reached over and pulled me closer, his other hand weaving long fingers in my hair. He was dressed in a cotton button-down shirt with the sleeves rolled up and well-worn jeans. I liked the soft feel of the fabric against my skin.

"I'm not curvy like most women."

"You're built like a cheetah: sleek and sexy." He nuzzled my ear, sending tremors down my body.

I grinned against his shoulder. "I'm covered in sand and I smell like coconut from all the sunscreen I lathered on. You smell wonderful, however." I buried my face in his neck, catching a delicious breath of his sweet scent as he wrapped his muscular arms around me. I rested there, perfectly content for a moment, then pulled away to ask, "What do I usually smell like to you?"

"Like a field of wildflowers the day after a rainstorm. Like cheetah." His eyebrow arched as he realized something. "You smell like the home of my childhood."

"I'm glad I remind you of happy times."

He wove his hand through my hair and smiled his most enticing smile. "I'm taking you home to get cleaned up. You and Ethan have to appear before the Shifter Council tonight." My eyes grew wide in surprise. "Some of the more conservative shifters have convinced the council you and Ethan may be a danger to the population." His eyes glinted with humor. "I think we have a few surprises in store for them."

"What about the others?" I was looking down the beach for Ethan and Sinc. Kyle was still swimming.

"I found Ethan and Sinc before I came to you. They'll tell Kyle." He chuckled and I wondered what exactly they'd been doing when he found them. "They'll meet us at 10:00 tonight. Let's go." We gathered up my towel and backpack and walked hand in hand to his car.

Chapter Twenty-Six

FIFTEEN MINUTES LATER, I WAS DELIGHTED to be pulling into the driveway of Garrett's lovely Victorian style home. After helping me out of the car, he opened the large front door and waited politely while I entered first. Walking through the foyer, we entered a living room with an enormous fireplace. The mantel was intricately hand-carved in a rich dark wood, so I inspected it more closely. Cheetahs in various poses shared the lovely relief amid a variety of assorted exotic flowers and trees. It was magnificent and I wondered if Garrett had designed it himself. Meaning to ask, I saw him looking up, so I followed his gaze instead.

A painting of a man, a woman, and two children hung above the mantel. The man looked so much like Garrett I knew instantly this was a family portrait. The auburn hair, strong jawline and build were identical to Garrett's. His father looked extremely serious in the painting, as if he'd refused to smile for the artist, but you could detect tiny laugh lines around his sparkling hazel eyes. The woman was lovely, with wavy dark red hair and Garrett's sapphire eyes and special smile. His little sister was so sweet, with her mom's red hair and her dad's large eyes. She looked around ten years old and was wearing a long smock dress in a pretty print with a matching bow in her hair. Garrett was trying to look serious in the portrait like his dad, but only succeeded in looking worried. He wore an old fashioned long jacket, a long vest, and knickers with hose and seemed to be about fifteen in the painting. His thick hair was pulled back and tied in a ponytail at his neck.

"It was painted in 1790. My father was French and my mother, Irish. They met in Quebec and fell in love instantly. They were passionate and argued about many things, but my sister and I never doubted they loved each other deeply. When the British forced the French Canadians to leave Canada, we settled in Louisiana. Marie mated with a lion shifter and her mate, her children, and her many grandchildren and great grandchildren still live there. They're mostly lions, from what I hear, although I might have one great-nephew who's a cheetah shifter like me."

His expression changed from nostalgic to sad. "They don't want anything to do with me. They blamed me for surviving when the rest of my family died and for continuing to live as a vampire. They told me I should have walked into the sun the moment I was able. To them I'm the worst kind of traitor."

I wrapped my arms more tightly around him and felt him lean against me, burying his nose in my hair and taking a long calming breath. He'd shared something very personal with me, something still causing him great pain, although it was so many years later. I wanted to comfort him, to heal him, but all I could do was hold him. It didn't seem enough.

I would have stayed in his arms for hours, but we had to prepare for the meeting. He pulled away and cradled my face in his hands, kissing me gently. The pain in his eyes touched my heart and I wished again I could help him.

When we broke apart I took his hand and looked around

the rest of the room. There was a large brown leather couch in front of the fireplace and two armchairs in a rich brocade fabric that matched perfectly. The walls were decorated with various paintings, some of which looked vaguely familiar. Along the wall was a bar with three tall stools and in the far corner of the room, near a picture window, was a violin and guitar case both leaning up against their own music stands designed for that purpose.

He saw where I was looking. "I'll play for you sometime. No time tonight."

He handed me a garment bag and a small shopping bag. "You can use my bedroom to change; second door on the right. There's a private bathroom attached where you can shower. I'm going to cook for you tonight." He gave me another sweet kiss on the lips, pushing me gently toward his room. I passed a doorway with stairs which probably led up to additional bedrooms, and could just see the kitchen at the end of the hallway.

I had to smile when I entered his huge bedroom. It was the perfect retreat for a single man. A king-sized bed fit out in burgundy satin sheets dominated the room but a reading area with two comfortable chairs and an enormous bookcase near the picture window made the room more homey. An antique unit on the right held an MP3 player and a speaker dock. The carpeting was a deep pile in a very warm brown, luxurious under my bare toes. All the wood was rich with an antique feel, appropriate for my dark angel.

I tried to suck in his delicious scent and thought about what the aroma actually reminded me of. Dark chocolate with a hint of sweet oranges: two of my favorite flavors. His cheetah smelled like the sea, churned up and full of life. I shook my head, laughing, and wondered if Garrett knew he could bring me to my knees just by standing in front of a fan.

Giggling, I headed to the shower and was not surprised

to see it could easily fit three or four people. I glanced at the bathtub on the other side of the room. Same story. I really didn't want to fantasize about him with other women because I'd get myself all worked up and I needed to keep my cool tonight. He must have had countless lovers throughout the decades. How could I ever compete?

I showered quickly and concentrated on thinking only happy thoughts.

Wrapped in a large white towel, I crawled mischievously onto the huge bed. It was so soft and luxurious, covered with lots and lots of pillows. I picked one up and buried my face in it, wondering if he'd smell me there when he slept that morning. Liking the idea, I did the same thing with every pillow on the bed.

When I opened the shopping bag he'd given me, I was a little embarrassed to find a matching bra and panties in black silk and wondered when he'd shopped for them. Of course they fit perfectly, which made me smile. I guess when he'd carried me naked he must've gotten a really good look. A devilish part of me enjoyed the idea.

In the garment bag were black leather pants, so soft I could sleep in them, and a green silk halter top with a V-neck, not too deep, but enough to show a little cleavage. I stood before the mirror amazed at my reflection. The emerald color suited my skin and hair and brought out my green eyes dramatically. Definitely kick-ass. I applied some makeup and used the comb and blow dryer sitting on the sink, leaving my hair down. I glanced at myself one last time, took a deep breath and followed the delicious scents emanating from the kitchen.

When I entered the room, still in my bare feet, Garrett was facing away from me. I hadn't realized how hungry I was, so I pressed myself up against his back and wrapped my arms around his waist exclaiming "Food. Now. Please?"

"Hunger reduces you to single syllables? I'll have to remember." I giggled against him. "I recommend you back up slowly unless you want your dinner to decorate your outfit instead of fill your belly." Backing away obediently, I gave him some room to turn and look at me.

My heart raced. I so wanted him to like what he saw.

His expression broadcast his delight. "Oh yes, I think the council will be in for a very big surprise tonight. You look sophisticated, sexy, and powerful. They'll think twice before messing with you. Do you like the look?"

"It's amazing, Garrett. Thank you!" I spun around showing him every angle.

He kissed me gently on the lips, but I grabbed his shirt and pulled him closer, wanting more. His lips, still nestled against mine, turned up at the corners.

"Don't laugh. Just kiss," I mumbled against his mouth. He responded by deepening the kiss, opening his mouth and exploring mine.

When he nudged us apart, I was dizzy, hot and cold and grinning like a silly girl. He smiled, speaking again in his practical way, as if nothing earth shattering had happened. "There are shoes. I bought several pair. You can pick later." Shoes. He was talking about shoes. Maybe my kiss didn't affect him the way his had affected me. I frowned and looked away.

A gentle grasp of my chin turned my face back around, as a stray lock of hair was tucked behind my ear. He spoke softly. "Eat now. I'm taking a quick shower. Then we'll talk, my sweet cheetah." He touched my nose, teasing me into smiling back.

I sat with a dreamy sigh and followed his orders, savoring each bite of steak, baked potato and asparagus, being very careful not to drip anything on my silk blouse. Fifteen minutes later, Garrett returned wearing a black suit and a dark gray button-down shirt without a tie. He sat in the chair right next to mine sipping on a glass of red wine and leaning back to watch me eat. When I got some of the juice from the steak on my fingers I decided to tease him by licking it off. He shook his head and chuckled. "Focus on the meeting."

I sighed and swallowed down another bite. "Do we know any more about the wolf pack who kidnapped you?"

"A good friend did some investigating. The pack leader of the Pine Ridge Pack was up in arms about my killing the three wolves who'd attacked us the night before. He hired Miranda to help him capture me. From the evidence gathered, it appears he'd had a lot of unsavory dealings with her in the past, a fact which upset many of his pack members. My associate told me most of the wolves seemed relieved that John and his second, Hank, were dead. Only the wolves at the lodge and the witch, Miranda, were directly involved in my kidnapping."

"They could be lying."

"He interviewed them in person. He'd know if they were lying."

"Is he another vampire?"

"Definitely not." He laughed, his beautiful eyes sparkling. "You'll meet him soon."

He didn't seem to want to go down that path so I changed the subject. "What's going to happen tonight?"

"The Crescent City Shapeshifter Council is made up of three shifters: Maya, a cheetah, Brad, a leopard, and his mate, Sylvia, a lion. They'll ask you questions and you'll have to prove you're not a loose cannon. Once they find out you're a cheetah, you should be in the clear, especially since you can already manipulate the ley lines. We will have to be careful how we explain your special talents, but the council members all respect Rob's skills as a trainer and also his instincts.

I put my fork down, suddenly feeling anxious. He reached over, weaving his fingers between mine in support. "I would never let any of them hurt you." His face was paler than usual and I wondered when he'd fed last. It was only eight thirty. We wouldn't be leaving for another hour.

"Have you eaten, Garrett?"

He grinned. "I'll call a donor after the meeting."

"Why don't you feed from me?"

"I told you I wouldn't, but I appreciate the offer." His cool fingers brushed back and forth against my arm. My heartbeat quickened.

"What about the second part of the mating bond: sharing blood at the same time. We could share tonight." I corded my fingers through his hair, then over his ear.

"If I had blood pressure it would be very high right now." His smile was adorably crooked.

"I'll feel safer tonight if our bond is stronger." I lifted my wrist to his mouth and smiled teasingly.

He brought my hand back down to the table and shook his head. "The bonding ritual shouldn't be taken lightly. This second step is more meaningful. I don't feel right about sharing blood with you unless you're serious about our relationship. It's not a game, and you were being playful when you offered me your wrist just now. Think seriously about what you're offering, because it will bring us closer than you can imagine."

It was clear for him this was more than the act itself. This was a promise to work together toward something permanent between us. And permanent for a shifter and a vampire was a very long time. I smiled because down to my bones I wanted to give him that promise. There was nothing in my life I'd ever wanted more.

I lifted my wrist again and spoke to him seriously. "I understand what it means and I want this. I'm in love with you." His eyes widened and I felt a little surprised myself. Blurting out the L word might scare him off, but I hoped he felt the same way, even if he didn't say it out loud. "I didn't mean to treat it lightly."

He smiled and lost his worried look. "We'll exchange a few drops of blood, but I'm not going to feed from your vein. You're not ready." The huskier tone of his voice and the sparkle in his eyes were a siren's call to my body. I leaned closer.

He laughed, grasping both of my hands. "We'll complete the spoken ritual and I'll take a small amount of your energy the way I do with my donors." He fished a thick golden chord from a closet, sitting beside me again. I moved my chair closer to his, then nestled my forehead against his shoulder, lifting my wrist once more to his lips.

Never taking his eyes from mine, he bit into his own wrist, leaving two perfect holes already beading with blood. Before biting into mine, he licked the sensitive skin on the underside of my wrist, numbing it slightly before he bit down deeply, pulling out one long swallow to get the blood flowing. I whimpered with the first pain, but when his saliva mixed with my blood, a warm serenity drifted throughout my body.

He placed our wrists and wounds together, tying them with the soft chord and whispering a few phrases in French. He translated: *"Joined in blood, power, and life."* I sighed in pleasure as he wrapped his arms around me and pulled energy very gently from my body.

"I could stay like this forever," I sent to him, kissing his shoulder and breathing in his intoxicating fragrance. I peeked at his face, waiting for a response. He was watching me carefully with narrowed eyes, probably concerned he'd weaken me too much before the meeting.

"It wouldn't be wise. You need your strength to deal with Maya."

"I'm rarely wise." I yawned.

"Enough, I think."

The sensation ended as he untied the chord. His skin was no longer pale, however his fangs were still fully out and his eyes swirled with a silver fog. It took a great deal of strength for him to stop taking energy after only a minute. With any other vampire I'd probably be in serious danger right about now.

"Just a drop." He held his wrist to my lips and brought mine to his. We tasted the other, his blood a familiar friend to my body. When he leaned in and kissed me, the blood on our lips and tongues mingled together. Our minds opened in a sweep of magic, and I felt his love and his desire wash over me as mine must be washing over him.

After too short a time, he pulled away, his voice deeper, "How are you feeling?" He laughed softly at my wide-eyed expression.

"You're worried about me and … and I can feel it. As if I'm feeling it myself." I must have looked a little spacey because he sat and pulled me down into the chair next to him.

"We can still keep our thoughts private, that's one of the advantages of our shields, but we'll be more in tune with each other emotionally. At times I'll know when you're angry at me and you'll know when I'm particularly captivated by you." He ran his knuckles lightly down my cheek.

"And vice versa." I giggled, a light-headed fool. "Do you feel stronger?"

"Oui, ma jolie Jacqueline. Yes, my lovely Jacqueline." He seemed to get a kick out of mentally sending me the translation. *"Your energy is a potent blend and your blood is more delicious than any other's."*

He sounded so sexy when he said such sweet things to me. "I don't speak French but I kind of love it when you do." I twisted my fingers through his hair.

"My father was born in Paris in 1582 and taught us all to speak Parisian French. Even Aaron. My cousin was at my house more than his own."

"But you sound like someone raised in California."

He shrugged. "I always try to fit in. If I ever go back to Louisiana for a visit, I'll fall into the drawl, I'm sure."

Gracefully, he moved to the fridge to pour me a glass of orange juice. "Drink this, you'll feel better." I drank it down, the rush of sugar relieving some of my shakiness. "The effects of our bond will fade in a few months, unless we share again, or unless we complete the third part of the ritual. The connection between us will help tonight at the meeting. Keep yourself open to me but make sure you're closed to Maya. She'll be testing you. Her questioning may become intense."

"What's the worst that can happen tonight?"

He sat next to me again. "You're an adult. If they judge you to be dangerous, they might issue an order of execution. Or they could mandate special training with Maya. If execution is the decision, I'll get you out of there and safe, somewhere far away. You have nothing to worry about." I trusted him completely but I wasn't an idiot. Being judged by strangers was frightening. Plus I didn't want to think about having to move away from my new friends and my new life.

He stood, pulling me into his arms. "I'll protect you with my life. Je t'aime aussi. *I love you, also.*"

"Je t'aime." I repeated the words as closely as I could: my new favorite expression.

He smiled. "I think you need shoes, correct?" Garrett walked to the closet and brought out six pairs, diverting me for a few minutes. I picked a pair of black sexy boots, bringing me closer to his 6' height.

"Are you ready to go?" I nodded even though my stomach was in a knot. He helped me into a green leather jacket that matched my shirt exactly, then took my arm in his and led me to the door. I stole a glance at the house as we pulled away in his car and spun a quick private fantasy of a possible future living with Garrett in his lovely home.

CHAPTER TWENTY-SEVEN

T HE MOOD WAS RIGHT OUT OF "THE Crucible," only the scene was set in a large office with the usual long table surrounded by uncomfortable chairs. Across from Garrett, me, Rob, and the team stood three shapeshifters: a woman with long wavy brown hair, hazel eyes and full lips, a man with short, spiky black hair, dark eyes and a muscular build, and another woman with light blonde hair cut short in layers, large green eyes and high cheekbones. Although no one had spoken, I could already tell by her hostile stare the blonde was Maya. They all looked to be in their early twenties, but by now I knew better than to go by appearances.

When our team had first met outside the office, I'd caught Kyle looking at my wrist. His disapproval and disgust were easy to spot.

"Kyle, this isn't the time," I warned him.

"I didn't say anything, did I? Jackie, this is Peter Bain. Peter, Jackie Crawford." He indicated the young man standing next to him who'd smiled warmly and stuck out his hand.

"Hi Jackie, it's nice to meet you." He was tall, slim, dark

skinned, handsome, and smelled like cedar. I liked him instantly.

"It's nice to meet you too, Peter." I smiled back as I shook his hand.

"Kyle tells me you're a cheetah. I hope you decide to stick around and become part of Garrett's permanent team. Crescent City can use your special abilities."

I snuck a quick gaze in Garrett's direction. He was talking quietly to Rob. "I have no plans to leave. Have there been problems lately? Garrett hasn't told me much about the work the team would be doing."

"In the past we've had some incidents with a couple of blood witches. Lately we've had to deal with the odd werewolf showing up, trying to drag off one of our female shifters." He shook his head in disgust.

"Freakin' wolves behave like they're living in the dark ages," Kyle interjected, looking angry, as usual.

Peter gave Kyle's hand a squeeze and an enormous smile spread across Kyle's face, the tension in his body melting away. Wow. It was obvious they were perfect for each other. "Only a couple of local packs are giving us trouble," Peter continued. "The rest are fine." He stole a quick glance at Garrett and lowered his voice. "Eleanor's nest has been causing problems, too." Kyle scowled, but this time Peter ignored him.

When we were told to sit, Peter left to wait in the hall. Rob had argued for Kyle and Sinc to be able to attend, but he didn't want to push his luck and insist on Peter attending as well, even though Peter was Garrett's lawyer.

The blonde spoke. "I'm Maya, this is Sylvia, and Brad. We're the elected members of the Crescent City Shifter Council. We're here this evening to decide the fate of Ethan and Jacqueline. Will you answer our questions honestly?"

"Yes," we replied together.

"Jackie, is it true you're a cheetah?" Brad asked.

"Yes."

"Who are your birth parents?"

"I don't know. I've been brought up with humans in foster care. The Crawfords adopted me almost two years ago."

They continued by asking Rob some questions regarding our training. He spoke about Ethan's accomplishments and his propensity toward leadership. He emphasized my ability to adapt under stress, my speed, tracking skills, and basic willingness to work with a team. He also mentioned he felt I had the ability to illicit trust and that people were comfortable opening up to me.

Maya nodded. "Her aura is a rich green. It's extremely rare." She glanced at Garrett, who didn't look surprised by this information. I'd have to find out later what a green aura meant.

"Jackie, tell us about what happened when Garrett was kidnapped." I described finding his car, tracking him to the lodge, Kyle saving me from Hank's attack, and Garrett's rescue by the group.

"You mentioned four wolves, yet you only saw two. How did you know about the others?" asked Sylvia.

Here was the tricky part. I turned to Garrett and asked, "*What can I say?*" He was about to answer when Maya interrupted.

"You're conversing mind to mind?"

I was shocked, answering automatically, "Yes." I'd forgotten to strengthen my shield against everyone but Garrett. I took care of it quickly, just in time to feel a strong push to gain entrance. The wall held and it was Maya's turn to look shocked.

She recovered her poise, saying, "Garrett, could you please describe Jackie's psychic abilities?"

Garrett went into detail about how he'd noticed I was feeling the effects of the ley lines at Carly's small cottage and how he'd tested me and trained me in using the energy to protect myself.

Maya stretched out her hand. "Jackie…."

I looked once more at Garrett for guidance. He sent, *"Keep our channel open,"* squeezing my shoulder.

I smiled sweetly and complied by touching her hand. She was trying to speak to me mentally, nudging at my shield, but instead of letting her in, I focused on holding strong. In my mind, Garrett stood beside me on the bluff above the sea, an arm around my waist. I looked back at the table surprised to see him still sitting there, smiling. *"This is so cool,"* I sent.

"Open your mind to me." Maya was pissed, but then so was I.

"I'm sorry, but no." Garrett had warned me this might happen.

Garrett leaned forward, catching Maya's eye. "She has not been charged with a crime and like all of us, has a right to privacy. My lawyer, Mr. Bain, is outside. I could ask him in to discuss the law with you."

Maya released my hand, obviously irritated with Garrett and me. She wasn't used to being blocked.

Sylvia asked, "Were you able to communicate with Garrett mentally while he was in the building?"

"Yes. He was very weak and I thought he might be dying, so I let him feed off me."

Maya asked Garrett, "You were able to take energy from her—from a distance?" Her eyebrows were practically even with her hairline.

Garrett nodded. "She sent me energy through our mental connection. I was in very bad shape and might not have survived without it." He turned toward me, smiling proudly. "I've only just begun her training."

Brad asked him, frowning, "So you can feed from shifters from a distance now?"

"Only from Jackie. We have a unique connection." He took my hand and met my gaze, my muscles loosening, my heart warming. Garrett seemed to have the same effect on me that Peter had on Kyle. If we could bottle it, we'd make a fortune. I'd call it "Angel's Touch."

"Garrett." Maya's tone had turned sharp. When she asked her question she was staring at me, not him. "What's your relationship with Jackie?"

"That's not really…." Sylvia began.

"It's fine, Sylvia. I've claimed Jackie as my mate." He'd woven his fingers through mine, resting our clasped hands on the table for everyone to see. It was a starkly possessive move, reminding me I was in a room full of animals who lived by different laws and customs than those I'd grown up with. In their furry form, they hunted and killed their enemies and rivals, although shifters seemed to be the supernatural race most like humans.

Of course, when you got right down to it, humans weren't all that different.

We were now officially *outed* as a couple, the expressions on my new team's faces when they heard the news was priceless. Too bad I still didn't have my phone. I would have loved to snap a picture.

And despite the seriousness of the circumstances, I couldn't resist giving my man a peck on the cheek.

Brad was smiling, as was his mate, Sylvia. "Congratulations." They seemed genuinely happy for us.

Maya huffed out a breath. "Yes, very nice, but can we please continue?" Maya asked me, her eyes narrowing, "In what ways can you manipulate magic?"

This was the root of their concern. "I can protect myself

with a shield and share magic with Garrett. I'm not trained to do anything else."

"You haven't experimented on your own?"

"No. I wouldn't."

"Who's training you besides Garrett?"

"No one, only Garrett."

The three council members conferred quietly for a moment, then Maya spoke. "We're going to take a ten-minute break to discuss this information. Please wait here or in the hallway." They left without speaking further.

Peter came in to get an update from Garrett while Ethan and Sinc whispered together. Relaxing back in his chair, Kyle asked me, "So what's it like, reading each other's minds, always knowing what the other one is thinking and feeling?"

"We're tuned in to each other's feelings, but we can keep our thoughts private." I put my hand in Garrett's and he pulled me closer, wrapping his arm around my shoulder.

Kyle wrinkled his brow. "I don't think I could stand it if someone were reading my thoughts all the time."

"What thoughts would those be?" teased Peter. "What's for dinner or why don't I have any clean socks or maybe, who changed the channel?" Kyle laughed and pushed against Peter's shoulder playfully, their affection for each other glowing in their eyes. Rob sat alone, smiling at their antics, and I wondered if someone waited at home for him.

The council returned and Brad remained standing. "We've reached a tentative decision. Ethan is approved as a member of the shifter community without reservation. Congratulations, Ethan."

I was trembling visibly, so Garrett tried to reassure me. *"No matter what they say, stay calm. Nothing will happen tonight. You're perfectly safe."*

Brad continued. "Jackie is required to train under Maya's

supervision for two hours every evening at dusk beginning tomorrow. At the end of one month, her case will be reviewed. Tonight's meeting is adjourned and we'll reconvene in one month." They walked out without a backward glance.

I sat there in shock. They thought I needed special training? What, like anger management? Garrett crouched in front of me, his hands on my knees. "She wants to make sure the community is safe. If you can relax, you'll learn a lot from her." He laughed and hugged me, apparently feeling relieved.

"But I'll get to see you less and less," I complained.

"I've already thought this through. We'll talk in the car." Grinning, he snatched my hand and led me to the parking lot behind City Hall. I was still pretty shaky. When Garrett pulled the car out onto the street, I fisted my hands, saying, "I'd like to stay with you for a while tonight and not go back to the cottage right away."

"How do you feel about moving in with me?"

The largest grin I'd ever managed to pull off decorated my face as I threw my arms around him, dragging him sideways so I could kiss his cheek. "I'm in." I laughed.

"Driving here." He straightened up, laughing. "But gentle cheek kissing is not against the California drivers' code."

"Why did you change your mind?" I kissed the corner of his mouth, playing with a thick strand of his hair.

"Ummm. Much better. You want the truth?"

"Always."

"My feelings are stronger since we shared blood this evening. I can't handle thinking of you sleeping next to Ethan tonight or any night. You're mine now." Those last words had come out kind of growly.

"He's mad about Sinc. Aren't they adorable?" I sighed, leaning against Garrett's shoulder.

He snorted. "Oh yes, *adorable* is the word I'd choose."

I punched him in the side and his eyes glinted with humor. "Most importantly, you'll be safer in my house. If there's an emergency while I'm resting, you can still contact me mind-to-mind. I won't be at my best, but even then I'm fairly strong."

"Don't vampires…? Aren't you dead to the world?"

"We sleep very deeply. We don't breathe and our bodies grow colder. To be at our strongest, we feed as soon as we can after waking. But our connection is strong, Jackie; I would hear you if you needed me."

We pulled up to the little house I'd shared with Ethan. It was empty and quiet since Ethan had gone to Sinc's, so I quickly gathered up my things. Grabbing paper from a drawer, I left Ethan and Carly notes. Taking one last look around and leaving with Garrett, my heart pounded with excitement. Soon we'd be together.

CHAPTER TWENTY-EIGHT

A PERFECT GENTLEMAN, GARRETT HELD the door of his lovely home open for me and I stepped inside. A fire was already burning in the fireplace, and the shadows dancing around the room reminded me of the way the embers had reflected on the cabin walls the first night I'd spoken to him on the island.

He took my hand and my backpack. "C'mon." He led me into the kitchen and showed me he'd had the refrigerator and cupboards stocked with food. I looked around surprised to see the mess I'd left from dinner was cleaned up. The place was spotless. "Elves," he teased, and we laughed.

Tonight he looked his twenty years, carefree and excited and so hot I almost jumped him right there, but I figured we had all night to get serious. Because of our emotional connection, he could feel my heat too. He looked at me with an amused expression, then shook his head and started walking. "This way." I followed him down the hallway toward his room, only instead, he turned me into the room across from his, another bedroom.

The queen-sized bed was a four-poster, draped with a

lovely blue fabric that coordinated with the custom window blinds. The light teal sheets matched the fluffy down comforter, a very feminine and inviting combination. The furniture was a light oak and my bare feet sank comfortably into the rich cream carpeting. It was quite lovely, but definitely not what I'd planned on for this evening.

Irritation colored my tone when I turned to him and said, "Garrett, I thought you wanted … I thought we'd be sleeping together."

"We've talked about this." He sounded irritated himself as he dropped my backpack on the bed and ran his hand through his hair. Because of our emotional connection, I could sense his desire for me. Here we were in my bedroom, so wicked woman that I was, I sauntered over and pressed myself against him, leaning in to kiss him.

He grabbed my shoulders a little too tightly and held me away at arm's length, forcing me to face him. "Let me be clear." He spoke softly but I could feel tension and frustration rolling off of him. "If you continue to throw yourself at me, I'll eventually cave. I may have lived over two hundred years, but physically, I'm a healthy young male."

Who didn't want me, no matter what his body was telling him. His words bit into my heart and I began to tremble, humiliated and horribly embarrassed. He pulled me closer to stroke my hair, trying to be reassuring. "You've gone through a lot of crap, some of it sexual abuse. You need time to heal, my love."

"You've healed me." A tear ran down my cheek and he caught it with his finger as if it was something precious. "You're the only man I've ever wanted to touch me. I wasn't sure I'd ever want to be touched again after…." I looked away from him, shamed by my confession.

"Come into the living room and sit with me." He took my

hand and I followed him reluctantly. Some of my old uncertainty had started spinning around in my mind. It was clear he didn't want me the way I wanted him. I'd practically thrown myself at him and he'd refused. What did I expect? I wasn't a virgin. He probably thought I was damaged beyond repair. Maybe I was. But then why did he say he loved me and why did he invite me to stay with him?

A few more tears raced each other down my cheeks. We sat in front of the fire and he put both of his arms around me and spoke softly into my hair. "I'm not rejecting you. Please don't take it that way." His voice vibrated through my body, calming me. "I love you and I want you to trust me." He turned my face so I was forced to look at him. "You're so beautiful and strong—incredible in so many ways." He stroked his knuckles along my jaw, moving them gently over my lips. "I only want us to wait until you're ready—until what happened in your past no longer affects the choices you make." He nuzzled my ear and ran his lips down my neck. "You're worth waiting for."

With a moan, I hugged him, burying my head against his chest. Tears were flowing more freely now, my anxiety pouring out in streams. Garrett wrapped me in strong, consoling arms, whispering words of love and encouragement. I didn't know exactly why I was crying, only that I felt safe doing it with him. I didn't feel like a loser or a freak when I opened my heart to Garrett.

We held each other in front of the fire and after some prodding from Garrett, I finally felt able to talk about the foster father who'd beaten me and his seventeen-year-old son who'd raped me. I talked about it more calmly than I thought possible, but Garrett could feel my past terror and guilt as if they were his own. Rage built in him once more.

I reached out with my mind. *"If you kill these men to avenge me, I'll feel responsible for their deaths. They aren't fos-*

tering children anymore."

His emotions spun between fury and concern. He sighed and pulled me into his lap, turning my face toward his and leaning his forehead against mine. I tried to turn away, knowing my eyes looked red and puffy and my hair was an ugly tangle, but I couldn't twist out of his firm grip. "I cried all over your silk shirt. I probably ruined it." I wiped my face with the tissue he'd handed me.

"It's just a shirt." Long fingers combed through my hair, passing over to my shoulder and down my bare arm, finally grasping my hand in his and kissing my palm. "Mon joli guépard, *my lovely cheetah*. I love you when your eyes are red and your hair is messy and you're too stubborn to listen to my excellent advice." He kissed my nose. "But I especially love you when you trust me enough to speak from your heart and cry on my shirt." I clutched at the soggy shirt and pulled him toward me, the taste of my tears mingling with his delicious lips. I opened my mouth, needing the tangible reassurance of his love and he responded with passion.

When we pulled apart, I spent a moment enjoying the aftershocks. This kiss was…. Well, how do you describe physical seismic upheaval? After opening my heart and talking about my most painful experiences, our emotional connection seemed to have strengthened, allowing me to feel every solid wave of his love for me. At first it covered me gently like a soft warm blanket but when the electricity got plugged in, I was on fire everywhere. Maybe my heart was never going to slow down again.

Garrett played with my hand and smiled his sexy smile. I was probably broadcasting my emotions out to Mars. "What happened with those men really doesn't matter to you? You still love me?" After the rape, I'd believed I was never going to find someone who could love me, damaged the way I was.

"For all time, my love." He smiled, whispering, "It's almost dawn." He got up gracefully and led me to my room.

"So where do you sleep?" I looked down at the floor, thinking there must be a windowless basement in the house.

"In my bed; no coffin required." He laughed at his silly joke. "The windows have metal shades that seal. My door is strong and locks automatically so no one can get in. I'm quite secure. The house is fireproof as well. There's a key to the house in the top drawer of my desk, but you should never leave my property unless you have permission from Rob or me. I should be up around three. I'll drive you to Maya." He hugged and kissed me gently and I melted against him.

"Will Maya be tough on me?"

He smiled a sly smile. "I can handle Maya."

After he'd gone to his room, I undressed and crawled under the covers of my comfy new bed, feeling safe and loved. I sent out a wish into the universe that I might spend every night of my long life with this incredible male —not sleeping separately of course—but curled up together the way mates should. I grinned into my pillow. His cheetah wasn't going to be able to hold out for long.

CHAPTER TWENTY-NINE

I WOKE UP AROUND NOON AND CALLED ROB from my cell phone to see if he wanted to come over for brunch. He was happy about the invitation and said he'd be at Garrett's house in twenty minutes.

I walked into the kitchen and stopped dead in my tracks. A young man I didn't recognize was watering the plants near the window. He was my height with extraordinarily vibrant purple eyes, a heart-shaped face, thin lips and a slightly turned up nose. His shoulder-length golden hair floated around his head as if a steady breeze blew through the room from all directions. Recognizing the warm buzz, I connected to the lines and saw thick tendrils of energy wrapping around him, flashing in a rainbow of colors. His lean build and pale skin made him appear almost delicate, but I knew better than to underestimate anyone who could pull in so much power. And the guy was just watering plants. Whoa.

He turned to look at me and smiled warmly, his hair settling back down. "You must be Miss Jacqueline. It is very nice to finally meet you. I am Liam." His voice was delightfully musical and soothing and I couldn't stop myself from smiling back. He wore a light blue button-down shirt with the sleeves partly rolled up, and jeans. He was barefoot.

I didn't quite know what to say, but managed a, "Nice to meet you too, Liam." I was at a total loss. Was this one of the people Garrett fed from? Was he from some paranormal cleaning service? He noticed my confusion and smiled a little wider.

He really is adorable when he smiles.

"I guard Master Garrett every day while he rests and I also clean and cook when he has guests. I am Seelie Fae, of the Cascade Sidhe.

I started laughing and had to turn away before I made a total ass of myself. "It would have been nice of him to let me know you'd be here." I chuckled. "He did tell me last night elves had cleaned up the mess, but I thought he was joking. No offence, Liam."

"No offence taken, Miss Jacqueline, but we do not refer to ourselves as elves. My mother is human, but my father is a fae lord—the eldest child of the former King of Faerie. I will be gone shortly after Master Garrett wakes, usually around two or three." I glanced at the clock. Happily, I didn't have long to wait to see him again. Liam took two hesitant steps in my direction. I think he was trying not to scare me. "Are you hungry? Perhaps you would like me to cook something for you?"

My mind whirled with happiness around the idea of someone else cooking brunch. "Can you make omelets and ham or bacon? I have a hungry guest coming. Oh, and coffee please?"

"Of course." He seemed pleased to be asked to cook, not something Garrett required him to do too often, I guessed.

"Who is your guest? I only ask because I must ensure Garrett's safety."

"Rob."

"Excellent." His smile was genuine.

I decided to take a look outside the patio doors to see what the weather was like. The back garden was delightful and the sunshine spreading over the patio reached out with a comforting blanket of warmth. An outdoor table and four chairs were placed adjacent to a white and red rose garden, along with some calla lilies, lilacs, and a small fountain. Around the borders was a large patch of multicolored wildflowers. Blown away by the beauty of his garden, I went back to let Liam know we'd eat outside.

Rob arrived ten minutes later and I escorted him to the patio where Liam had placed a carafe of coffee, a small pitcher of freshly squeezed orange juice and some fresh fruit salad. We sipped coffee and chatted about the lovely weather, my various adventures on Solo Island and my move to Garrett's house. Liam glided in gracefully bearing omelets, toast, bacon, and ham. He greeted Rob with a nod, wished us *bon appétit* and left to clean up the kitchen, his hair floating in the air around him.

We chuckled, watching him leave. "Liam was unexpected."

"He's been with Garrett for over a hundred years. I don't know the whole story, but I know Garrett helped Liam's half brother, Aedus, out of a bad situation. Since then, Liam's father, Lord Caelen, a powerful fae elder, has become an ally, and Liam has pledged service to Garrett." He turned back to look at me and I must have seemed confused because he laughed. "Garrett will explain it all. The fae are a complicated race." He took a bite of food, swallowing and then smiling with pleasure. "You know, it does make sense for you to stay here, you'll be safer and he'll be a lot less stressed out."

We both dug in as I puzzled over what Rob had said. "Does he stress out a lot?"

"He takes on too much responsibility, as if the whole community were under only his protection. I worry about him." His mouth turned up at the corners. "I think I'll be worrying less."

"Do you know what the third part of the bonding ritual is? Garrett hasn't said."

"The ritual for shifters and wolves is very similar, but I'm not sure about vampires. Shifters first claim their mate, then share a kill during the full moon. The last part is a ceremony in front of the council and the community. For weres, males fight to claim a mate." He rolled his eyes. "Very violent. Then the couple shares a kill and has sex during the full moon, *then* there's another bloody ceremony led by the alpha. Weres always take everything to the extreme." He smiled wryly. "I think you should ask Garrett about the vampire ritual."

I watched him as he sipped his coffee and stared at the trees. "Do you have a mate, Rob?"

"Not anymore." Pain tightened his mouth and narrowed his eyes. "When I'd recovered from the torture, I decided to stay here in town. I took a job with a construction company and got an apartment. Lynette was a professor at the local college and we started dating. We were crazy about each other and we went through the ritual, then married and planned to have a family. But the werewolf who'd originally imprisoned me found out where we lived. He kidnapped her. He was angry he'd been strong-armed into letting me go."

"What happened?" I was afraid to ask, but felt he deserved my support if he wanted to talk about such a painful part of his life.

"He killed her. Then Garrett killed him. Slowly."

"I'm so sorry, Rob." I put my hand on his.

"It was fifty-five years ago. I still miss her every day." I got up and went over to Rob to give him a hug. "Thanks, Jackie.

You're so easy to talk to. That's a gift, you know."

Liam was clearing away the last of the dishes when he turned to say, "Her aura is a rich green, Robert. It is in her nature as a healer to listen with compassion." He walked away and we both stared after him feeling more than a little confused. Robert laughed and kissed me lightly on the cheek.

"While the cat's away, Rob?" Garrett was standing by the patio door grinning and looking incredibly hot, wearing only black jeans and holding his shirt. Yum.

"We're all cats here, Garrett. The mice live two towns over." They cracked up and I rolled my eyes. *Ugh. Corny shifter humor.* "Anyway, if I wanted to play, you wouldn't be able to take the competition." He jokingly tried to put an arm around my shoulder, but I ducked out just in time, pushing him away with a giggle.

"Depends on the game." Garrett winked at me.

"My Sicilian good looks would win over the signora." Robert patted his chest.

"Have you looked in a mirror, Robert? You dress like a lumberjack," Garrett teased back. "I don't think your ancestors would approve. In case you haven't heard, some of the best designers live in Italy."

"And what about when you vamp out?" returned Rob, sticking his fingers out like fangs and hissing.

By now we were all laughing and the somber mood brought on by Rob's tale had reversed completely. I wondered if Garrett had heard what we were talking about and had wanted to cheer Rob up.

My chin practically dropped to the ground when I noticed he was standing directly in the sun and didn't seem to be affected at all. I sent, "*Don't you feel weaker in the sun? Doesn't it burn you?*"

"*If I was in the direct sun for an hour or so, it would kill me, but a few minutes feel great. Older vampires can tolerate the rays for longer."* He shrugged. *"I miss it."*

Not realizing we were speaking to each other, Rob said, "Well now you're up and my plans to steal Jackie away have fallen apart, this lumberjack will be leaving. Next time I'll bring my chain saw." He gave me another quick kiss on the cheek, thanked me for lunch, gave Garrett a playful punch on the shoulder and left.

I took in Garrett's muscular chest and hard flat stomach and sighed. "You know, if you want me to control myself, you should keep your shirt on around me." He grinned, as I sauntered past him. "I'm getting a glass of OJ, do you want anything?"

"I'm fine." He laughed quietly but I could feel his eyes glued to my back, taking in every movement as I walked into the kitchen. I made sure to sway just a little bit more than I normally would, the frisky cat in me coming out.

I came back with a glass of juice and asked, "What should I wear to meet with Maya? Will she ask me to shift?"

He was, unfortunately, listening to my advice and buttoning his shirt as he said, "Wear something comfortable. I'm coming to make sure she behaves herself and doesn't ask you to do anything too difficult. She won't like me hanging around but I'm the equivalent of your fiancé, after all."

The word made me smile. *Fiancé.* He seemed to know Maya really well and it was strange how she'd seemed kind of jealous. I decided to just blurt it out. "Were you and Maya…? Were you lovers?"

He took a moment to assess my mood before answering. "Yes, around forty years ago. She was another cheetah, so it made sense, but we fought all the time about everything. She wanted a permanent commitment and I couldn't see us lasting more than a couple of years. We had practically nothing in common."

"She's a lot like me though, isn't she? She's a cheetah and she pulls power from the lines."

"She's nothing like you. She's ruthless and—demanding would be a nice way to put it. She likes to be in charge and doesn't share authority easily." He grinned widely. "I won't let her bully you." He wrapped his arms around me and kissed my ear. "Thank you for inviting Rob today."

I tilted my head in the hopes he'd kiss it again. "He's been patient and kind to me, even when I acted like a brat. Speaking of which, I'm sorry about how I've been acting with you lately. I'll try to control my libido."

His mouth turned up in a sexy smile, crinkling the edges of his eyes. "Patience comes naturally to a vampire, while shifters can't help but live more in the moment. Your life energy is potent and delicious," he teased, kissing me gently and then playfully pushing me toward my room. "Get ready. We have to go soon."

CHAPTER THIRTY

MAYA WAS SEATED AT HER LARGE WALNUT desk typing away at her laptop as we entered her office holding hands. I wasn't surprised to find her office beautifully decorated with expensive art and pottery. Apparently, being a member of the Shifter Council paid well.

"Hello, Maya, how have you been?" Garrett's greeting was forced as he lowered himself gracefully into one of the expensive leather armchairs facing her desk. I decided to remain standing, waiting to see how this interaction between them played out.

She gestured around the room so we'd be sure to take note of her prosperity. "I've been very well, and you?" She smiled in my direction but no warmth shone in her eyes.

He pulled on my hand to bring me closer, never taking his gaze off of Maya's. "Better than ever." I was surprised Garrett was flaunting our relationship, but then I didn't know much about their history together. Still, this encounter was turning into a pissing contest.

Her eyes narrowed for an instant and then swung back toward me. I kept my expression neutral, hoping to avoid conflict. She decided to get down to business. "Jackie, we're going to start working on your psychic skills this evening. Please sit down." I sat in the matching chair next to Garrett. "I'm going to have to ask you to leave, Garrett. She'll never be able to concentrate if you're here."

"I'll be as quiet as death." He smirked and didn't budge.

"I have to insist. If you don't leave, I'll be forced to report to the council that she refused to cooperate." Her threat wasn't lost on either of us. If he didn't leave, I'd be screwed.

"She's here on time and cooperating fully." He stayed where he was, but his eyes had darkened to navy, usually a sign silver dots were about to follow.

"Cooperation is such a general term, subject to interpretation, isn't it? The council will believe whatever I tell them." Her anger was building. Great, this session was going to be so-o-o much fun.

Garrett scowled at her and sent to me, *I'll be right outside. Keep a line open to me. I'll come immediately if anything gets out of hand. You're safe.*

He kept telling me I was safe, but something about Maya made me wonder if he was right. He must know me well enough by now to know I wasn't gonna let her freak me out, no matter what. *I can take what she dishes out.*

"Of course you can, my love." He stood, kissed me on the forehead and left without a word of goodbye to Maya.

Her smile never touched her eyes. "It's such an intimate experience, communicating psychically, isn't it? Garrett and I used to spend hours exploring each other's—minds."

She was baiting me and I wasn't falling for it. I sat in silence and waited for the lesson to begin.

When she saw she wasn't getting a rise out of me she shrugged and said, "Forgive me. Garrett and I have a history and we seem to enjoy tormenting each other. It's become a game of sorts." She sat up a little straighter and pulled out a yellow legal pad. "I know you can build a strong wall to protect yourself, but there's much more to learn. At the meeting I couldn't pull out all the stops, so to speak. Let's begin. Please pull up your shield."

I tapped into the lines to strengthen my wall and placed myself on a hill surrounded by farmland. I felt it was a defensible position because no one could sneak up on me. I really wasn't sure how this worked but I resisted taking her to my cliff. That was a private vision I shared only with Garrett. This grassy hill was neutral and the illusion was easy to maintain.

I felt her nudge my wall. "It's remarkable you're this strong after only a few day's training. I'm going to speak to you now, so you need to let me in."

I felt her gently push on my wall, so I allowed a section of my shield to melt away. Immediately, I noticed her power felt very different from Garrett's. His was a cool refreshing stream; the illusion of himself he projected was always tinged with his comforting blue aura. Maya's was hot and dry, a desert valley. Her aura was a bright orangey yellow, burning with excitement.

"Lesson number one. Never open a hole in your shield to communicate. You can simply fine-tune your aura's magical pulse to mine to absorb what I send to you. Then, if I attack, your wall would still be able to protect you. Right now you're completely vulnerable." A hot jab of energy hit my back, knocking me forward. I opened my eyes to find myself kneeling on the floor of her office, my hands on the carpet in front of me.

"*Jackie?*" Garrett's concern came over my mental airways loud and clear.

"*I'm good.*" I stood up, not taking my gaze off Maya. I could see her at her desk, but also on the hill behind me, the two realities making me dizzy. To get some relief, I shut my eyes and concentrated only on maintaining my vision and defenses, reinforcing my wall. As adrenaline began to pump through my system, my heartbeat quickened, my initial shock turning to anger.

I was surprised when the vision in my mind smiled. "Excellent. I sense no fear, only a readiness to do battle. You might become a fine warrior with the correct training. Try to keep your eyes open, even though it's strange at first. Some of our enemies have the ability to fight psychically and physically, so you need to be aware of all that is going on around you."

When I opened my eyes she was positioned in front, facing me. "Keep your wall strong and try to match my aura's rhythm as closely as you can. Then you should be able to send to me and hear what I send to you without leaving yourself vulnerable."

In my mind I watched her saffron haze pulse with power. I reached out to feel its rhythm in my chest and after a few tries, matched my aura's tempo to hers. She sent, *"You learn quickly."*

"Why don't I have to do this with Garrett?"

"Your natural auras are congruent. Your emerald green and his sapphire blue are harmonious and blend naturally together. Yours is the aura of a healer, a lover, someone in perfect balance with nature. His signifies clarity, truthfulness and a loving nature. You balance each other beautifully." She sent this to me in a straightforward way without any feeling of resentment or anger.

"What does your orangey aura signify?"

"My aura demonstrates an intelligent scientific mind with a tendency toward perfectionism. All true, I admit. Much tougher to blend with."

"How do I … fight with the magic?"

"*To attack someone, we draw the ley line power into our-selves, shape it as a weapon and, using your own unique pulse, push it toward your enemy. The difficult part at first is con-trolling the intensity.*"

"*You can fight using magic?*"

"*Yes, because I'm a cheetah. But I'm no healer. Liam is the only other healer I've come in contact with, and he's fae. 99% of shapeshifters and wolves use magic instinctively when they shift, but can't control it in any other way. The older undead can pull from the lines to some degree along with some sorcerers and witches who learn to connect when they spin a spell. You must study each of the races so you are able to fight them efficiently if it becomes necessary.*"

"*What about the fae?*"

"*The fae are unique. Magic permeates their cells. They feed the lines because they are the lines.*"

She sighed as she relaxed back into her chair, speaking out loud again. "There's great evil in the supernatural world. My best advice is to learn quickly how to use your powers. If you stay with us, you'll be called upon to protect others who can't protect themselves. If you're not willing to help, there's no place for you here in Crescent City."

Maya's gaze locked on mine in challenge, but I didn't flinch. "I'd like to help."

She nodded, accepting my response with cool efficiency. "Please sit down. Some scientists believe cheetahs are the most ancient of the big cats. Perhaps this explains our mystical con-nection to magic. We're natural warriors, which means that because you're also a healer, you'll constantly have to work to balance between your urge to fight, to defend your loved ones, and your urge to heal, to repair the damage. When we meet next, we'll begin working on your fighting skills."

I must have started to glaze over from the overload of

info, because she smiled. "This is overwhelming, I'm sure. I'll dismiss you for tonight and give you homework to work on with Garrett. I'll need to take time to decide how best to approach your special situation."

Relief washed over me. "Thank you."

Her face grew curious. "Do you find yourself reaching out to touch people when you talk to them?" I nodded, surprised. I guess I hadn't realized it. "This is one way a new healer transfers her energy to someone. Not everyone appreciates it. You may want to talk to Liam."

"I'll see him tomorrow morning."

Maya continued to speak with a professional tone. "Although we'll never be friends, I'd rather you don't think of me as your enemy. Please call or email me if you have questions. I'll set aside time to answer them." I respected the honesty, even though the delivery was kinda bitchy.

I jumped when Garrett flashed into the room and laid a hand on my shoulder. Maya wasn't fazed at all by his vamp speed, continuing to write on her legal pad. Handing him the top sheet of paper, she returned her attention to me. "Garrett's done a competent job, so he may as well continue." She ignored Garrett's annoyed grunt. "Work on solidifying your shield and the basic drills I've put on the list. I'll have you back for a test in a couple of weeks. Control is our major concern. If you can demonstrate you won't be a danger to the shifters and others in this community, we'll be happy to let you stay."

She turned to Garrett. "If this team of rogues can truly work together the way you and Rob say they can, I'll be your strongest supporter." She allowed herself a half smile and this time Garrett smiled back. "Go on, get out of here." She turned away to her computer and began to type. Garrett and I headed out the door without a backward glance.

CHAPTER THIRTY-ONE

ROB AND GARRETT HAD DECIDED THE team should meet to discuss our next move, so Garrett and I pulled up in front of Kyle and Peter's house ten minutes later. Everyone was there, and since Peter had barbequed enough ribs to feed a pride of lions, we sat around in their backyard sucking on rib bones and licking our fingers while we talked. I'd noticed Kyle was in a snit for most of the evening. He'd glare at Garrett, then look away when he saw me watching him. Ethan had volunteered to load the dishwasher and Sinc was clearing the table when Kyle started in on me.

"Did Maya tell you about her and Garrett? From what I heard they had some wild affair. Half the town could hear them...."

"Shut the hell up," growled Sinc. Everyone was looking from me to Garrett to Kyle and then back to me again.

Oh boy.

"I was gonna say fighting." Kyle scowled at Sinc.

Garrett unfurled his body from the chair next to mine. He stood directly in front of Kyle's chair, seeming even larger than his usual 6'. "What is between us, should not affect how you treat Jackie. I expect you to apologize." His voice was cold, his eyes darkening. Rob was also glaring at Kyle, although he didn't speak.

Peter came out carrying a tray of assorted desserts and coffee. After glancing around at everyone's serious expressions, he put the tray down and walked to Kyle, appearing extremely annoyed with his mate. "You need to let Lily go. Garrett can't help her and you're giving Eleanor the power to fuck up your life and your relationships." His meaning was crystal clear.

Kyle winced at Peter's words. This might be a bone of contention between them. I decided it was time to have a little discussion with a particularly annoying leopard. Standing up suddenly, I snatched at Kyle's hand and said, "Is there someplace we can talk privately?"

He glared defiantly at first, then shrugged, "Sure, sure … c'mon." He led me into the woods behind his house. We walked in silence for a few minutes until we reached a small clearing. I sat on a downed tree branch and he sat across from me on a large rock, our knees almost touching.

"So what's really going on here? Why are you so angry at Garrett and why are you freaking out at me?"

"I'm sorry, but shit, Jackie. He's a low-life bloodsucker. How can you stand to let him touch you?" He shook his head. "I don't want you to get hurt. What if he turns you?"

I ignored him, sensing there was much more he wasn't saying. "Do you hate all vampires or just Garrett?"

"Mostly Garrett and Eleanor." He didn't hesitate at all, which surprised me. So this was personal.

"What happened?" I touched his knee without thinking, sending a gentle probe into his mind. He looked at me, shocked at first, but when our gazes locked, his expression changed. I felt the exact moment he began to trust me.

Heartbreak vibrated off of him in painful waves.

"Eleanor took my adopted sister, Lily, and turned her. She wasn't a shifter. She was human—the sweetest kid in town." He smiled sadly, lost in memories. A moment later, his expression grew grim. "The last time I saw her she almost killed Peter. Eleanor thinks it's funny to watch me suffer."

He rubbed his face in frustration. "It's my fault. I helped kill one of Eleanor's nest four years ago. He'd been hunting and killing shifters in our territory. That's why Eleanor keeps trying to hurt me. It's a game she plays."

Kyle eyes were pleading. "I want Garrett to get her away from Eleanor and kill her, for real. I'm sure she doesn't want to be like this. He says he won't do it 'cause he thinks Eleanor will kill Peter or me in retaliation. Can you talk to him, Jackie? I can't ... I can't bring myself to kill her."

His emotional turmoil had turned his healthy red aura into a muddy swirl. I wanted to help him but wasn't sure how, so I tried to do what Maya had suggested; to synchronize our energies. I was supposed to be a healer and now was the time to prove it. Keeping my hand on his knee, I worked to make my emerald waves move to his red tempo. When I felt them sync, I gave a gentle push in his direction.

His eyes widened, but he didn't pull away. "What's that feeling?"

I ignored the question and started speaking in a soothing tone. "Maybe Eleanor would release Lily and you could reconcile. It must be hard for you to see her as a vampire." While I was speaking I was sending him strong waves of my energy, tuned perfectly to his. Slowly his aura brightened and began to clear. "The team is here for you; you're not alone. You can talk to us."

He lifted his chin, "I failed her."

As the anger he'd hidden behind slowly left him, Kyle's lip trembled and his eyes glistened. I sent to Garrett, "*Please send Peter,*" keeping my energy flowing into him. In less than a minute Peter was there, holding Kyle as he cried softly. I left them alone and walked back to the others. Garrett put his arms around me and pulled me into his lap.

"Liam said her aura is green. She's a healer, isn't she?" asked Rob. Garrett nodded and hugged me closer. "This is great news," Rob continued. "The council will never banish a healer."

"A powerful healer can destroy with the same intensity they use to heal. Maya may try to force her in that direction. It's not an easy path."

He kissed my head and I sighed. "Mmm."

I closed my eyes and nestled more deeply against his chest, not really paying attention to the conversation. I was sleepy, even though it was only around nine. Garrett stroked my hair. "*How's Kyle?*"

"*I think he'll be okay. Don't be mad at him. He's grieving for Lily.*" I breathed in a lungful of Garrett's scent and smiled when he buried his face in my hair. We both found comfort there.

"*Lily is lost. She's Eleanor's new pet. She tortures and kills as often as her maker, and she enjoys those sessions just as much. There's none of the innocent girl left in Lily.*" He sighed and I heard great pain in the soft sound. "*Maybe if we'd taken her when she was first turned, she might have been able to join another nest. Kyle wants me to kill her, but I won't endanger us all by attacking one of Eleanor's progeny, unless they attack us first.*"

Kyle and Peter reappeared and Kyle walked directly over to Garrett and me. He looked at Garrett. "Hey man, I was a jerk. I can't keep blaming you for what Eleanor did. I'm sorry." He stuck out his hand and Garrett shook it solemnly.

"It's behind us now." Garrett seemed genuinely relieved.

Kyle turned to me next. "Thanks, Witchy Woman. I feel much better." He kissed my forehead, a sweet gesture from someone who wasn't particularly touchy-feely. His shining dark gaze and clear red aura had me feeling pretty damn proud.

"Anytime you want to talk…." I offered. He nodded, gasping when Sinc grabbed him from behind and hugged him tightly. Despite their constant bickering, we all knew they cared about each other.

"Thank you." Peter spoke quietly over the sound of Kyle's laughter as he took my hand and squeezed it. How wonderful it was for Kyle, who always seemed to be at a high or a low, to have steady Peter in his life. Peter's aura was a clear, rich violet. I'd have to make a note to ask Maya about that particular color.

I rested in the hollow of Garrett's shoulder and yawned again.

"I'm taking you home, *chatonne*." Garrett unfolded himself gracefully from the chair with me still in his arms, and set my feet back on the ground. "We'll see you all tomorrow. Jackie needs to rest." They said good night. Sinc took a look at Garrett's show of affection and gave me a discreet wink before she parked herself in Ethan's lap. In her mind, Garrett and I had become more than roommates. I sighed and indulged in a short little fantasy concerning the rest of the night. Unfortunately, once in the car, I only had enough energy left to lean against him as he drove.

An hour later I was lying on my bed with Garrett propped up next to me, typing away on his laptop. I'd managed to stumble through a shower, dress my exhausted body in PJs, and drag my sleepy ass into the bed without doing a face plant, a great accomplishment, I'd decided. I turned onto my side, leaning on my bent elbow to face Garrett, and noticed a curious combination of emotions rolling around in his aura.

"What are you thinking?"

"I'm thinking back to when I first saw you running down a dark deserted road at one in the morning; a fourteen-year-old girl out by herself, but not afraid. When I saw your speed I suspected you were a cheetah. When your permanent aura formed eighteen months ago I was concerned, because healers can easily turn into killers if they're twisted by circumstances. You've had more than your share of rough times."

"I thought about killing my foster brother." This was something I'd never told anyone else. "I might have tried if he hadn't been convicted and sent to jail, just to keep him from doing the same thing to another girl." I looked at my hands, the knuckles turning white.

"I'm sorry I wasn't always with you when you needed me." He stroked my hair and kissed my cheek, putting aside his laptop.

"You saved my life, Garrett. Those men would have killed me." I reached for his hand. "Stay with me Garrett." He started to say something, but I put my finger over his lips.

"Just till I fall asleep. Curl up with me like shifters do."

He kissed my finger and whispered. "Roll over and face the other way." I did and he scooted next to me in the perfect spoon position, his arm wrapping over my waist, our knees bent and nestled together. His skin felt cool again. "Did you feed tonight?"

"When you fall asleep I'll go out. I have plenty of time." He kissed my hair and my ear, sending serious shivers down my body. "I'll ask Liam to guard you."

"He's gone home hasn't he?"

"Liam travels the ley lines. He can be here in two seconds." He kissed my throat.

His kisses were warming my body low in my belly. "The bed is going to burst into flames in a minute."

"Sorry," he chuckled. Only he wasn't sorry at all.

"What's a *chatonne*?"

"A kitten."

"Very funny." I closed my eyes, purring contentedly.

CHAPTER THIRTY-TWO

T HE NEXT DAY I GOT UP EARLY, SHOWERED, dressed, and hunted through the house looking for Liam. I had quite a few questions I wanted to ask him and was slightly annoyed he seemed to be nowhere around. My mood was greatly improved, however, when I saw the fresh pot of coffee, so I took a mug out to the back patio and sat in the sunshine. He popped up about ten minutes later to ask me if I'd like some breakfast. Instead, I asked him to sit.

"Do you know Maya?"

"Yes, I do."

"She told me your cells have magic. Is this true?"

"Yes. We are made of magic and can drift in and out of the lines as you would step in and out of a gentle rain shower."

"Can you help me learn to use magic?"

He sat silently for a few moments, his forehead creased in thought. "The fae are comprised of multiple races, all of them powerful, some much more so than others. There are Seelie or Unseelie royals who would kill us both if I tried to teach you our ways. Secrecy is essential to our survival."

I could see the strain in his expression. "I understand.

I'm sorry if I asked for something I shouldn't have." I nodded my head slightly, the way I'd seen Rob greet Liam, and he acknowledged the courtesy with an amused smile and nod of his own. There was something about Liam that made me switch into a more formal mode of address, whether it was the way he spoke or the fact Rob told me he'd been around for fifteen hundred years and would possibly live for many millennium.

Liam continued, "What I *can* do is come to your aid if you are in danger. I am much more than I seem—a trained warrior pledged to serve Garrett, and now you. This I promise, Jacqueline Crawford."

He bowed his head again and I acknowledged his generosity saying, "I accept your kind offer, Liam, of the Seelie Court." His laugh was musical and so infectious I joined him. When he asked again if there was something I'd like to eat, I requested french toast and orange juice, moving inside to relax into a kitchen chair and watch him cook.

My cell phone rang. It was Ethan.

"What's up?"

"Hi, Speedy! Sinc, Kyle, and I are doing some impromptu training. Can you meet us at Route 204 and Longview Road in about an hour?"

"Sure, sounds like fun. Does Rob know?"

He hesitated. "No. We want to try out the weapon Kyle and Sinc have been working on in the lab. It's not perfected yet. Once we know it works, we'll surprise Garrett and Rob."

The idea that Rob should probably be told about our little excursion swirled around in my head for a few seconds, but was quashed by my excitement over doing something cool on our own, without "teacher supervision." "I'm in. See you soon."

Liam was bringing out my breakfast as I was hanging up.

He put the plates on the table and looked at me with a worried expression. I had a few bites of food, hoping he would leave. When he didn't, I asked, "What's wrong?"

"Master Garrett will not be happy if he hears you four went off on your own. You must call Robert."

"We're going into the woods to train, what could happen? Kyle will have his weapons, Ethan is as strong as any werewolf, Sinc is a genius and can camouflage herself like a ghost and no one can run me down." I crossed my arms smugly and met his violet gaze with my emerald one.

He scowled and spoke sharply. "I believe in your very limited experience you have only encountered humans, underfed werewolves and shapeshifters. Master Garrett is the only vampire you have met and I am the only fae you have come in contact with. There are deadly creatures roaming the forests of your world and many of them are your enemies. Your ignorance and your arrogant attitude are dangerous, not only for you, but also for the rest of your team."

My mouth dropped. What happened to the sweet fae who cooked and watered the plants? He continued, still frowning. "And no, your cheetah would not be able to outrun even a newly-made vampire or the weakest of the fae."

Whoa, well that was unexpected. Liam was starting to piss me off. "Liam, I appreciate your concern. I'll leave Garrett a note." No response. "I'll take my cell phone and call here if there's any trouble at all. We'll be back before dusk. We'll be fine." I glared at him, ready to continue the battle.

He left the patio without comment while I ate for another ten minutes, carrying my plates to the sink. I threw two sports-sized water bottles, four apples, four granola bars, my cell phone and a hooded sweatshirt into my backpack and took off walking down the road to the intersection about half a mile away. Clouds were beginning to roll in from the West and the wind was picking up. I hoped the approaching storm would hold off until dark.

CHAPTER THIRTY-THREE

S INC AND KYLE WERE ARGUING ABOUT *him* driving *her* car as Ethan shook his head in disgust. I was really glad to see them and hoped we could get through the rest of today without any serious temper tantrums, hurt feelings, or injuries. I considered what Liam had said, but shrugged it off. Today I was with the team, and that made it a good day.

We parked on a side road out of sight of the highway and walked deeply into the forest following a narrow trail. Kyle and I took the lead, Kyle carrying his duffle and me with my backpack slung over my shoulder. Bringing up the rear were Sinc and Ethan holding hands and whispering. For fun I pulled on the lines and reached out toward the couple just to see their auras. Ethan's was a vibrant turquoise and Sinc's was a clear red, slightly brighter than Kyle's. Maybe that's why she and Kyle fought a lot. They were so similar.

We came to a clearing and Kyle dropped his duffle with a loud thump, reminding me Kyle was very strong, despite his smaller frame. I sat on a stump and took a swig from my water bottle, then passed it around to everyone else, along with three of the four apples. Ethan helped Kyle set up his little experiment and Sinc strolled over to me and whispered, "So, how are things with you and Garrett? Has he bitten you yet? It's supposed to be erotic."

"Garrett and I are doing fine." I ignored her other question. "How are things going with Ethan?"

She pouted and looked in his direction. "I'm trying to get him to move in with me. He's very sweet and he makes me laugh." She sighed dramatically. "I'm kind of falling for him."

I laughed softly. "I'm pretty sure he's falling for you too."

Kyle's voice broke into our conversation. "We're good to go." He'd assembled an elaborate crossbow with a power pack attached.

He looked at me. "I'm turning this sucker on and you need to tell me if you can mentally connect to the mechanism."

I raised my eyebrows as he explained further. "I'm trying to create weapons that can be controlled through one person's unique connection with the ley lines. Once it's synchronized to your energy, you would be the only one who could fire this baby. You should be able to make the shaft go wherever you decide it should go, even if it's pointed straight up in the air when it's fired. Eventually I'm hoping I can develop a weapon all shifters can use, even if their connection to the magic only happens when we change forms. Some of us may be able to learn to use that part of our brains at other times too. Of course, it won't be a crossbow, this was just the simplest weapon for us to program."

My throat felt dry, so I swallowed to soothe it, feeling just a little nervous since I didn't want to ruin all their hard work. "Okay, tell me what I need to do."

"Since I can't use the energy, I've had to research how it works. I did get a better feel for it when you touched me last night, so I'm pretty sure this is gonna be awesome. Open up to the lines and give me a signal when you're ready."

I tapped in to build my wall, and waved at Kyle. He flicked a switch and I immediately felt an oddly familiar pulsing vibration pushing out from the computerized pack. It wasn't the same as an aura, but it was similar. No one else seemed to be feeling anything at all. I tentatively reached out with my mind, felt a sharp jab and heard a computer come online. Kyle, Sinc, and Ethan started jumping around, whooping and hollering.

"Don't do anything yet. I'm going to load it and hand it to you. Ethan, you and Sinc go behind those trees to the right. Jackie, when I give you the go, aim it at the fir tree straight ahead. Try to make it hit where the bottom branch connects to the trunk. You don't need to pull a trigger or anything. Your mind should do it all."

At first I couldn't figure out how to get it to release the bolt. Eventually I could get it to fire, but it didn't go where I wanted it to go. After about seven or eight tries, and several lost bolts, I was getting tired, but I also knew I was close. I started visualizing the target instead of the bolt and amazingly that was all that was needed. The bolt flew home time and time again. Kyle and Ethan were dancing around and Sinc was laughing at them. I lowered the crossbow and sat down on the stump, exhausted beyond words from using the lines for almost an hour. I pulled out my granola bars, threw one to each of them and ate to get some of my energy back.

Although it was only around three, it was getting much darker. Grey clouds moved through the sky and a strong breeze had picked up, making the leaves rustle on the surrounding trees. A potentially heavy storm was coming in, so Kyle and Ethan packed up quickly and we started back down the trail. I stumbled a few times, feeling dizzy, but Kyle tossed the duffle to Ethan and picked me up, throwing me onto his back. I started to protest, but he interrupted. "Relax, you worked hard. I forgot how draining the mental crap is. Just hold on."

Carrying me didn't seem to strain him at all, so I closed my eyes and rested my head against his shoulder. His lemony scent was pleasant and he moved with the same shifter powered grace I'd come to expect from most supernaturals. When a flash of lightning was followed by the usual distant rumble, we picked up the pace.

I smelled something and dug my nails into Kyle's shoulders, my body growing tense. He'd felt my reaction put me down gently, his eyes instantly on the woods around us. "Something's watching us," I whispered. The familiar smell wasn't human or shifter.

Garrett answered on the first ring. "Vampires," I whispered into the phone.

"I'm coming, stay open to me," he answered.

Ethan and Sinc had run up beside us as Kyle pulled weapons out of the duffle: long knives for Ethan and Sinc and a deadly katana for himself. To me he hissed, "Change and run."

"Give me the freakin' crossbow," I insisted.

"We don't have time to set it up," he growled back.

"Then give me a knife." I stared stubbornly at him refusing to budge—refusing to leave my teammates. He grimaced and handed me a long silver knife with an ivory hilt. It felt comfortable in my hand, but I had no experience using it. I remembered to reinforce my mental shield then crouched down and waited with the others.

A beautiful young woman appeared on the path ahead. She had lovely Asian features, dark eyes and looked to be around my age. As the wind grew stronger, her thick, straight black hair blew out in a silky cloud behind her. She wore a long purple tunic with a plunging neckline along with skintight black pants and boots.

Kyle stepped away from us and started down the path toward her. "Lily?" he called in a pleading tone. His sword hung useless by his side.

"Sweet Kyle, you and your friends look particularly delicious this evening." Kyle stopped where he was. Her fangs showed when she spoke and her scent, which carried on the breeze, smelled rotten with old blood. Her skin was as pale as porcelain and looked just as brittle.

"I smell two new recruits." She jabbed at me mentally but my wall was too strong for her to penetrate. The sound of dropping weapons chilled my blood faster than the sight of her fangs. To my left Ethan and Sinc stood unusually still. Dread filled my heart when I realized I was the only one not affected by her powerful glamour.

She moved closer to Kyle, using a speed too fast to track. Without thought for anything but protecting him, I rushed to position myself between them. Kyle was completely helpless, unable to defend himself. I clutched the knife a little harder, holding it up in front of me, realizing too late I was every bit as helpless as Kyle.

"So what are you?" Lily took a sniff and smiled. "Another cheetah? Eleanor will be so pleased." She swayed the last few yards, as graceful and deadly as a viper. She took her time, convinced I couldn't outrun her, and I was pretty sure, now that I'd seen her speed, she was right.

Lily could smell my terror, her eyes filling with silver as she fed from my fear.

She was next to me now, her horrid scent bringing up a taste of bile. Her delicate hand slowly reached out to touch my ponytail, pulling it toward the front, playing with my long locks the way a cat might play with its prey before taking the first bite. I tried to take a step back, pointing my knife at her chest in a weak gesture of defiance, but she yanked hard on my hair and I clumsily dropped the knife.

I whimpered from the pain as she twisted my hair around her hand. Lily whispered in a tone so unnatural it sent shivers creeping over my skin. "You smell so delicious, pretty girl. Eleanor will want to eat you up. She'll share you with me when she's done. We'll have such fun together, pretty girl. Tell me your name." She'd used Influence in that command but it didn't breech my defenses. When I didn't answer, she hissed in frustration and dropped my hair.

"*Give her a push with your mind. Aim it at her chest.*" Garrett was here somewhere, but I didn't let my relief show on my face. If I gave away his location she might go after him.

Even though I was exhausted, his voice caused adrenalin to pump through my system. I pulled in some extra energy from the lines, formed it into a brick and slammed it at her chest. She stumbled backwards, eyes wide, giving Garrett all the time he needed to grab her from behind and hold her immobile.

The action had cost me in energy. I swayed and stumbled backwards into Kyle who grabbed my arm at the elbow to steady me and keep me from falling. I was relieved to see my friends had come out of Lily's spell as soon as Garrett had restrained her. They scrambled to pick up their weapons and the four of us hovered together away from the action.

"Lily, Lily." His condescending tone, brought a harsh growl from the female in question. "Why are you here causing trouble?" Garrett whispered into her ear as she hissed and struggled. "I'm sure Eleanor has not approved this little side trip. You may not hunt in shifter territory, surely you know my rules." To me he sent, "*She's probably not alone. Stay alert.*" I nodded and scanned the trees, giving Ethan a sign he relayed to the others.

She pouted, her fun ruined. "My new playmates are outside their territory, as you well know, Garrett. They crossed over the highway. Maya's pitiful bubble of protection doesn't extend this far." Lily's tone turned harsh. "You're slacking off. Has your juicy little cheetah distracted you?" She fixed her eyes on me. "I bet she's yummy. I can smell you all over her."

Her fangs had grown longer, saliva dripping from her mouth. Garrett twisted her arms in an unnatural way and she snarled at him. "Let me go Garrett, I'll be good. I wasn't *really* going to hurt them. I was going to bring them back to the villa as my guests." Lily continued to stare only at me, silver streaks swirling in her black eyes. She licked her lips and I trembled.

"You-will-not-touch-them." His voice held a deep resonance, using his Influence to control her. When he released Lily, she crossed her arms looking petulant and angry, but didn't take another step in our direction. Because of his age, Garrett was near the top in the nest's hierarchy and had some power over his younger nest mates. He leaned over to whisper in her ear. "If you touch them I'll take great pleasure in ripping out your throat, Lily. Not even one little finger." He held up her hand and started to bend her fingers back.

She snatched her hand away. "Fine, I'll leave them for now. But you should know, Eleanor sent me here. She's heard about your new toy and wants to play, too. You have one week to share with us. If you don't show up with the new cheetah, Eleanor will come after her personally and you'll end up locked in a box for ten years. But first you'll watch her die like you watched the rest of your family die." Lily looked at me with hunger, running her hand down Garrett's chest and laughing. "He's delicious isn't he?" When I didn't respond, she took an intimidating step toward me. I backed up automatically.

Garrett shoved her so hard she flew across the path and into a large fir tree. In a silent blur he took a protective stance in front of us, his darkened eyes flashing silver and his mouth curled up in a wicked snarl. "Leave now, Lily, or it will be only your head crashing into the next tree."

Lily hissed at Garrett and turned to smile at me. "Sweet cheetah, enjoy your week. Goodbye, Kyle. Antoine, we're leaving." A male vampire appeared at her side just as the rain began to fall. He was bald, just under six feet, with lots of tattoos up and down his arms and around his neck. He turned back to me and smiled wickedly, his sharp fangs glistening and his mouth and clothing covered in fresh blood. I flashed on him feeding from a helpless human and retreated another step.

If these two were typical of the vampire race, I could live a long and happy life never coming into contact with another one, Garrett being the exception of course.

When they'd left, Garrett turned to us, his eyes still smoldering with anger. His voice was hoarse when he spoke. "You'll drive back to my house immediately and we'll discuss the stupidity of today's adventure." All four of us stared at the ground, ashamed we'd been so careless. We'd played into Lily's hands like ignorant children. If Garrett hadn't come…. We shivered, rubbing our arms and shuffling in place, trying to warm up our limbs. The wind had picked up.

Ethan spoke first. "It's my fault, Garrett. I should have looked at the maps, made sure we stayed in our territory." He pushed his dripping hair out of his face and pulled his collar up in a feeble attempt to protect his neck from the cold rain.

Garrett directed his glare toward Ethan and spoke, his voice as icy as the wind. "As you are the team leader, I could put the blame entirely on you, but I won't. Each one of you acted irresponsibly." He paced, maybe trying to keep himself from going ballistic. "What worries me the most is you never thought to call Rob. This could have happened even inside our territory. Vampires don't always pay attention to boundaries set by shifters or even other vampires."

In the silence that followed, he locked gazes with each

one of us, holding mine the longest. He was right, we were idiots who could all be dead or worse right now. "I'm going to make sure they've gone. I'll see you at my house in forty-five minutes." He left before I knew he'd even moved.

My friends stared at me, probably wondering why Garrett hadn't taken me with him. He knew I was exhausted and that the trek back to the car would be rough in the cold rain. I sighed, put on my hooded sweatshirt and started walking. *Payback's a bitch.* Halfway there, Ethan picked me up and threw me on his back the way Kyle had. I'm not sure I would have made it on my own. By the time we crawled into the car, we were soaked, cold and miserable.

When we arrived back at the house, the door was unlocked and a fire was blazing in the fireplace. Pizza and hot coffee was laid out along with a stack of towels. We dried off as best we could and dug in, grateful for the food and the fact Garrett wasn't glaring at us while we ate. Despite the warmth of the flames, the mood was somber. We knew he was pissed and none of us were looking forward to facing him, especially me.

He entered the room after we'd finished eating and sat in an armchair facing us. "How did this stupid plan unfold?"

Ethan and Kyle took turns explaining their idea of testing out Kyle and Sinc's invention as a surprise. They told him I was able to make the weapon work using my psychic abilities after only a few tries. They were getting very excited as they rattled on about how accurate my shots had been and what this could mean in the future, when Garrett raised his hand to stop them.

He turned to Sinc. "And why were you there?" he asked.

"I did a lot of the programming. I wanted to be there to see if it would work." She was nervous around Garrett, probably more in tune than the guys were with what might be coming.

He turned to me. "And so Ethan called you, and you simply agreed to go? It didn't occur to you Rob should know where you were?" Our emotional connection was in full swing, his disappointment, anger and concern making me squirm. "I know that Liam tried to discourage you." Another well-deserved jab.

I nodded and stared at the floor, remembering my reaction when Liam had objected to my leaving. "Liam thought it was a dangerous idea. When I told him I'd be safe with the team, he said I was being arrogant and should tell Rob. But I was sure nothing could happen if we were all together." I lifted my chin, watching the anger glow in his eyes. I was ashamed I'd played a part in putting us all in danger, including him.

Garrett wasn't yelling. That would have been easier to take. Instead his voice was calm with an intensity that made the hair stand up on my arms. "You foolishly put yourselves in danger. You've been told previously these two vampires had been seen in the area causing trouble." "Lily likes to drain her victims slowly as they scream and struggle. She particularly likes to torture shifters because your life force is so strong. You usually take a long time to die. Your deaths would not have been easy."

He looked back at the others, and I let out the breath I didn't realize I'd been holding. "I know how Eleanor trains her nest. Lily would have drained Ethan on the spot and given Sinc to Antoine, since he likes to rape his female victims as he feeds." He looked at me and Kyle. "You two would have been forced to watch them die. Afterwards, they would have taken you to Eleanor. There you would have wished you could have died like the other two."

We sat in silence, our faces pale, while he watched us. Kyle made a move to protest how Garrett had described Lily, but when those silver-streaked eyes met his, Kyle thought better of it. Ethan and Sinc were holding hands in support while I thought seriously about crawling under the rug and hiding there for about a month.

Garrett continued. "I don't doubt you would have put up a fight today. One of you might even have escaped, but over time, living with the memory of your friends dying because of your stupidity would have been a worse fate.

"Rob and I saw great potential in all four of you. Were we mistaken?" No one spoke. Really, what could we say? We all felt we'd let Rob, Garrett, and each other down. "Go home and rest. I'll see you here tomorrow night at eight. Bring the crossbow."

Ethan, Kyle and Sinc quietly filed out the door, mumbling their apologies to Garrett. Their eyes were sympathetic when they said goodnight to me, since I'd have to face him alone. He closed and locked the door behind them and turned, but all I could do was stare at the rug I wanted to climb under. Or maybe I'd fit under the couch. One thing I knew I couldn't do, was see the look of disgust he was probably wearing.

He touched my cheek, turning my face, and I was quickly drowning in the depths of those incredible eyes. Tonight they were filled with pain and concern. I'd done that to him.

"I'm so sorry. I made things worse for you." My voice could only conjure up a whisper of volume.

"It would only have been worse if you'd been hurt. Eleanor's plans mean nothing to me." He sighed and released my chin. "But now she knows you exist and I care for you. You've become a target. This was my greatest fear."

"I'm sorry…." Was he going to send me away?

"You ask me to treat you as an adult, but today, by refusing to listen to Liam's advice, you behaved as a child."

"I did. I'm an idiot." I rubbed my head where Lily had

yanked on my hair. It still hurt, but I'd deserved it.

"Not an idiot, but you should have used caution. The other three knew better." He slid a quick glance toward the front door, frowning. "They've all encountered vampires in the past."

"They were excited about the invention."

"Which is not an excuse to endanger your life." He trapped my chin firmly between his thumb and index finger keeping my gaze locked with his. "In the future, I must insist that you take Liam's advice seriously. A fifteen hundred year old fae knows when a situation is dangerous." He stood, pacing. "Your ridiculous stubborn streak could have gotten you killed."

He stopped when he saw my wide eyes, rubbing his face and huffing in exasperation. "I haven't felt this protective toward anyone since I was with my family." He sat beside me and grasped my hand. "I'm trying not to overreact, but it's impossible when I think you're in danger. Today the entire team was in severe danger." He pulled me closer again, not able to make up his mind if he needed some space or more contact. "It's imperative I be able to trust you to make intelligent decisions regarding your safety." He rested his chin on my head, taking in my scent, squeezing me a little too tightly.

I felt awful that he was so upset, but I was happy as a clam in his arms. "Why didn't Liam wake you up and rat us out?"

"He waited as long as he could, hoping you'd change your mind, but when he sensed vampires might be in the area, he woke me and took off after you. He would have killed Lily if she'd attacked before I got there. For me, he would have protected only you. You might've been the only survivor. The Fae Council of Elders has allowed him to remain with me as long as he doesn't interfere in the affairs of other races. Killing a vampire who is not an enemy of the Fae race would go against their laws. He'd be forced to return to Faerie."

I shivered, hugging him tighter, wondering how I would have coped if my three friends had died violent deaths—deaths that possibly could have been prevented by me. "Should I thank him or apologize, or what? I don't really know much about the fae."

"Tell him his actions were appreciated and his advice will be heeded the next time he offers it. And mean it, Jackie. He can smell a lie as well as I can. I'm inviting him to tomorrow night's meeting. I think he'll be interested to see the crossbow." I wasn't looking forward to seeing Liam tomorrow, although I owed him the apology.

He offered me a gentle smile so I reached for his hand and kissed his palm. His skin felt much colder than usual. "Have you fed?" My meaning was clear.

"No." He didn't pull his hand away, but his smile curled up crookedly. "I'll go out later, after you're asleep."

"Feed from me, Garrett. I'm feeling fine now I've eaten. You can curl up next to me and feed and I'll just fall asleep and be fine in the morning."

He was blocking me from his mind, but his eyes couldn't hide his desire. I was certain my blood was just what the doctor ordered. "We'll see." He kissed my cheek and turned me toward my bedroom, patting my behind playfully

I showered quickly, threw on a pair of PJ pants and a tank top and got into bed. Garrett crawled in next to me, barefoot, dressed in dark sweatpants and a tee shirt.

Sitting on the bed, I smoothed my hand down his arm, feeling how cool he was. He hadn't fed because of me. I could do this for him. My cheetah purred deep in my core. I could do this for me too.

He leaned over, smiling his very sexy smile, and whispered in my ear, sending shivers down my body. "It's not too late to change your mind." I shook my head. "I can still take energy like I do with my donors."

"I want to give you blood tonight, not just energy." I ran my hand more firmly over his biceps and he shivered too. "My blood is strong, isn't it? Let me do this for you."

He arched an eyebrow, slightly wary. "Because you feel guilty?"

"No, because I love you."

He grinned, looking younger again. "And I love you, my sweet. But the saliva from my bite will make you feel slightly… euphoric."

"Sinc said it's erotic." Whoa. That just popped out of my mouth. *Oh, boy.*

He laughed full-out this time. "So you've decided to run your own little experiment?" My face heated to record temperatures. "Your blushes are so beautiful. I'm very tempted to take you up on your offer."

"I want this."

Trailing his knuckles along my jaw and down my throat, his expression turned serious. "We've shared two parts of the mating ritual. Giving me blood, enough to revive me, will be a sensual experience. More than you might imagine."

"I want you to need me. To rely on me. To trust me. I messed up today. I won't mess up like that again." I kissed him deeply to seal the deal and we were lost in each other for a few delicious moments.

Garrett leaned against me, forehead to forehead, his eyes beginning to sparkle. His sweet breath warmed my face as he spoke. "I was terrified I might have lost you." The kiss he gave my nose was playful. "I need you more than life, my love and I trust you completely. My concerns are only for your safety."

He urged me to lie back on the bed then turn on our sides to face each other. He lifted my wrist to his mouth.

"Don't you want to take blood from my neck?"

"I want to watch your face. Tonight we're going to play." He kissed my palm. "When you feel it, open your mind to the lines."

My heart beat in record time as he pressed his nose under my wrist, smelling my skin. I trembled as he licked at my pulse, biting down swiftly, attaching his lips and sucking rhythmically. The pain was sharp at first, but my wrist grew numb and the pain was followed by a comfortable warmth which spread up my arm, down my chest and over every inch of my skin. I floated as if rafting on a peaceful stream under a sunny sky. We stared into each other's eyes—his a swirling silver pool, mine an emerald forest, each of us full of love and desire for the other.

The warmth from his bite changed to a tingling heat, traveling everywhere over my already sensitized body. My skin craved his touch in an almost painful way, my shields dropping without hesitation to take in his magic, hoping for relief. Power looped between us, the rhythm of each wave matching the pull of blood from my wrist. His free hand slid to my waist, finding my skin under the hem of my shirt, the touch of each finger sending lightning to my center. As his feeding grew stronger and more urgent, my free hand moved up his arm, my fingernails digging into his skin.

I couldn't kiss his mouth, because he was feeding, but I wanted to taste him, so badly.

The magic between us moved in tangible waves, the pleasure in our bodies building until we reached the peak, exploding in exquisite release. In my mind, Garrett's pleasure had wrapped around mine, his eyes glittering with warmth and need. His mouth on my wrist had become a connection not simply to my blood, but also to my heart. In that moment we were one creature, one soul.

We returned to reality cushioned in a blanket of ley line magic, sharing breaths, sharing sighs, sharing smiles.

Garrett pulled away from my wrist, licking the last of the blood that had beaded on the surface. He kissed me deeply as the pulses slowed and we let go of the lines. When our kisses ended, I nestled into him and sighed out loud against the warmth of his chest.

Eventually I found the strength to speak. "If that's what your donors feel when you feed from them, I'm mad jealous." I wasn't really. I felt so loved at that moment it would have taken a naked woman crawling out from under him to make me even the tiniest bit jealous.

Okay, so that's an exaggeration.

He kissed my head. "I don't take blood from them. Taking blood is a hundred times more intimate and I only want that experience with you. *Tu es mon coeur. You are my heart.*" He licked my wrist once more to close the wound. "Sleep, my love."

I closed my eyes and snuggled even closer, obeying without argument.

CHAPTER THIRTY-FOUR

I DREAMED.

I was in a doorway looking into a bedroom. Garrett was facing away from me standing in front of an exquisitely beautiful woman. Her golden blonde hair fell in long wavy tresses over voluptuous curves, and her striking gray eyes shone with a silver desire. She looked at me and smiled a wicked smile, her fangs extended as she bit into his neck. Garrett was groaning with pleasure as he raised her wrist to his lips, beginning to drink. With Garrett's blood smeared on her mouth, she pulled away from his neck and said to me, "Jacqueline, come share with us. What belongs to Garrett is mine also. I will see you very soon." Although the blood dripping from her mouth made me sick with fear, her magic pulled at me to join them. I took two hesitant steps forward.

I bolted upright and cried out. Garrett appeared in a flash. "Jackie, what's wrong?" I glanced at the clock. It was still two hours before dawn.

"I dreamed you and a beautiful vampire were feeding

from each other. What does Eleanor look like?" I described the dream and the female vampire who'd beckoned me to join them.

He frowned. "We need to check your mental defenses before you fall asleep each night. Lily must have given Eleanor a full report, so now she's intrigued. Surprise is really our best defense if she moves in to attack, so it's probably best if we keep information regarding our more advanced powers under wraps."

He started to pace, thinking out loud. "She'll leave the rest of you alone if I show up at her Carmel villa. Once I'm there, I can get into her mind and convince her to release me. I'll have to be very subtle so she doesn't know what I'm doing, but I've pulled it off a few times in the past." He glanced at me, then away again. "I might have to spend a few days with her, but I'll be fine." He didn't look as confident as he tried to sound, which worried me.

"Can she force me to come, too?"

"No, as long as you're here in my house, you're protected. Liam will make sure you're guarded at all times. If she's not patient and comes after you in person, I may have to kill her. I've already contacted my lawyer to add your name to the deed of the house. Don't ever give her permission to enter under any circumstances. As part owner you can keep her out. And if your wall is up, she can't glamour you."

I watched him carefully, surprised he'd thought so much of this through already. "Can you kill your maker? Are you strong enough?"

"Yes. I think so. She's over four hundred and has access to strong magic, but I've been working to strengthen my powers, which include my abilities as a cheetah." His gaze grew wary. "I have a few friends in the nest. If I kill her, I'll have to take them on as mine."

"Start your own nest?"

"Yes. If I defeat her, I'd have to either kill them or create my own nest and take them in. I could never let any of them loose on the world the way they are now, but I'd like to give a few of them a chance to change. Some of us tried our best to watch each other's backs, even under the worst circumstances."

At this point, we were sitting cross-legged on the bed, knee to knee. Wanting to get even closer, I leaned my forehead against his and whispered, "Tell me how I can help you."

Gentle fingers raked through my hair, stopping to hold my head in place so he could kiss me. It was sweet and needy. He was worried. "We'll start working immediately on Maya's list. The more you can use the lines, the safer you'll be, and the safer the team will be." His rich blue gaze burned into mine, pleading. "You have to promise me you won't follow if I go to her."

"I can't promise." I shook my head stubbornly. "If you're in danger, I'm coming to help you. The whole team will come." I was sure they would, maybe even Aaron and his pack.

His voice was soft, but a touch of real fear made it husky. "If you follow me, you'll die. She'll torture you in front of me and make it last as long as she can. She's done it before. She has a nest of over ten vampires. I won't be able to save you." He tenderly brushed a strand of hair out of my face. "If she comes here, I can protect you."

"Then make her come here. Talk to Rob and Maya and all the shifter families. You've helped them out for years. Talk to Liam and your cousin Aaron and his pack. Kyle, Ethan, and Sinc will develop more weapons. We'll fry her ass with the lines. Please, please don't go to her. I can't even think about her hurting you." I scooted closer, wrapping my arms tightly around his chest and leaning against him, breathing him into my lungs and filling my heart with his steady presence.

He held me quietly for a few moments. "I don't believe the community would agree to put their families in such extreme danger. If we can draw her away from the town, they might send some of their better fighters."

"To solo Island?" It was the first place that popped into my head.

He was kissing me before I had a chance to take a breath. "You're remarkable." He jumped up. "I'm calling Rob, then I have to get some rest, it's almost dawn and I want to rise early today." He leaned back and kissed my palms. "*Je t'adore. I adore you.*"

After he'd shut the door behind him, I shivered. Eleanor was a much older and more experienced vampire. What chance did he really have against her? Sleep was hard to come by.

CHAPTER THIRTY-FIVE

WHEN I WOKE AT NOON, I DRESSED and hunted around for Liam, wanting to get the tough job out of the way first. I found him pruning a rose bush in the backyard. As I opened the patio door he turned and put down the clippers. We stared at each other for a few moments and then I took the plunge, keeping my tone as respectful as possible.

"Thank you, Liam. I appreciate the risk you took for my safety." He waited. "You were right. I was arrogant and childish and I didn't show you the respect you deserve. I can't swear I'll never act that way again, because I'm pretty stubborn, but I promise I'll treat any future advice you share with me as a gift to be taken seriously. I'm sorry." I'd practiced this speech in front of the mirror and hoped he believed me because I meant every word. I waited quietly for his reaction.

His violet eyes sparkled with what looked a little bit like humor. "Miss Jacqueline." His tone was formal. "I acknowledge your statement as truth and I hope I may be of service to you in the future. I have never seen Master Garrett so happy. I begin to understand the reason." His mouth curled up in a gentle smile. "There is food warming in the oven. My sage advice for today is that you eat."

"But is everything all right between us?"

"Yes." His eyes narrowed and he took a step toward me, sniffing twice as if testing the air. "Do you know you are using the lines right at this moment? Are you attempting to use magic to heal our earlier disagreement? Or is this done without intention?" He flattened his mouth in irritation.

I must have looked as bewildered as I felt. "I'm not … I'm not trying to influence you in any way. And I'm not touching you." I lifted my hands, puzzled. Didn't Maya say I had to touch someone to heal them or calm them?

He motioned for me to sit on the bench as he sat pretzel-style on the wide wall surrounding the fountain. "I know how difficult it is to learn to control your gift," he began, "but it's imperative you attain those skills quickly. As you were able to send Garrett ley line magic from a distance, it's now apparent you are able to send healing energy without requiring physical contact.

"Most supernatural creatures will dislike your magical intrusion if done without permission. My people in particular find it offensive, even though your motives may be pure. Your spirit's goal will be to create a balance where you sense there is turmoil. However, it is extremely important you are always aware of when you are using magic. You must *never* allow the magic to control you, as it just has."

"Garrett said Maya might want me to use my power to become a fighter."

"You have the ability. Healers like you and I can reverse the flow of the ley lines and drain the health from a weaker enemy, pulling their life force into our bodies and adding to our strength. Not many can stomach the consequences of such a skill, because if carried far enough, we leave behind an empty husk. Powerful vampires, like Eleanor and Garrett, can pull in a creature's life force as well." He sighed sadly and looked away. "To be a strong healer is a wondrous gift and a terrible burden, because we can injure as easily as heal. We are constantly forced to choose between the two paths."

I imagined over the hundreds of centuries Liam had lived he'd had to make those difficult choices many times. I managed a shallow nod in reply, feeling a little overwhelmed by this information. "Thank you, Liam." He'd trusted me, opened up to me—a gift I would never take for granted. I rose, dished out some pancakes as ordered and sat down to eat.

His words tumbled around in my head like fall leaves in a brisk wind, my mind taking his information a step further. With magic, control was essential, that was obvious. My nature was to heal, but I must never force my energy on someone, even if I only wanted to help. Going into someone's mind without permission was a kind of rape, after all, even if the purpose is to heal.

Kyle had accepted it, but Liam hadn't, and I was fairly sure most powerful supes wouldn't appreciate it either.

And what about the destructive side of my nature? If I can learn to drain an enemy's energy, I'd be an enormous asset to the team and the entire shifter community. But could I take away someone's life force, even a creature like Eleanor? Like dirty water down the sink drain or sipping through a straw to nourish my body, leaving only the dregs at the bottom of the glass.

I decided to call Maya to talk to her about what Liam had told me. No one else might understand. "Maya, could we meet somewhere? I have a few questions about my psychic healing abilities."

"Your healing abilities haven't manifested themselves quite yet. Wait a few months and then we'll talk."

"Liam thinks I'm healing subconsciously. He thinks I'm using the lines without realizing it to calm people. I've already used my healing with Kyle and I think I helped him a lot."

I counted three beats of silence before she said, "I'll meet you at Bette's Diner in one hour. Go to the back room." I breathed a sigh of relief. Whatever I thought about her abrasive personality, at least she was true to her word.

An hour after telling Liam where I was headed, I was drinking a coke at a small round table in the empty back room of the local diner. Maya was sitting across from me nursing a cup of coffee and studying my face. I'd already explained everything, so I stayed quiet while she twisted all the possibilities around in her keen mind.

Her expression grew determined. "Let's see what you can do. I don't have anyone for you to heal like you helped Kyle, but there are other forms of healing. We'll start with a simple, yet practical experiment." To my surprise, Maya took a Swiss army knife out of her bag and ran it across her palm drawing a thin line of blood. "Focus your energy and heal me."

"But I don't think Liam was talking about healing physical injuries." I was shocked and upset by her pain. This was not what I expected.

"Jackie, now's the time to get over your 'I can't do it' attitude and just focus the damn energy and heal me. I'm bleeding, in case you haven't noticed."

She sounded very calm for someone whose blood was dripping on the table, so I took a breath and did what she suggested. I stared at the wound, drew in the magic and focused. The heat from the lines built up in my stomach and chest, the way it had when I'd struck out at Lily in the woods. I reached across to hold Maya's injured hand in both of mine, feeling the need for physical contact.

"Send the warmth of your aura out like a bandage to cover the wound, then pull it tightly together to seal it."

The visual helped, so I concentrated on my breathing, pulled again on the current and pushed a flat wave of emerald energy toward her bleeding palm. I felt it make contact with the surface like a second skin and was amazed when I saw the bleeding start to slow down. I sent another strong pulse to push the edges of the skin together.

I was horrified when I saw her wince. "Ow, shit! It felt like you were healing my cut with a soldering iron. You can definitely use some practice." I flinched at her harsh words, but she scowled, saying briskly, "Don't turn away, look!" She held out her hand, palm up. It was perfect.

I gulped down a few sips of soda, the caffeine clearing my head. "Your trust in my abilities is a little—extreme. What if I couldn't do it?"

She shrugged, appearing as calm as I'd ever seen her. "I know power when I feel it, and you're buzzing like a hornet's nest. Worst case, I would've needed a few stitches. Or I could always shift to heal."

I wasn't sure how I should be feeling about this newly discovered ability. I was embarrassed I'd worked my magic so clumsily, amazed I could actually heal a small wound at all, and scared about what this meant. Garrett, Liam and Maya had mentioned a healer could kill using the same energy. But when would I ever need to kill? And could I kill if I had to? My stomach did a backflip. Living in a supernatural world was getting very complicated.

"I see you've put two and two together, so let's give it a try, shall we?" She laid her hand palm up on the table. "Cut me. Cut me the way I cut myself. Try not to make it too deep; I'd like to survive the day, if that's all right with you."

"I can't...." She put her other hand up to silence me.

"We had this discussion three minutes ago. Cheetahs

don't run from what we are. We take our natural gifts and make them stronger. Now do it." There was no fear in her eyes or in the relaxed way her hand rested on the table in front of me. In fact, she looked eager, and almost hungry. Maya, the scientist and magic user, was aching for another challenge. Looks like I was prime guinea pig material.

I didn't argue further. Taking in three deep breaths and drawing in power, I shaped and sharpened the magic to a fine point and pushed it out to flick across her palm. Maya winced, but didn't make a sound. The shock of seeing her skin open up without anything touching it was surreal. Not wanting to wait, I grabbed the edges of her palm with both hands and sealed the skin once more. This time when I finished she was beaming. Of course, I was happy too, just still too shocked to show it.

Odd how I was able to cause hurt from a distance, but preferred to touch someone to heal them. I was too tired to put much thought into that particular puzzle. Maybe Liam could shed some light on it later.

I attempted to stand and stretch my legs, but my knees wobbled so much I had to sit again. I plopped down in the chair rather ungracefully. Maya huffed in annoyance. She'd probably wanted to keep experimenting on me. "You need to eat something before you pass out. I'll call Ethan to pick you up and take you back to Garrett's." She signaled to the server and ordered me a cheeseburger and a side salad, never asking what I wanted. "Rest tonight. No strenuous training. No strenuous anything, understand?" I nodded, common sense telling me that arguing with the alpha female would get me nowhere fast.

Her gaze held some respect. "You've accomplished quite a lot today." Yeah, the ability to heal was an amazing gift, but I couldn't take pride in the other. She continued with a scowl,

42

"Don't you dare feel guilty about your power. You'll be able to save lives and protect the people you love. Think about that before you start whining."

"But … but how do I stop myself from sending out healing energy when it's not wanted or appreciated. Liam was pissed."

"I'm not surprised. The fae find it offensive if you can't control your magic around them. You need to practice doing it over and over until your body and your mind are keyed in to what it feels like when it's happening. It'll take a while. Ask Liam to help you. He will."

"He said he wasn't allowed."

"He'll help you. Trust me. I've already seen it."

Before I could ask what she meant, Ethan strode in with the rest of the team. Maya greeted them coolly, leaving through the back door, having already paid for my meal. I shook my head watching her leave. Maya had such confidence. I wondered if I'd ever feel that way about my power.

Ethan sat next to me and rubbed my back, probably noticing my rattled composure. "Eat your burger and talk to us." I told them everything. Even though Maya's pain had been relatively mild, I was troubled by what I'd done.

"I hated hurting her."

"The team can use you as a tracker and you can patch us up afterward. No one will force you to fight." He smiled his beautiful smile. "It'll always be your choice to make."

"I'm not afraid."

"We understand. You grew up with humans. Sinc and I grew up with supernaturals. Kyle's lived in a supernatural community for ten years. Injuring someone—killing someone—it's not easy for any of us. We've all killed to protect others. It stays with you."

Sync spoke softly. "I killed a child. Kyle and I were chasing a wolf who'd raped and killed a young girl. The gun was knocked from my hand and went off." Sinc's eyes held unshed tears. "He'd pushed her into the line of fire. She was twelve years old. I see her face every day."

Kyle nodded his head. "Even with Hank, who was torturing Garrett and was probably gonna kill you. I mean, if he'd been in another pack like Aaron's, he might have turned out an okay guy. I ended any chance he had to change."

I looked from Ethan to Kyle to Sinc and found myself strangely reassured by their words. They held themselves accountable for those deaths. Stupid, I guess, but I'd worried that living for centuries with the power to destroy so easily would somehow diminish my ability to show mercy, or worse, to feel remorse. I shuddered at the thought and promised myself to follow Maya's advice and learn to control this *gift*.

I remembered what Maya had said about seeing Liam helping me with the magic. "Can Maya see the future?"

Ethan nodded. "Yes, sometimes. It's kinda spooky. I guess cheetahs end up with different powers."

"I wouldn't want that gift." I looked around the table and smiled gratefully at them. "Thanks for the help. I think I want to go home now." They drove me to my new home, Kyle and Sinc arguing about something they were working on together in the lab. Later it morphed into trading quips about what they were wearing, neither of them appreciating the other's taste in fashion. I sighed and smiled, happy to be in the back seat leaning against Ethan.

CHAPTER THIRTY-SIX

I TOOK A NAP WHEN I GOT HOME, WAKING UP around six, thrilled to see Garrett propped up on the bed next to me, working on his laptop. "Hey sleepy. Maya emailed me. You had yourself a busy afternoon. How do you feel?"

"I feel fine, now that I got a couple more hours of sleep."

I automatically brushed my fingers along his arm, this time finding his skin warm to the touch. I adjusted my body so I could sit, leaning against my fluffed up pillows. I watched his graceful hands moving across the keys and allowed my gaze to wander up his long arms to his flawless face. His eyes glittered with energy in the late afternoon sunlight streaming through the window. I wasn't terribly surprised to feel a tinge of jealousy. Should I insist on meeting his donors? Somehow I knew they'd be women. Did he kiss them when he fed from them? Did they feel like they were gently floating or did they feel the heat and the passion I'd experienced last night?

He chuckled softly. "You're very easy to read this evening, especially since your shields are down. Yes, they are all female shifters. I switch off between six of them so they can fully recover. No, I don't kiss them. There's nothing sexual about the experience for them or me. Basically I glamour them so they relax, then I feed for a few minutes and they fall asleep.

I'd popped my shields back in place. "Do you touch them when you feed?"

"I find it's fastest if I hold them." My incredulous expression made him pause from his typing and ask, "What is it? They're fully clothed and fast asleep!"

"Garrett, if you think these women aren't getting off on your closeness or your hugs or your feeding from them, then you are a very naïve 234-year-old male. I mean look at you. Women must throw themselves in your path and beg to be fed from. You probably have a twenty-person waiting list." I was laughing as I said the words, but the infamous green-eyed monster was starting to prowl around inside my head.

He continued to type. "Closer to fifty." He smiled, turning in my direction but not seeing the response he'd hoped for. "C'mon, that was a joke. They know the rules—it's all very professional. No groping allowed." He gave me an impish grin and brushed his lips across my cheek. "But I like that you're just a little jealous."

"Hmph. Just a little doesn't cover it. Do you pay them?"

He kept typing and didn't respond right away. "I did promise them our arrangements would remain private. None of my donors know each other." He sighed at my determined expression. "Of course, I'll tell you. I don't want secrets between us, but you need to keep this information private as well." I nodded. "I pay for their health insurance, for them and their families. Full coverage with dental."

His body relaxed when I finally smiled. "I figured it was something like that. You must know helping them out in such a generous way makes you even more attractive in their eyes. None of them have mates, do they?" He shook his head.

"They're definitely getting off on the whole *look into my eyes while I embrace you and suck your energy until you fall asleep thing.*"

Garrett barked out a laugh, allowing his voice to go all deep and soft. "Ah, but isn't it more important to you that I'm not getting off on it? That I only get turned on by my lovely cheetah with her delicious mouth," he brushed my lips with his, "and her perfect body?" He'd put down his computer and was leaning closer, running his hand up and down my arm and nuzzling my ear.

I had to admit he was right. That was way more import- ant. But I wanted to have some fun, so I tried not to smile when I shrugged. "Yeah, I guess so."

"You guess?" He grasped both of my hands and gently pulled me out of bed, wrapping them around his waist to rest on his lower back. One of his hands wove into my messy hair and the other landed on the waistband of my jeans, looping a finger playfully through a belt loop and pulling my hips even closer.

He whispered, "You're the only one I want to be with." He kissed me with passion, my whole body singing with heat. He was mine—every delicious, sexy inch of him. What happened when he fed from those donors meant nothing.

"You made your point, Monsieur." I teased, closing my eyes and melting against him, wishing that all the stress caused by Eleanor would evaporate so we could go back to our relatively peaceful life.

Of course my stomach picked that very romantic mo- ment to growl, so he laughed again and led me toward the kitchen. "Time to feed my perfect cheetah." As I watched him move in his graceful way toward the fridge, I sighed and bit my lip. Yeah, I was definitely hungry, and I knew from our close embrace he was too. And he thought I was the stubborn one. *Huh.*

We grilled a chicken breast and some veggies for my dinner. Garrett got a lot of joy out of "manning the grill" while I sauntered back and forth finding the various implements, sauces, plates, etc. He'd told me he enjoyed watching me eat, so I took my time and made sure to lick my fingers just to tease him. After all, he was the one who wanted to wait, and though I'd promised to be good, I was only human … or close at least.

As the meeting time grew closer, he paced, on edge about something he wasn't telling me. I did my best to worm it out of him, but his answer only scraped the surface.

"I'm working out in my head how best to discuss our plans with the team."

Hmph. That definitely wasn't the whole story, but I figured he'd tell me when he was ready.

At eight, we met in the woods behind the house so the team could demonstrate how the new crossbow worked. Liam showed up to watch as well, walking out of the forest just as we were beginning. Kyle and Sinc glowed with pride as I hit the target every time, even when Garrett made it tougher and more specific. Kyle discussed how the technology could be used with all kinds of weapons and that eventually he hoped people who only had a weak link to the lines could find a way to use it. Because their life force was strong, shifters were often victims of more powerful magic-using supernaturals like dark witches, sorcerers, and vampires. Weapons that could access magic would always be in demand.

We moved into the living room, all of us taking seats. Sinc had her laptop perched on her lap, the clicks and clacks of her typing filling the temporary silence in the room. Liam sat next to her, quietly observant.

Sinc spoke. "I've sent out emails to every shifter household on our list. The council is meeting tonight to decide what, if anything, they'll do to help. I've also contacted our wolf allies. How many volunteers do we need to take down Eleanor and Lily and the rest?" Her eyes sparkled with eagerness. According to Ethan, Sinc hadn't liked how easily Lily had controlled her and was itching for a rematch.

"We'll need at least fifteen volunteers plus our team. On top of that we'll have Aaron and a few of his pack. Eleanor will probably bring Antoine, who's older than me and very strong, Lily, Sasha, Yvette, and perhaps Heinrich. I don't believe she'll come with more. The much older members of her nest are in Europe or South America and she would not see us as a large enough threat to call them back. She'll never believe we have a chance against her, even if we do organize."

Rob spoke up. "I'll take on training any of our shifter volunteers. Most don't know much about vampires or how to kill them."

Garrett looked at me for a moment then turned back to the group. "We need to be prepared for any eventuality, but I've made a decision which might solve our problems. I plan to challenge Eleanor to a personal duel to be held on the island, which is still considered neutral ground. Vampiric law for dueling states no one else can interfere while we're fighting. When I take her out, the rest of her nest will be under my authority. They'll have to join me as part of my own nest, pledging loyalty with a blood oath, or I'll be forced to execute them. This plan keeps all of you, along with the volunteers, safe."

He swallowed hard, his nerves showing. "If she kills me, and makes a move toward any of you, you'll have to fight. She'll be in a weakened state from our duel, so it shouldn't be too difficult to take her out." While he spoke, he kept sneaking peeks in my direction, but I kept myself perfectly still and shut down tight, not looking at his face or letting him into my head.

When he finished, Ethan, Rob, and Kyle started talking at once, the gist being, "That's a crazy idea … too dangerous … we can take care of her together, etc." Sinc sat quietly watching my reaction, which was probably what you'd expect it to be.

First, I was furious he hadn't mentioned his little plan beforehand. We'd had plenty of time to talk when I woke up from my nap or when we were cooking and I was eating dinner. Second, I was terrified. How could he fight *alone* against Eleanor—a female vampire twice his age—and win? When he'd mentioned fighting her before, I'd figured he'd be bringing some help. But this plan? This plan was just crazy. Eleanor was going to kill him and I was going to lose him forever. I finally stole a glance, but his determined expression as he listened to the others told me we wouldn't be convincing him to change his mind. I felt helpless—triggering another wash of anger.

I took in a breath, ready to send a rather scathing mental remark his way, when I felt a sharp nudge at my wall, and it wasn't from Garrett. I turned to the only other psychic in the house, Liam. He lifted an eyebrow and I let him into my mind.

"Garrett is doing the right thing. He knows what he is risking. He understands that you will be angry and may turn away from him. He also knows he may die, but he is thinking about your safety and the safety of his friends and the entire community. He is being selfless, according to his nature. Try to consider this before you attack him with your hurt feelings and your fear. Garrett needs your support more than he ever has before. To win against Eleanor, he must know you are all behind him, especially you, Jacqueline. He is more powerful than you know, perhaps more than he knows, but your trust and your acceptance of who he is and what he must do, will give him the energy and the will necessary to beat her."

I closed my eyes and allowed the sharp magic I was aiming at Garrett to float away, then turned again to stare into Liam's alien violet eyes. He was right. As terrifying as it was, this was how I could help my mate. I'd been a big talker, telling Garrett I was a woman and not a child, that I wasn't someone who required saving, that I wanted him to need me as a partner and not always be the needy one. Well, I needed him to live and I'd do everything I could to make sure that happened, but right now, he needed my help to gain support for his extraordinarily brave and dangerous plan. I clenched my fists and squared my shoulders. I could do this for him.

I nodded at Liam and sent to him, "*Thank you.*" Holding my fear in check, I attempted to smile, but I couldn't hide my feelings from Liam. My face was probably an open book, the table of contents a lineup of mixed emotions. But the ancient male met my gaze and nodded solemnly, and although his expression was serious, a warm respect glowed in his eyes. It gave me the courage to do what I needed to do next.

Garrett, Ethan, Rob, and Kyle were still arguing, and even Sinc had joined the fray. I took a deep breath and stepped into the middle of the argument. "Could I say something?"

"Jackie … I'm…." Garrett began.

I put my finger on his lips and sent, "*Please give me one minute to talk and please, please try not to interrupt me.*" He nodded and started to step away but I grabbed his hand and pulled him next to me, looking directly into his amazing eyes with all the reassurance I could muster. "*We must form a united front, general.*" I smiled and he gazed back at me, bewildered.

I faced the others. "More than anyone else in this room, I want Garrett to live and not get hurt." I squeezed his hand so hard I might have broken a bone if he wasn't a vampire. "He's been tortured by Eleanor for over a hundred years. She won't hesitate to use all of us against him. She needs to die, right?"

The others nodded, waiting for the rest. "His plan makes sense. If he goes into her territory he'll be killed or locked up and she'll still come after us. If she shows up on our island with her nest and we all battle it out together, we might beat her, but a lot of us would die. We're willing to do that for him, but how will those deaths affect us and the community?"

No one spoke for a moment. "This way, she has to accept the challenge, which puts us in control." A small shiver ran down my spine and suddenly Garrett's hand was there supporting my back, holding me steady. "Surprise is our best defense," I quoted his earlier remark. "Garrett is so much stronger than Eleanor realizes. My vampire will kick her ass from here to Hawaii." I wrapped his arms around me, my back pressed against his chest. "I support his plan."

Silence filled the room for only a moment. "We're in," said Ethan, grinning at me. Sinc had a tear running down her cheek and even Kyle nodded and looked impressed. Rob gave a small salute in our direction and started laughing. Liam came over and spoke a few quiet words in Fae with Garrett, then nodded to me and left.

The rest of us sat around for two more hours discussing strategy. When we finished, Rob took Garrett and me aside and said, "Jackie, you should think about running for council in a few years." We laughed and I hugged him goodbye, then I walked over to Kyle to ask about Peter. Rob's voice was quiet but our ears were very sharp. "When you finish with Eleanor, I want to be your best man."

The room got really quiet, really fast. Looking a little uncomfortable, Ethan, Kyle and Sinc waved their goodbyes and left.

"We haven't actually discussed marriage, Robert." Garrett looked just as uncomfortable as the others.

"Ask her, Garrett." He turned away, winked at me and followed the rest out.

"That was awkward." I'd never expected Garrett to propose to me. In fact I didn't think shifters or vampires actually married. I figured the three-part mating ritual was it. A lot of them might marry for legal reasons and others for religious reasons, but none of it was necessary for me. I walked to the window and looked out at the waning moon. Marriage wouldn't change anything between us, but I'd go through the whole dress/cake/ceremony thing if it made him happy. I turned and smiled so he'd know I wasn't upset by what Rob had said.

He stayed where he was, hesitant. "Rob was married to his love, Lynette. He wants us to be happy like they were. My parents were mated, not married, and they were the happiest couple I ever knew." He walked to me slowly, still unsure, and reached out to hold my hands. "Marriage isn't a requirement for happiness, at least not for me. I'll give you a huge wedding if it's what you want. I'll do anything to make you happy, although I don't think you'd accept my proposal if I asked you tonight."

He ran his warm knuckles down my cheek to my chin, neck and collarbone and on cue I shivered, my body making it clear what it desired. I thought about a life without Garrett and tried to gather up my courage.

I took his hand in mine and turned once more toward the moon, bringing him along with me. He stroked my hair and kissed my head so I leaned back against him and wrapped his arms tightly around my body crossing them over my chest as we stared out the large window at the woods beyond. "I don't need a wedding. The mating ritual will be perfect."

"What you did tonight, supporting me, even though you're afraid and angry, meant everything. I've never loved you more."

I faced him, my need impossible to hide. "I love you. If you're going to take this risk and face Eleanor alone.... If I might only have one or two weeks with you...."

"I'll destroy her and then we'll be to—"

I put my finger gently on his lips and spoke softly. "Please hear what I'm saying. I'll support you with my whole heart. But tonight we're together, and I need you. I need to be yours in every way possible." I leaned in and kissed him, my arms around his neck, my brain shutting down as my body warmed up. I moved away and smiled at my handsome mate. "I need you to cave," I teased him, wondering if he'd remember his little speech when I'd first moved into his lovely home.

His expressive eyes were starting to darken, glistening with silver sparks like the stars I'd wished on as a sad child. Leaning closer, he whispered next to my ear, "You shine like an angel in the moonlight, and I would never refuse my angel anything." His smile had turned wicked, my heartbeat quickening like a rabbit's. My toes curled up when he grabbed a handful of my hair and drew me in for another kiss.

"Not feeling too angelic at the moment," I managed to pant out before the next kiss scrambled my brain and set my body on fire.

He led me into his bedroom with the huge bed and satin sheets, moonlight streaming in through the large windows. We stopped when we reached the foot of the bed and he took the band out of my hair, letting my blonde waves fall across my shoulders. He held me tightly against him, his whisper husky. "I've never brought a woman to this bed. I want tonight to be perfect for you." Through our connection, I felt his desire but also his fear that he'd hurt me.

I took a step away so he could see my face. "I trust you." It was a simple statement, but it meant more to both of us than we could ever put into words. I hoped he believed me, because I *did* trust him. I trusted him with my body, my mind and my heart, even though I was scared that I wouldn't be enough. The only experience I'd had being intimate… I shook off the memory of that boy. I was in my lover's arms and I was his tonight, and he was mine.

I smiled and smoothed my hand across his chest. "You are my dark angel." He chuckled at the name. "That's what you looked like to me when I first saw you at the cabin on Solo Island."

Enjoying the name, he grinned and translated, "*Mon ange sombre.*"

When he slid a hand under my shirt at my lower back and pushed my body against his, I almost stopped breathing. He kissed my hair, my ear, my neck, my collarbone then brushed his lips back up to my mouth where he kissed me hard, his fangs tugging at my lower lip when we finally pulled apart.

"*Je t'aime, mon ange.*"

In the silver glow of the moonlight we undressed each other, crawling into bed to love and laugh and deepen our commitment. The magic of the lines pulsed with the rhythm of our lovemaking, connecting our spirits and enhancing our pleasure. Garrett made love to me with a gentle skill and an urgent passion, and all bad memories dissolved with every kiss and tender touch. We fell asleep utterly content: two lovers, two rogues.

CHAPTER THIRTY-SEVEN

I WOKE UP IN MY OWN BED, ALONE BUT relaxed and glowing with pleasure. Stretching languidly, I took the time to remember each precious moment from the previous night. Now I was his mate in every way possible, so when I jumped in the shower, I found myself humming a song and making a fool of myself as I did a silly happy dance. If I had anything to say about it, this was going to become my morning ritual.

After dressing and drying my hair, I went looking for Liam. He was sitting on the patio reading what looked like a very old book with a thick leather cover, written in a strange language I didn't recognize. Liam put the book down as I walked outside to join him.

His mouth turned up in a small smile when I sat across from him. "Your aura is a more vibrant emerald. Your support empowers your mate. Eleanor will have a very difficult fight on her hands, especially now that you have bonded physically."

Liam always got right down to the essence of things. I tried very hard not to blush and changed the subject. "I can't help him during the duel, can I?"

"No, but you have done much already. You give him faith and a reason to win. He has always had the ability, but not always the confidence or the motivation." I felt a nudge on my wall, so I opened to Liam, curious as to why he wanted to converse mind to mind.

"*Jacqueline Crawford, I would like to offer you my assistance in learning to use the magic of the ley lines and the powers with which you have been gifted. I must tell you that if you accept my offer, you may not speak of our work together to anyone except Garrett. This will be a serious agreement between us and if our secrecy is breached, then death may result. An agreement of this kind with a seelie fae is a magical binding and not something to take lightly.*"

I held my expression in check, but my heart was racing with fear and excitement. "*May I ask why you're offering me this astonishing gift? I don't mean to be disrespectful, but I can't make a decision without knowing.*"

"*I am a warrior, but also a healer, just as you are both. My mother is human, my father, a fae elder, a royal, the first-born son of the former King of Faerie. Maintaining a balance of power between the supernatural world and the human world is important to me. If you are trained correctly, you will naturally work toward this end as well. It has been clear from the beginning that your innate instincts are to heal and not to fight. Maya and Garrett are great warriors, but not healers, and understandably, they can only see the world from their perspective. If you are trained solely by them, you may not retain your balance. That could be a dangerous thing for you and our two worlds.*"

"*You mean I could cross over to the dark side?*" I laughed but saw quickly that Liam wasn't amused at all. "*Please forgive me. This is all so new.*" I switched gears. "*How long would this training last?"*

"We could set our initial agreement to last for no more than three cycles of the moon, six hours per week. I would be your teacher and would expect your focus and your compliance during our training sessions, even when the work is difficult. Our relationship outside of those six hours would be as it has been, Miss Jacqueline." He smiled. Somehow I knew he wouldn't be addressing me that way during our lessons.

He sat quietly while he waited for my response. I'd be an idiot not to agree, but I had no experience with the fae. The amount of magic that surrounded him on a daily basis was staggering. He was probably more dangerous than Garrett, Eleanor, and her entire nest put together.

In the end it was his long-term loyalty to Garrett that convinced me. He wanted to help us. *"I accept your offer. How do we seal this agreement?"*

"With magic."

Oh. Big surprise there.

He grabbed my hand and led me quickly over the patio and into the woods. We walked down a path I'd traveled several times in the past week, but it looked nothing like what I remembered. Instead of the usual conifers and oaks, trees with shining white trunks and iridescent leaves that looked like tiny fingers framed the narrow lane. Instead of the usual pine needles, flower petals covered the ground, their movement beneath our bare feet filling the air with a pungent bouquet.

I was pretty sure I'd been wearing flip flops in the kitchen.

We came to a lovely clearing where a gently flowing stream was fed by a golden waterfall, the sound of the moving water making a glorious music. Where was this place? Was this Faerie? I found myself too awed to ask a question, afraid that the sound of my voice would shatter this beautiful illusion.

As if he'd read my mind, he answered. "We're in a sacred place in your world, where fae magic is strong." Liam's golden hair floated around his head in a wondrous manner, his eyes glittering like violet diamonds. I felt lightheaded, as if I'd fallen down the rabbit hole, so he seated me on the banks of the stream and sat next to me.

He sang a few short phrases in an exquisitely beautiful language and I lost myself in his music and his eyes and his spirit. It took me a moment to realize he was speaking in English again. "Jacqueline Crawford, by magic, do you agree to be trained by me, Liam, Son of Caelen, to use the power of the ley lines and to keep this secret from all but your mate, Garrett?"

"I agree."

A rune-covered goblet appeared out of nowhere, filled with glistening, rainbow-colored water from the stream. He offered it to me and I drank without hesitation, certain it would be the most delicious water I'd ever tasted. And it was even more: the finest wine, the sweetest juice, the most powerful potion. Gold sparkled in his eyes as he watched me drink greedily, only taking the goblet away when he felt I'd had enough. He downed what was left and I stared at his throat as he swallowed, annoyed he'd denied me the rest.

The goblet disappeared and he looked at me curiously. "Not many non-fae can drink more than a few sips."

"I was so thirsty."

He laughed and suddenly we were standing on the patio behind Garrett's house. I automatically looked down, delighted to see my flip flops cushioning my feet once more. "We begin tomorrow at noon." He nodded in the fae manner and turned away to continue his work in the garden as if nothing out of the ordinary had happened. I pulled up some power and watched the tendrils of rainbow colored energy still spiraling around him. I had to admit, Liam was spooky, especially outside of Garrett's house. I could only imagine what kind of power he pulled in when he was battling an enemy.

Still feeling the effects of the potion, I smiled goofily. Liam's scent, which somehow covered me, was exotically fragrant and enticing. I shook my head to clear my mind and walked inside quickly. Coffee should help.

CHAPTER THIRTY-EIGHT

I SAT DOWN TO A SMALL BOWL OF CEREAL AND a cup of coffee, not feeling very hungry, even though I hadn't eaten since last night's dinner. Still, it was probably a good idea to put some real food in my stomach. The amount of fae magic I'd ingested made every nerve-ending tingle in a very pleasant way. Plus all my usually acute senses were going into sensory overload.

A few spoonfuls of cereal and sips of coffee later, I began to have second thoughts. Maybe what I'd done wasn't so smart after all. It wasn't drinking the potion that bothered me—I trusted that Liam wouldn't poison me. It was that I'd just made a binding agreement with a fae. A fae of the royal house. A kick-ass powerful fae.

I'd signed off on an agreement that could get me killed if I messed up. *Holy crap.*

Garrett wasn't going to be happy. Liam had enticed me with his purple eyes and floating golden hair and his adorable smile. Garrett trusted him with his life and I was growing to like him too, but Liam was dangerous in a way I couldn't quite grasp. What was his true motivation? I sighed in frustration.

I couldn't take it back now, so I was going to have to trust that Liam truly meant to help me.

After breakfast I got my mind off of things by calling Carly to see how she was doing, then Sinc to plan a possible lunch date. Still feeling buzzed from Liam's magic, I decided to go out for a run along the beach. I called Rob and he joined me, his long legs keeping pace fairly well, especially since I couldn't run full out with humans in the area. We chatted as we ran, and I was happy to hear that many shifters had agreed to help the team if it became necessary.

After dropping Rob off at his house, I found Garrett sitting at the desk in his study working at his computer. When he saw me, he reached out and pulled me into his lap.

"Any regrets?" he whispered as he nuzzled my ear.

I gave him a gentle kiss at the corner of his mouth. "Last night was perfect."

"For me too." He took a sniff and his eyes widened. "I smell fae. Liam?" His eyebrows arched in curiosity.

I swallowed. "I kind of … have to tell you something. I hope you won't get upset." He waited patiently. "You absolutely can't tell anyone else, okay? Please, you have to promise me."

He nodded. "I promise." He didn't seem angry, but I hadn't actually told him anything yet.

"Today Liam offered to train me in how to use the ley lines. He said I could only tell you, on pain of possible death. The agreement is for three months, six hours a week. He took me down the path out back; only it looked nothing like it does normally. We drank some kind of water that was infused with fae magic."

This time I waited. And waited. He was pissed. I knew the signs. *"And you didn't think that I should have shared in a decision that could theoretically cause your death?"* His eyes darkened. Not a good sign.

"Wait a minute!" I said out loud, and then switched back to mind speech. *"Who just announced last night that he was fighting a duel to the death with a vicious vampire without consulting me first? I'm trying to be a grownup here. This is to help you and the team. I have a sneaky suspicion that Liam's class isn't going to be an easy A."*

"The fae rarely do anything without getting something in return. What did you promise him?"

"Nothing, really. He asked for my compliance when he was teaching me and he said our relationship the rest of the time would be the same as always. He wouldn't force me to do anything…evil…would he?"

"Liam has been loyal to me for over a century and I trust him completely. He'd never harm you. But the fae are a strange collection of beings. He'll use you if it suits him."

"So I messed up?" I glanced at his face to see if he was still angry. *"Again?"*

"No, but be aware. What you see is a handsome young male with perfect manners and a warm smile. But he kills as viciously as any vampire, and he's more powerful than all the other supes put together. The fae are made of magic. And Liam is an unusual case."

"Unusual, in what way?"

"Until he came to me, Liam had spent fourteen hundred years in Faerie, only venturing out to do battle with supernatural enemies. He'd had absolutely no contact with humans, except for his mother, who may as well be fae at this point, and very little normal contact with other supernatural groups. This is common for his people.

"Now that he's spent a century with me, he's fascinated by other races. He wishes to learn as much as he can about how others live and work and love. Having you here must be like a dream come true for him."

"He's fond of you."

Garrett smiled. *"Like Rob, he's a brother to me. Just do me a favor and don't make any more magical bargains without discussing it with me first."*

"He wants to help me because he thinks it will help you win."

"Oh, so you think you understand his motives after knowing him for … um, how many days has it been?"

"I understand more than you think." I pouted.

"A terrifying thought," he teased back. He lifted my wrist to his nose and spoke out loud in his sexiest voice, "Are you going to share?"

"Share what?" I teased, grinning.

"The fae magic." He grazed my wrist with his fangs.

"What happened to 'I'll never drink from you unless you offer it?'"

"I'm asking nicely." He kissed up my arm, ending at my earlobe, which he nibbled.

"Very nicely. Unfair tactics." I pulled my wrist away playfully. "I was on my way to take a shower when you accosted me."

He grinned in that boyish way I loved and stood, pulling me up with him. "Accosted you?" His voice lowered an octave. "Would you like to be accosted? That can be arranged."

"I've created a monster." I giggled.

"My desk…." He arched a questioning eyebrow.

"Wicked male. I need a shower." I spoke firmly, even though his desk did look inviting.

"Great idea." His grin was all mischief and heat.

His hair was damp. "Didn't you just take a shower?"

"I might have missed a spot. You can't be too clean." He leaned in and whispered, "If you're lucky, I might wash your back. I'm very good at it."

"I'll just bet you are." Without another word, Garrett scooped me up and carried me to his huge shower where we played and loved together. He washed my back and shampooed my hair and in return, I shared the fae blood.

Later, after a yummy dinner of lasagna that Liam had left for me, we sat in front of the fire wrapped in each other's arms. I watched the reflection of the flames dancing in his glowing eyes, filled with energy and excitement as he described a funny adventure he'd shared with his cousin Aaron when they were kids. Aaron had been a wild child and the story was a good one.

As he spoke about his past and the things he enjoyed in his life today, I came to realize in so many ways Garrett was my peer. He was a healthy young guy who liked to listen to music, drive his car fast and surf the net. When he had the time, he'd watch sports on TV, talk with me about the environment or the latest book he was reading. I'd forget for an hour or so what he was. But then, something would happen and he'd grow angry or worried or very, very still. I'd notice he wasn't breathing, or his eyes were filling up with silver or his skin was like ice. Those moments still shocked me. It didn't change the way I felt about him, but it kept me on my toes.

It was midnight when we both became aware of another presence nearby. Garrett was instantly in battle mode, his fangs and eyes sharp. I pulled on the lines, arming myself as well as I could, standing behind him so he'd have room to maneuver.

"*Eleanor,*" he sent to me just as someone knocked. "Who is it?" he asked out loud, sounding perfectly calm.

"It's Eleanor, dear. You know it's me. You must let me in." The last was an order, spoken with the influential magic of a four hundred year old vampire.

Garrett sent to me, "*Don't allow her over the threshold. If we can keep her out, we're safe. If not, change and run like the wind. Do NOT argue. I've put in a mental call to Liam. He'll be waiting in the woods to help you escape, if necessary."*

"*I understand.*" I was trembling, but still level-headed enough to reinforce my shield.

Garrett opened the door, prepared to attack if she got past him. Her steely gaze took me in with a hint of amusement.

"The house is mine." I was surprised by how steady my voice sounded.

"Invite me in, dear." The pull was magnetic, urging me to give in and act the perfect host, at least until she eviscerated me. My shields were wavering. I took a tiny step closer.

Garrett sent, *"It's a trick, Jackie, she'll act sweet, then she'll eat you for dinner."* I pulled in more power and snapped out of her spell.

"Sweet little cheetah, you want me to come into your home, don't you?" She spoke again with Influence.

Only this time—nothing. "Not really, Eleanor."

She glared at me then, realizing her glamour had stopped working. "You're strong and very pretty. Of course Garrett wouldn't mate with just anyone, not after he'd been with me."

"He's mine now." I smiled meaningfully, one woman to another, making it clear Garrett was mine in every way. Garrett backed toward me with caution, putting an arm around my waist. I leaned against him and smiled, trying not to look as terrified as I felt.

He scowled, allowing some fang to emerge. "What do you want, Eleanor?"

Eleanor's eyes darkened dangerously. "Come to the villa and bring the cheetah so we can all play together. I won't make a coat out of her, at least not right away."

He fought against her control with all his strength, his hands clenching in anger and his face grim as they battled mind to mind. Pulling in power, I touched his arm and sent him a strong wave of my healing energy. Eleanor's eyes widened in surprise as his muscles slowly relaxed and he regained his control. He put his hand over mine. "I'm never coming back to you."

She was livid. "I'm your maker. Your Mistress."

"I will never refer to you as Mistress. You killed my family and tortured me, forcing me to become a monster like you. You don't deserve my respect."

She glowered. "If you don't come to me, I'll kill your healer bitch. I'll make her death last a long time. She'll scream and bleed and beg and I'll enjoy every second. And when I'm bored, I'll give her to Lily or perhaps Antoine. Lily has such a wonderful imagination, doesn't she? Antoine would be more brutal."

Her gaze grew feral, making it crystal clear the pain and suffering of others fed her dark spirit just as the blood taken from innocents fed her body. She was completely turned on by her violent vision of my painful death. I found her repulsive and pathetic and I lost my fear and grew angrier, thinking about all the innocents she'd murdered. "I'm not afraid of you."

"Then you're very foolish, child."

Garrett took a step forward and spoke to her with a clear voice. "Eleanor Howard, my—Maker." He couldn't conceal the disgust he felt when he used the title. "I challenge you to a duel to the death on Solo Island one week from tonight at midnight."

A slow, evil smile spread across her face as she realized his mistake. "I eagerly accept your challenge, foolish Garrett, but who is your second?" Her voice dripped with menace.

Garrett hesitated, then said, "Robert...."

"Robert is not here, and according to our laws, your second must be here when the challenge is made. Antoine will be my second." The bald vamp I'd seen with Lily appeared next to her. He smiled at me with the same disturbing hunger I'd witnessed before and I couldn't stop myself from shivering.

"*Shit!*" Garret was furious with himself. He'd made a serious tactical error and was probably thinking he'd blown the whole deal.

"I'm his second." I was livid and in no mood to put up with anymore of her crap. Eleanor's smile was triumphant.

I felt Garrett tense and turn to face me, holding my arms tightly enough to bruise. "*You are NOT my fucking second. Antoine will challenge you and he's as powerful as I am. You are not putting your life on the line because I made a stupid mistake.*"

He was frightened for me and honestly, so was I, but I narrowed my eyes and made him listen. "*I can take him. He can't use the lines like a cheetah and he can't shift form. He's a powerful vampire, I'm sure, but I'm much more than a vampire. I'm a cheetah shifter, a magical warrior. Most importantly I'm your mate, which makes me stronger still. I have a week to get ready. Maya will train me and I'll have twelve hours with Liam under my belt. I trusted you when you decided to challenge her, so trust me. I can do this.*" I hid every ounce of terror tightly behind my wall so all he would feel was my confidence.

Eleanor asked, "Is the precious little cheetah your second? If not, then the challenge is null and you'll not get another opportunity." She was leaning against Antoine, tracing one of his tattoos with her sharp nails, leaving behind a trail of blood. He'd snaked his arm around her waist, pulling her closer, obviously enjoying Eleanor's creepy attentions.

Garrett was stuck. Many would die if he didn't go through with the duel. If he did, I might die, and he couldn't bear that. But I might die either way. "*Tell her I'm your second,*" I urged, hoping he'd say it before I lost my courage.

I watched his fists clench and his jaw tighten as he warred within himself. Finally he made a decision. "Yes." He took in a deep breath. "Yes. Jacqueline Crawford is my second."

"Antoine, now." Eleanor turned to watch my reaction as Antoine said in a husky, accented voice, "Jacqueline Crawford, I challenge you to a duel to the death which will take place immediately before the duel of Eleanor and Garrett one week from today." His voice was deep and gravelly, his sharp fangs still glistening from his recent feeding.

I wouldn't let them see my fear. "I accept your challenge, Antoine. Bring it on." He glared and hissed, looking quite ferocious with his arm muscles bunching up and his fangs poking out. Beside me, Garrett blew out a frustrated sigh at my bravado. He obviously thought I should be taking this much more seriously. Oh yeah, I was scared shitless, but I also felt a tinge of joy, glad I'd be more than just a bystander on the day my mate destroyed his enemy.

"Next Saturday at midnight, Garrett, I will rip out your throat. But first Antoine will drain and torture your juicy little cheetah while you watch. Until then, my dear, au revoir." They disappeared, leaving behind the scent of rotten blood, their laughter dying in the distance.

I closed the front door and turned back toward the room. Garrett had lowered himself onto the couch and was staring into the fire, his eyes flat, his skin looking even paler than normal. His hands were trembling slightly from pent up tension, so I crouched down next to him and held them in mine. They were so cold.

His mental standoff with Eleanor must have wiped out any benefit he'd gained from our activities earlier in the evening. "Feed. You'll be able to think more clearly." I was trying to be practical, but he kept staring straight ahead, not really hearing me. I tried to reach into his mind but his walls were up and he wouldn't let me in. I was getting worried.

"Garrett, you need to feed now." I shook him but he still wasn't responding.

Crap! I crawled into his lap, took a breath and forced healing energy into him. "I'm going to be really pissed off, if you don't start taking my magic. I don't like cuddling with an iceberg." His expression changed as he started to pull in energy. I snuggled into his chest and closed my eyes allowing the floating sensation to take over my body, hoping this would be enough to bring him back to himself.

A few moments later, he stroked my hair. "I'm so sorry, my love. I've made an enormous mistake and now you're in terrible danger. I tried to protect you by challenging her and now you're—"

"Glad I have a chance to help you. To help everyone. I want to do this."

"Jacqueline…."

"Stop beating yourself up. Liam and Maya will teach me everything I need to know to take down this asshole." He looked skeptical. Couldn't really blame him. "Have a little faith. I'm gonna channel Buffy."

When Garrett started to laugh, I joined him. "Does that make me Angel?" he asked.

"Depends on the season." I tried unsuccessfully to suppress the yawn. He picked me up effortlessly and took me to my bed where we cuddled and allowed our fear for each other to drift away with each sweet kiss. I fell asleep in his strong, loving arms, my favorite place in the whole world.

CHAPTER THIRTY-NINE

THE NEXT SIX DAYS FLEW BY IN A FLURRY OF activity. Garrett would rise around three o'clock and take off for the island with Rob and Ethan. They were setting up traps and defenses in case things got out of hand and the vampires decided to forget the rules of the duel and attack us all. They also spent time training the twelve or so shifters who'd volunteered to fight. Garrett usually didn't get back until around midnight, so any alone time we could squeeze in was precious.

Sinc and Kyle spent days in the lab hunched over computers and experimental weapons. I had training sessions with Liam every morning at nine.

"Jacqueline, I will train you to use magic to move like a vampire, faster than a human can see. This will be your best defensive weapon against Antoine because he will never expect it. But you must use it sparingly, two or three times at the most, as it will drain your energy and make you weak. When you've mastered this, we will move on to your offense."

Because of my upcoming duel with Antoine, Liam had agreed to train me every day this week, so we worked together for two-hour sessions. At the end of each one, I collapsed into bed and slept for another hour, always waking up completely famished. Liam would have food prepared and waiting for me and would usually keep me company while I ate.

"You are doing well," he would say, "but there is much more to learn." I'd nod in understanding, eat what he put in front of me and take a few seconds to wish Garrett would hold me for a while. The closer to the duel we got, the more I felt I was in over my head.

Maya would show up later in the afternoon, never friendly but always professional. The first two days were spent on defensive maneuvers to divert projectile weapons as one weapon for each combatant was allowed in the ring. Psychic cutting, pushing and throwing were next. She'd always bring a couple of shifter volunteers who were frightened at first, but who started to trust me when they saw I felt worse than they did about hurting them. Plus I was getting much better at the healing part, which helped all of us relax.

Two days before the duel, Maya arrived with four shifters instead of the usual two. "Today we're going to work on using your mind to drain Antoine's energy. Liam is going to supervise because this isn't one of my areas of expertise. It's probably a good thing. There'd be a few very weak ex-boyfriends walking around town if I had your skill." I laughed, but she didn't bat an eye.

Liam and Maya showed me how to darken my aura and create a void, then described how to pull in an enemy's energy to fill it up, turning it emerald green again. Since my brave volunteers had no psychic connection to the magic, I needed to touch them in order for the drain to work. I realized this must be similar to what Garrett did when he fed from his shifters, and I hoped as I practiced, that the volunteers were feeling the pleasant floating sensation and not anything painful.

When the volunteers left, Maya spoke to me in her serious way. "I'll be at the duel. I don't mean to add to your stress, but for Garrett to have the strength to win against Eleanor, you need to beat Antoine. The Shifter Council has decided that Crescent City needs you. This is your last official lesson with me, but you are always welcome to call me with questions."

A glimmer of respect shown in her eyes, probably all I'd get in the way of encouragement. She nodded and left, still looking twenty after two hundred years as a shifter. I heard a noise and turned, surprised to see Garrett standing in the doorway, up a little earlier than usual. I ran to him, holding him tightly, trembling from a combination of tension and exhaustion.

"Liam and Maya have been working you hard, but they wouldn't bother if they didn't feel you were capable. You've earned their respect." He lifted my chin and kissed both of my tired eyes. "You're working too many hours. I'm worried about you."

"You're working non-stop on the island and getting up earlier every afternoon. How can I do any less?"

He took my hands, an excited gleam in his eye. "Let's take off tonight, just the two of us. We'll take my boat out and watch the sunset. I know a private cove where we can drop anchor away from the world. We'll spend the night on the water and sail back before dawn." After giving Garrett an excited hug, I and ran off to pack a few things for the sail. Garrett made several short phone calls and we were ready to go.

We sailed out of the harbor at five in the evening on his thirty-five foot sloop named *Spotted Lady*. Garrett showed me how to tie off the lines and crank up the sails and even trusted me to steer, once we were in open water. The rocking motion of the boat was so peaceful I fell asleep outside on a cushioned bench, only to feel Garrett kissing me awake and laughing a little when I clung to his mouth like Velcro as he tried to pull away. We let the wind guide us south as we enjoyed a glass of wine and watched the sun go down over the Pacific, the glorious streaks of pink, orange and gold our own private Impressionist painting. In the twilight, Garrett turned us back toward the coast, maneuvering the sloop into a quiet cove and anchoring in a secluded spot where we could be alone.

I'd watched him as he'd worked around the boat, bringing down the sails, steering into the inlet, stowing equipment, and releasing the anchor. He seemed truly happy, adding to my own inner glow. The strain of the last five days, so evident in our faces a few hours ago, had drifted slowly away along with the ocean currents. When he'd finished his captain's duties, he sat next to me, one long arm over my shoulder, his fingers playing with my hair.

Now was as good a time as ever. "What's the third part of the mating ritual for vampires?"

"The third part is of no concern."

"Why? You've decided you don't want me? Am I too much trouble?" Since our lives had turned so serious, I particularly enjoyed these rare playful moments.

He smiled. "*Ma petit provocateur, My little troublemaker.* You're the kind of trouble I will always want to sink my teeth into." He nibbled on my ear and as usual, my heartbeat raced.

"Answer my question please, Monsieur."

"Or?"

I narrowed my eyes. "Or I will torture it out of you."

His voice lowered. "There's some torture that's quite delightful."

"Then it isn't torture."

"I assure you, it is." Now he was laughing at me.

"You've changed the subject, but I won't be put off. Please

tell me."

He sighed. "Eleanor would have to approve my 'selection' and drink your blood. She'd use a knife to cut a small wound into our skin in a pattern of our choice and it would leave a matching scar, similar to a tattoo."

"What? Did you say Eleanor cuts us? And drinks my blood?" I shook my head in confusion.

"I tried to explain. It's of no concern because she'll be dead soon."

"How do we complete the ritual if she's dead?"

"Eleanor has a maker, Francois. He's much older and much more reasonable. He's in town to support me at the duel. I'll speak to him about it."

"You've never mentioned him before. Do you speak to him often?"

"I contact him at least once a month. He lives in Paris."

"And have you told him about me?"

"Yes, and he's quite happy for us. When Eleanor murdered my family and turned me, he punished her severely. Francois called it an immoral act, although it wasn't theoretically against vampiric law."

"Too bad he didn't kill her," I grumbled. Unsure, I reached to touch his hand. He smiled and wove his fingers between mine. "Why can't we just do the shifter's version of the ritual? You used to be a shifter."

"Unfortunately, the shifters wouldn't agree. To them I'm a vampire, and as antiquated as the idea seems, the ritual that's performed is according to the male's race, not the female's."

"And Francois is really okay with us?"

He stood and pulled me to my feet. "I didn't bring you out on the boat, under the stars to talk about Eleanor or Francois." He nuzzled my ear, kissing in a line down my cheek and neck.

I'd leaned my head back to give him better access. "Why

did you bring me here?"

He cradled my face in his hands and kissed me with a passion I'd only dreamed about. His desire for me was as clear as the night, as mine was for him. I used my flattened palms to brush over the broad plains of his chest, continuing down to his firm abs. He made a contented sound, so I did it again.

"I wish to forget for a few hours—to lose myself in your arms. I need you tonight." He kissed me urgently and I opened to him, pulling in magic and mixing it with desire and love. It was a potent brew, which carried us below deck. We spent the next precious hours as he'd predicted: banishing our fears and strengthening our sweet connection. Sharing our bodies and our blood worked its magic, because as we sailed back to the Crescent City Marina, Garrett and I were feeling almost carefree.

CHAPTER FORTY

ROB WAS SITTING ON OUR STOOP LOOKING grim when we got back to the house. It was two hours before dawn. "Carly's been murdered. A witness described a male coming out of Carly's driveway. The description fit Antoine perfectly. I'm sure he wanted to be identified, otherwise he would have escaped using vamp speed. Carly was beaten and drained. Samson was knocked unconscious."

Garrett reached out for my hand. "Have you called her family?" he asked, draping his arm around my shoulders when he felt me start to tremble.

"Yes. They've asked me to tell you the service will be held at Trinity Chapel on Sunday evening."

"Is the rest of the team safe?"

"Yes, I've given everyone else a heads up. They're all staying the night with Peter and Kyle. Fortunately, their house is warded." Rob looked toward the SUV. "However, there's another rather large problem needing immediate attention."

"What?" Garrett

"Samson doesn't get along with anyone except you, Jackie. Carly's family doesn't want him and he doesn't like me either. I don't want to take him to the pound."

"I'll take him." I looked at Garrett pleadingly as tears continued to chase each other down my cheeks. He dabbed at them gently with his shirttail.

"Yes, we can take him. He seems to tolerate me fairly well and no dog can resist Liam. Carly would be happy to know Jackie has him. Not too sure about me, though." He shook his head sadly.

"She'd want him to be cared for. He'll be happy here with us. Where is he?" I glanced around.

"In my truck." Rob tossed me the keys. Samson started to whine pitifully as soon as I got close.

I could hear Garrett's angry tone as he spoke to Rob. "This is obviously part of Eleanor's strategy. She wants to break our concentration before the duel. Also, Antoine got a good dose of two-hundred-year-old shifter blood." Garrett was pacing back and forth. "I don't think there's much we can do about it. It'll be up to Jackie to avenge Carly."

They both looked at me with concern as I walked back holding Samson by his leash. "Do you think he needs a vet?" I couldn't see any obvious wounds as I crouched to give him a hard squeeze around the neck. His enormous tongue laved my cheek. I giggled, which was totally inappropriate, but neither of the guys seemed to think so.

"No, he wasn't hurt. The big brute has a hard head. But he's going to miss her terribly." The renewed vision of Carly beaten and drained brought on another crying spell in Garrett's arms while Samson lay at my feet, his huge head resting on his paws. Rob returned to his car and brought out Samson's bowls, food, blanket, and toys, and carried them to our door. We filed in and Rob put Samson's few possessions on the floor in the living room.

"I'll call you in the afternoon. I'm sorry you had to hear about Carly like this." Rob left, his face tired and drawn.

We put water in one of Samson's bowls and a little dry food in the other and left them in the kitchen. Garrett and I decided to let Samson sleep in my room this morning, thinking he might be more comfortable if he wasn't alone. We laid his blanket on the floor by the foot of my bed and put one of his toys near it. He settled in and seemed to make himself comfortable, although his eyes looked so sad. We left a note for Liam explaining about the dog and that I would probably not make my lesson at nine. I changed into pajamas and dragged Garrett into bed with me, desperately needing to cuddle up and feel safe in his arms while we mourned the loss of a gentle spirit.

CHAPTER FORTY-ONE

I WOKE IN THE AFTERNOON AROUND ONE. Samson was sprawled across the foot of my queen-sized bed taking up a whole lot of room. I scratched him behind the ears and he wagged his little stubby tail, perhaps trying to make the best of being handed over to people he hardly knew. I could so relate to that. "Good boy. We'll all miss her, but we'll take very good care of you. I promise."

I jumped in the shower, dressed in jeans and a tank top, and went out to see what Liam was up to. He was working in Garrett's office. I plopped myself down in a nearby armchair.

He smiled. "Good afternoon, Miss Jacqueline. I am very sorry to hear the news about your good friend, Carly. She is gone long before her time. Terribly young."

What was it like to be so old that two hundred and thirty-three is considered terribly young to die? "Thanks Liam," I answered. "I'm still in shock."

"Miss Jacqueline, you must train today."

"Yes, of course, *Sensei*." The corners of his mouth twitched at my feeble attempt at a joke.

"There's food on the stove. Please eat something. We have

much to do."

After dishing out the homemade chicken soup Liam had prepared, I sat at the kitchen table. Samson trotted into the kitchen and lay down at my feet, looking at me with those large, sad eyes. I petted his head.

"Do you need anything, Samson? Do you want to go outside? He wagged his little stubby tail. Before I could open the sliding glass door to the patio, Liam was there, crouching by the dog and speaking to him in his musical language. Samson seemed enthralled, then barked a few times as if they were carrying on a conversation. After a few minutes, Liam walked back inside. To my horror, Samson had run off into the woods.

"What did you say to him?" I asked, a little unsure of what I'd just witnessed. "Should he be in the woods? What if he can't find his way back?"

"He knows what is off limits and what is permitted when he is in the backyard or the nearby woods. I've already explained the house rules to him. He's quite intelligent and will have no trouble finding the house again. He wishes to protect you above all others now Carly is gone. The beast has fae blood."

"Fae blood? I thought your people weren't shifters."

The look he gave me could have frozen the fountain. "The fae breed dogs just like humans do. They're used primarily to hunt our enemies. Their blood is infused with some of the magic of the lines. Samson is a descendant of one of those dogs."

Not much surprised me anymore. "Did you feed him?" His food bowl was empty.

"Yes, I made my own recipe. Much better than the store brand. The dry food will do for now." I managed to hold in a giggle and sat down again to finish my soup. The phone rang just as I swallowed the last bite. It was Sinc.

"How are you, Jackie? I've been thinking about Carly all day. She was always so sweet to Kyle and me. I hear you guys have taken Samson in."

"Yes. Liam is training him. It's a riot."

"Jackie, I just wanted to say ... well, we missed our shopping date but I still want to go sometime soon."

This was her way of saying she knew I'd still be around after tonight's duel. "Sure. Maybe next week. I'm kinda busy tonight." My feeble joke died when we both heard the anxiety in my voice.

"You'll blow him away." I didn't know what to say, so she continued. "Look, I know we started off a little rocky, totally my fault, but I'm glad you're part of the team."

"Me too. Thanks."

Liam supervised my normal routine. I stretched my body to warm up my muscles, drawing in and focusing the line magic, then using it in various ways. He wouldn't let me overexert myself, because the fight was tonight, but he insisted that I do everything he'd taught me at least twice. He also had me go over what I'd learned from Maya. We finished by discussing various attack scenarios and how best to handle them.

At the end of my final lesson, Liam stood and held out his hand to me. Since he rarely touched me I felt this was a great courtesy, so I took his hand and stood facing him. He looked so lovely, almost feminine, yet cloaked in a wild masculine strength. Magic surrounded Liam, permeating his aura with a golden fire. His hair floated around his head and his violet gaze pierced my green with shafts of tingling energy. My body trembled from the power flowing between us and I thought I could actually see the currents of the lines coursing through him the same way my blood flowed through my veins.

We were exactly the same height, so when he leaned in to kiss me, I only had to tilt my head a little and our lips were touching.

Suddenly, I became the magic too. Although my body remained standing in the kitchen, my spirit traveled inside lines of crackling force, my ghostly heart beating to the pulse of the power that enveloped us. I became one with the energy of life and death, because here time and place were meaningless. Liam's calm presence guided me over currents and through eddies of magic, limitless in scope as all boundaries fell away and I became everyone and everything and no one and nothing. My *self* was left behind and I was free.

Slowly, although it could have been centuries or a millisecond, I became aware again of his soft lips touching mine. He stepped back and smiled before I could speak. "Jacqueline, Antoine used violence to kill and drain Carly. Through blood magic, he has gained in strength. To counter him, I have given you a touch of fae magic, life magic, infusing it into every cell of your body. I offer this to you willingly, as a friend. Trust your instincts, remember your lessons, and yes, you may share with Garrett."

He smiled more broadly and said out loud. "I will be there watching." He stroked my hair once, then turned away and walked out the patio door, disappearing completely before he'd reached the edge of the woods.

Our kiss had been chaste, just lips touching, one of his hands holding mine, and no more. Yet I was amazed by the intimacy and the generosity of the gesture. Awed, I took a moment to breathe calmly and find my center. When I became aware of another presence, I looked to my right. Garrett was standing in the archway that led into the hall, leaning against the wall, a warm smile on his face.

"I think Liam has a crush on you." He laughed out loud, not exactly the reaction I expected.

"He gave me some of his magic for tonight."

Garrett took in a long breath. "I smell it all over you. You're a delicious morsel." He pulled me close to him and kissed me deeply, pricking my tongue with a fang and sucking in the fae magic and Liam's spell.

When he pulled away, a silver whirlpool spun in his eyes. He forced himself to back up a few feet to lean against the wall. I rested against the opposite wall breathing heavily, and we watched each other across the narrow hallway.

"Are you jealous he kissed me?" I wanted him to be.

"Yes, a little. But I'm also very turned on." His eyes ran over my body, heating me up in all the right places. "Unfortunately we have to restrain ourselves. If we show up totally depleted, it would be a grave misuse of the extraordinary gift he gave us."

"It was strange, because I'm not attracted to Liam. But when I was looking into his eyes and his hair was doing the spooky thing..." I wiggled my hands in the air, "...and he leaned in to kiss me, I leaned in too. I wanted the magic, not really him. And it wasn't like he glamoured me. It was completely my choice."

"Faerie mojo is powerful stuff." Garrett ran a hand through his hair—what I'd come to know as one of his nervous gestures. "Some people get addicted to it like a drug. And actually, he did glamour you. The fae are like that. If they feel it's justified, they just go ahead and do whatever they think is right. In this case, he did it to save your life, so I can't be angry with him."

"The fae must have lots and lots of babies." I laughed.

"They have lots and lots of sex, but very few babies. They have trouble conceiving, which is why they mate with humans or shifters once in a while, like with Liam's mother and father. The fact he's half human hasn't affected the extraordinary powers he's inherited from his father." His eyes narrowed in thought. "Perhaps his attraction to you has something to do with you being a healer."

"You know you have nothing to worry about don't you? I know you vamps get all territorial, but Liam didn't mean anything. He was trying to help us."

"Believe me I know exactly what Liam was doing and so does he." His expression turned serious and I could feel his uncertainty. "I'll never take you for granted. There are other men, like Liam, who would be good mates and wouldn't put your life in danger. I'll always have something to worry about."

I think my jaw dropped six inches. "And what? Do you really think I'm going to run off with someone else? Someone *safer*?" I was across the hallway in two steps. "Stop it, Garrett!" I grabbed his hands and squeezed them. "Please stop telling me you're not good enough for me. I don't want to hear it anymore. And don't insult me by imagining I'm using you while I wait for someone better to show up. There will never be anyone else. You are my heart and my soul. If my life is in danger, it's Eleanor's fault, not yours. I know the risks, but I've chosen to live my life with you. You say you can smell the truth? Well use your nose."

I took a step back and let go of his hands, suddenly realizing what I'd been doing. Green waves of energy were flowing from my body into his; trying to make him believe once and for all that I wanted with all my heart to be his lifemate. His aura was blazing a vibrant blue, his eyes wide with surprise.

Angry with myself, I backed away and ran through the patio doors and into the yard. The sun was setting and a pinkish glow was reflected on the marble fountain, drawing me there. I sat on the scrolled iron bench and listened to the water, breathing deeply to try and calm myself.

I was ashamed I hadn't been in control of my healing energy. This was exactly what Liam had warned me about. I didn't have the right to force my power into him, no matter how frustrated I was with his unfounded insecurities.

When I looked up, Garrett was standing in front of me, his eyes still dotted with silver. I spoke softly, but his hearing was sharp. "Maybe I'm the one who's not good for you. The healer in me takes over and tries to fix things. I think it was even stronger because of Liam's magic. I don't even know I'm doing it. I'm sorry."

He sank to his knees in front of me and wrapped his arms around my hips, laying his head in my lap. I hugged him and buried my face in his silken hair, wishing I could make my broken angel see he deserved to be happy. But instead of the pain I'd felt rolling off him a minute ago, his aura was bathed in joy.

"I believe you," he whispered so softly I could barely hear him. He lifted his head. "I believe you, Jackie." He spoke a little louder this time, cradling my face in his hands, so he could look into my eyes. "You've chosen me, as I've chosen you." His smile lit up his face and my heart.

I laughed. "You're pretty dense for a two-hundred-year-old guy." He laughed and kissed me playfully, gently biting my nose like his cheetah had all those days ago. "I'm your mate for all time, Garrett. Nothing can ever change how I feel." As I spoke, I jabbed my finger into his chest for emphasis. He covered my hand with his and held it there securely.

"Apparently I've done something in my life to deserve you, although what it was I can't imagine." He kissed me with passion, pulling me off the bench and onto my knees in front of him.

With a sigh, I leaned my forehead against his, then jerked away, a sudden epiphany slapping me upside the head. "Is Francois around? Can he come now?"

"I'll call him, but only if you're absolutely certain."

I laughed and nodded." Yes, I'm sure, just call him."

He pulled me to my feet, making the call that would alter our lives for all time. Fifteen minutes later a tall, extremely handsome vampire was at the door smiling at me. He took my hand in his and kissed it seductively. "It is a great pleasure to meet you, Jacqueline." He spoke with a sexy French accent, mischievously doing his best to work his glamour on me. Garrett had warned me Francois was an incorrigible flirt, but also he'd never step over the line with anyone who wasn't interested. I had a sneaky suspicion he was testing me, checking to see if I was worthy to mate with one of his line.

"Please come inside, Francois." He moved with perfect grace into the living room, turning to look back at us both. Appearing to be in his late twenties, he had that same charismatic seductive power Eleanor and Garrett possessed, and it didn't hurt that he was absolutely gorgeous, with dark blonde wavy hair, crystalline blue-gray eyes and the kind of broad shoulders women probably loved to wrap their arms around.

Garrett explained what we wanted and Francois burst out in laughter, his sparkling eyes glittering with excitement. "Eleanor will be enraged when she sees your mark. This is a perfect revenge. She's always wanted you for herself, exclusively, but you've made it obvious from the beginning that you loathed her. *Magnifique!*"

His expression turned serious as he sat gracefully in one of the armchairs, speaking in a voice tinged with the authority born of living over seven hundred years. "Stand before me please." Garrett took my hand, stilling my trembling as we faced Francois together. This ancient master vampire held our future in his hands.

He smiled at me with real warmth. "Of course I approve your choice in mate, Garrett. You are exquisite, Mademoiselle, and I can sense the depth of your power. It is quite unique."

I was able to feel him playfully nudge at my wall and I must have looked a little surprised before I remembered that Eleanor could use the line magic, too. "I am her maker, much to my chagrin. Older vampires are able to use the lines, but a well-trained cheetah can be a fearsome opponent. I prefer to defeat my enemies with my wits. I find it much more gratifying and less messy."

Garrett bowed slightly. "Thank you, Grandsire, for coming to help us with such short notice. You've always supported my efforts to distance myself from Eleanor. I know there have been times when your interventions have saved my life."

"You may repay my efforts by wiping the earth clean of that depraved bitch. I turned her at a vulnerable time. I take full responsibility for spoiling her in the beginning. She was so lovely, but her beauty turned sour as her true personality surfaced. I regret the havoc she's caused here in your lovely country."

His apologetic expression disappeared as he got back down to business. "Have you chosen a shape for your mark?" We handed him a sketch. He nodded his approval and produced a six-inch blade covered in beautiful etchings, spinning it around in his hand like an experienced wielder. He must have seen my expression because he shrugged and said, "One's survival depends on the ability to defend oneself in all circumstances. Tell Garrett to train you to use a blade. You may be surprised how useful the knowledge will be." He smiled at me. "So who will go first?"

It wasn't the most pleasant experience, but Francois was careful with his blade and his magic and I only cringed a little when he threw salt on the wound to prevent it from healing and disappearing as most scars do on a vampire and a shifter. Garrett had held my hand and smiled at me the whole time, kissing me when Francois was finished.

Then it was his turn, and after only a few minutes we were marked and sealed together forever. The final part of the ritual made me anxious because I wasn't too keen on Francois drinking my blood.

He must have seen my worried expression. "I will not take your blood, because you have a battle tonight that will require all your strength and resources, although I can smell the fae magic and it is quite tempting. You need to prepare for the duels, so I will leave you for now, but I will be on the island later and will help in any way I can." He kissed my forehead and patted Garrett's shoulder.

Feeling overwhelmed by his generosity, I hugged him. "Thank you Francois. You're always welcome here in our home." He looked a little surprised at first, but then laughed at my audacity.

"Not many shifters would have the courage to embrace a seven-hundred-year-old vampire, especially a shifter who smells as delicious as you do."

My face flamed with heat, but he lifted my chin gently with his fingertips and smiled. "*Trés charmante et trés courageuse. Bonsoir, Madame Cuvier, et merci.*" Francois walked to the door and turned back toward us. "You should share a bit of energy. It will add magic to the mark." He left in a blur, leaving behind the sweet smell of vampire along with a touch of fine wine.

I sighed and Garrett laughed at me. "He's…." I began, having trouble finding the right words.

"Yes, he is. Are you all right, my love?"

I looked at the mark on the top of my wrist, a place visible to everyone, and smiled, beckoning him to come closer. "I'm great, but I think we should follow his advice, don't you, Monsieur Cuvier?"

He grinned deliciously. "*Oui*, Madame Cuvier, I do, but

just a taste."

"Just a taste," I agreed. He kissed me oh so perfectly, drawing a drop of blood from my lips and also his, and for a wonderful moment we shared our life force as we'd pledged to share our lives. As we looped magic between us, we watched the shapes carved into our wrists take on color: mine emerald and Garrett's sapphire.

"I feel like I can beat five Eleanors right now."

He smiled his sexiest, most evil smile. "Eleanor is mine, my lovely cheetah, *mais Antoine est le tien.*" I didn't need to ask him to explain that he meant Antoine was all mine. Garrett's fangs had extended and his eyes had turned cerulean silver. He was ready to do battle.

I started to giggle. "Good thing there aren't any humans around 'cause you already look pretty terrifying. All you need is a Dracula cape."

"This reminds me, we're dressing up for the duel tonight. I've picked something special for you to wear."

"Let me guess, black leather?"

"No, that's for me. Yours is red."

CHAPTER FORTY-TWO

PPARENTLY, WHEN DUELING, IT WAS traditional among the vampires to wear something white. I guess so the spilled blood would brighten your outfit and add some entertainment value, or perhaps some reason equally macabre. For me, Garrett picked out skin-tight white leather pants plus a form-fitting red leather sleeveless tunic with a deep cut neckline. I surveyed my appearance in the mirror and had to laugh. I looked sexy as hell, but was this ideal for a battle? I went through some basic moves and found the lightweight leather moved beautifully with my body, plus nothing was dangling for Antoine to grab onto. I'd French braided my hair up and out of the way for the same reason. I wore boots, but would fight barefoot, my footwear of choice in a battle on sand. I could change my feet and hands to use my cheetah claws if necessary, but I prayed it wouldn't come to that.

Garrett knocked and walked in looking like a Renn Faire fan. He wore tight black leather pants and a loose white leather tunic with a black leather belt tied on the side. In his belt he carried a sheath holding a silver knife with an ivory-colored handle. Words were etched into the blade and the handle, but I didn't recognize the language.

"It belonged to my father. Even though the blade is silver, it's been warded so I don't feel its effects." He saw me looking at the writing. "The words are a curse upon the enemy of the knife bearer written in an ancient French language. It translates into something like, "May the enemies of the rightful bearer know the fire and the abyss."

"In other words, go to hell, Eleanor." I smiled at him, trying to ignore the tight knot forming in my stomach.

"Quite fitting don't you think?" He must have seen the fear in my eyes, because he tried to distract me. "You're perfect. My very own angel of death." He held me tightly, both of us realizing this could be our last moment alone. He whispered in his most reassuring voice. "We'll be home together again in a few hours, my love."

As we clung to each other, I selfishly hoped that if only one of us survived, it would be Garrett, because I wouldn't want to live my life without him. He grunted and turned us toward the front door. "The troops have arrived."

"Hey guys, we're here!"

I heard Sinc telling Ethan in a much softer voice, not to yell. It was just the two of them since Kyle had decided to travel over to the island early with Peter and Rob, planning on making sure everything was set up properly.

We joined them and made appreciative noises regarding each other's battle wear. Ethan and Sinc had chosen to wear loosely fitting clothing so they could fight or shift more easily if the duels went badly and the vampires decided to attack the spectators.

Garrett cocked his head. "Liam's in the kitchen. I think he'd like to speak to you." He smiled and squeezed my hand, then turned away to talk to the others. I walked tentatively into the kitchen.

Liam was dressed in royal blue and gold, looking very handsome in a fae kind of way. "Good evening, Jacqueline." He nodded. "I've brought you a weapon to use at the battle. This is only a loan. I must get it back from you after you've killed Antoine."

"I wasn't planning on using anything, Liam." We were allowed to bring one weapon of our choice to use during the duel. I'd decided against it because I wasn't trained to use weapons and I felt my ineptitude would distract me from the mental attacks I'd be dishing out. I saw a glimmer of disappointment in his eyes, so I remembered my promise about listening to his advice. "But if you think I should carry it, I will."

"I do." He smiled and pulled a shining metal blade from a sheath on his belt. Holding it reverently, he handed it to me hilt first. I took it from his hands and studied the elaborate etchings on the blade. The handle was made of some kind of strange stone, painted with various shapes and designs. They'd glowed with a golden fire in Liam's hands. I watched curiously as the etchings changed to green as I held it, the handle warming in my hand.

"It's beautiful, Liam."

"Already it tunes to your aura." He seemed very pleased. "Although it is a silver blade, forged with deadly Magiks, it has been warded for your safety. It will act according to your desires, wounding or killing. If you lose contact with it, the blade will come to you when you call to it, and it will never miss its target if your magic is well focused."

I felt a mental tug, urging me to look him in the eyes. They shone with a violet fire. "*It is crucial you do not wait until you are too tired to use it. It requires great mental strength.*" I looked a little leery. "*You do have the strength to wield it. You must trust yourself. I would never give you such a gift if this were not the case.*

I nodded solemnly. "Thank you, Liam." I glanced down at my sleek outfit. "Where can I wear it? I don't have a belt." My gaze remained locked on his as he untied his own belt and looped it around my waist, pulling it tight and fastening it in front. We stood only inches apart, breathing in each other's breaths. I could smell fae magic on his, as his hands worked deftly to secure the sheath. He positioned it perfectly and slid the knife in place. His hair brushed my cheek, and I stared at his lips, wanting so much to taste the magic one more time, to forget the duel and feel the freedom of the lines once more.

His voice whispered in my mind, his speech changing from formal to intimate. *"Jacqueline, I know it's the magic and not me you desire."* I blushed and stepped away but couldn't take my eyes from his. *"You're a remarkable female and many fae lords would take you to their beds and make you their Lady, but not me. You love Garrett. Your bond has been sealed and you're stronger now than ever before."*

He looked down at my wrist with its emerald green symbol and smiled, saying out loud, "Antoine and Eleanor will not see the next sunset. You'll use the blade wisely." He nodded with great formality, his hand on his heart, then turned and disappeared. Poof.

So I hadn't been hallucinating when he'd run into the woods before. Whoa. That must be some totally awesome way to travel. A moment later, Garrett was holding me and enjoying the smell of fae magic. I confessed, a little shocked at myself. "I almost kissed him again."

"You vixen," he laughed, playfully poking my ribs. "Liam would have politely pushed you away and probably scolded you for being greedy. I suspect he'll try to win you if I truly die in this duel. You're both healers and would make a good match for him. Your children would be powerful."

"I don't want Liam."

"I believe you."

"And I don't want children."

"Not now."

"Not ever, Garrett." I hurriedly changed the subject. "Did you know Liam can talk normally? I mean, using contractions and all?"

"Liam can speak hundreds of languages, so why wouldn't he be able to speak English the way we do? He does everything for a reason. If he sounds like a servant, then he's perceived as one and underestimated by our ignorant enemies." He brushed a hand through his hair, a sure sign of his tension. "Let's get to the island."

CHAPTER FORTY-THREE

THE FOUR OF US SAILED ACROSS THE channel in *The Spotted Lady*, tying up at the dock where Rob had kept his boat weeks before. We hiked along the path to an open area cleared of debris by volunteers, Garrett and I holding hands but not speaking. Maya, Sylvia, and Brad were standing by a large tent set up on the far side and we greeted them warmly.

Brad turned to me. "On Maya's recommendation you are officially welcome to join the shifter community of Crescent City. No further testing is necessary. Congratulations, Jackie." Brad held out his hand and I shook it, a little amused at the circumstances. If Antoine had his way tonight, I'd be the shortest-lived community member ever.

Garrett's cousin Aaron, his mate Catherine and his second in command, Franklin, had already arrived, along with ten other pack members. Aaron introduced us around, gave me a hug, and clapped Garrett on the back. "Cuz, you two attract trouble like a black hole sucks in galaxies." He laughed and winked at me. "You're perfect for each other." He gave me a good sniff. "Why do I smell fae magic?"

"We had a little help from a friend," Garrett said.

Now that I was here where the actual duels were going to take place, my mind and stomach had decided to torture me. An icy knot had formed low in my belly, expanding as each moment passed. *This might be the last time …* kept looping through my overloaded brain, as precious memories of my short time with Garrett dissolved, perhaps never to be recalled again. I sidled closer to my mate, not wanting to leave any space between us, needing his warmth to melt the cold dread.

"Nice matching tats," Catherine said. I looked up, surprised to hear conversations still continuing around me. Garrett squeezed my shoulder, sending, *"We'll survive this day, my love, and begin our life anew when our enemies are dead."* He raised my hand so everyone could admire our mating marks, but kept his arm tightly around my shoulders, as if he knew I needed the physical as well as the emotional support.

"Thank you." I'd managed to pull off a pretty good smile, despite my growing terror.

"Congrats, guys!" bellowed Aaron. He kissed me on the cheek while clasping Garrett's hand. "So when's the party? The holiday party you had a year and a half ago was awesome!"

"I had to replace three windows and several pieces of furniture," Garrett replied, giving him a playful shove.

"Wolves are enthusiastic, what can I tell you?" His grin was so much like Garrett's, they looked more like brothers than cousins, and even in these tense circumstances, I laughed at their antics. I wondered what they'd been like growing up together. The dynamics of their relationship was so much fun to watch. A part of me was envious. It would've been amazing to have a brother or a sister or even a cousin to confide in.

The thought of planning a party to mark our mating took my mind to a happier place and away from the duels. "We'll have a party next weekend, Aaron, and you're all invited." I'd included the rest of the pack, who thanked me and started talking and laughing about the last party and what had caused all the damage. Apparently one of the drunker wolves had been thrown through a window. *"We can have it somewhere outside,"* I sent to Garrett.

"Good plan." He hugged me and we heard a few awww's. I didn't mind at all.

I recognized other faces in the crowd: Peter and Kyle, Chloe, the waitress from the diner, Joe Rinaldi, our mechanic, and Denis, the gas station owner. Garrett introduced me to Elizabeth, a young woman who smelled like thyme. She grabbed my hands and said, "It's wonderful to meet you, Jackie. A healer in the community will be an enormous blessing. I've done what I can to protect you, but your auras are already very strong." She smiled and walked away.

"Let me guess. A witch?"

"Yes, a hedge witch. She's powerful without using dark magic."

Finally, after making their own rounds through the crowds, Ethan, Kyle, and Sinc made it back to us, followed closely by Rob. They hugged me and wished me luck, Ethan clinging to me the longest.

"You'll be great. Everything's set in case the vamps ignore the rules. Maya or Garrett will send you a signal." He kissed my cheek.

Maya got our attention. "You two can rest in the tent for a while. Eleanor and Antoine are expected to arrive within the next twenty minutes."

Garrett and I walked into the extremely large tent and eased our tense bodies down on the small couch I recognized from the cabin. Wordlessly we took in breath after breath of our combined scents as we wrapped our arms tightly around each other, lost in our own thoughts. It was warm and stuffy under the nylon roof, but I ignored the sweat beading along my hairline and continued to lean against his chest and just breathe, and breathe. Garrett shifted position, putting his head on my chest so he could listen more closely to my heartbeat while I stroked his auburn hair, the steady rhythms calming us both.

I wondered again if this would be my last few minutes alone with him for all time and what I should say or do if that were true. I could smell his fear, not for himself, but for me.

I sent, "*Promise me you won't blame yourself.*"

"I can't. I—"

"*Shhh.*" I leaned down and we kissed.

I teased him to lighten the mood. "*The fae magic is still messing with me. If we didn't have a couple of vampires to kill I'd rip your clothes off and jump you right here.*"

He didn't laugh, but he managed to sound deeply sexy. "I'll remind you later tonight." *Later tonight* hung in the air between us.

I was desperate to continue to hear his voice, so I thought up another question. "Besides me fighting Antoine, what would you change?"

He was silent for a few beats of my heart. "I'd protect you from your attackers when you were younger." He kissed my hands and arms where the old scars used to be. "I'd tell you more often how precious you are to me and I'd work on being more patient with you and the team."

"We needed you to kick us in the butt that night. And if I hadn't been attacked, you wouldn't have given me your blood."

"I'd still have claimed you. I believe we're together for a reason—this is our path—we're meant to make this journey together, wherever it leads us."

I smiled, even though my heart was breaking. "I believe

the same."

"But you haven't told me what you would change, my love."

I tried to make it simple, knowing if went too deep I'd end up sobbing. "I'd ask you to play the violin or the guitar for me. I never got to hear you play. And I'd make sure we had more time for fun stuff, like hunting together. Besides that, I'd do everything the same—except for the day with Lily. I'd listen to Liam." We were smiling at each other when Garrett tensed up.

"They're here."

CHAPTER FORTY-FOUR

THE DIFFERENCE IN THE ATMOSPHERE OF the crowd was dramatic. Our supporters no longer laughed, or even spoke. All eyes were on the newest arrivals.

On the opposite side of the clearing, Eleanor and Antoine smirked at Garrett and me, their eyes sparkling with bloodlust, their fangs beginning to show. They looked about as terrifying as vampires can look, and that's saying a lot.

I trembled, my gut clenching. Garrett sent, "*Start your calming and focusing exercises.*" I nodded and moved into a lunge position, stretching out quads, gluts and hamstrings. I continued with exercises to loosen my back and shoulders and upper arms, but I never moved my gaze away from Antoine, silently praying he couldn't smell my terror.

Eleanor was wearing a short white leather dress with a low neckline and a slit on the side. It stretched to fit her shape perfectly, making the high boots look even more amazing. Antoine was dressed in cream leather pants and nothing else. Jeez. I guess he figured I'd swoon and drop dead after one glimpse at all those muscles. His mouth was bloody, as if he'd just fed, so I tried to ignore the gore and looked to see if he carried a weapon.

Seeing me watching him, he pulled out a wicked looking ten-inch knife. He played with it, tossing it around skillfully and slicing it through the air in practiced maneuvers. My hand automatically went to my belt where Liam's smaller blade rested. I swallowed, my throat feeling dry, but was relieved when the hilt of my dagger warmed, then vibrated in my grasp.

Eight other vampires were spread out behind Eleanor and Antoine, more than Garrett had anticipated. Lily was there and Garrett pointed out others: Sasha, William, Heinrich and Yvette, and three newly-made teenaged vampires, probably no more than fifteen years old when they'd been turned. The young ones hissed at us like feral cats.

Maya moved into the middle of the clearing and spoke. "We are here to witness two duels: the first between Jacqueline Crawford Cuvier and Antoine DuLac, the second between Garrett Cuvier and Eleanor Howard. The duels will be fought in accordance with vampiric law. There is no time limit. Torture and the drinking of an opponent's blood is allowed. Only one fighter in each duel will leave the ring alive." At this point the crowd had become completely silent, the serious nature of the night's events sinking in.

"Each fighter may bring one weapon into the ring with him, but it must first be presented to our judge for approval. If a weapon is enchanted, it must have been created with its magic and not altered unnaturally for the purpose of the duel. This includes the use of poison. Our judge will determine whether a weapon is acceptable or not.

"No one outside the ring may interfere in any way, on pain of death. This includes the use of mental powers." As she spoke she scanned the entire crowd, but the seriousness of her words was clear.

"The duels will be judged by an outside neutral party. Kennet, Fae Lord of Cascade, has agreed to take on this task." I looked toward the woods and saw a tall, slender man with a glowing golden aura emerge. It was hard for any of us to look at him at first because his aura was so bright his facial features were unclear. Many of the people who'd come to support us took a few steps back, obviously afraid. When he reached the center of the clearing, his glowing aura dimmed and he greeted Maya with a small nod of his head. Some entrance.

His hair was long and very light in color, a platinum blond bordering on white. He had sharp features, thin lips, and deep purple eyes, his gaze taking in the four of us with only a mild curiosity.

After Maya had left the ring, he turned to survey the crowd, speaking in a rich melodic voice, free of any fae accent. "Jacqueline Crawford Cuvier and Antoine DuLac, please come into the ring to present your weapons."

Antoine moved quickly to the center, pulling out his knife and handing it hilt first to the fae lord. Kennet examined it and nodded, returning it to Antoine who then left the ring to kneel at Eleanor's feet as if he were a knight asking for his queen's favor. I moved hesitantly into the center and handed Lord Kennet Liam's blade. His eyes met mine and instantly he was past my psychic wall and in my head.

"Who gave you this blade?"

"I borrowed it from a friend."

"A powerful friend?" He arched an eyebrow and smirked.

"Yes." My mouth felt dry. He was every bit as frightening as Antoine.

"Tell me his name." I felt a strong nudge pushing me to tell him. I strengthened my wall in response, but instantly realized how stupid I was being, since he'd already breached it so easily.

"No, I can't. I promised to stay silent."

His eyes narrowed and yet I felt him withdraw, deciding not to push harder. He could have forced me to tell him, or he could have taken the information without my permission. *"You choose not to betray your source. I will not weaken you before a battle by forcing you to be honest. Did he offer it to you freely?"*

"Yes. I wasn't planning on using any weapon."

"Then why did you accept his extraordinary gift?" Kennet was handling the blade as if it was a rare and exquisite artifact, but the weapon did not take on his aura as it did mine and Liam's.

"I accepted it because he advised me to take it. I've learned to listen to his advice." My answer seemed to amuse the fae lord because he smiled at me, yet the action was cold—detached. He was nothing like Liam. Were all full-blood fae more like Lord Kennet? If so, I'd make sure to avoid taking a trip to Faerie.

"To wield this blade, one must be powerful indeed. I will watch your duel with great interest, Jacqueline Crawford Cuvier." Lord Kennet returned Liam's weapon with a nod and I spun and walked quickly to Garrett, still shivering from the encounter. I wrapped my arms around my mate, snuggling against him and shutting my eyes as his embrace calmed my fears.

"Remember our date," he whispered. I smiled against his chest.

"In one minute the duel will begin." Kennet spoke loudly so all would hear.

Garrett sent, *"Francois is here. He'll heal you if you need help when the duel is over. You may have to drink his blood, but you can trust him."* He lifted my face. *"Je t'aime, mon ange."*

"Je t'aime." I managed to smile as I turned away, allowing

my hand to run down his arm until only our fingertips were touching. With one last step I was on my own, moving into the clearing where Antoine waited, his lips curled in a vicious sneer.

We circled each other, glaring and waiting for the battle to start. I pulled in a slow breath, allowing a deathly calm to replace the fear in my heart. I thought about Carly's violent murder and allowed my anger to build inside me. Antoine hissed and moved his knife back and forth between his hands, but I left my enchanted blade in its sheath, thinking of Liam's words as he'd slid it into place.

"You do have the strength to wield it. You must trust yourself."

Magic pooled around my feet, so I drew it into my center and shaped it to my will. The sounds of the crowd died away, as all of my mental focus, energy and power was held in readiness, aimed toward Antoine's destruction.

"The duel will begin now!" Lord Kennet's voice rang out.

He was on me before I took another breath, biting viciously into my shoulder and ripping off a chunk of flesh. I avoided his knife by striking his wrist with a brick of my energy, but the pain from his bite was excruciating and my attack wasn't as strong as I'd hoped. I managed to jab him near the heart with another sharpened shaft of power and he backed off, looking surprised but pleased.

Yes, Antoine, I'm going to give you a good fight.

He rushed me, attempting to smash his fist into my face. I turned away at the last second so he only grazed the side of my mouth, splitting my lip. I responded with a flat wave of energy, sending him flying across the clearing and crashing into a tree. Unfortunately, he was on his feet immediately, wiping the blood off his mouth and smiling.

Antoine raced forward again, using his vamp speed this

time, so I slashed out immediately with a mental slice across his neck, causing him to growl, but not slow down. Although I tried to avoid him, he hacked at me, ripping through my pants and leaving a long gash in my thigh. I tripped him at the last second, pushed out another wave of energy, sending him rolling once more to the far side of the clearing where he jumped quickly to his feet. He touched his wounded neck, lifting his bloody fingers to his mouth and rubbing saliva on his injury. He sneered at me as the wound closed and disappeared.

I was bleeding from three places now and I didn't have much time left if I was going to have the strength to kill him. The steady blood loss would eventually weaken me so much I'd be unable to defend myself, let alone attack, but I didn't want to use up my strength healing my wounds just yet.

We began to circle once again. Antoine spoke, his deep voice taunting me to act. "So, Cheetah, you use the lines well. But it won't mean a fucking thing when I rip you apart piece by piece and drain you in front of your lover and your friends." I didn't reply. "Carly begged me to stop. *Please stop ... please.*" He imitated a woman's voice, mocking my friend's death. "Then she screamed and screamed."

His laughter burned a hole in my gut as I dug my nails into my palms to pull in my focus. He'd made a deadly mistake, because now I was seething with rage, and nothing brought my focus to a point better than anger. Liam's knife vibrated against my hip, responding to my fury. Without any plan on how I'd use it, I slid it out of its sheath. It felt pleasantly warm in my hand as its energy merged with mine with an almost sentient desire for blood. Antoine's blood.

My eyes narrowed—glaring at my enemy in anticipation of avenging my friend. Opening my mind to accept the unique magic the fae blade offered up, I braced my body for his next attack.

Antoine raced toward me in a blur, his fangs fully out and his knife slashing through the air. I ducked behind him in my own blur of vamp speed, jabbing him in the kidneys with Liam's fae blade. When he stumbled I raised my blade to strike again, but he threw himself away from my intended strike, roaring with fury and pain.

I'd been fighting for only ten minutes, but it felt like hours. My muscles ached and I was bleeding badly from the wound on my thigh. I was using a great deal of energy and needed to find a way to conserve my strength until the right time came to strike the killing blow. Magic continued to wrap around me, so I used it to darken my aura, allowing anger to suck energy from Antoine the way he'd sucked blood and strength from Carly. The first flicker of fear flashed in his eyes as I grew stronger and he weakened.

Knowing he was in trouble, Antoine barreled into me, knocking me down hard. Liam's blade flew across the clearing, completely out of my reach. My head bounced off the ground, stunning me, my vision blurring. When it cleared a few seconds later, Antoine loomed above me, hissing with fury, his lip curled into an angry snarl. He lifted his foot and stomped down on my left hand with his boot. I cried out as bones shattered and muscles tore. Excruciating pain took away my ability to focus and defend myself as I watched helplessly as he lifted his heavy boot once more. He kicked me solidly in the ribs and I went flying across the clearing, landing in a heap not too far from the fae knife.

In the throes of my agony, I heard its magic call to mine. The blade craved more of Antoine's blood, demanding I draw on the power it offered up and use it to kill him. Finding strength in desperation, I pulled more magic into my center and promised it Antoine's life. The cool stone handle materialized in my palm, as a sudden burst of energy gave me a more focused confidence. My enemy sauntered toward me, grinning with malice and taking his time. Blood was dripping from my mouth, leg, shoulder and hand as I raised myself to a kneeling position and faced Antoine with a focus that left the rest of the clearing behind.

I'd have only one chance, so I hid the knife by my side, willing it to remain unseen and waited for my prey to come closer.

"Antoine," I rasped. "Please…." Groaning, I spit out blood and coughed. His kick had probably cracked a rib or two, but I forced myself to ignore the pain and clutched the hilt of the blade. It thrummed with power. Antoine didn't see it there. His entire focus was centered on my anguished expression. I was sure he thought the blade still lay where it had landed before.

His arrogance would kill him.

I kept my agonized mask in place as I opened myself to the darkest part of my psyche, feeling only a warrior's blood-lust, the darkness inside my core drinking in my pain and fear like it was a magical tonic. I'd feared this part of me for as long as I could remember, terrified I would lose myself to violence if it was released.

Antoine snarled. "What is it, Cheetah? You want mercy?" He crouched and grabbed my crushed hand, squeezing it hard, forcing me to scream. He laughed at my agony. "Beg for it. Beg for mercy. Beg for a fast death." He bit down savagely on the inside of my elbow and drank, viciously squeezing my shattered hand.

But despite my groans and sobs, my inner darkness was smiling as I called upon my rage to pull as much of the ley line magic into my center as I could bear to hold. He was so close I could smell his rotten stench, bringing up the vision of him beating and draining my friend, Carly. The fae blade hummed and melded with my magic, becoming an extension of my dark desires. Together we pulsed with power as my healer stepped aside and my warrior took complete control.

"Antoine," I sobbed again for effect. He laughed between the gulps, getting off on every moment of my pain. My heated rage spread its fire into the blade, the warrior I'd hidden from for years commanding the weapon to do my will and kill him. I leaned closer to his ear and whispered, "For Carly."

I swung the knife up between us, stabbing him low in the stomach. He released my arm and roared with pain as I twisted the blade and viciously ripped a gash from belly to sternum. The magical weapon had burned a trail through his body, his organs bleeding, his skin blackening.

Dark blood gushed out of his jagged wound, covering us both. His silver eyes rose to meet mine, widening slightly in surprise.

"Your eyes, Cheetah ..." he croaked.

The bright orange glow reflected in his silver gaze startled me, but his expression held no fear, only a brief flash of an emotion that struck at me hard. Antoine must have seen my own surprise, because he sneered at me a moment before I gathered my strength, willed the blade to lengthen and sliced through his thickly tattooed neck with one smooth stroke. His head dropped and rolled several feet before turning to dust.

His body collapsed on top of mine. I groaned and cried out from the burning heat of his skin and the weight putting pressure on my injuries. A moment later the fire was out and he was only a powdery ash disappearing with the steady wind off the sea.

"Jacqueline Crawford is declared the winner," rang out Lord Kennet's voice. Most of the audience cheered, but I didn't have the strength to even smile. I lay there in pain, covered in blood, yet proud that I'd destroyed Antoine and given Garrett the chance to take down Eleanor.

But I could no longer hide from the darkness inside myself that I'd loosed against this monster. For now, I clung to that black warrior with all my strength, because when it was gone, I'd have to face my healer self again.

Thinking back to Antoine's last moments, I'd recognized relief in his eyes. He'd yearned for death in the end, a release from the life he'd led. Even a monster like Antoine had once been human. What was he before Eleanor, an even crueler monster, had turned him? I shuddered and locked away those thoughts, only dredging up the strength to close my eyes.

I was lifted by unfamiliar arms and taken into the tent. Garrett was there along with Francois, who'd been the one to carry me and lay me on the couch. He examined my shattered hand, turning it carefully to see the damage. I whimpered and Garrett tried to soothe me with sweet words and gentle kisses. Francois turned to him and spoke in French then translated for me. "You must accept my blood. Garrett cannot give you his before he meets Eleanor."

"I can heal myself, at least I think I can." I tried to pull my hand away, but the pain was too much and I cried out.

Garrett pleaded. "Please, Jackie. You're exhausted. Francois' blood will heal you quickly. Then I won't be worrying about you while I'm fighting her."

"I'm sorry. Of course it's okay. I'm an … an idiot." I managed to gasp out.

"You are the most brave, beautiful, perfect female." He kissed me again, this time with passion.

Francois was smiling. "I hate to interrupt, but Kennet is going to call you into the ring in exactly three minutes and you have to ready yourself."

"Go, Garrett. I love you."

"*Je t'aime.*" He disappeared through the tent flap just as

Lord Kennet announced that he and Eleanor should bring their weapons into the ring in two minutes for his approval.

Francois sat quietly, holding my hand in his. A few stray tears trickled down my cheek from the pain and the tension. "Will you drink my blood to heal properly? I promise I will not bite you back." He smiled, but all I could manage was a shallow nod. He bit into his wrist and held it to my mouth. I steadied it there with my uninjured hand and began to drink, noticing his blood tasted slightly sweeter than Garrett's.

He watched me carefully, measuring exactly when I'd had enough. With the first few swallows, my shoulder, elbow, thigh, and hand stopped bleeding, the jagged cuts closing up quickly. The pain from my cracked rib lessened as well. He took away his wrist and licked it clean. Garrett's was high octane, but Francois' blood was like rocket fuel. When I tried to stand, he put a hand out to stop me.

"Not yet. Another minute. May I prevent scarring by licking your wounds?" I nodded and watched as he bent down to lick the top of my thigh, my shoulder and very carefully, the inside of my left elbow. My hand had improved, but was not completely back to normal, so he suggested, "If you shift your hand to your animal form, it will heal faster." I pulled on the lines and shifted both hands, not sure I could do just the one. Francois was still holding the left one and seemed completely enthralled by my fur, claws, and markings. He stroked it gently.

"Of course, you are a cheetah. *Charmant!* Has your hand healed sufficiently?"

"Yes, Francois, thank you." I smiled at him with gratitude as I transitioned my hands back to human, pleased to see that I could wiggle my fingers and form a fist with only a little stiffness. I kept glancing at the entrance to the tent, wondering what was happening.

"Garrett has a few more minutes. I must see to your lip. We don't want anything to mar your lovely face." He kept his eyes on mine as he placed his finger in his mouth to wet it, then rubbed it slowly on my healing lip. He sucked off the blood, then smiled his very sexy smile. "You are quite delicious." He winked. "Come, Madame Cuvier. Garrett will need to see you before the duel."

"Thank you, Francois." I'd managed to hold in my laughter at his unashamed flirting, but wasn't quite as successful at hiding the smile. After quickly replacing Liam's knife in the sheath on my belt, I took Francois' proffered arm and we left the tent together.

CHAPTER FORTY-FIVE

ARRETT HAD JUST LEFT THE CLEARING after showing Kennet his weapon, when he saw me healed and smiling. He picked me up and spun me around as our supporters in the crowd all cheered. "I'll destroy her and our lives will be perfect."

"Mine is perfect already." I kissed him quickly, pressing my forehead against his, locking gazes and sending him bursts of my love and my energy. His confidence soared. Tonight, he'd free himself of this bitch forever.

I felt him switch to vamp mode as he turned and gracefully swayed into the ring, fangs out, lips pulled back in a snarl that raised the hairs on my arms. She matched him step for step glowering and hissing. Her sexy demeanor had completely disappeared, replaced by a violent beast; her true colors for all of us to see. Antoine's death had perhaps surprised but not unbalanced her and I watched with fascination as Eleanor's tremendous power charged the air, tendrils of energy reaching out toward her nest.

My team had moved to stand beside me in support, so I took Ethan's hand as he put an arm around Sinc who was already clutching Kyle's elbow. We knew instantly something was up when Eleanor's nest grew unnaturally still. Lily, Sasha, and the rest began to sink to the ground and weaken before our eyes. She was draining them of life force so she could beat Garrett. As she grew more powerful, her black aura cleared and her eyes turned a solid silver, much sharper in tone than Garrett's.

To distract her, Garrett held up his wrist and showed her the mark of our mating. Her eyes widened and she whipped her head around to glare at me, so I held up mine, along with one prominent finger. She answered with another hiss, her rage adding to her monstrous aspect.

Lord Kennet's voice rang out once more. "The duel begins now."

Eleanor and Garrett moved in a blur practically invisible to shifter eyes. To see them more clearly, I tapped into the lines. Garrett was already in trouble. He was barely able to defend against her attacks and could make very few of his own. I saw a few slashes across his face and arms where she'd used her blade, fangs, and nails. She was a windstorm of fury and blood lust and I quickly became afraid for him.

The frenzied action stopped as rapidly as it had begun. They continued to circle; taking a moment to rest and adjust to each other's fighting styles. Garrett looked worse than Eleanor, A chunk of flesh was missing from his cheek, his shirt was ripped to pieces with bloody red gashes visible through the holes, and his arms were badly bitten. In a fluid motion he removed his shirt and pulled out his knife, never taking his gaze from Eleanor, his maker, the female who'd forced him to become a vampire against his will, who'd forced him to watch his family die. I wanted to help him…

"*Jacqueline, stop!*" Liam had pushed his way next to me. "*If you let your energy heal him you will both die.*" I kept very still, absorbing the tendrils of emerald magic floating toward Garrett. They hadn't touched him, but they were very close. *"Your ignorance and lack of control won't matter to Kennet. You'll still die."* I stole a glance at the fae lord. He was watching me intently as my power dissipated.

"Thank you, Liam." I undid the belt and handed it to him along with his blade, never taking my gaze away from Garrett.

Liam touched my shoulder. "He has a plan. He will succeed in killing her."

While Garrett bled and fought, I forced myself to think about his incredible abilities.

He's a master strategist, I told myself. He hasn't pulled out his trump card yet. He hasn't used the lines. He'll beat her. I took in a deep breath, let it out again with a shudder and forced myself to simply watch. Liam placed his hand on my shoulder, maybe needing the contact as much as me. I sometimes forgot he was half human, and had been Garrett's close friend for over a hundred years.

Eleanor arrogantly tossed her sword outside the ring, seeming to perfer using her nails and teeth to draw blood. She was sure she was winning, and on the surface, it looked that way to everyone. The crowd near me had quieted and some of the shifter fighters were picking up their weapons, readying themselves for the battle to come with Eleanor and her nest after Garrett's death.

Racing toward him again with her amazing speed, Eleanor sunk her fangs into his shoulder, ripping deeply and exposing some bone. Garrett managed to dole out a few wicked punches, hitting her stomach, ribs and then her kidneys as she turned away, but she retaliated by ripping into his chest with her sharper nails. When she swung her other arm toward him he managed to pull away at the last second, avoiding her long nails as they slashed at his throat. But a well-aimed kick to his stomach sent him flying across the clearing.

Although the odds seemed to be in Eleanor's favor, she was tiring. She'd grown cocky, taking more chances, expending much more energy than Garrett and leaving herself open to attack. Not a smart move around someone as skilled as my mate.

As she raked her nails viciously across his face, she stumbled, her momentum carrying her away and leaving her back exposed. He jumped on the opportunity, using his father's blade to slice across her flesh. A sharp growl erupted, as fury and pain distorted her features even more, turning her into more beast than vampire. The smell of burning flesh filled the air and the gash continued to bleed, not healing as her other wounds had.

Garrett was taking what she was delivering, all the while conserving his strength. He hadn't used the lines yet, so I held my breath in anticipation, eager to see him kick her ass with his magic.

This time, Garrett didn't give her a chance to recover. He ran in and grabbed her arm, twisting and breaking it, bringing a startled gasp to her lips. She ignored the pain and forced him back with a shove, snarling and attempting to bite into his neck again. Garrett jabbed her in the stomach with his fist, breaking ribs and forcing her to let go of his arm and stumble backward. His blade ripped through the air, this time slicing a burning gash across her shoulder. She hissed and the fighting stopped as they each took a moment to gather their wits and recoup. They moved in a circle, silver gazes locked together in hate.

Eleanor straightened, drawing all eyes to her beauty, transformed once more from the feral beast into the exquisite monster who'd sucked in so many innocent victims over the centuries. When she spoke to Garrett, her voice was a silky seduction, brushing against our senses, enticing him to obey.

"Come home to me. You've always been a favorite. I won't punish you or your sweet cheetah. She and her friends can live out their lives as they please. None of us will touch them, I promise you. I only want you back where you belong. Come to me, Garrett."

I heard a few shifters in the crowd whisper, "He should go back. She's so beautiful." Her Influence was incredibly strong, spilling over into the crowd, but my mate was used to her deceptions.

Garrett curled his lip back in a sneer, the first small vibrations strumming through me as he began to pull magical energy into his body. "Eleanor, I've never believed your lies. You plan to kill them all, just as you killed my family, just as you're planning to kill me the moment I let my guard down. But tonight it will be my pleasure to end your depraved existence." He spit on the ground at her feet and she growled in rage at his act of disrespect. "I claim my independence from your nest. I'm no longer your property."

I felt a change in the air as Garrett stopped moving, his voice echoing with power and his own brand of Influence. "You're my maker, a position which should have earned my respect and obedience. But you're only interested in your own sick pleasures. You even torture your nest." He indicated the figures crumpled on the ground on the far side of the clearing. "You've taken hundreds of innocent lives and forced your nest to participate in your perversions. I've witnessed many of them myself. Tonight I have people to avenge. I hope you find no peace on the other side."

Eleanor tried to act nonchalant, but fear burned in her eyes for the first time. She was an older and more powerful vampire than Garrett, but she'd forgotten in accepting his challenge, Garrett was not only a vampire. Her voice was shaky when she answered, although she put on a good face. "Garrett, you and your little cheetah are quite amusing. I think I shall skin her alive when I'm through with you: like I did to your sweet little sister."

Enormous amounts of magical energy spun into the clearing as Garrett's aura cleared and grew brighter. He picked her up in a blur and threw her across the ring, cracking the trunk of a tree. She jumped up immediately, but her fear and shock was obvious to all of us.

Garrett stood perfectly still—the blue of his eyes completely hidden by the silver of his rage. His body pulsed with a power that crackled around him in a magical circuit. He reached out to her with his mind, his magic and his unbound anger, his hand tracing a shape in the air. Garrett's rich voice rang out, "*Se soumettre*. Submit!"

Eleanor was on her knees in the sand a moment later, her arms frozen at her sides. She struggled madly, but couldn't rise. She snarled and hissed in fear as Garrett circled her, his smile devoid of warmth. Holding his knife in front of his body, he swiped his finger over the sharp blade and blood flowed down its length, dripping into the sand at his feet. He cut a shape on her forehead and rubbed his blood into it as if completing a ritual. Her eyes grew wide with terror.

"Eleanor," he hissed. "I will drain you slowly."

"You will not do this. I am your maker. Release me." When he didn't respond, she said, "I love you, Garrett." Her desperation drew no pity from anyone watching. Eleanor had sent her vampires to shifter and even werewolf communities to murder entire families. No one would save her from my avenging angel.

He laughed quietly, the sound as cold as winter. "With each minute of your pain, I'll remind you of the innocent lives I witnessed you destroy."

Eleanor glanced toward her nest, only to realize she'd left them too weak to help her. She moaned and screamed, her skin tightening painfully. Garrett's blue aura brightened with each magical pulse as her body slowly shriveled and dried up. As long as she was able, Eleanor cried and pleaded while Garrett whispered to her in French, cursing her and reminding her of past treacheries. Her skin, bones and organs burned and cracked causing her excruciating pain, but denying her death, Garrett took his time.

At one point, he reached out to transfer small jolts of magical power into me, Francois, who stood across the ring from me, Liam, Maya, and even Eleanor's depleted nest of vampires. We all gasped from the sudden shock, then fed on the energy, using it as we wished. I stored some, in case a battle with his nest came later, releasing the rest back into the lines. He could only share this power with those of us who could connect to the lines, but perhaps the non-magic users could feel health returning to the island, as Eleanor's dark power was extinguished.

Almost at the end, Garrett shifted into his magnificent cheetah, ripping her throat out with his sharp teeth. The people in the crowd who hadn't known Garrett had once been a cheetah, were struck dumb, but soon a shout rang out in support of his final actions. The shifters and wolves who had come to see the duel, had known their families would not be safe as long as Eleanor lived.

Garrett's cheetah tore at her neck with his claws and his fangs until her head rolled on the ground. A moment later her dust blew into the sea and dissolved in the currents.

He had avenged his family in a most fitting way, his cheetah delivering true death to his vicious maker.

"Garrett Cuvier is declared the winner." When I glanced over at Lord Kennet, I was surprised to see he was looking at me.

CHAPTER FORTY-SIX

FTER A FEW SECONDS OF STUNNED silence, cheering erupted from our side of the clearing. But while Ethan, Kyle, Rob and Sinc were laughing and shouting, I was watching Garrett. Francois was by his side when he transitioned back, helping him into a robe and crossing the clearing together. To keep us all safe, Garrett had to quickly control his former nest mates. The energy he'd shared had strengthened them enough to stand and talk, so he and Francois confronted each one, insisting they pledge loyalty to Garrett by sharing blood and taking an oath, or else face immediate execution. The few who refused, the newly made teens, were beheaded instantly by Francois. Lily was the last one they approached.

"You traitorous piece of shit! You'll never be able to take her place. I'd rather die a true death than live under you."

"You have a brother who still cares about you despite your cruelty. And your life will be different if you pledge your loyalty to me. I'm not Eleanor. You'll have to change, but you'll be treated well if you do."

Lily snarled, "You tortured her. You tortured our maker."

Her eyes glistened with emotion.

"It's over now. Share blood with me and join my nest."

"Garrett, let her die, she doesn't want to be a vampire." Kyle had run over to see what was up.

Lily turned to face him, emitting a slow, snakelike hiss. Her fangs dripped with saliva and her face had taken on a dangerously feral look. "Stupid, Kyle. I love to torture weaklings. My life began when Eleanor turned me." She hissed again at Garrett. "I won't live like you do. Kill me so I can join my maker in death."

Garrett turned his gaze in Kyle's direction.

Kyle's expression showed nothing but his aura had turned muddy with pain. "Goodbye, Lily. I'm—I'm sorry." He nodded at Garrett and turned back to where Ethan, Sinc, and Peter waited for him. Peter led him away as Francois' sword sliced through her neck with a slick sweep. Lily turned to dust, her last wish granted.

Exhausted, Garrett sat down hard on a nearby stump and put his head in his hands. I ran to him and knelt by his feet wrapping my arms around his legs, pouring my healing energy into him.

He threaded his hand in my hair but didn't speak. Francois sat on a large rock nearby.

"I have arranged to take your surviving nest to the house I am renting on the outskirts of town. I will see they feed and I will interrogate them more thoroughly to determine if they have the ability to adjust to a radical change in lifestyle. You will make an appearance tomorrow evening?" Garrett nodded and Francois rose, placing a hand on his shoulder. "I will support your choices, but they must not be made in haste."

"Thank you." Garrett was still shaky but he managed to rise and hug his grandsire. "Thank you for all you did here tonight."

"It was a very great pleasure, believe me. *Vous étiez tous les deux magnifiques.*" He smiled charmingly in my direction. "Your hand?"

I laughed. "It's fine, thank you."

He kissed it with care. "Bonsoir, Jacqueline, Garrett."

Garrett drew me closer as Francois walked to the small group of vampires, the nest still weak from the death of their maker and nest mates. "Does Francois have a boat?"

He kissed the top of my head. "He can take all of them through the lines."

"All four?"

Garrett nodded. "He is an ancient."

We leaned against each other, staring out at the ocean and the stars, too wound up to talk about what had taken place in this small wooded clearing. No one interrupted our moment together, although a flurry of activity was taking place behind us. Shifters and wolves chatted about the duel, then made ready to head back to the mainland.

"Jacqueline Crawford. A word with you?" Lord Kennet was standing on the shoreline twenty yards away. He looked less alien in the moonlight, but not a bit friendlier.

"Go ahead. I have things to take care of." Garrett kissed my forehead and returned to the clearing as I moved nervously toward Lord Kennet. I kept as much distance between us as I could manage without insulting him, but I was curious as to what he wanted.

"I was most impressed with your use of the lines. Who has trained you?"

"Garrett and various other friends."

"Liam allowed you to borrow the fae blade he has claimed as his own. Have you returned it?"

"Yes."

He looked me over in the way males do. "Has he expressed interest in you as a mate?"

I was surprised by the question. I took a step backward. "No. I'm bonded to Garrett."

I watched his curious expression turn scornful. "A shifter made vampire. He isn't worthy of you."

"*I'm* a shifter, Lord Kennet." I was starting to get annoyed, but giving a fae lord attitude would be reckless.

"*You* are a manipulator of magic with great potential. I could help you reach your potential and more."

I remembered Garrett saying that the fae always wanted something in return. "At what price?"

His smile was beyond creepy. "A very pleasant one. I will take you as my lover and train you personally to use your magical gifts. We will have powerful children. I have no heir."

My heart hammered in my chest. I looked away so he wouldn't see my horrified expression and tried to organize my thoughts. If I said the wrong thing I'd be in deep shit, if I wasn't there already.

I dug for courage and faced Lord Kennet, praying I could avoid angering him. "Lord Kennet, I'm overwhelmed by the compliment and I sincerely thank you, but I'm mated to Garrett and plan to remain with him for the rest of my life. I love him." I showed him the mark on my wrist.

His eyes flashed with a golden fire. "I could force you to go with me now, wipe him from your mind." Moving closer, he touched my cheek with only the tips of his fingers. The desire to touch him, to kiss him, to please him, plowed against my shields. I dug my nails into my palms, bit my lip hard and automatically reinforced my wall as much as I could against this alien force of nature. Kind of pathetic, really, but he surprised me by pulling back, amused by my efforts.

When I could speak again, I forced my voice to hold steady. "I see... I see you could destroy me, but you would also alienate two valuable allies of the Cascade Sidhe." Meeting his gaze took every ounce of my courage, more than walking into the ring with Antoine.

"You do not fear me?" He tilted his head in surprise.

I was grateful he couldn't read my emotions as well as Garrett. "I fear your power, Lord Kennet, but not you." I forced my body to relax, trying with all my might to appear brave.

He smiled slowly. "It has been a long time since someone separated the two." Turning away, he looked out at the sea for a moment while I held my breath. "It is true your chosen mate is considered an ally. I disagreed with the decision, but could do nothing. You however, have not been so designated. You are not protected in that way."

In desperation I was sending out waves of calming energy, hoping he wouldn't notice, hoping it would be enough to send him away, content. His eyes narrowed and he tilted his head in curiosity, suddenly throwing it back to laugh. I jumped, a little shocked by his reaction.

"I am a Fae Lord of the Seelie Court. Your use of magic on me, even healing magic, is considered confrontational in fae society. You have...attacked me." He chuckled, his expression turning serious a moment later. "You are an ignorant child. You should have proper training if you wish to have dealings with us."

Did I ever say I wanted to have dealings with the fae? The answer was a big fat *no thank you!* Hanging with Liam was as close as I ever wanted to get to Faerie. I waited for him to speak again, not wanting to say anything that could dig my grave any deeper.

"I will recommend to the Elders that Liam instruct you. You will hear from me again, Jacqueline Crawford." He nodded, turned away and disappeared. Like poof.

The last comment had sounded too much like a threat.

I shuddered and searched for Garrett, finally spying him talking to Rob and Maya. He'd taken off the robe and dressed in sweatpants and a tee shirt.

"How do you feel?" Maya asked me in her cool, professional way. "Antoine was vicious."

"I'm okay. A little shaky, but not in pain."

Rob gave me a gentle bear hug "You were amazing. We're all proud of you."

Hearing Antoine's name again iced my core. I'd killed for the first time and even though Antoine deserved what he'd gotten and more, I still felt dirty. Garrett wrapped me in his arms. *"It doesn't ever get easy. It shouldn't."*

Rob could sense our need for some alone time. "I'll take the rest of the team in my boat." He left to gather up the others.

"Let's go home." I'd prayed to hear those exact words all night, but now that Garrett spoke them, I was afraid. He'd killed his maker and was now the master of his own nest. Would that change things between us? Had I handled Lord Kennet competently or had I made more trouble for him? I'd thought winning against Antoine and Eleanor would be the end of our problems, but it seemed life in this supernatural world just kept getting more complicated.

He led me up the path to the dock and we prepared the boat for the hour-long sail back to Crescent City. Garrett sensed something was upsetting me so he quietly set about doing the mundane tasks to put us out into the channel. I knew he'd ask me about it once we had some privacy, but for now, I locked my doubts and fears in my usual box. It was getting pretty full.

The sky was clear, and the starlight reflected in the ocean seemed to ripple and race with the currents. Garrett was guiding us home with a hand on the wheel and a thoughtful expression. "Will you talk to me, angel? Are you angry with me?"

"Why would I be angry with you?" I sat on the starboard side bench, avoiding Garrett's face, not brave enough to look him in the eye.

"My taking on the responsibility of leading what's left of Eleanor's nest is going to complicate our lives." He glanced at me sheepishly. "You didn't sign on for this."

I got up and wrapped my arms around him. "But I did. When I said I'd be your lifemate, I signed up for a lifetime with you. It's made me happier than I could have imagined. Except," I swallowed, "I need to tell you something."

"Tell me." He draped his free arm around me and squeezed my shoulder.

I told him about Lord Kennet's strange proposition and my response. I saw minute changes in his eyes and the line of his mouth, but he listened without interruption. "I'm afraid I screwed everything up."

"Kennet is an arrogant windbag, but he won't go against my alliance with Cascade." He stroked my hair to put me at ease. "If the elders agree to allow Liam to share his knowledge with us, then it's all good. Liam's father is an ally of mine, but I would never presume to ask him directly for Liam's help. Liam stays with me of his own free will."

His stroke continued down my bare arm to my injured hand. He lifted it to his lips and kissed it gently, examining my palm and fingers for any remaining damage. I flexed each digit and demonstrated their agility by massaging his back with firm motions.

He hummed with pleasure as I worked on a knot. He grunted when I attacked another tight spot, asking, "Did Francois behave himself?"

"Yes. He flirted with me a little but it was all in fun. He's rather charming."

Garrett barked out a laugh. "He's had centuries to practice

the art of seduction. He's very much a master." His smile was warm. "I'm forever grateful for his continued support. Francois tends to treat me as a younger brother in constant need of his guidance. He seems quite taken with your charms," Garrett teased.

"Whatever *charms* I have are only for the use of a particular vampire. In fact I seem to recall being asked to remind you about something. Hmm, what was it?"

He snatched twisted and maneuvered me around to face him. "I haven't forgotten." His voice sent happy chills down my spine. I leaned in to kiss him but he pushed me gently away and winked. "We'll be home in thirty minutes."

"Waiting is not my best thing." When I pretended to pout, he laughed, a sound that rang through my heart, reminding me that complicated or not, we'd been given a chance to share a life together. I had no intention of wasting one minute of it.

CHAPTER FORTY-SEVEN

CARLY'S FUNERAL SERVICE WAS IN A LOVELY chapel decorated with pink tulips and white roses, Carly's favorite flowers. Many friends got up to share stories. Maya spoke about a meeting where Carly helped her with her first shift, then gave her extra homework for talking back to one of the teachers at the school. I was surprised when Garrett talked to the group about some of their funnier childhood experiences. His face was drawn and I knew he felt badly they'd never reconciled their differences.

Rob told a story about a double date he'd gone on with Lynette and Carly and her boyfriend at the time. They'd spent a nice evening bowling, eating pizza, and drinking beer. Carly's boyfriend had wanted to show off so he threw the bowling ball too hard and it actually made a hole in the back of the pin machine. They'd ducked out of the building pretty fast and Carly had reamed him out for getting drunk and not controlling himself around humans and then thrown him through his own windshield. They'd all walked home that night.

Outside after the service, many of the shifters spoke to Garrett and me about the duels. Most of them simply wanted to say thank you because they knew that the killing wouldn't have stopped with Carly's death. Some actually hugged us and offered us a free dinner at their restaurant or a free oil change or whatever they could afford to give us. They knew by now that my ley line magic had surpassed Maya's, but it seemed more important to most of them that I was a healer. They seemed more trusting of Garrett, too, asking him about his cheetah background and also for advice on how to better protect their homes and families. Shifters were a peace-loving race, and Garrett's bravery against Eleanor would allow this community to live in safety, at least until the next threat came along.

It occurred to me because of Eleanor, Garrett's playful cheetah side had been forced to turn violent and seek out blood daily from humans or shifters to survive. As a newborn vampire, he'd been completely under her power, killing and possibly torturing innocents at her command. It must have taken him time to gather the strength to oppose her will and survive his own torture. This went on for over one hundred and twenty years.

Garrett's surface emotions were clear to me: sadness over Carly, relief over my safety, and excitement over heading his own nest. But he kept some feelings behind his wall, feelings too hard for him to share. He was very good at control and not so great at trust. My inner healer stretched her muscles and grinned at the challenge.

As we were leaving, Sinc gave me a huge hug saying, "Shopping? Friday?"

"I'll be pretty busy organizing things for the party. I was going to ask…."

"Of course I'll help. I'm bringing the most delicious chocolate mousse cake. You'll want to roll in it, it's so good." Visions of Sinc and Ethan covered in chocolate made me giggle.

Garrett hung his arm loosely over my shoulder. "What's so funny?"

"It involves a chocolate mousse cake," I wiped a tear from my eye.

"You two should try it." Sinc winked and slunk away to Ethan.

I grinned. "That snow leopard mojo is powerful stuff."

"Nothing's better than cheetah." He kissed my forehead and squeezed my hand.

We spent the hour-long drive to meet with his new nest by going over party details. We'd decided to have the mating party at the Smith River Campgrounds and were able to rent the western campsite for the night. We'd be setting up six large barbeque grills, which Garrett's cousin Aaron and his pack had agreed to man, and were also catering in pasta, veggies, the works. Beer and wine would be provided, but nothing stronger. Swimming was allowed in that section of the river so we'd also bought dozens of towels and blankets for drying off and relaxing under the stars. Several shifter volunteers who owned or worked in local bakeries were providing desserts.

We drove down a curving driveway and stopped in front of the double doors of a very large two-story brick house. "Francois and I have only spared the four who seemed the most willing to adapt to my rules. They've pledged loyalty to me and we've shared a few drops of blood in the usual ritual, so I'm connected to each of them more strongly than before.

"However, they're in a dangerous state. Their nest mates have been executed and their maker is dead. They have a difficult path ahead of them. If you're quiet, they'll ignore you. If you have questions, we'll speak mind to mind." I nodded in understanding. "Thank you." He kissed my hand, leading me up the front stairs and through the unlocked double doors.

Francois was there, looking elegant in a dark designer suit

and rich purple silk shirt unbuttoned at the collar. He gave Garrett a friendly hug and took my formerly injured hand in his, kissing it gently. He looked a little less put together, some strain evident in his eyes. Eleanor's death must have affected Francois as well.

His voice was sultry. "Bonsoir, Jacqueline. I'm so pleased to see you again." Garrett laughed softly. Eleanor must have gotten her seductive powers from her maker. She'd used hers to lure in the innocent, but Francois seemed to use his as any charismatic, attractive man would.

"Thank you, Francois." I smiled. "I see you're as charming as ever." Francois smiled widely in response and winked, his eyes sparkling with mischief. Garrett, never one to be outdone, arched an eyebrow and snaked his arm around my waist. I glanced at his adorable turned up smile and breathed in his delicious scent. It occurred to me Garrett had plenty of his own inherited seductive powers, which I'd willingly fallen prey to. I should make sure to thank Francois for passing on those as well.

He led us to a large room with two enormous couches, several plush armchairs and a grand piano placed near a picture window overlooking the ocean. The fireplace crackled, taking away the chill of the rainy night, and the cozy scent of burning logs blended well with the sweet scent of vampire.

Seated silently on one of the couches were a male and a female. Their expressions remained neutral, only their eyes moving as Garrett led me to an arm chair indicating with a tilt of his head I should sit. I did, never taking my gaze away from the couple. Garrett sat gracefully in the adjacent chair, resting his hand over mine.

He spoke with his usual tone of authority, the one he used when the team trained together. "Sasha, Yvette, this is Jacqueline Crawford Cuvier, my lifemate. Jackie, this is Sasha Vodinski and Yvette Blanc."

I recognized them now from the duel, picturing them hissing and snarling. I was happy to see they wore more submissive expressions tonight. The duo glanced at me, maybe uncertain as to why I was present, quickly returning their attention to Garrett.

Sasha was blond with deep-set light blue eyes, sculpted cheekbones, and a strong jaw. He wore a sienna brown well-fitted suit, and a tan shirt, unbuttoned to mid chest. He was barefoot and very handsome. Yvette wore a low cut black silk dress with spike heels. She was lovely, with thick dark curly hair, very dark eyes and light mahogany shaded skin. These two felt old to me, near Garrett's age, so the three of them must have been nest mates for a long time.

Two more vampires, both males, entered and sat on the second couch. Garrett introduced them as William Carlyle and Heinrich Schultz. William had red hair and blue eyes and very pale skin, and wore jeans and a button-down navy blue shirt. He was thin and had a slightly desperate look about him. My guess was he'd been turned recently. Heinrich was a huge man, very tall and broad with light brown hair and brown eyes. He wore a black muscle shirt, black jeans and a leather vest. He was definitely older than William but not as old as the other two.

Francois joined us, lowering his body elegantly into a third chair. "*I informed your new nest they needn't kneel before you.*" Francois winked at me, so I was left wondering if the head of a nest was treated like a king or queen. I glanced at Garrett, but he was trying very hard not to laugh at Francois' comment. Thank goodness.

Garrett began. "Francois and I believe you four have the strength and the desire to change your behavior. It's going to rough at first, but I'm giving you a new set of very clear rules to follow. You can ask any questions you like." They glanced at each other first, then nodded in Garrett's direction.

"There will be no killing. The only exception to this rule would be if you're attacked by an enemy, or if I've given you permission to kill. I will not deny you the right to defend yourself. There will be no torture allowed except during interrogations to save innocent lives, and then only if I've ordered it and am present. You'll feed daily from volunteer donors. No more hunting for innocents."

"There are volunteer donors?" Heinrich looked skeptical.

"Yes, hundreds. Sex with your donor is allowed. You're adults and I have no desire to police your private lives, but rape will never be tolerated. You will glamour your donor to protect them from the pain of the bite, but not to force them to do something against their will. After you've fed, I expect you to heal their wound and ensure they've returned to a healthy state.

"Eleanor kept you with her at all times unless you were hunting for victims, but when I feel you're in control of your impulses I'll allow you out. Vamp bars and clubs are the best place to find donors, but again, you must be careful not to feed too often from the same donor. It will weaken them too much, and addict them to your blood only. Those donors grow ill and often don't recover.

"You'll rest here during the day here. The bedroom windows have been blocked and the house will be guarded. When our grandsire returns to Paris, with his permission you may petition me to join his nest and accompany him. I'll allow it as long as you don't return to my territory—ever."

"What if we want to stay in this area after Francois leaves?" Sasha asked in a lightly Slavic accent.

Garrett hesitated. "We'll take this situation one day at a time and see how it goes. But understand this. You'll live by my rules or you'll be executed. This isn't negotiable, although I promise to give you a fair hearing before making a decision. Do you have any questions?"

Heinrich spoke first. He had a slight German accent. Eleanor must have traveled the world. "Master, I don't have a problem feeding from willing donors, but how do I control my cravings for violence?"

I hid my smile and sent to Garrett, "*Master, huh?*"

"*Quiet, lowly shifter.*" His mouth twitched, but he held onto the stern gaze he was directing at Heinrich. "The craving will lessen with time. If you're interested, I could train you to fight with my team. You might save some lives in the process."

Heinrich nodded, his shoulder muscles relaxing. "I was a soldier before I was changed and did well in battle. I accept your leadership, master." The big one was surprisingly polite.

"I'd prefer you all call me Garrett."

"Will you execute us if we slip up and harm a human? In the heat of feeding, I may—forget the new rules." Sasha leaned forward, speaking softly.

"I remember what she did to you, Sash." The tall blond frowned, turning a shade paler. "And I remember what she forced you to do to others in the nest. I'll never torture you. I'll never starve you or burn you or poison you to teach you a lesson. I'll never force you to harm one of the others. That goes for all of you. I'm not Eleanor. If I decide to execute you, it will be fast and clean. I know you'll make some mistakes. If your control is weak, ask Francois to stay with you when you feed. He can stop you if it goes too far." Sasha nodded and relaxed back into the couch cushion, the lines of tension on his face smoothing out.

Yvette frowned. "When you killed Eleanor the severing of the bond was painful and isolating. I feel empty now." She didn't hide her grief. "She's all we've known for so long." She lifted her chin. "I'd like to go home again to France. I need the distraction of a large city. I don't know if I can survive in this small town."

"I felt the same pain when she died, but I'll never regret killing her." Garrett looked out the window at the tree-lined yard, lit brightly by moonlight. "This is the community where I live, where I'm happy." He squeezed my hand. "If the new rules are followed, I'll release you to Francois. He and I believe you can adjust, Yvette." He scanned their faces. "I'm going out on a limb with all of you. Trust isn't easy on either side, but you've known me for many years. My goal is to eventually re-lease you. You'll be able to stay or go as you please. But first I must be certain you'll live by the rules I've devised, and not only when you're in my territory." He finally cracked a smile as he glanced in my direction. "I have family now. Ruling a nest was never part of my grand scheme."

Suddenly I had everyone's attention. I tapped into the lines for security and looked back at each of them. They turned away when they saw they had no ability to glamour me. I guess trying is something automatic with a vampire. I checked out their auras, all of them a nasty looking shade of gray. I'd have to mention that to Garrett later.

Yvette asked, "Is the shifter above us?" Her voice bor-dered on contempt.

"Yes." He didn't hesitate. "Jackie is my lifemate and is under my protection. She killed Antoine who was above all of you in age and power. You won't be able to glamour her, and I'm warning you now, if you decide to fuck with her, she's more than capable of helping you meet final death." His eyes flashed silver. "You'll treat her with the same respect you show me or Francois." Garrett rarely cursed, but hearing him talk me up to his nest made me feel pretty awesome.

Garrett turned to William. "Do you have any questions,

Will?"

William had been sitting and staring at his shoes. Now he lifted his head to speak. "No, Garrett. I'm hungry is all." His fangs were partially out and he was shaking slightly. "I'll follow your rules. I just need to feed every day. Eleanor left me hungry a lot. You saw how it was with her."

Francois stood. "I have lined up volunteers for tonight. They are waiting in your rooms. Talk to them first. Find out what they are willing to give. And please remember the rules. I'll be available if you feel you need my help."

They stood, nodded at Garrett, ignored me and left. I heard various doors opening and closing.

"Stay as long as you like. I am going to see to the others. I will call you later, Garrett. Bonsoir, Jacqueline." When Francois moved into the next room, I got up and sat in Garrett's lap hugging him tightly and nestling into the comfort of his long arms.

"I'm sorry if that upset you. I feel responsible for them." He kissed my cheek.

"Why is Francois helping you? He's acting like your assistant. And why didn't he automatically take them on and make them part of his nest?"

"He feels responsible for Eleanor's behavior. Also he gets bored easily. I think he's having fun. He told me running my own nest would be good for me."

He was staring into the fire. It had been a difficult evening for him. I had an idea. "Can I drive your car?"

"Yes, of course. Where are we going?" His forehead furrowed with curiosity.

"It's a surprise." I yanked him out of the chair and out the door to the car. I drove up into the Cascades and pulled off the main road and parked. We both jumped out and walked to the front.

"What now?" He was grinning like a cat with a bowl of cream.

I grabbed him by his belt and pulled him closer. "My cheetah wants to play. Let's hunt."

We undressed and shifted, spending the next two hours hunting, sharing kills and chasing each other. His handsome cheetah was stronger, so when he caught me he could pin me to the ground to nip at my nose and my ruff, but he rarely caught me. We collapsed near the car and transitioned back, laughing and happy. Garrett was still a little weak, so I let him feed from me, which led to other amazing moments. Finally we dressed and he drove us back to our home and to Samson, our furry companion.

CHAPTER FORTY-EIGHT

I WOKE UP AROUND NOON THE NEXT DAY TO find Liam busy in the garden.

"Hello, Liam."

His posture was stiff, his tone reserved. "Good afternoon, Miss Jacqueline. You and Master Garrett did well at the duel."

"Did Kennet speak to you?"

"Lord Kennet did speak to me." His violet eyes held mine as he waited to hear what I would say next.

"I swear to you I didn't tell him about you lending me the knife. He just seemed to know." Liam nodded, seemingly satisfied with my response.

I stepped closer to him and sent, *"He asked me to be his lover and give him an heir. I refused him as politely as I could and instead suggested we could be allies. Are Garrett and I in danger?"* I'm not really sure why I told him this, but once I'd blurted it out, I felt better.

Liam was silent for several moments, processing what I'd said. *"It will depend on how much he desires you and how much he is willing to risk war to have you. Shifters and vampires might declare war against the fae if he is so foolish as to kidnap you. Francois' line is powerful, as is Aaron's pack council. The fae are more powerful but your people are much more numerous and extremely determined. It could end in disaster for both sides. The Fae Elders will not look kindly on Lord Kennet if he starts a war over a female."*

I started to respond, but Liam continued. *"He knows this, and yet he has no heir, despite the fact he's had several wives over the centuries. No woman has given birth to a fae child in seventy-five mortal years. In a fae lord the desire for an heir surpasses all others. Still, I do not believe Kennet will attempt anything so extreme."*

I thanked Liam and curled up in a chair on the front porch, soaking in some sunshine. My life had changed so much since my first night on the island. I had real friends who I'd never have to move away from. I had a home where I could stay forever, and a wonderful male who loved me, a mate for life. There was no way I'd let Kennet disturb what Garrett and I were building together.

Ethan called to challenge me to another backgammon tournament, so on Thursday I invited him over for lunch. He beat me, of course. Afterward we sat in the backyard and talked for a while. I'd avoided asking him about his first change, and now seemed like the perfect time.

He was reluctant. I touched his hand and he laughed. "The witchy woman wants to fix me?'

"There's nothing to fix. You don't have to explain…."

"You have a right to know who you're working with, who you're trusting your life to."

"I'll trust you no matter what."

He sighed and began. "I grew up a shifter, psyched to know I'd be a cougar like my parents. But I didn't change when everyone else did and it pissed me off. Things had always gone my way and I wasn't used to being left out. My friends were off hunting and I was stuck at home. No one else seemed worried about it. They just shrugged and said I'd change eventually. I got kind of depressed and started hangin' with some kids I knew who used.

"At first, it was just pot and a lot of booze. No big deal, I thought. Then I started taking pills, like valium and oxy. My grades in school went down. I was seventeen and still hadn't changed, but I was jittery and getting headaches, all the signs. I was just too wasted to realize it."

Ethan looked down at his hands, not wanting to meet my eyes. "My parents were freaked of course, so we ended up arguing all the time. I quit school, left home, moved north to Portland and was living on the streets dealing, turning tricks, stealing, whatever I had to do to buy more drugs. They called Rob who knocked me out, threw me in the back of his truck and actually took me home to live with him. I was a freakin' mess and he wanted me near a hospital just in case. He helped me clean up. Those were a couple of really bad weeks." Ethan shuddered, raking both hands through his hair.

"He fed me healthy food and made me exercise. He was pretty tough on me." He smiled and rubbed his chin as if remembering a punch Rob had landed. "Mostly he talked to me about what he'd gone through and he listened when I talked to him. Rob saved my life. When I still hadn't changed, he took me to the island to shoot me up with the drug Sinc had developed. I was still being a pain in the ass 'cause I didn't want to be there. That's why I tried to run away."

He looked at me with his large amber eyes. "I bet you don't think I'm such a great guy now, right?" The pain and fear in his expression were heartbreaking as he waited for me to tell him to leave or maybe that I wouldn't work with him. Instead I leaned over and hugged him, pushing my love and my energy into him. He hugged me back, his muscles finally relaxing. We moved apart and smiled at each other.

"You being there on the island with me, made me feel useful. Someone else needed me. Someone I could help. I wasn't the only fucked up one." I rolled my eyes. "And I liked feeling like you … you kinda looked up to me."

I smiled. "I still do. I was a mess on the island and I'd never have gotten through everything if you hadn't been there with me. But Ethan, your past doesn't have power over you unless you let it. Have you talked to Sinc about any of this?"

"Not a good idea." He shook his head.

"She's crazy about you."

He grinned like a kid. "I'm crazy about her, that's for sure. I mean she's definitely high maintenance, but she can be really sweet and generous and funny. She's so bright. I'm amazed every day she's still with me and hasn't kicked me out."

"Kicked you out?"

"I moved in with her a week ago."

"And you were going to tell me this, when?"

"We thought you had enough going on in your life. It just never came up. Anyway, she still wants me there."

"Let me tell you a secret about women like Sinc and me. We really like to feel needed by our partners rather than total-ly dependent on them. If you tell her what you told me, she'll be there for you. She'll be happy you trusted her and she won't turn away. Her love is going to heal you faster than anything I could ever do for you. It's like Kyle and Peter and me and Garrett. We heal each other. Just tell her."

He grabbed my hand and squeezed it. "You really are a witchy woman. Thanks, Speedy, for the food and the therapy." I laughed again as he leaned over and kissed me on the fore-head. I caught a whiff of eucalyptus as he winked and headed out the door.

CHAPTER FORTY-NINE

O

N THE MORNING OF OUR PARTY, I TOOK Samson out with me for a run. We ran along the main road and turned into the woods on a path I wasn't too familiar with. After a couple of miles, I saw a female twenty-five yards ahead of me standing under a huge oak. Samson started to bark and growl, but like Liam, one glance from her silenced him. Her long dark hair blew around her body as she moved gracefully down the winding path. Her violet gaze took me in without a hint of emotion. I could smell the magic of Faerie all around her.

"Jacqueline Crawford Cuvier, I am Kaera, a representative of the Fae Council. You and your mate, Garrett Cuvier, are invited to Faerie to be the guests of Lord Caelen and his family on the evening of June 19th. You are invited to dinner and then to a meeting of the Fae Elders where various topics will be discussed pertinent to our alliance. An escort will arrive at your home in Crescent City at dusk on the day of the meeting to guide you to the Cascade Sidhe. You will stay with us until dusk on June 22nd. Liam, the son of Lord Caelen, will also be accompanying you.

"Lord Caelen and Lord Kennet have both extended invitations for you and your mate to join them at Midsummer on the evening of June 20th." She'd made a face when she said Kennet's name, making it clear who she thought we should join. "All correspondence between us can be through Liam." She handed me an envelope. "Good journey, Jacqueline." She nodded and dissolved. Poof.

I ran home clutching the envelope. Liam read the invitation quickly.

"I will, of course, accompany you. Don't allow yourself to worry over Lord Kennet. My father can arrange it so you never have to see him the entire time you are there." I was relieved I'd told Liam about my encounter with Kennet. I'd also confided in him about my fractured emotions regarding Antoine's death. My healer/warrior nature was something only he could relate to. We were becoming more than teacher and student. I felt a strong friendship growing between us.

He took my hand, smiling. "Tonight you will enjoy your party. Tonight you will laugh and dance and take pleasure in the company of your friends. Tonight Master Garrett and you are sealed as lifemates in the eyes and the hearts of all the people who love you and whom you love."

As Liam predicted, the party was a glorious event. It seemed at least a third of the shifter population of Crescent City showed up along with quite a few of their human partners. The wolves: Aaron, Catherine, Franklin, Tony from Sacramento and at least fifteen others, barbequed enormous amounts of ribs, steaks, chicken, and burgers, and then spent the rest of the night throwing each other into the Smith River and flirting with the shifters. Aaron managed to toss Garrett into the river, but Garrett got his revenge later when some of Sinc's chocolate mousse cake ended up in Aaron's face and down his shirt. Of course that prompted another shove.

We'd hired a local shifter DJ who kept the night hopping while Ethan and Sinc encouraged everyone to dance, showing off the latest moves. They managed to attract a crowd when they danced, mostly because they were a spectacular couple and moved like professional dancers. Peter and Kyle were glued together all night and I couldn't help but smile when I heard Kyle laugh heartily over something Peter had whispered in his ear. Kyle seemed so much happier since Eleanor's death.

Aaron and Catherine tore up the dance floor with some ballroom salsa. Very hot stuff! Garrett managed to get me to dance some of the slower dances, the only kind of dancing I was any good at. He held me close and led me gracefully and people started to clap like it was a wedding. I looked into his radiant blue eyes and knew he was all I needed. No fancy wedding would change anything. We were completely committed to each other and would be forever.

Maya, Brad, and Sylvia arrived together and enjoyed themselves kayaking and socializing with friends. Rob showed up a little late, but insisted we follow him to a quiet table near the river. Maggie and Justin Crawford were there. At first I was shocked, but then I ran to them and we hugged and kissed. They apologized over and over and I forgave them over and over. They seemed so pleased for us and we promised to call often. Before they left, I asked them about my birth parents, but they could only give me the names of the lawyer who'd handled my adoption and the social worker who'd represented the state.

I had a chance to meet Ethan's parents, who hugged me and thanked me for looking after their son. I told them what a great guy he was and they beamed with pride. Ethan and Sinc seemed closer than ever so I guessed maybe he'd taken my advice and opened up to her.

My favorite part of the evening was when Garrett grabbed

me away from a conversation with Catherine and sat both of us down near the dance floor. He whispered in my ear. "This is for you, mon ange." He kissed me sweetly on the lips.

While the DJ was on a break, a drum set had mysteriously appeared in the corner and a wolf from Aaron's pack took his place on the stool behind it. To round out the band, Garrett walked out carrying his violin, Aaron appeared holding a small accordion and finally Peter showed up with an acoustic guitar. All of our guests had gathered around, chatting excitedly, some of them pairing off and moving out onto the dance floor, ready to move with the music when it started. Garrett tapped his foot and bobbed his head in four rhythmic beats and they began to play … Cajun music!

When I'd first seen the violin, I assumed he played classical music, but this was so much fun. Peter sang with a strong voice in a language kind of like French but not exactly: the meaning always clear in the music. Kyle ran over to me and pulled me out onto the dance floor, explaining Peter had taught him how to do the Cajun two-step. After looking like an idiot through the first song, I started to really get into it, turning under his arm and dancing side by side with my funny, lively friend. Ethan danced with Sinc, so the four of us switched partners a few times, bumping into each other and giggling hysterically. I guess if any of our enemies had seen us this night on the dance floor laughing together, they wouldn't have thought the four of us to be much of a threat. They'd have been wrong. It was more obvious to me than ever before our team of rogues was going to kick ass … just not tonight.

According to Kyle, the four musicians had spent many years in Lafayette, Louisiana, which was a Cajun stronghold in the south. They'd learned to play this warm-hearted soulful zydeco music when they were fairly young, in supernatural years, and continued to get together to play whenever there was a nearby gathering of shifters or wolves. After four songs, the drummer left and Peter handed Aaron his guitar. Garrett and Aaron played an amazing Irish reel as a tribute to their mothers who were sisters, off the boat from Ireland. The music started slow and then got faster and faster and soon the whole crowd was hollering and clapping. Garrett watched me enjoying the upbeat music, clapping along with everyone else and then running to hug him when he finished. He grabbed me up and kissed me in front of everyone, which brought on another cheer from the crowd.

Around 2:00 a.m. the party started breaking up. Garrett and I spoke to everyone we could, thanking them for coming and also supporting us in our battle with Eleanor and Antoine. The wolves and some of the shifters had already cleaned up the mess, but we stayed until everyone had left. As we were pulling away in the car I caught a whiff of fae magic, so I hoped it was Liam and not Lord Kennet who'd been observing the festivities.

We'd invited Liam of course, but he felt having a fae present would put a damper on the festivities, since so many shifters feared the fae. Francois also declined the invitation because someone had to keep an eye on Garrett's nest. I put aside all thoughts of Kennet and the new nest and leaned against my handsome vampire for the ride home.

As we walked hand in hand up the path to the home we shared, I pushed my hip playfully into his. "How do you feel?"

"I'm the happiest I've ever been, all because of you, little cheetah." He played with my hair, running his hand down my arm to come to rest on my hip. He arched an eyebrow, the imp making an appearance. "How do *you* feel tonight?"

"Deliriously happy," I sighed as he unlocked the front door, "and a little excited to see what's coming next."

"What would you like to happen next?" He pulled me

into the foyer, kicked the door closed behind us and kissed my ear, which he knew would send tiny shockwaves down my body and get me thinking about where else I wanted him to kiss me.

I decided to start with something serious which had been on my mind for a long time. I took his hands in mine and stared into the glorious eyes that had worked their magic on me all those weeks ago. "I'd like to look for my birth parents."

"I'll do anything for you. We'll find them together." He buried his nose in my hair and took a long deep breath, pulling away to kiss the mark Francois had cut into my wrist. Our matching symbols had healed well, taking on a rich luster— more like a tattoo than a simple carved outline. We'd chosen the shape of a cheetah's eye with its black tear stripe weaving its way down our hand to disappear beneath our index fingers. When we'd shared our magic that evening, mine had taken on my rich green hue and Garrett's his sapphire blue, mimicking our eyes when we shifted. We'd both agreed unusually powerful magic had definitely been at work here.

I wanted to tease him a little so I ran my hand through his silky auburn hair as I thought about how else I could answer his question. "Next week, I think we should take a few days off. Maybe we could drive north to Oregon or Washington, to hunt a little?" I brushed my hand down his sculpted chest to rest on his hard stomach. He closed his eyes and made an encouraging sound, so I started to back up toward his bedroom, drawing him willingly along by pulling on his belt. "Tomorrow we should take Samson to the groomer, he needs a bath and he's hard to manage in the tub." Garrett's stomach jerked under my hand as he started to laugh.

I had my back to his bedroom door, my left hand turning the knob. He whispered in my ear. "And what about tonight, angel?" I bit my lip as I thought about how I should answer.

Tiny silver specks danced in his amazing eyes, a universe of stars all for me. I lifted my finger to trace along his full lips. "Tonight there's you and me." Garrett gently kissed my finger, sucking it into his mouth and allowing it to scrape along one of his fangs as I drew it out. I shivered in a good way.

His mouth twitched at the corners. "And lifetimes together, my love."

"Lifetimes might not be long enough." I threaded my fingers in his hair, pulling his face even closer, angling it just right. He smiled, loving the more confident me. Finally alone with my mate, I breathed Garrett into my soul and kissed my dark angel, opening my mind and my body and letting in the magic.

ACKNOWLEDGEMENTS

I'd like to thank my two editors, Emily Schiller and Anneli Purchase, both of whom worked very hard to help me create the best book possible. I'd also like to thank Reba Buhr, for her hard work in narrating the audiobook version of Rebirth. You brought my baby to life! To Nicole Blanchard at Indie Sage, I thank you for helping me with promotion and marketing and to Stacy at Champagne Formats I'd like to offer up another round of appreciation.

A very special thank you goes to my daughters who inspire me every day and to my brother Rudy, who loves to hear all the crazy stories I carry around in my head. And as always, I'd like to express tons of gratitude to my readers, who stick with Jackie on her long journey and root for her to find happiness. Thank you.

About the Author

I'm fortunate to currently be a resident of a lovely town in Northern California, a magical place within the context of the mortal plain, where flowers bloom all winter long and people actually smile and say hello when they pass you on the sidewalk.

I've spent most of my professional life working with community theatre groups in NYC as a costume designer, production manager, stage manager, etc. Over time I've adopted the philosophy that life is one enormous theatrical extravaganza and I'm merely doing my best to keep it interesting for myself, my family, my friends and hopefully my readers.

I've read fantasy most of my life and still read into the wee hours. Steven King said something about not having the tools to write if you don't spend a good amount of time reading. I'm continuing to strive toward perfection on that front, although I've expanded my list of genres to include other genres. I hope you stop by my website, Facebook or twitter page to say hi or leave a comment. Happy reading.

Visit Gayle at www.gayleparness.com
Or on Twitter: twitter.com/gayleparness
Or on Facebook: facebook.com/gayleparness-author

Here are the links to contact my dream team:
Editors: Anneli Purchase at www.anneli-purchase.com
Emily Schiller
Cover Designer: Tatiana Villa: www.tat-94.wix.com/viladesign
Promotion and Marketing: Nicole Blanchard: www.indiesage.com
Print Book Formatting: Champagne Formats: www.
champagneformats.com
Audiobook Narrator Extraordinaire: Reba Buhr: www.rebabuhr.
com

Other Books by Gayle Parness

ROGUES SHIFTER SERIES

BOOK TWO: *Stalked* Jackie and Garrett travel to Faerie to celebrate the Midsummer Solstice Ceremony with their new fae allies, only to become the hunted enemies of a powerful fae lord who wants to claim Jackie as his own. At the same time, Garrett's team of rogues go undercover to find a female fae warrior who's disappeared without a trace. What and who they find instead, turns everyone's life upside down, forcing Jackie to have to choose between family and friendship.

BOOK THREE: *Twisted*

BOOK FOUR: *Blown Away*

BOOK FIVE: *Caught Between*

BOOK SIX: *Torn Apart*

BOOK SEVEN: *Cut Off*

BOOK EIGHT: *Blood Spelled* (releasing March 30, 2016)

TRIAD SERIES

BOOK ONE: *Breaking Out* Charlie sets off with his best friend, Jay, a grizzly shapeshifter, excited to finally be making his own choices and following his own path. After taking time to rough it in the Sierras, he and Jay finally make it down to

LA, where they figure they can enjoy some R & R of a more civilized kind. However, before long, they're caught up in a dangerous mess involving a girl with a secret, a violent pack of werewolves, and an irritated king. As the two friends try to handle this convoluted situation without endangering the human population, they are being watched and followed by a dangerous being with an agenda all his own.

BOOK TWO: - *Falling Out*

BOOK THREE – *Spinning Out* – Releasing Fall, 2016

THETA SERIES

BOOK ONE: *Playing with Passion*
Review from the Pedantic Punctuator: *Gayle has created an amazing world, filled with characters you will both love to hate, and some you will grow desperately attached to. Throughout the book, the growth of the characters was realistic and entertaining, and I found myself utterly engrossed in their adventures. I desperately wanted to see the theta troupe escape their enslavement and the relationships between the various members of the troupe was enjoyable and fun to read. As an editor, I was impressed with Gayle's writing – as a reader, I was engrossed and can't wait to read the second book in the series. 4 1/2 stars.*

BOOK TWO: *Yielding to Pleasure*

BOOK THREE: *Teasing the Heart* (Releasing August 10, 2016)

Excerpt from *Stalked*:
Book Two of the Rogues Shifter Series

STALKED

CHAPTER ONE

THIS WAS ONE OF THOSE DAYS WHEN I HAD to keep telling myself I was not hallucinating, even though I'd questioned my sanity several times in the last six weeks. I was truly riding in a white limousine, holding hands with an extremely attractive vampire, sitting across from two high-seelie fae on my way to celebrate the Midsummer Solstice Celebration with a group of ancient fae lords and ladies. Yep, Jackie Crawford, that would be me, was going to Faery. No lie.

As we drove through the Cascade Mountains in northern California, Garrett Cuvier, the aforementioned gorgeous vampire, was making lazy circles with his thumb on my palm as he discussed tonight's meeting with the other two passengers. Across from us sat Liam, an adorable and powerful half-fae/half human, my teacher and my friend, and Kaera, a lovely but serious representative of the Fae Council of Elders. I hadn't seen her smile once.

Spread out across my feet and cutting off my circulation in the process, sprawled Samson, a protective Rottweiler Garrett and I had inherited after the death of our friend, Carly. Liam had insisted the sweet natured mutt accompany us. I'd argued against bringing the dog at first, but I'd learned the hard way not to take Liam's advice lightly.

Samson grunted and stretched his huge body across the floor of the limo, taking up even more room and covering my feet completely with his black and tan belly. Garrett and I laughed out loud. Liam smiled good-naturedly while Kaera continued to stare out the window, her expression bordering on glum.

I sent to Liam mentally, "*What's up with her?*

"*She is worried about a family matter, but it is her nature to be reserved around non fae.*" Not having any blood relatives of my own, I could only guess at how family problems could mess with your head. I felt bad for her, but I wouldn't let her gloomy mood ruin my happy one.

I snuggled closer to Garrett and peeked again at Kaera, who seemed a million miles away. She tapped her foot impatiently, probably irritated the trip was talking so long. She and Liam could have transported us to Faerie instantly through the ley lines, but because it would have been my first time to travel inside the magic, they decided a car trip would be a much gentler journey and that I'd arrive in a healthier state. Apparently, many non-fae had trouble traveling directly through the hidden energy that crisscrossed the human world, feeling nauseous and weak at the end.

Hey, I'd been willing to give it a try, in fact I was kind of looking forward to it, but since they were all against it, I'd agreed.

Thinking about traveling through magical rivers of energy to get from one place to another would've had me doubting my sanity just a couple of months ago. Back then, I'd thought of myself as a human girl with several extremely odd and uncomfortable abilities. I could run faster than any Olympic track star, and my senses were so acute I could hear a baby cry ten houses down the block or see a bird dive for the ocean a few miles away. I'd struggled daily to keep these *talents* hidden from the world and live as normal a life as possible, but it hadn't been easy.

On the evening I learned the truth, my life began to corkscrew in a roller coaster ride of new experiences. Rob, a black leopard shapeshifter, informed me I was also a shifter. My initial reactions had run the gamut from disbelief to terror to fury, until I met another shifter, Ethan, a large cougar, who was also learning from Rob. In the end, being faced with the irrefutable evidence of seeing them shift in front of me, I had no choice but to agree to my own forced change.

Turns out I'm a rare cheetah shifter and able to pull energy from the magic that courses through the earth in rivers of power. Since that first transition, my new life has moved forward at an amazing rate until I've felt at home with myself in a way I never had as a human.

We passed yet another glorious view of the sun setting over the forest which spread out west of the mountains in gorgeous shades of gold and pink and purple. Contented, I stretched my arm across Garrett's slim waist as I took in a deep breath of his delicious scent, something I did to combat my nerves, but also as a reminder of how lucky I was.

Garrett, my sexy vampire, has been the main reason for my unrestrained happiness. Two years before, he'd saved me from a vicious attack by giving me blood to heal my extremely serious injuries. Six weeks ago I'd battled with the painful physical effects of the ley line magic. He'd taught me how to build a shield to protect myself and then how to use the power that the lines offered up. Through that energy, we connected to each other on a primal level, now living in each other's minds and emotions in a wonderfully intimate way, bonded together in love by ritual, but also by magic.

Kaera's musical voice broke into my thoughts. "We will be there soon. You must agree to be blinded, Jacqueline."

"Do you mean blindfolded?" I asked, sitting up in the seat.

"No, it is a temporary blinding that only lasts a few minutes. There is no pain."

"I've had it done, it's nothing. I'll be right here holding you." Garrett tightened his embrace.

"I can close my eyes. I won't peek." I turned quickly toward Garrett and said in a slightly annoyed tone, "Wait a minute. She's not blinding you?"

Kaera answered, frowning. "Garrett is an ally of an Elder, Lord Caelen, Liam's father. Blinding is not necessary in *his* case." She spoke with a sharp edge to her voice, seemingly annoyed I didn't already understand the rules.

I twisted my mouth. "I'm his mate. His *lifemate*."

"There are no exceptions." I gave her another appraising look. She was at least three inches taller than my 5'9" with long dark wavy hair and lovely amethyst eyes, which were currently flashing with gold, a sign of strong emotions. Yep, she was pissed. "You will not be allowed inside unless you consent."

I glanced at Liam who nodded his agreement and held up a hand in a calming gesture. "Fine, get it over with." I shrugged, not happy, but willing to grin and bear it and Liam immediately lost his worried expression. I have a tendency to be stubborn on occasion, but I wanted into Faerie in the *worst way*. I'd grilled Liam on the subject and his descriptions were so lovely, I couldn't wait to see all the amazing colors and the magical landscapes and people. My heart was pounding with excited anticipation.

Kaera reached over and placed a smooth hand on my

forehead. Samson growled a warning, but a look from Liam quieted him. I felt a sharp jolt of energy and my vision faded slowly to black. In reaction I drew on the magic and reached out with my mental senses to see if I would be able to *see* in that way. In my mind, I was on my familiar rugged cliff with waves of ley line power crashing against the rocks below me, a made-up place I went to focus my energy. I attempted to stretch my senses out in sneaky tendrils to discern shapes or shadows in the real world, but it remained dark.

"*It's only for a few minutes.*" Garrett sent to me mentally. "*I won't let go, my lovely cheetah.*"

I smiled and leaned against him once more. "*I'm a little nervous about meeting the fae, especially seeing Lord Kennet again.*"

"*You will enchant them all.*"

"*Exactly what I'm afraid of.*" Lord Kennet, the judge at the duels, had actually proposed I leave Garrett and become his consort, even going so far as to suggest I give him an heir. "*I really didn't want to be doing any enchanting in Kennet's direction.*"

Garrett laughed and hugged me tighter. "*Caelen and I will protect you from the pretentious jerk.*"

My vision cleared as Liam announced, "We are here, Jacqueline." I glanced at him curiously, when he nodded in the fae manner. "I will not be addressing you as I do in your home. I am the son of a Council Elder and must behave as such." Liam had pledged his service to Garrett after Garrett had saved his brother, Aedus from some kind of undisclosed danger, so at home he referred to us as Miss Jacqueline and Master Garrett.

Liam was my height, with delicate, almost feminine features and shoulder length golden hair. However, the power emanating from him was all male and quite seductive as I'd learned in the past. His violet eyes sparkled with excitement and his whole body seemed to relax as the car slowed. I guess he was pleased to be home.

"Sure, Lord Liam," I teased. He laughed gently, a musical sound which made us all smile, except for Kaera. *I hope the others aren't so stick-up-your-butt serious.* I kept that particular thought to myself, just in case Kaera was listening.

The car had come to a stop, so Garrett vamp-speeded it over to my side to help me out in his usual gentlemanly way, adding a sweet kiss on the cheek as an extra bonus. Samson hopped out after me with a grunt and a vigorous shake of his head and body. I snatched up his leash and took a look around.

We were in a narrow valley, the mountains surrounding us cloaked in thick forests. I pictured Garrett and myself hunting together under those trees in our cheetah forms, possibly taking down something large and then feasting on the fresh kill. Standing next to me, he caught a taste of my hunger and squeezed my hand in agreement.

We stood in a large field without buildings or even a pathway. Instead, tall grasses and fragrant wildflowers spread out for hundreds of yards in every direction. A heavy buzz throbbed in my chest, marking this as a strong hot spot of ley line magic.

Garrett pulled me in front of him and wrapped his arms around me, pressing his chest into my back. "Watch this," he whispered in my ear. I leaned back against him, loving the feel of his warm breath on my neck. Samson obediently sat by my feet as I watched, enthralled.

Liam and Kaera walked twenty yards into the field and stopped at exactly the same moment, as if there were some unseen barrier blocking their way. They stretched out their arms with their palms facing down and I felt a pure burst of energy flow from their hands into the heart of the earth. An enormous tugging sensation came next as the power rebounded, bringing massive amounts of magical energy up through their bodies and out through their outstretched hands. Their physical forms almost disappeared in a shimmering golden haze, as shafts of magic in dazzling golds and purples and reds exploded outward, bouncing from mountain peak to mountain peak, surging into the heavens. A towering white stone archway appeared in front of the two fae, brilliantly reflecting the colors of Liam and Kaera's magic. As their bodies reformed and became visible to my eyes once more, they turned and motioned for us to follow them through the arch.

Garrett had to nudge me to get me moving, 'cause I was pretty much blown away by what they'd done. That amount of power would have burned me to a crisp, but Liam and Kaera seemed unfazed by their efforts. A little shaky, I picked up Samson's leash and clutched at Garrett's hand as we followed them into the world of the fae.

Stalked is available at all the regular vendors. To find out more about Gayle's books or to sign up for her newsletter, check out her website: www.gayleparness.com

Made in the USA
Charleston, SC
15 March 2016